BETWEEN TWO THIEVES

Roberts and Bradley Private Investigator Crime Thriller series book 1

Solomon Carter

Great Leap

Many of us crucify ourselves between two thieves – regret for the past and fear of the future.
--Fulton Oursler

One

Thursday night.

Two men walked in the darkness, their feet padding carefully on the beach. They walked in silence, their eyes occasionally turning to the sparkling black sea. It was almost time – almost but not quite. In the far distance across the water, a few studs of light marked out the Kent coast. Much nearer were the lights of Southend Pier, stretched out in a line like a garland of Christmas lights pulled tight across the water. The two men trudged together, their breathing light with anticipation.

"Think you're ready?" said the taller guy, his voice gruff and curt.

"Of course I am," said the shorter man.

"You sound nervous," said the taller one, in a cutting tone.

"I've always done my bit," he replied.

"Haven't you just..." said the taller one, shooting his companion a look. The small guy chewed over the words and shook his head. They were a good long way from the lights of the town centre and the beach this end was quiet. The men approached their target positions from the empty Southchurch side of the beach. Their target was a single storey, white-painted huddle, the Marine Activity Centre, and more specifically the long wooden jetty jutting out from the back of the building across the wide sand and above the dark depths.

"We'll be there in a minute," said the taller guy. "So, get yourself together," he whispered.

"I am together," said the short man. He stopped walking. "Hold up. I think I can hear him coming..."

"Already?" The tall man strained his ear to the water. "Let me check," he said, hearing a mere hint of sound, but still indiscernible. "We'd better get in position then..."

They parted ways, the shorter man aiming for the white marine centre, the taller aiming for the jetty. The sparse beach grasses fluttered around their ankles.

Nearby another man watched and waited in silence. Unseen, he stood alone on the town side of the marine centre building, his big body absolutely still but for the breeze tugging at his thin hair. The man's stillness was a talent learned from practice. So far none of them were aware of each other. Only the darkness and the sound of the water filled their senses. Behind him the seafront parade of houses and pubs were grey and silent. The lone watcher's eyes roved the waters and his ears strained against the breeze. His name was Carl Renton. Carl Renton was forty-seven years old, a man of large dimensions, overweight yet strong. He had never been considered cool, nor did he desire to be. He knew people thought he was strange, but then being strange was his calling and he knew it. Being different was what made him do what he did – what brought him out standing alone on the beach in almost all weathers. Besides, what did other people's opinions matter when a man was committed to his mission? He stood a little way from the town-facing side wall of the Marine Activities Centre. In the short time since the council had sold it off, the marine centre had been given a lick of white paint and a rebranded logo but it was essentially the same thing, and security had gotten worse not better. Which Carl reckoned had made his mission even more essential. By day, kayaks, canoes, windsurfers, dinghies and mini-yachts, buzzed around the marine centre's jetty to access the water. By night the jetty should have been silent. Contrasted against the pier, the jetty was a just a child's toy, but it still offered easy access to the water, and it didn't come under anything like the same scrutiny as its enormous neighbour. Which was one of the reasons Carl Renton needed to stand close by, following his calling, watching the waters as he did nearly every night. But tonight Carl felt uneasy. He held a crumpled jiffy bag in his big hand without really wanting to hold it at all. Carl told himself he didn't want to know what was inside. But then that wasn't altogether true.

His lifted the jiffy bag to his eyes. The contents shifted inside with a metallic clink and rattle. Curiosity stirred in his belly, but the thing simply had to go. It was a distraction from a project which had cost him too much already.

Carl shook his head and whispered under his breath. "See what's inside when this is done… but for now you concentrate."

He lowered the envelope by his hip – out of sight and out of mind. The breeze dipped, and Carl cocked his ear towards the estuary. He caught a hint of movement in the blackness and narrowed his eyes. Despite all the practice he was tired, feeling it in every bone. He was getting too old for all this, but someone had to do it. Not all things were to be accepted meekly. Not all things were good. And some were so bad that Carl knew he had to fight them with every fibre of his being. Breaking though the sounds of the water and the wind, the low buzz of a motor rose to meet his ears. The faintest buzz… it came and went and rose again as it did battle with the elements. Staring out to sea, the adrenaline of the mission stirred in him again. So, they were coming in again tonight. He had to make sure his efforts were not wasted. Carl kept still and listened so hard that nothing else mattered. He tuned everything out, so that he simply didn't hear the few cars passing behind him on the esplanade. Nor the late-night stragglers walking along by the sea wall. Southend was a big town, and there were always people out late at night. Drunks and junkies – the kind of people Carl knew well. He heard nothing but for the lap of the waves on the shore, and the ting-ting-ting of ropes rattling against yacht masts on the breeze. But the buzz was coming nearer. And getting closer, still quiet as mice, two sets of feet padded on the sand, unheard and unseen. Three men, and their full attention was devoted to the sound on the water. And then something changed.

Behind the sea wall, out on the street, one of the lone stragglers slowed down his pace and turned his head towards the sand and the darkness. His body hidden by the dark grey wall, he was nothing more than a head and shoulders. The man's eyes were turned to the water, but he stopped altogether when he glimpsed Carl Renton's broad back. He studied the man's build and shape and saw the jiffy bag dangling from his hand. Still Carl Renton didn't hear anything aside from the buzz of the motor coming from the water. He didn't see the man climb the short flight of concrete steps to cross over the sea wall. He didn't notice the man drop down onto the soft weedy sand. The newcomer took a breath and wiped his clammy face with the back of his hand. He started walking, taking care not to make a sound. When he got close to Carl Renton's back, the man opened his jacket, slid something from it down into his hand and slowed his feet.

Carl frowned as the motor buzz rose and fell on the breeze. He felt disconcerted but didn't know why. He supposed the evening's events had gotten to him and tried to dismiss his feelings.

Behind him, the newcomer licked his lips and his eyes scanned the back of the big man's head, and the package in his hand. As he stared out to sea, Carl Renton felt a deep sudden need to turn around, to face something behind him. It was a stupid and childish sensation, but he knew better than to dismiss any so-called gut feeling when it was this strong. Because he knew where those feelings really came from. Carl started to turn around, but by the time he did, it was already far too late. Renton's eyes flared in recognition as he saw a set of bright, narrow eyes close behind him. The very moment he saw them, it began. Frenzied. Angry. Strategic. The blow struck hard and fast in a way no man could have defended, no matter how big they were. A blinding crash of pain filled Carl's head and sent him staggering back as the breeze rose again. He knew he was hurt, but barely cried out. Renton gathered himself. Blood filled one of his eyes, but he still turned to face his attacker. Renton was caught between a choice to fight or offer the man another way out, when a flash of gleaming metal clunked into the side of his head. This time it bit deep. The man pulled the sharp edge free, swept it down and the metal bit deep again. Carl reeled and turned his eyes skyward. He mouthed a few silent words and his body started to fall. The attacker tried to snatch the big padded envelope from his hand and tried again to pull it away as Renton sank to the ground, but Renton kept it clasped tight. The attacker gritted his teeth and shook his head. Two more vicious strikes and Renton was down and ruined, but somehow, the man still clung to the envelope. The attacker crouched over Carl and delivered one last swiping cut deep against the big man's gut. Finally, Carl Renton fell. His big arm jerked up in the fall. The jiffy was cast into the air, and glittering contents flew across the weed-strewn beach. The attacker looked wildly about the sand. With a shaking hand he slid the weapon back under his jacket and began to scramble around, raking the pebbles and grasses with his fingers to ensure he had retrieved every last item. After twenty seconds, he stood up quickly and glanced at the dark silent houses across the street, at the big bloodied body at his feet, and then at the darkness and water behind him. The buzzing motor was coming ever closer on the waves. The man took one last look, scanning the darkness for anything he had missed and then broke into a run. He ran for the wall as fast as he could. Just as he started to drop down to other side of the sea wall, the man felt the jiffy bag snag on the concrete. A single round, shining gold item tumbled to the sand and rolled into a clump of weeds. The man didn't see it. He took a quick glance at the insides of the envelope but couldn't see anything wrong. The motor was getting closer… he took a deep breath and then he quickly and carefully stalked away. For better or for worse, the deed had been done.

The motor on the water became a roar as it came closer. Other sounds came with it. The sound of the slap on the water and the quiet lift into the air as the smooth fibreglass hull bounced on the waves. When the sound was close at hand, the tall man, Clive Grace, stood up from his crouching position on the edge of the jetty. He leaned left and right until he saw the curved spout of water shooting from the back of the jet ski, rising and falling in a big arc, faintly illumined by the distant lights. Just as bright were the glints of light in Tommy Pink's eyes. Tommy Pink, the market trader, the man riding the jet ski, was his employer and comrade in arms. Dressed from head to toe in a black wetsuit, complete with a snug black snood, Pink always reminded him of some cheap Bond villain on nights like this. But Grace knew the light in Pink's eyes came from the thrill of the job. The excitement of another big payday coming their way. Grace couldn't blame the man. He was excited too. The engine switched off and the jet ski glided the last few metres in silence before it bumped gently against the end of the jetty. Pink leaned up and away from the handlebars, standing up on his steed. He was dressed in black and bore a matching black rucksack on his back. It looked full. The smile on Pink's face told the rest of the story. Pink leaned over the handlebars and opened the storage compartment door on the front of the jet ski. With a gloved hand he pulled out two more rucksacks and a rope. Clive Grace took the rope from Pink and lashed the jet ski to the end of the jetty. Little Norman Peters appeared to assist him.
"I saw you out there," said Grace. "I even heard you speeding up at the end. You bloody love all this, don't you?"

"And you're saying you don't?" said Pink. "Anyway. I like riding on the water. But landing's always the riskiest part," he said. "I think we're okay now though, don't you?" He waved a full rucksack in his hand to prove the point and let out a laugh.

Pink clambered up from his jet ski onto the end of the jetty and sat down. As soon as his backside touched the wood, he peeled the rucksack from his back and unfastened the top. Tommy Pink knew Grace and Peters would have carried out all the necessary checks, but Pink reckoned it never hurt to check again. He groaned with effort as he stood up on tiptoe and peered left and right around the jetty like a meerkat. He walked quickly and quietly along the jetty, looking back to the shore and sea wall on the other side, taking care to glance towards the pier to make sure he hadn't been seen by any late-night stragglers. He was almost done. Pink had pulled the bag open, ready to get on with dishing out the contents, when he noticed a large dark hump dumped on the middle of the sand, on the town side of the beach. "Not another bloody waster sleeping on the beach," he muttered. But then he saw the dark patch on the sand, and all thinking stopped. Pink turned cold and stopped moving. The hump wasn't far from the edge of the marine centre building, not far either from the wooden platform at the end of the jetty. Something like that would be a ruddy homing beacon for the law. Pink moved between the empty metal canoe racks kept outside the marine centre building and using them as a hide, he stared at the hump on the sand until he was sure. All night his mind had been on one thing. The Uber run. But now he could only think of the trouble coming their way. Tommy Pink left Grace and Peters in his wake as he scuttled down the jetty, doing his best to keep out of sight from the street

"Norm! Get that jet ski out of sight and secure, then come and check over here will you?"

"Why? What's up?!"

"Keep it down, you stupid sod," said Pink. "Just get your arse over here pronto."

Peters didn't like Pink's tone, but he did what he was told and skulked along the jetty until he stood at Pink's side. He saw Pink's deep frown and followed his eyes to the sand. Fresh moonlight picked out the oversized body. "Oh no," said little Norman Peters.

"We're gonna have to clear that up," said Pink. "And by we, I mean you. You and Clive."

Norm Peters' mouth dropped open.

"Is that an actual dead body?" he said.

"Just take a bloody look, man. And once you've worked it out, fix it, will you? You and Clive."

"Fix it? How do we fix that?"

"It can't be seen here, can it? Or we're finished, right? So use your brain and use it fast."

The taller man, Clive Grace, joined them on the platform as Norm Peters leapt down and skipped across the sand. Grace stared at the body with narrow eyes and a narrow-lipped mouth. "Damn it," he said. Pink looked back at him. "You help him too, Clive."

"Me? Help him with what?"

"Yes. He'll need help to deal with all that mess. You know what Norm's like… dumb and sloppy."

"Why deal with it at all?" said Grace.

"Seriously? Surely you've got a bit more brains than him?" said Pink.

They watched Norm Peters drop to the sand, kneeling alongside the body as if in prayer.

Clive Grace turned away, swore under his breath, and shook his head. He leapt off the jetty and started off in the direction of Norm and the corpse.

Norman Peters stared down at the man's bloodied head. At his lifeless eyes. He looked at the blood on the sand and took a sharp intake of breath when he heard footsteps coming behind him. He looked back to see Clive Grace padding along towards him, face grim as ever. With shaking hands, Norm Peters reached for the man's dead face and touched his skin. Before Grace could reach him, Peters slipped a small deft hand into the man's pockets to see what he could see. His small fingers came free with a leather wallet, a pocketbook and pen, and a small silver tin, covered in slick warm blood. The man hadn't been dead long. It must have only just happened. Peters snatched a breath, slipped the cash and the tin into his own pocket and put the rest back. He wiped his hands on the sand. But the blood and sand crusted his hand, and his fingers stayed soiled.

"Nasty," said Clive, staring down at the dead man's head.
"You recognise him?" said Norm.
"Yeah. Same as you do," said Grace.
Norm nodded slowly, but caught something in Grace's tone of voice
He glanced back up over his shoulder, his eyes searching Clive Grace's face for more. Grace was always curt, always inscrutable. But the tall man's grim, pinched face revealed nothing at all. Grace's eyes flared at Norm in reply to his gaze.
"You'd better get moving him, then, hadn't you?"
"Move him? But why, Clive?"

"Ain't it obvious?"

Peters kept looking at Clive's face until the taller man got annoyed. He hissed and kicked some sand at Norm.

"Unless you want this sweet spot to come to an end, muck in and get it done."

Peters swore under his breath. Clive Grace crouched down at his side and they started what had to be done.

Two

Friday.

"As another deadline passes..." The TV newsreader was in full flow as Eva walked into the living room, but within four words she had already heard enough. Eva sipped her strong morning coffee, picked up the remote control from the coffee table and switched off the widescreen TV. Behind her on the sofa Dan Bradley threw up his hands in disgust
"Hey! What did you do that for?" said Dan, still chewing on a mouthful of buttery toast.
"You know why," replied Eva. "Brexit overload."
It was seven fifty on a Friday morning. Most weekdays Dan Bradley and Eva Roberts would have already been downstairs in the office of their private investigation agency. But as today was a rare scheduled day off, they had been taking their time to get ready. Red-haired Eva had abandoned her usual tweed suit ensemble for a summery lace-frilled blouse. Her tweed skirt was still safely in place. Those who knew Eva only by her work often thought she was a little too serious for someone of her beauty and intelligence. But her business partner, and long-time boyfriend knew her better than most. He knew there was joy beneath her severity, smiles with the beauty, and everything else a man could wish for besides. And Eva was nothing if not a fighter. As a former boxer, Dan was a fighter too, albeit of a different kind. Dan took another big bite of toast and shook his head.
"The newscasters seem to have forgotten anything else goes on in the world."

"Brexit is still news, Eva."

"Dan, let's not go there." She sat down and opened her laptop.

"But I like the news," said Dan, slurping his coffee.

"I know. But this isn't the news. It's torture."

Dan gave a shrug. He had to admit she had a point and he sensed Eva was battling a bad mood. He had no intention of adding fuel to the fire, especially seeing as it was supposed to be a day off. He swallowed his toast and put the plate down. He cast an admiring eye over Eva's lacy-edged summer blouse as she switched on her laptop.

"Seeing as we're on a news ban… and as it's a day off, maybe we could entertain ourselves some other way… we could take advantage of a morning alone…"

"We have every morning alone, Dan."

"Hey. You know what I mean. Besides, you've taken away the last of my distractions."

Eva gave him a well-practiced look. "The last thing you need is any more distractions, Dan. Or fixations, obsessions, or addictions."

Dan's eyes stayed on hers and Eva angled her head like she was looking at a cheeky kid instead of grown man in his mid-thirties.

"Bedtime's over," said Eva. She looked at her laptop screen. "Besides, there's other news out there if you need it. You just have to look around for it."

"On the web, you mean? But you used to say that was full of conspiracy theories."

"And it is. But these days so is the TV."

"Yep. It's a confusing world," said Dan.

"Safer to stick with toast and coffee," said Eva.

Dan grinned and took another bite. "At least a man can rely on toast and coffee. And the love of a good woman. Well, sometimes," he added quickly. Eva glanced up over the screen of her slowly waking laptop. Dan took it in his stride and smiled.

"It's okay. I got the message. If you do find some real news out there, let me know. You can be my curator, or my censor, depending which you prefer."

"No thanks," said Eva. "I'm just checking emails and then I'm switching off the machine because this is a day off. Why would I want to spoil it with someone else's nonsense?"

Eva peered out of the living room blinds onto a blue sky as she waited for the damned slow machine to finally wake up. When it did, she opened her webmail application. The email list popped up and she deleted the junk right away. After that, she saw almost nothing left. Not good. There were no new work inquiries, and the office badly needed some new business. In good news there were no new invoices, either. Eva was about to close down the laptop as a dead loss when she saw a strangely familiar name buried in an email address somewhere lower down the stack. It was a way down the list, so Eva guessed she must have missed it the day before. She double-checked the sender's email address and saw she was right. Mixed feelings burst like fireworks in Eva's chest, most of them unpleasant. Her cheeks burned like she was sixteen all over again. Eva didn't open the email. She just stared at the sender's name, her mouth wavering in an uncertain line as she considered the implications. Eva had given up on ever hearing from Lauren for the rest of her life. She'd accepted it. And by now, she'd learned to welcome the fact. Lauren Jaeger. Her former *best friend forever*. It was a distant memory and yet somehow it was as fresh as ever. Back then they had been girls who had everything going for them, young women who were going to set the world alight with their good looks, intelligence and willingness to put in the hard yards. But that was before Lauren Jaeger had so abruptly cut her out of her life, like a gangrenous limb. The young Lauren had been blessed with better looks than Eva, and a personality to match. Eva was able to live with that, but what happened just before they turned seventeen hurt like nothing else had in her entire life. Thankfully, Lauren had never met Dan, and so the crazy years of chaos and bliss that followed certainly helped dull that bitter pain. But Eva was certainly in no mood to go back there. Not to that dark place. She didn't even want to think about it. But the name still sat there, front and centre on her computer screen. *Lauren Jaeger? Seriously?* And how come she was still known by her maiden name? They were close friends almost twenty years ago. That Lauren hadn't been married in all that time seemed unlikely. Eva's finger hovered over the laptop mouse for a few seconds before it swooped down. She clicked once, and Lauren's email disappeared from her list, still unopened, sent straight to the delete file for imminent wiping. Eva closed her eyes and a furrow of regret appeared in her brow. The deletion gesture didn't feel good either – Lauren was reaching out to her after all – but in terms of her best options, deletion still seemed the best way to go. She sighed, picked up her coffee cup and took a long gulp.

"You did it, didn't you?" said Dan.

Eva turned her elegant head and cast a weary eye Dan's way. She'd made a great swap in exchanging Lauren for rugged boxer Dan. But all the same, he still drove her half mad every day.

"Did what?" she said.

"You read the news, didn't you?" said Dan. "I can see that look in your eye."

"What look?" said Eva.

"That *what's the world coming to?* look. So come on. What happened to make you look so heavy?"

Eva shook her head. "Nothing. I read my emails, that's all. Now I just want to get on and enjoy my day."

Eva folded her laptop screen down and shoved it aside.

"You and emails," said Dan. "See. You've got your fixations too. Next I bet you go down to the office and check the answerphones. And then the post."

Eva shook her head. "Nope. Not today. We promised Mark and Joanne a lunch in the sun and that's exactly what we're going to do. And we're going to stay cheerful and enjoy it. I mean it." Eva tried for jolly and breezy and knew she was trying too hard. Damn Lauren Jaeger. Why did she have to show up today of all days? Just her name seemed to carry the residue of all those bad old feelings. Eva stood up and left her computer behind.

"I'll get a shower," she said.

"You already had one," said Dan. She grabbed her cup and walked away.

"I want another one."

"Need some company?"

"Nope," said Eva, and the door clicked shut behind her.

"Can't blame a man for trying." Dan picked up the remote control and switched on the news.

"…Brussels really doesn't know what to make of London's latest Brexit announcement," said the reporter.

"Does anyone, Katy?" said the anchorman.

Dan grinned. He picked up the last half crust of toast and stuffed it between his teeth like coal into a steam engine.

***

"So, where are we going to eat?" said Joanne, leaning forward from the back seat. The young blonde gripped the headrest and leaned close as Eva drove them to Leigh in her red Alfa Romeo Giulietta. The car windows were down, and Eva's long red hair wisped and billowed back over her seat. Joanne, the girlfriend of their young apprentice, Mark, smiled brightly. She looked excited to be going out. Seeing the girl's enthusiasm, Eva willed herself to cheer up a bit.

"Is pizza okay with you?" said Eva.

"Fine by me," said Joanne.

"And me," said Mark. Eva noticed the proximity of their bodies. The young couple sat close together in the back seat leaving plenty of empty space around them. Quite a feat in her hatchback, so she guessed their relationship was still going well. If anything, they looked closer than ever. Eva wondered what Mark's mother thought about it all. Joanne's too for that matter. Chances were their parents probably knew little about anything. By now Joanne had helped them on a few cases, always on an ad hoc basis, and rarely rewarded with any cash. In many respects, Eva thought Joanne the better equipped of the two for work in private investigations. Mark was sensitive and prone to overthinking, whereas Joanne was always up for taking a risk. She was smart, good at thinking on her feet, and knew how to use the power of persuasion. Mark had been in danger a few times and ended up hurt more than once. As a result, he seemed content to play safe, taking risks only when forced to. He had drifted more and more into a paperwork safety zone and they had let him do so. For all Joanne's impulsiveness and trouble, Eva would have hired Joanne in a heartbeat if she could. But as ever, money was the issue of the day.

"Pizza? Where?" said Dan.

"The pizza place next to the fancy hairdressers. Today we eat posh pizzas," said Eva.

"And tomorrow we open the credit card bill," said Dan.

"You have to spend it somehow," said Eva.

"Yeah. And you have to earn it too."

"We'll earn it. We always do," she said.

"That sounded almost convincing," said Dan. "Why? Are there any new gigs on the horizon? I'm assuming that's what you checked your emails for this morning…?"

"Amongst other things," said Eva.

Dan waited. Eva shook her head. "No. Nothing yet."

Dan folded his muscular arms and turned his head. Eva left her eyes on his profile. He had almost totally recovered from last year's ordeal. His bodyweight, musculature and toning was returning, and he seemed healthy and strong. After taking a shot in the gut, it was a miracle he wasn't complaining about his digestion anymore. Eva noticed one or two grey hairs appearing in his short dark hair, but Dan still looked good. She knew he looked a damn sight better than most men of his age.

They hurtled all the way to Leigh, before slowing down for the inevitable catwalk of the Leigh Broadway. It was a hot, sunny day and all the coolest cats were out strutting their stuff. Ladies in short skirts clutching expensive designer handbags, young men in Ray Bans, Dolce & Gabbana, Versace and Armani, with labels virtually hanging off every conceivable garment, right down to their canvas pumps. Even with the ice caps melting and plastic pouring into the seas, flashing the cash still seemed to be the order of the day for good old Leigh-on-Sea. Pedestrians walked out into the road, mobiles pressed to their ears, not wasting a glance at the oncoming traffic. Top speed was twenty on the Broadway. Maybe fifteen. A Lamborghini cruised by and a bright red Ferrari followed. Dan's eyes were taken by each one in turn.

"I prefer something a little more understated," said Eva.

"You always do," said Dan. "I like something that roars."

Eva saw his eyes sparkling her way and raised her eyebrow in warning before Dan could say something risqué in front of their young helpers. Dan smirked and bit his lip. A moment later his eyes were caught by a handwritten newsagent's signboard at the side of the road. He turned his head as the car breezed by.

"Did you see that?" said Dan.

He looked back at the reverse side of the same A-board. Beneath the handwritten print was the red and white logo for The Record newspaper. The local rag.

Uber Drug Craze Claims More Youths.

Eva glanced in her wing mirror and worked to make sense of the writing.

"Another death from that awful new ecstasy?" said Eva.

"Yes, but that wasn't it," said Dan. "There was a different headline on the other side. Something about a local hero going missing. I wondered if it was anyone we knew."

"And did you hear about the Saxon Gold?" said Mark, suddenly leaning forward in the back of the car. "One of the councillors borrowed some of the artefacts from the Saxon Tomb exhibit and managed to lose them during some fundraiser at his house! Sounds like The Record are trying to get the guy sacked for it."

"If that's true, the man deserves what he gets," said Eva. "They were calling the Saxon King the UK's own Tutankhamun. Trust some local big ego to blow it all at the first opportunity."

"That's if you trust what The Record says about anything." Dan made a face at Eva. She pulled one back.

"Now you see what happens when you make me miss the news?" said Dan.

"Hang on. You probably just read it wrong," said Eva. "Missing persons don't ever make the news. They're ten a penny, always have been."

"But I didn't read it wrong," snapped Dan.

Joanne and Mark shot each other a look in the back of the car. Sounded like a tiff was brewing. Joanne loved the tittle-tattle of Eva and Dan's relationship.

"Look," said Dan. "Just stop when we get to the next newsagent. I want to see what's happened."

"Certainly another Uber death from what I saw," said Eva. "It's a shame when you start to get blasé about yet another young life lost to that rubbish. Those pills have killed enough people already."

"I don't know why anyone would want to take the risk," said Joanne.

Dan's brow dipped over his eyes as he strained to recall the headline. Eva pulled in to the side of the road as they were about to pass a Costcutter convenience store. "You can get a newspaper in there," she said, nodding across the street. "But you're not to sit there reading it all the way through lunch."

"Deal. Though it might be wise to see what our mutual friend is writing about these days," said Dan.

Eva frowned. Their mutual friend: Alice Perry. Perry was the vicious little harpy who was The Record newspaper's most high profile reporter. The young hack seemed to be writing every salacious story she could find in the effort to get noticed by one of the big London newspapers. But with the kind of junk she wrote, it wasn't likely that the FT or The Telegraph would be calling anytime soon. Aside from her writing, Eva had good reason to want to scratch the girl's eyes out. A year back, the girl had tried to force Dan into bed with her, using blackmail tactics to make him play along. Thankfully, Dan didn't, and the only reason the girl still had both eyes was because Dan had managed to reverse the blackmail and they still held some collateral against her to use whenever they liked. But Eva knew the value of that collateral would soon be waning. She even wondered if Perry might profit if they used it. A photograph of a young female journalist caught naked in her kitchen might become the fast track to career advancement in modern journalism. With Alice Perry anything was possible. And Perry was just one more person they needed to be wary of – one in a very long list.

Dan got out of the car and, mimicking the swagger of other arrogant pedestrians, he skipped across the street in front of an oncoming Merc. Eva's mobile buzzed in her handbag. A new job inquiry, maybe? She hastily grabbed the mobile, and saw the call was from an unknown number. But the unread text message beneath the incoming call alert was what really took Eva by surprise. She jerked up in her seat, read the text, and frowned.

"But how?" said Eva out loud.

Joanne looked at Eva in the rear-view mirror. "What's the matter?"

"Um… Nothing," she lied. From the look on her face it was plain to see the text message was a lot more than nothing. *Hi Eva. How are you? I know it's been a seriously long time, but I really need your help. I sent you an email. I hope you got it, but maybe you didn't. Please, please, please call me when you can. Lauren J x.*

Eva's body swirled with sudden discomfort and a spurt of anger. *What the hell?!* Lauren Jaeger, her cold-as-ice former-friend – the woman sends her an email and expects her to jump to attention just like that – after well over fifteen years of radio silence and complete ignorance. And Eva noted the passive/aggressive tone of the statement about the ignored email "Maybe you didn't get it." As in 'I know you got it, *so why the hell didn't you reply*?' As if she didn't know why?! And the kiss! The whole thing was a joke. With a whole heap of anger in her head, Eva looked out to the street. She saw Dan emerge from Costcutters, with a Record newspaper wide open in front of his face, his hands flipping fast through the pages. He walked out onto the busy pavement, and a few irritated strutters tutted and walked around him. He reached the kerb, the newspaper still open and started to step out into the street. Just as he took his first step, a short guy dressed in trendy clothes sped past him. The guy was walking forwards but looking back over his shoulder the whole way. He looked about forty but was dressed like he was twenty. Too much colour and his clothes too tight. Just as Dan planted a foot into the road, the guy swept in front of him, jumping down into the road, his shoulder almost barging Dan's newspaper from his hands. Dan dragged his newspaper back. He watched the guy panic as he turned his head to see a single-decker bus gliding towards them, slowing down to pull in at the bus stop right by their feet. Dan stepped back to the kerb, but the little guy was committed. People around stopped what they were doing and stared as if watching a disaster unfold. But in the last moment, the little guy found enough pace to jog clear into the street, and the bus driver found enough brake to avert a tragedy. The bus shuddered and groaned and the man raced across the street, jumping up onto the kerb in front of Eva's parked Alfa. The three in the car watched the little man run on, turning down a side street towards the sea front. A moment later they saw a taller man cross the street, moving purposefully after him, his clothes much lower key, and from the look on his face, he was in a very bad mood.

"What just happened?" said Mark.

"I don't know," said Eva.

"Maybe he's with the fashion police," said Joanne, with a smirk. "Did you see what that guy was wearing?"

Dan opened the car door and got in.

"You see that?" he said. "That little guy almost got himself turned into a pancake. I think that tall guy was after him. It's like Leigh Broadway's turned into Southend High Street."

Dan looked at Eva and saw a hardened look in her eye. She started the engine.

"What's the matter?" he said.

"I just got a text message from an old friend."

"That's a good thing, isn't it? So, what's the matter?" said Dan.

Eva took her time and pulled the car out into the traffic before she replied.

"We're not friends anymore, Dan. We haven't been friends for almost twenty years."

Dan nodded but she saw he didn't understand.

"Think about that," said Eva. "How did she get my number?"

"Oh." Dan nodded his head, his eyes tempted by the newspaper in his hands. "Hang on. Didn't I tell you?"

Eva cast a glance to the front passenger seat.

"Some girl called you few days back. You were out. Said she was an old, old friend of yours and was trying to track you down for a get together. You were out. So I gave her your number."

"What?" said Eva.

"Eva, she was your friend. She even mentioned a few places you used to hang out. She sounded pretty nostalgic for the good old days, you know. I gave her your number so you two could catch up."

"Damn it, Dan!" said Eva, working hard to keep her driving calm.

"Then you're not friends?" said Dan.

"I told you, we're ex-friends. As in former. As in I don't like her."

"But she said—"

"Then she played you just like she once played me. I don't know what she wants, but you can bet it won't be anything good."

"How do you know that, Eva? She sounded friendly enough to me. She said some very kind things about you. People can change a lot in twenty years."

Eva blinked, recalling the Dan she'd met back in her college days. Since then he'd lost half a finger, gained a few grey hairs, survived several deadly attacks and acquired the scars and wrinkles to prove it. Other than that, Dan Bradley was the same man-child he'd always been. Eva shook her head. "I don't think so."

"Eva," he said.

She shook her head. "It's okay. I'll deal with it. Let's just go and get some lunch, okay? I'm sure I'll forget all about it soon enough."

Dan sighed and turned the newspaper over on his lap.
"Sorry to tell you I was right about the headline I saw. There is a missing person mystery, but The Record are jumping the gun. The guy only disappeared last night. Alice Perry must be desperate to write about something other than Ubers."
"Who's gone missing?" said Mark, shrugging dismissively in the back seat.
"He disappeared last night, which means the guy might not be missing at all," said Dan. "But the type of guy he is, it'd be pretty strange to just vanish like that. He runs a rehab, and a Christian charity. He's the stable as they come type. That's her angle."
"Alice Perry was always desperate," said Eva.
"True. But she knows what her readers like. And from what this article says about this Carl Renton guy – she could well be right."
"There's a first time for everything, I suppose," said Eva. "But if Mr Renton turns up today, the least she'll have is egg on her face." Eva smiled at the thought. Mark and Joanne crowded in from the back seats to read the front page headline. Eva's eyes flicked from the Broadway traffic to the newspaper on Dan's lap. Today was supposed to be fun, and yet Lauren Jaeger had appeared to spoil it. Eva felt on edge. There was only one thing for it. A decent sized glass of ice cold Italian white to go with her pizza.

Eva glanced at the headline, and the write up. LOCAL HERO GOES MISSING. The photograph below showed a happy middle-aged man – from a holiday in Israel, so the text beneath said. The man hardly looked like a typical hero to Eva, but then, Perry was behind the article. Poetic licence and all that. As she scanned further, Eva got the gist. Carl Renton was a single man, a devout Christian, who had spent the last fifteen years getting drunks dry and junkies clean. The article said the man had invested his own money and had received a grant to a second rehab. And in recent months, Carl Renton had personally taken up the fight against those bringing wave after wave of drugs into Essex, drugs such as Spice, which turned people into living zombies, and the new Uber form of ecstasy, which offered youths a celebrated almost manic high, followed by a crashing low. But Ubers were far worse than the earlier versions of ecstasy. Deaths seemed to follow wherever it was taken. The newspaper quoted the pastor of Renton's local church. The pastor described Carl Renton as "a selfless man who goes out on a limb for the lost. If not for Carl's help, an awful lot of people in this town would already be dead. Carl has always been a brave, fearless and loving man. He decided to try and take on the town's drug problems when most turned a blind eye. Because of that we are already greatly concerned for his safety. Carl was due to attend our regular church meeting this morning but he didn't show up. Carl wouldn't have ever missed one without calling." Perry went on to say that Carl Renton also failed to show up at either of his rehab houses for the late night shift. More behaviour which was distinctly out of character. The article ended with a neat appeal for anyone with news of Renton's whereabouts to give the news desk or the police a call to reassure the friends, rehab users and staff that the man was alive and well. The article was a heartstring puller with more than a hint of purple prose. Perry made Eva sick but it sounded like she wasn't wrong about Carl Renton. Whoever he was, he sounded like a good man. And his sudden disappearance, even for one night, was against the man's character.

"Let's hope they find him," said Eva. "Alive and well," she added.

Dan was already halfway through the flimsy newspaper by the time Eva parked the car outside Leigh's fancy pizza house. Eva watched him fold the newspaper under his arm as he got out of the car. He was going to bring the damn thing with him after all. Eva shook her head. Looked like it was going to have to be a large glass of white wine after all. Today, small just wasn't going to cut it.

Three

A Hawaiian for Joanne – sweet and savoury, much like the girl herself. A Four Seasons for Dan, – the man who wanted everything, all dowsed with extra chilli oil. An olive and anchovy for Eva, a woman who always opted for the most savoury of tastes, balanced by a glass of cold white wine which amounted to a third of a bottle. Mark opted for beef and mozzarella – plain and maybe a little too safe. Eva smiled. The wine wasn't enough to make her drunk, but it was enough to take the bitter edge off her mood. The pizza restaurant's chatty ambience helped too. Even Mark seemed to be loosening up. Dan flicked through the newspaper between slices of pizza, and Eva drank her wine to prevent herself complaining. She watched as he glanced through from front to back, and then started over, only reading the articles which had piqued his interest. Eva reclined in her seat. She took her glass in hand and pushed thoughts of Lauren Jaeger to the back of her mind.
"Now you've digested the whole newspaper, you should tell us what we're missing."
Dan laid the paper down and picked up the vegetable portion of his pizza. He eyed it with a carnivore's suspicion.
"Well, to start with you've got Carl Renton," said Dan.
"The missing hero," said Joanne, sipping from her own glass of white, a hint of pink already showing on her cheeks.

"Yep. There's even a profile piece on him inside – but he only disappeared last night. Perry must really think something's happened to the guy. She must have had a tip-off. This Renton guy looks safe and boring from the outside, but it seems he's actually a pretty interesting man. He sounds like a good guy out on a limb. I hope this story gets a happy ending."

"I'm not sure that's the ending Alice Perry would want."

"Alice Perry only wants to sell newspapers," said Dan. "And bad news is what sells."

"That's not all she wants," said Eva.

Dan looked at Eva, seeing her serious eyes. "Hey. We're past all that and we've got her under control."

Eva's eyes flicked to the newspaper. "So. What other craziness is going on in this town?" Dan knew she was changing the subject.

"This Uber Ecstasy craze is causing a lot of problems. A&E has been flooded with kids OD'ing on the crap." Dan flicked back to the paper and began to list the items he'd read.

"And, after that dumb-arse councillor managed to lose some items from that Saxon King treasure trove, Southend Museum is putting out an appeal for their return."

"What was he doing with them anyway?" said Joanne.

"They were the centrepiece for Councillor Audley's fundraising dinner. The councillor was no doubt stroking his own ego and it looks like we all paid the price." Dan patted the newspaper.

"Feel better for your news fix?" said Eva.

"I'll feel better when I finish this pizza and get another beer to wash it down. Are you still the designated driver?"

"So long as I stick to just this one," said Eva, tapping her glass, "I should just about manage it."

"Then another Kronenbourg it is. Anyone else?"
Joanne nodded, a mischievous glint in her eye. Mark hesitated before asking for a half.
"Suit yourself," said Dan. As he waved at the nearest waitress, Eva noticed Mark's eyes drifting off.
"What's on your mind, Mark?" said Eva.
"Me?" His eyes returned to the present and picked up a forkful of spicy beef. "Oh, just thinking about the past."
"*Oh please*," said Joanne. "Just when I was enjoying myself too.. Maybe you should go for the full pint instead."
"Um, no thanks," said Mark. "Actually, I was hoping that we could stop off somewhere on the way back into town – if you don't mind."
Eva shrugged. "I don't think that'd be a problem. Why? What do you want to do?"
"It's this." Mark shuffled in his seat and slid his hand into his pocket. When his hand came back it was carrying a bright red nylon wallet with a colourful 'Hang Loose' logo on the front.
"You brought *that* thing with you? Why?" said Joanne. She turned to face Eva. "He's been banging on about this stupid wallet for days. Because he'd stopped talking about it, I thought it had been forgotten."
"Not at all," said Mark. "I just thought it was a bit weird, that's all."
"Weird?" said Eva. "Why? Who does it belong to?"
Dan's hand still hung in the air. He hadn't been served. He leaned over the back of his chair and snapped his fingers for attention. "Hey."

"I found a provisional driving licence card inside," said Mark. "And an old gym membership card. Expired. There was no cash or anything else. I guess any cash could have been stolen and the wallet discarded."

Eva nodded for Mark to go on.

"It belongs to a guy called Joe Clancy," he said. "We were in the same class at school. We were similar kids. I mean, Joe wasn't exactly popular, either, but he was confident, smart, just a bit of a loner. But unlike me he always had plenty of money. His dad was a wealthy jeweller. They said Joe only insisted on coming to our school because he wanted to piss off his dad. I got the impression they never got on."

Eva did her best to follow Mark's story and sipped her wine. Joanne gave Eva a look, which seemed to say *'see what I have to put up with?'*

"Okaaay…" said Eva.

Mark picked up on the nuances and decided to sum up.

"Joe Clancy was a rich kid in a rough school. My school. He didn't need to be there, but there he was. After we left I never saw him in my part of town again. I mean, no one really ventures to that part of Southchurch anyway, unless they've got a very good reason. Basically, you either go there for the adult college or the adult entertainment, if you know what I mean. You're a kerb crawler coming for the ladies of the night."

"Ladies of the night?" said Joanne, raising an eyebrow. "Is that what you call them."

"I was trying to be eloquent about it."

"Well, you came close," said Joanne, grinning.

"And that's where you found the wallet? Near your home?" said Eva.

"Kind of. I found it in that little old park. The one we always used to call the duck park, the one on Park Lane."

"I know it," said Eva. "It's a very pretty looking place, but some very unscrupulous types use it by night," said Eva.

"I know," said Mark, "And that's where I found Joe Clancy's wallet. Right there in the park, thrown to the side of the path."

"So where does this Joe Clancy live?" asked Eva.

"Not far from here, actually. On Kings Road."

"Now that's a very decent street," said Dan, having placed his order with the waitress. "Big houses, fancy cars. You never know, the kid could even give you a reward for your trouble. I assume that's what you're after."

"No," said Mark. "I just thought we should get this back to him. And it'd be interesting to see how he's doing. It's been years.

Dan picked up the dregs of his glass with a thirsty grin.

"You want the little rich kid to get his wallet back? No problem. We can do that.. But first, we relax and we drink." Dan raised his glass. "Cheers!"

Mark sipped his half lager, his eyes glazing over the top of the glass. He felt the lump of his old schoolmate's wallet in his pocket, pressing against his chest. Old feelings and new questions had a hold of him. Soon he'd find out what it meant.

Four

After a hot morning, a large salty pizza and an oversized glass of white, Eva wasn't in a great state for driving. But then again, everyone else had drunk more than her with the exception of Mark. And there was no way their apprentice was driving her car. The two strong lagers were beginning to show in Dan's exuberance, and Joanne seemed to find everything hilarious. Finally Eva found herself enjoying the atmosphere in the car. The whole long afternoon lay ahead of them like a blank canvas. She could feel the beach calling. It was a rare day indeed that they skipped work to enjoy the local sands. But at the weekends, any hot day ensured most of the beaches were far too busy to be enjoyed. If ever there was a day for ice cream at the seaside this was it. Eva lowered the driver's side window all the way down and turned up the radio.

"Kings Road, remember?" said Mark.

"I know. I haven't forgotten," said Eva, glancing back in the rear-view. "Do you know where this Joe guy lives?"

"It says right here," said Mark. He opened the big red wallet and glanced at the driving licence. He read out the door number and Eva took it in.

"And after that?" said Dan. "How about a spot of beach followed by some sundowners at Chez Roberts and Bradley."

"We're certainly cutting loose," said Joanne, smiling.

"If not us, then who?" said Dan, with a theatrical tone. "If not now, when?!"

"What's that from?" said Eva.

"Ronald Reagan," said Dan.

"Who?" said Joanne.

"Forget it," said Dan.

The car pulled up at the foot of a steep slope, where the princely Kings Road stretched down from the back end of glamorous Leigh, into the neat affluence of Chalkwell. They were in the centre of Kings Road, a place of spacious white mid-twentieth century houses, all detached, all with big driveways, and many of them had two cars apiece, most paid for by lucrative city jobs just up the train line. Dan eyed the parked cars all around with a hint of envy. Then he looked at the house immediately before them with no car in sight. The driveway looked naked in comparison.

"Thought you said this guy has money," said Dan.

"He does. Just look at his house," said Mark.

Dan scoped it out. Eva turned down the stereo. From what they could see through the window the interior looked part minimalist and part cluttered. The balance in one room was in favour of clutter. The house looked well kept, as did the front garden and borders.

"Still, money shows itself in a man's car."

"Or a woman's car," said Joanne.

"Works either way – but no car."

"Joe lives with his father. His dad probably has the car."

"His mother doesn't live here?" asked Dan.

"No. They split up years back," said Mark. "His dad's freewheeling."

"And daddy got the house? Those odds are like winning the lottery."

"I get the idea she was the one who cheated," said Mark.

"Okay then. Go and give him his wallet back," said Dan.

"I'd kind of like to see what his house is all about. What did you say his dad did for a living?"

"I said he's a jeweller. Joe once boasted he was a bit of collector too. A collector of rare shiny things."

"Rare *and* shiny?" said Joanne. "*Now* I'm interested."

"So am I," said Dan, looking at the house. He noticed a curtain twitch in the leaded-light window of the first floor.

"Someone's in," said Joanne.

Mark got out of the car. The rest of them watched what was likely to be a brief exchange. Mark pressed the doorbell and its shrill ring was audible from the car. He waited a minute, then pressed it again. A moment after that, Mark turned back and started walking to the car.

"Well… it looks like he's not at home," said Mark.

"Someone is," said Dan.

"Then it can't be convenient for them. We can call back sometime."

"But how often do we come to Leigh?" said Joanne. "If you want him to get that wallet back maybe you should try one more time."

Mark sighed. A faint shadow flitted past the downstairs window as he approached the front door for the second time. This time, the big brown wooden door opened even before his finger reached the doorbell. Mark got ready to make his rehearsed statement, but when his eyes landed on the young woman who answered the door, words failed him. She had a serious, earnest expression, with big wide blue eyes, dark hair, and the kind of pretty elfish face which looked like it would flourish into a full lustrous beauty in a few years' time. But from the near haunted look on her face, she seemed unaware of her potential. She looked shy and awkward and her hair was a little lank.

It took Mark another few seconds to realise that he recognised her. The spark of recognition was mirrored in the girl's eyes. She tugged a lock of brown hair and tucked it behind her ear.

"Georgie?" said Mark.

A hint of pink lighted the girl's face. She nodded.

"Mark. I don't think I ever expected to see you again. At least not around here."

"Kings Road you mean?"

The girl shook her head. "At Joe Clancy's house."

Mark smiled. "You know, I could say the very same thing about you."

The girl's smile warmed a tad, and she looked at the others, waiting in Eva's gleaming red Alfa hatchback.

Joanne's leather seat creaked as she shifted in the back. The beginning of a frown settled on her face. "Who is she supposed to be?"

A thin smile appeared on Dan's face but he didn't say a word. He watched Mark step away from the doorstep and gesture towards the car.

"Uh. We came to bring this back to Joe." As he spoke, Mark backed away towards the Alfa, trying to bridge the gap between the house and the car, trying to draw the girl down from the doorstep. She hesitated a moment before she stepped out.

"What is it?"

"It's his wallet. I found it. I was just out here with my boss and my friends…"

Joanne raised an eyebrow in the back seat. "We were nearby so we thought we should bring this back. Nobody likes losing a wallet after all."

"No," said Georgie. "But that's odd. Joe didn't mention losing anything to me."

Mark paused when he was at the edge of the driveway. "So, um… you and Joe are…?"

"An item?" said Georgie.

She smiled and then the smile fell away and she said nothing for a moment "Kind of. And sometimes kind of not. But we're close enough." She didn't look sure about her last statement. Mark saw her discomfort and raised the wallet in the air.

"I'd love to give this to him. Is Joe here? I haven't seen him in years."

"Really? I never had you two down as friends…"

"I can't ever say we were best buddies, but there were a lot of worse people in the class."

"You can say that again," said Georgie. "Like Morris Murphy, and his little tribe of scumbags."

"Exactly," said Mark.

"Um," said the girl. "You can't give it to him now. He's not here."

"Oh. But if he's not here why are you?" said Mark.

The girl blushed again. "Me. Oh. I'm always hanging around here. These days it's what I do… You said you had a boss. What are you doing these days?"

The girl followed Mark close to the edge of the driveway and folded her arms. Mark nodded to the red car.

"Me? Oh. I work for a private detective agency. I'm their apprentice."

The girl looked at him with big-eyed wonder. "No way?! You're shitting me!" she said.

"No shit at all," said Mark.

"No shit," muttered Joanne in the back seat.

"Wow. And these are your bosses…? They're private detectives?"

Mark nodded. Eva smiled and Dan flicked a wave. "Hi."

"And that's my girlfriend," said Mark. "Joanne."

The girl looked at Joanne and seemed impressed by her looks. "Hi."

Upstairs in the house, Eva saw a net curtain flap once before it dropped back into place.

Eva narrowed her eyes and switched off the engine.

"Someone's home," she whispered to Dan. "But they don't want to come out. I don't know why that rankles but now I'm getting curious."

"The way you are today, I'd say you're ready to rankle at anything."

"I'm getting rankled too," said Joanne, glancing at Mark's awkwardness around the girl.

Eva and Joanne opened their car doors and stepped out into the afternoon sun. The girl appraised Joanna and Eva afresh and took a backward step onto the drive. Eva sensed her intimidation and offered a warm smile.

"Hi," said Eva. "It'd be great if Joe could just come down and get his wallet back. Just so as we know it got back to the rightful owner."

The girl blinked. "Joe's not in right now. I could take it for you and—"

"Someone's in," said Eva. "That room up there on the right. Maybe Joe's back already."

The girl looked up at the window behind her. When she looked back at Eva, Dan, Mark and Joanne, her defensive arm-folding became two wringing hands at her waist.

"Um. Sorry about that. Joe isn't exactly feeling himself today. I don't like to mislead anyone, but he told me to say he wasn't in."

"Why?" said Dan from the car.

"Because he's not so good with people when he's not well. And because he's shy like me, maybe," said Georgie.

But Eva could see the girl was being economical with the truth. Mark winced. Georgie had always been a bright spark, not far off the smartest girls in the class, but still far enough beneath the summit so no teacher had bothered in pushing her to excel. If she had been pushed, Mark had no doubt she wouldn't have been so stoop-shouldered or shy or have been caught telling foolish lies in the middle of Kings Road. He almost felt like covering for her.

"It's okay, Georgie," said Mark. "We only wanted to make sure he got this back. If he only comes down for a second, that would be fine."

They heard the sound of footsteps descending a wooden staircase, feet rattling fast down the stairs. A moment later, a young man with a pale, stubbly face and slim build stood in the doorway, one hand reaching up behind his head to scratch his back. He looked self-conscious. On the spot. Caught out.

The young man's hair already seemed to be thinning on top. He was Mark's age, but he looked older, and pretty uptight. His face flashed from a polite smile, to confrontational grimace and back again.

His gaze settled on Mark. "Hi, Mark. I hear you brought something for me?"

The young men regarded one another, taking in what had changed, and what hadn't. Mark studied the serious look on his face. That part was new. Joe Clancy had always been a loner, but he had been confident too, a joker, a smart alec with a quick sense of humour. The new version of Joe Clancy looked worn out, and his smile looked a little frayed at the edges.

"I think you lost your wallet."

"My wallet?" said Joe.

Mark raised the red Hang Loose wallet and Joe Clancy looked it over without moving to claim it.

"Where did you find it?"

"At Southchurch, in a place I call the duck park. It's at the bottom of York Road. It's not exactly your kind of place."

Clancy smiled. "Maybe not," he said.

Mark offered the wallet across and the young man eventually took it. "So how did it end up down there?"

"No idea," said Clancy. "But thanks for bringing it back."

Joe Clancy offered a nod of thanks. He aimed the same vague look of gratitude towards Eva, Dan and Joanne. It was no more than a platitude. A neat way of turning a thank you into a goodbye. The young man backed away towards his house, but he moved slowly, like he didn't want to appear too eager about it. The girl stood her ground, her arms folded, but her eyes big and thoughtful, her mouth framing unspoken words. They all waited for her to speak. Behind her, Joe Clancy saw his girlfriend was about to say something. He jumped in quickly.

"We should go in, Georgie," he said.

"What's the rush?" said Dan.

The girl looked around the group and then turned back to face Clancy. The young man's face quickly became a look of resignation.

"They brought your wallet back, Joe. You lost it and they brought it back."

"And? I said thank you," said Joe.

"It proves these people could help you, Joe. And look. We know one of them. Mark here was in our class at school. He was one of the good ones."

"And I appreciate him bringing back the wallet," said Joe. "I thanked him for it, but look, I honestly didn't really care whether I got that thing back or not. No offence by the way."

Mark's face hardened but his words didn't. "None taken."

"But didn't you hear?" said the girl. "Mark works for a private detective agency. These guys are private investigators." The young woman said the words with excitement. Relish – like a chance meeting with private investigators was the most fortuitous thing that could have ever happened. Joe Clancy paused for breath and took his time to reply. Eva, Dan, Joanne and Mark waited for him to speak. There was no doubt about it – something *was* going on.

"I'm not sure we need that kind of help, Georgie."

"But you needed help before," said Georgie. "And you know you won't get any here."

Eva and Dan exchanged a glance.

"Damn it, Georgie!" said Joe.

"Excuse me," said Eva. "But would one of you mind telling us what's going on here?"

"I don't want to bother you with my problems. You must be busy people. Besides, it's not like I have the finances to hire private detectives."

Dan looked up at the pristine white edifice of the large detached house. At the neat, weedless driveway, and the proud palm tree. Joe Clancy followed his eyes.

"This is my father's house, not mine."

Dan nodded, but the look in his eyes said *"And?"*

Georgie spoke quickly, as if she had to push past a sworn vow of silence.

"Joe does need your help," said the girl. "I'm sure Mark wouldn't mind helping out a little bit, especially seeing as he's brought you the wallet."

Clancy held his tongue. There was no way he could complain any further without causing a greater fuss. The young man knew he was boxed in. So he watched and listened as Georgie elaborated.

"Joe's dad isn't here very often. He wasn't here much back when Joe was at school, and these days he's around even less. But a person always needs someone to look up to, someone to help and guide them, right?"

Mark gave Joe a sympathetic look, but he looked away.

"You're all the help I need, Georgie."

Georgie shot him doubtful look. "I'm here when Joe needs me. But until very recently he had one really solid guy looking out for him. A friend who looked in on him whenever his dad was away."

A furrow of intrigue formed on Eva's brow.

"But it looks like he's gone."

"Gone?" said Dan, shaking his head.

Georgie nodded. "He left in a hurry last night. And if we believe what the newspaper is saying, he's gone missing too. I really hope not. He was so good for Joe."

"Hey, Carl might not have gone missing, Georgie," said Joe. "I don't get why the newspaper would even say that. Who knows? Carl might have taken off for a day or two, he works harder than most people, after all."

"Not him, Joe. You know he wouldn't do that as well as I do. And if that newspaper says he's gone missing, then they must have a reason. They must have spoken with his family. Or his projects."

Dan's eyes narrowed. Projects – meaning rehabs. Dan dipped his hand through the open car window and pulled out his creased copy of The Record. He shook the paper and slapped the front page flat, holding it up for all to see.

"You mean this guy is your friend? Carl Renton? They splashed this missing hero story all over the front page like it's cold hard fact. Like you said, they must have a reason. A journalist can lose their job over getting a front page wrong."

Joe's eyes blinked at the photograph on the front page. What remained of his weak smile faded altogether. The girl saw his face change and tucked the same rogue lock of hair back behind her ear.

"I hadn't seen that," said Joe Clancy.

"Don't sweat it yet. It's only the local rag," said Dan. "But judging from what they say about Mr Renton's interests, I'd say the attention might be justified. This article says he wanted to take on Southend's dealers and drug traffickers."

Clancy nodded. "Carl is a devout Christian. And by that, I don't mean some mealy mouthed stiff. He liked helping people in all different ways. In fact, he had a big vision to change the whole town."

"And he was helping you?" said Eva.
Joe Clancy rubbed his forehead, opened his front door and walked into the big porch with a sigh. "You could say that. Carl has a heart of gold. He's always looking out for people. He came to help me because he thought I was a little lost soul too."
"You were," said Georgie. "Your dad has never really looked out for you like he should."
The young man shot her another look.
"Whatever. So Carl decided he had to come and help fill the hole in my life. I wasn't always grateful to him. But yeah, Carl helped me a lot. There. You know everything there is to know. Have I told them enough now, Georgie?"
"Not really," she said. "If Carl *is* gone then you're going to need help now more than ever."
Joe looked at Eva and Dan and saw they were going nowhere.
"I don't need any help, honestly, I'm fine."
Eva watched Georgie bite her lip. The look on her face spoke volumes. Joe sighed a final time before he walked away from the front door, leaving it wide open in his wake. He walked deeper into the house.
"You may as well come in then." He looked back at the door.
The others looked at one another before Eva led the way into the house.
"I think we'd just like to hear about what kind of help you might need," said Eva. Georgie closed the door behind them.

They walked into a plush house, as white inside as it was on the outside. Space seemed to be the defining characteristic. The furniture was large, but clean and minimalist. In spite of the emptiness of the first rooms they saw – all minimalism, the moment they walked into the living room, it reminded Eva of a knick-knack parlour, part trophy cabinet, part museum, part granny's house. Her eyes circled the room, taking in the framed prints, the stack of leather-bound books on a corner bookshelf, the strange jewelled animal skull mounted above the fireplace – it looked as if it belonged to an antelope or similar – and the small wall-mounted glass cabinets laden with golden trinkets and objet d'art. Georgie and Joe seemed oblivious to the sparkling mess. As Eva and Dan scanned the room with a mixture of curiosity and fascination, Joe and the girl looked at one another.
"Joe always says he doesn't need help, but he does."
"Please, Georgie," said Joe. "You mean well, but…"
"I always mean well but you never like it anyway."
"It's just that things are already difficult without making them any worse."
Eva read their faces and tried to pick up on the detail. Dan's eyes were all over the cluttered walls.
"Where does all this stuff come from?" Dan prodded a silver skull ornament which was mounted on a dusty red velvet cushion.
"Please don't touch anything," said Joe. "It all means something to my father. He'll know if someone's been prodding around and I'll get the blame for it."
Dan nodded but kept his eyes on Clancy, waiting for his answer.

"My father is a jeweller by trade and by hobby. He buys and sells jewellery, and he collects the more interesting pieces for fun. His hobby gives him a reason for all his foreign expeditions. As far as my father's concerned, the more exotic the better."

"And he brings things like this home from his travels?" said Eva.

"Yeah. I used to think that was why he went away in the first place," said Joe. "But these days, I think he goes to get away from me. But he always gets something on his trips. And every one of his holidays turns into a business trip. He buys stuff and sells it. His trips pay for themselves and then some."

"Yeah. They must pay him very well, from what I see," said Dan.

"And these… artefacts… are they just jewellery to him?" said Eva. Joanne and Mark walked around the edges of the room, perusing and inspecting as they went.

"Kind of," said Joe, looking tired. "So long as they contain some precious metal or gems, he loves them all the same. He has another cache of stuff like this upstairs in his study. Though I'm not really supposed to say that."

"A hidden collection. And I bet those are worth a fair few quid."

Eva cast a cautionary eye at Dan. The questions were mounting but nosing into the family wealth wasn't going to get them any answers. The Clancy house was intriguing – but Eva felt that the jewellery and gold on the walls weren't the substance of it. The intrigue came from the boy himself. Eva sensed she had to be subtle to get a clearer view, because the young man seemed to have no intention of being understood.

But there was no stopping Dan's current line of questioning. "So, let me get this right," said Dan. "Your old man is a jeweller? So where's his shop?"

"He's an online jeweller," said Joe. "These days he has other people run the business for him. Paid staff. His main interest is in the collectables."

"Interesting. Which means your old man gets paid twice. Once for the standard jewellery business and again for the more interesting stuff he picks up along the way. His holidays turn a profit too."

Joe Clancy's face clouded and turned pale. The young man left Georgie standing by the window and walked between Dan and the wall of objects in front of his eyes.

"My dad works hard and he earns well. I don't see a problem with either part of the deal."

"Neither do I," said Dan. "I'm interested, that's all. My line of work makes me interested in people. Does he get up to anything else?"

The kid read Dan's eyes and saw he was genuine. He lowered his guard with a shrug. "He's been trying to write a book too. Some kind of thriller or adventure, I think." There was a hint of pride in the young man's voice, but there was an equal hint of melancholy. From her position by the window, Georgie's eyes seemed to ask for Eva's attention. Eva felt there were words on the tip of her tongue. She gave the slightest nod of invitation and the girl broke her silence. "Joe's father is incredibly good at what he does," she blurted. "But the way I see it, that's always been part of the problem."

"Problem?" said Joe.

The girl nodded, refusing to be silent. "He's always away these days. And when he's not away at work, he's here, locked in his study or out at the library, finishing whatever he's working on until it's done. You only ever see him when he's between trips or business meetings or writing his book."
Joe winced and glanced at the floor.
"Then it's a good job he has you for company," said Eva.
"He's away now?" said Dan.
Joe shook his head. "No. He's between projects, like Georgie said."
"That's good then," said Mark, taking an airy tone to lighten the mood.
Joe and Georgie looked up at him, unconvinced.
"Isn't it?" said Mark.
"After this last gap," said Georgie. "I think Joe had gotten used to his father not being around. I think we both had... Carl Renton helped fill the void he left behind."
"Georgie!" said Joe, checking her. "There's no need to tell these people everything!"
"They're private detectives, Joe. They could help you. They could help us all."
"Help in what way?" said Eva.
"Help us find Carl, of course. Joe won't admit it, but he got close to Carl. He was like a second father."
"That's overdoing it, Georgie."
"You want us to find Carl Renton?" said Dan. "We could look at that. But I still don't understand. How come someone with your background had dealings with a man like him?"
The boy's eyes flared. "A man like him?"

"You don't strike me as the Christian type. I knew those types pretty well. I went through some hard times a few years back. I knew the down and outs, the junkies and alcoholics, all their self-inflicted misery and hard luck stories," said Dan. He looked around the room. "That's not you."

"Carl Renton is more than some sappy Christian who runs rehabs," said Joe. "He does that because he's kind. He does all kinds of outreach stuff. I first met Carl at some music event at my sixth form college about a year back. I got talking to him about music. He was funny and we got on from there."

"Then he started coming around here?" said Dan, making a face.

"Or I would go and see him at his office. I always got on better with the more eccentric types. You know that right, Mark?"

Mark nodded. "Yeah. I remember alright."

"Carl was real with me, so I was real with him. It was a mutual respect thing. Though I guess Dad being away so much might have been a factor in how we became friends." Georgie gave a thin smile at the admission. "Carl was good to him and good to a lot of other people too. But disappearing like he did. That's not like him at all."

"Yeah. From what I've read, I think the same," said Dan. "People like that, the kind who run rehab centres – dependable upstanding people, they don't just up sticks, and disappear. If they did, they would certainly have a serious reason for it. That's the first thing you need to establish, is why he had to go. Once you establish that, it should be pretty straightforward to find him. If he wants to be found."

Joe Clancy made a face and looked away.

"Is there a problem?" said Dan.

Joe looked up and met his eye. "What if he doesn't want to be found?"

Eva and Dan shared a momentary glance.

"And what makes you think that?" said Dan.

"Just the fact he's gone. Doesn't that speak for itself? Like you said, people don't disappear unless they have a very good reason."

"And do you know what that reason might be, Joe?" said Eva,

The young man met her eye. He seemed downcast, pale and weary. "No," he said. "No, I don't."

After studying his eyes, Eva gave a slow nod of acceptance. He seemed to be telling the truth.

"And that's not even the extent of our problems, is it, Joe?" said Georgie.

The young man looked up at the girl and shook his head. He was about to say something but she beat him to it.

"The break-in, Joe. The burglary. And the other missing stuff.

Joe Clancy gave the girl a sharp look.

"Come on," said the girl. "If there's a chance that these people can help, then you may as well tell them everything."

"I think I should consult my father on that first, don't you? They burgled his belongings after all."

Eva frowned.

"I'm sorry? Break-ins? Theft?" she said.

"Don't worry. My father is dealing with all that. There was the break-in last night, and a few other things are missing too. Having a collection like his creates risks in itself."

"You had a break-in here?" said Dan.

"Yes," said the girl. "They came in through the kitchen window and they stole a few things from the collection…" she looked at Joe. "So Joe told me," she added.

"Last night?" said Dan.

Joe nodded. "Late last night."

"And were you here when the house was robbed?" said Eva.

The young man shook his head. "Unfortunately, yes."

"It was pretty scary," he said. He looked at Georgie. The two of them exchanged a meaningful glance. Eva saw it. Dan's eyes narrowed.

"I was upstairs while it happened."

"You must have heard the glass getting smashed…" said Dan.

Joe looked suddenly embarrassed. "I'm a solid sleeper. But even if I had been awake, I wouldn't have risked my life to save a few pieces of shiny metal."

"What did they take?" said Dan.

"Oh… I don't know the details. I only knew that stuff had been taken. But my father knows about that."

A car pulled up outside on the driveway, and the engine shut down. Dan looked out and saw the grand black bonnet of a new Lexus saloon fill the window. The car door slammed and a raised voice could be heard. It sounded like one half of an angry telephone conversation. The words were hard to make out, but the tone was clear – irritated and frustrated.

"Your father?" said Eva.

Joe nodded. "Sounds like that's him now. Let's hope he doesn't mind you lot being here. "The boy stiffened as the key turned in the lock. Eva and Dan felt themselves tensing too. The door opened and a set of heavy, confident feet echoed into the hallway before the door clunked shut.

"No…" said the voice. "But my Celtic torq has nothing whatsoever to do with whatever items that preposterous councillor lost at his little soiree. Come on, man. It would only take a fraction of expertise to tell the difference between a piece of ancient Celtic gold and the pieces you're looking for. There's a clue in the name. What the councillor lost belonged to a Saxon King, and my gold torq is Celtic! That piece is mine and went missing in a burglary here last night. I'm happy you found it, but it's mine! Surely the museum staff, with all their expertise, could have explained that a Saxon belt buckle has nothing at all in common with a Celtic gold band! If you people won't take my word for it, surely you'll take theirs?"

There was more silence as the man kicked his shoes to one side. Eva, Dan and the rest kept silent and listened in.

"Now listen here. I've been robbed blind. You've thankfully found one of my pieces and all you want to do is give me incident numbers and claim procedures and now you're telling me you won't release that piece of mine until some bureaucrat with no expertise tells you that Celtic gold is not the same as Saxon gold. It's from a different era, from a different race of people, found in an entirely different country! Do the idiots rule the roost here or what? No, no. That wasn't an insult. It was merely a rhetorical question…"

The man on the mobile passed by the front room door and stopped walking. The phone was still pressed to his ear as he leaned into the room and his eyes widened as he took in all the faces ranged around him. His mouth fumbled to find words he no longer wished to say in public.

"Look, officer, I've got to go. That piece is mine, that's all there is to it. And if I don't hear from you by tomorrow then I'll probably have to contact my solicitor. Now please get me some good news. I could do with it."

The man took the phone from his ear and ended the call. Then he looked at his son and the rest of them, letting the silence rapidly fill with unspoken questions.

"More guests of yours, Joe?" said his father in a deep, well-spoken voice.

The boy looked awkward in the extreme.

"Yes, they found my wallet and brought it back to me."

"All of them? They all found it?" said the man.

"No. Mark here was in my class at school and he found it."

The taller man nodded at Mark. "Then he'll remember Georgie as well."

"I do," said Mark. "Pleased to meet you, Mr Clancy."

The man nodded but offered no further greeting.

"I had no idea you'd lost a wallet, Joe. You never mentioned it."

"I'd forgotten all about it. I think it happened while you were away," he said. The older, taller Clancy gave a nod. "Well, at least some people still believe in returning other people's belongings. For a moment I thought you'd managed to find yourself a new set of strange friends. My son is a collector much like I am," said the man with a smile. "Except where I tend to collect precious items, my son tends to collect people."

"The police have one of your items?" said Eva.

A furrow appeared in the man's brow. He cast a look at his son before speaking.

"Yes, unfortunately they do. It seems one of the items these ruddy thieves purloined from my house was either lost or discarded en route. It was found early this morning on the Southchurch seafront. Compared to some of the other items, that Celtic band certainly doesn't look worth very much. It's dirty and discoloured with age. But it was one of my first purchases. I bought it from a potholer in northern France. It has plenty of sentimental value, not to mention financial value. Somehow these fools have managed to confuse it with the museum's missing Saxon treasures. All because of some showboating councillor's almighty cock-up. The councillor's house got robbed while he had the Saxon haul on display."

"Did you have anything to do with the Saxon King find, Mr Clancy?" said Dan.

"And are the Saxon pieces still missing?" said Eva.

"Yes. They should never have kept the damn things at our little town museum in the first place, let alone loan them to some fool councillor for his house party. Damn fools. They should have gone straight to the British Museum. They know how to look after treasures up there."

The man's brow dropped low over his eyes.

"Excuse me for saying this, but seeing as this is my home, I'm sure you'll understand. Just what is your interest in all this? What with the burglary and the police holding my belongings, one tends to be a little cautious as to who one lets into his house – even if my son doesn't take the same precautions."

The younger man blushed and shook his head.

"It's not like that, Dad. They brought me my wallet…"

"So you said," said Clancy Senior, sticking a speculative tongue against his cheek.

"Of course, Mr Clancy," said Eva. "My name is Eva Roberts, and this is my partner Dan Bradley. We're private investigators."

The man's frown lifted a little. His eyes fell upon Mark and Joanne.

"And these are our assistants," said Eva. "This certainly wasn't a business call by any means. Mark wanted us to return the wallet he found, but then we learned that Joe here knows Carl Renton – the man the newspapers are saying is missing, You must know him too, I take it."

"What? They're saying he's missing, are they? But wasn't he here last night?"

Joe nodded with a pained expression.

"Then he can't be missing. The papers must have it wrong. Mr Renton is a friend Joe collected last year, while I was away on business. Yes, I know him. Seems a nice, upstanding fellow. Very different to me and Joe, of course. But I suppose Joe could have picked up with a lot worse than him while I was on my travels. I was a bit concerned the man was going to turn him into a tambourine waving church hippie at first…"

"Dad," said Joe.

"But over time I saw he had a stabilising influence on the lad. That's what he needs, of course. My work isn't exactly perfect in that regard, I'm afraid. Renton isn't the friend I would have chosen for him, but he is safe at least."

"Safe? He's better than safe, Dad," said Joe.

"But now he's missing…?" said Mr Clancy. "Are you working to find him at all?"

"No," said Dan. "We'd only just read about it before we came here."

"I see," said Clancy.

"And with your burglary it seems you have a problem of your own."

"Yes," said Clancy. His eyes narrowed and he sucked in air through his teeth, "Yes, I certainly do. It seems some chancer has decided to take my collection for himself. I'm sure it'll be one of the usual rogues doing the rounds. We live on one of those kinds of streets that the villains target from time to time. I don't mind so long as I get it all back."

"Were there other thefts?" said Eva. "I got the impression you lost a few other things."

"A few things have gone missing here and there, but nothing to worry about. But this was a big hit right at the heart of my collection and I'm not in the mood to let it happen again. Some of these were the centrepieces of the whole thing. Just holding them takes me back to the place where I first bought them. And they're effectively my life savings too. My son's inheritance."

"Perhaps they could help you find them, Mr Clancy," said Georgie, with big eyes. Her voice trailed into silence as the man looked at her. He regarded Eva and Dan with thoughtful eyes. Eva saw a moment of opportunity. Business was slow lately and here was a new job just waiting to happen. They both felt it. There was no need to pitch for the business. They'd expressed an interest, demonstrated their credentials through their questions and they were already on the ground. The rest was up to Mr Clancy himself.

"Hmmm. You've done this kind of thing before?"

"Located stolen items? Found a thief?" said Eva

"Found missing persons?" said Dan.

"Located stolen items, mainly."

"Yes, Mr Clancy. We've done that kind of thing before. Successfully too."

The man crumpled his chin and nodded his head. He looked at his son, at Georgie too.

"Then maybe you should come and see what's left of my collection. It might give you a feel for what's missing, and perhaps, give you an inkling where to look. If I were to take you on, that is."

Eva buried her excitement under a professional smile, but Dan saw the gleam in her eyes. Joanne noticed it too and beamed in the corner of the room.

"It certainly wouldn't hurt to take a look, would it?" said Eva.

Clancy shot Dan a look of caution.

"Ah," said Clancy. "I prefer to take one guest into the room at a time."

"We're trustworthy, Mr Clancy," said Dan.

"I'm sure you are. But allow me a mite of caution. I'm sure you'll be able to tell your partner what he needs to know."

Eva looked at Dan and nodded. "I can manage that."

Dan didn't look impressed but shrugged anyway.

The tall man led the way into the neat clean white corridor.

"Dad, wait!" called Joe.

Eva and Clancy Senior returned to the living room doorway. Clancy Senior looked serious and burdened.

"Yes?"

"If you do hire them," he said slowly. "Maybe… you could ask them to find Carl Renton too."

"I think those would be defined as two quite separate tasks, don't you, Joe? I want my collection back from that thief."

"They do seem like separate tasks," said Eva. "But seeing as Mr Renton has been such a help to you, we'll see what we can do."

Joe nodded his thanks and Clancy Senior gave him an 'are you satisfied?' look before turning away to lead Eva to the stairs.

Any idea of an afternoon at the beach had gone by the wayside, but there was a new excitement in the air which couldn't be expressed as long as they remained in the Clancy household. Dan decided to use the wait for Eva as best he could. His eyes tracked around the artefacts on the living room walls and he took in the odd, quiet glances between Joe and Georgie. The dynamic between them was weird, but Dan couldn't yet decide how. He resolved to try and crack the code with a few questions.
"So tell me more about Carl, Joe. When did he actually disappear?"
The young man's eyes glazed with a sad, tired look as he began to replay the events of the night before.

In the hallway, Clancy Senior led Eva to the staircase at the back of the hallway
"Your son seems quite affected by Mr Renton disappearing."
"Yes, don't think I haven't noticed," he said. "But when you've known Joe for as long as I have, you'll know that he gets affected by an awful lot of things. He's the sensitive type, I'm afraid. Highly strung. A trait he inherited from his mother."
"Sensitive? Some people would say that's a good thing," said Eva.
"I'm sure some would. Don't get me wrong, Miss Roberts. I want what's best for the boy. But becoming resilient to the slings and arrows are essential for success in this world, and Joe needs to get a lot more resilient than he is now."

"All in good time, I'm sure," said Eva with a smile. "He's still young."

"Hope springs eternal," he said, pointing the way for Eva to take the flight of stairs. Clancy followed on behind.

"What did you make of Carl Renton, Mr Clancy?"

"I only ever knew him in passing, you understand."

"So what did you make of him?" said Eva as she finished climbing the dark wooden staircase.

"Well, I knew the man was on something from the first moment I met him," said Clancy.

Eva's face flickered. "What?"

"All those fixed smiles and enthusiastic handshakes. He was high on religion. I'll admit, that bothered me for a while. But then I considered the benefits."

"The benefits?"

"The obvious benefits. I didn't have to worry that the man was some kind of pervert trying to groom my son. And Carl kept an eye on my son for me while I was away."

Eva frowned. "And does Joe need an eye on him?"

"I never gave him permission to get so close with Georgie, for example. Joe is a young man, Miss Roberts. And young men always need an eye on them, if only for their own good."

Clancy Senior led Eva along a short upper corridor before opening the door into a cluttered study much like the living room below. The study was modern and the furniture all neat and square but for a distinctive dark wooden bureau standing proudly against one wall. There was a side table with an old-fashioned telephone beside it. One of the kind you had to put your finger in to turn the dial. The room felt like the back room of a museum, a place where a curator might work and catalogue his pieces. On top of the bureau, not far from a wall-mounted trophy cabinet, was a book, open to reveal pages of handwritten numbers and notes. Beside it was a sphere, a little like a giant children's marble, but its swirl of colours were purples and pinks.

"I bought that one in India. It actually comes from a Hindu wedding. The Hindus do so love their gold and precious gems," said the man, seeing Eva's eyes land on it. "It's a more recent acquisition, so I'm not entirely sure of its composition. I'll have it checked and log it accordingly. To me it looks simply priceless either way."

"And this Hindu family gave it to you? Surely not?" said Eva.

"No, no. I paid them handsomely. India has quite a liking for money, you see. It can persuade most people to part with even the most sentimental things."

"Fascinating." said Eva.

"The stone?" he said, picking it up, weighing it in his palm. Eva shook her head. "Your life is what I meant. Part jeweller, part collector, part writer…"

He nodded. "Writer, oh please," said Clancy looking coy. "He told you about that, did he? It would be better to say part traveller. I have a wanderlust. The novel is just an itch I needed to scratch. But the trinkets I buy are a wonder to me. Like this for instance. It doesn't look like much does it?" Clancy hefted a small ingot in his hand. It was dull grey, like faded iron, or maybe tin or lead. He passed it to Eva.

"This is pure gold encased in a shell of base metal to disguise it. It was a means for the original owner, one of the original gold rush pioneers, to keep a secret of his find. The secret didn't last long, mind. The gold in that ingot could well be from Sutter's Mill, California, itself. The home of the California Gold Rush. Another very special item."

Eva nodded. Clancy clearly wanted her to be impressed, and she was. But Eva didn't intend to look starry eyed.

"If you want me to find what was stolen, Mr Clancy, I'll need to know exactly what happened – when they were stolen, and exactly what we are looking for. Do you have any idea who might have taken them?"

The man shook his head. "None at all. I've been back in the country for a few days now, but a few small things went missing a few weeks back, though they were nothing compared to this."

"Why?"

"They've taken the most obvious treasures – the gold and silver wrist bands, and masks from my Ethiopian trip and the cymbals and dishes from Syria. After what happened in Syria, it's possible there's nothing like them left in the entire world. Those items are precious indeed."

"Anything else?"

"Necklaces and rings too. The kind of thing one would keep behind glass rather than wear. I only hope the barbarians don't melt the things down for profit. That would be just as bad as what those savages did to monuments in the Middle East."

"You really think it would be that bad?" said Eva.

"To me at least. I love these things, Miss Roberts, and I'd believed they were safer here than anywhere else – particularly with my son always on hand."

"Always on hand? Then Joe doesn't work? No college or part time job?"

"College, yes, he was at college. Studying for his A-levels, if one can call it studying. My son, as you will have already seen, prefers company to study. And as for a job – he lives under my roof, all paid for by yours truly, he eats the food from the fridge, and I supply him with a small allowance. A kind of salary, if you like, for keeping house and looking after my collection. But it seems his company might have kept him a little more distracted from that duty than I would have liked."

"How do you mean?" said Eva, wanting the specifics behind the man's opinion.

"Georgie. Mr Renton too. I think he's been too busy to keep an eye on the house."

"Teenagers are the all same, don't you think?"

"I suppose so," said Clancy. "Though without any decent study, I don't see how Joe will be able to follow in my footsteps. Business is about keeping the mind sharp, and when making deals of this size, you need to be sharper still. But, ultimately, that's a matter for him."

Eva nodded. Clancy seemed a good man in essence, but stern all the same.

"Okay," said Eva. "So Joe looks after your collection."
"Yes, much as a security man or a caretaker might," said Clancy.
Eva gave him a certain look.
"I only mean to say that he has no expertise. I love my son, Miss Roberts, but the only kind of looking after he provides is his presence. His presence here is the deterrent, that's all."
"But the burglary took place while you were here, correct?"
"I was in the country, but I wasn't at home. My son was here. They broke in through the downstairs kitchen window, took a few items from the living room, then came up here and helped themselves to my wristbands, cymbals and dishes."
"When did it happen?" said Eva.
"Last night apparently. I had the window replaced first thing this morning. A broken window is an open invitation. It had to be seen that someone was dealing with the mess promptly. If not, maybe the blighters would have come back."
"So…" said Eva, carefully. "Joe was at home."
"Don't remind me. Yes. Joe tells me he was asleep. Which well he might have been. The boy has always slept like a log. His mother was the same. It used to take an age to wake her in the mornings, and even then she always complained about it."
"So he says he slept through the break-in."
"Miss Roberts, I know it sounds ridiculous, but I was here one time when the smoke alarms went off in the night. My son slept through two of the loudest alarms I've ever heard, and one of them is right outside his bedroom door."
"Really?"

"Yes. And since he's been hanging around with dear Georgie, I think those late nights of his mean he's sleeping in later too.."

"Ah yes, Georgie," said Eva. "What is the arrangement there exactly?"

"There is no arrangement. Georgie is my son's friend, that's what he says. By which I presume he means girlfriend. But I've given him ground rules there. The girl is not to stay here. She has her own home and her mother will be concerned, especially if she thinks I'm letting my son do whatever he likes with her under my roof. No way. The rules are she goes home."

"But she's here a lot, it seems," said Eva.

"He's a young man and I don't think Georgie's influence on my son is altogether negative. I even hope she might even motivate him towards aiming for something, or at least pulling himself out of his doldrums. Love can do that for a man, don't you know. In the beginning at least."

"Your son does seem a little in the doldrums," said Eva, "doesn't he?"

"He's a moody teenager and he doesn't look after himself. He eats junk and doesn't exercise, consequently he has a gnat's immune system. He's ill far too frequently for my liking. He needs to grow up and get out in the world."

"But you need him here, don't you?"

"Not all the time. He should have a life too."

"So he's ill a lot then?" said Eva.

"Yes. With all manner of bugs. You name them, if they're current, Joe will get them. Vitamin supplements don't seem to do a damn thing for the lad."

"Hmmm. And he was here last night.."

"Yes. And yes, he was ill again. Not severely ill, just under the weather, as always. Weak, pale and tired. He went to bed about nine and as I'd finished working, I was heading out to meet someone."

Eva gave him an inquisitive look.

"A lady friend," said Clancy.

"And was Georgie here when Joe went to bed?"

"No. She'd gone home already. I always make sure of that."

"Fine. So it was just you and Joe, and Joe went up at nine pm, feeling ill, and you went out."

"About a quarter of an hour later or so, yes. But before I left, I went up to check on him, brought him some medicine, but he was already half asleep. He seemed a bit feverish to me, but he was asleep so I left the cold and flu remedies by his bed in case he needed them."

"This Carl Renton thing must have upset him," said Eva. "But then Mr Renton wasn't missing at that point."

"Renton had only just left a while before that. Joe seemed upset about something, but he didn't want to talk about it. I put it all down to his mood swings and general poorliness and let the matter go. I suppose it could have been down to some foreknowledge about Renton but I'd only be guessing, I'm afraid. His mood swings could have equally been about a row with Georgie. Or the usual simple disapproval of my ways."

"Disapproval?"

"Yes. Haven't you noticed yet? Oh, I'm sure you will. Joe disapproves of a lot of things, and I am chief among them."

"But why would he disapprove of you?"

"He thinks I'm a let-down as a father. Who knows, he could be right. But then he doesn't remember what his mother was like." Clancy offered a smile and finally relaxed a little, visibly sinking into his shoes

"So your son is estranged from his mother too?"

"Yes, he is. And I can't say I'm sorry about that. But she chose her path, and I've worked hard to establish mine. Now, do you mind, Miss Roberts. I have a few things to do. I need to check in on my jewellery business and so forth."

"Just a few more things, Mr Clancy."

"Very well.

"Where were you during the robbery?"

"Why ask me?" said Clancy. "I'm the one who was robbed after all."

"If I can get the fullest possible picture of comings and goings last night, I'm sure it would help."

"Fine then. As I said, I've got a lady friend. Yvonne Parker. She happens to know a lot about jewellery and ornaments, and she's great company too. Soon as Joe was settled I went to see her for drinks and a spot of company."

Eva thought of asking if the man has spent the night with Yvonne Parker, but it seemed inappropriate to ask without being hired for the case. But Eva's hesitancy spoke for her. Mr Clancy scratched his chin before he spoke.

"I stayed until about five am. I always wake up early. Yvonne was going to be busy this morning, so I left her to it."

Eva nodded. "Thanks for being so candid, Mr Clancy."

"If it helps find what's been stolen from me, I'll tell you all I can. I suppose you'll want pictures of the missing items? Visuals to help you track them down?"

"That would certainly help, yes," said Eva. The man walked to the bureau and pulled down the writing flap. He pulled another leather-bound book – one of A5 diary size – from one of the pigeon holes at the back and laid it flat on the desk flap. Not everything was organised. Between the pigeon hole compartments was a mess of paper piled at all kinds of angles. Accounting and receipts, she guessed. An untidiness from disliking the financial aspect of his work? It was a common malaise. But everything else seemed orderly and beautiful. Eva looked at the pages of the book. There were images of gold bangles, cymbals, small bowls. Each one had been assigned a handwritten code number. And beneath the handwritten notes (all in nice blue fountain pen ink) a new pencil note had been added. It said 'Missing'. Eva noticed most of the missing items seemed to belong to the empty spaces in the wall cabinet, but there was one anomaly. Eva looked at the catalogue entry of a fine ornamental hatchet with a gold and copper criss-crossed handle. There was no 'Missing' word beneath it, but she saw its place on the display was empty.

"This seems to be missing too, Mr Clancy.

"Which?" said Clancy.

"The… um, Celtic hatchet?" said Eva, reading the note.

"Damn it. You're right I didn't even make a note it!" said Clancy, snapping his fingers with irritation. "Still, that you noticed the problem is very reassuring. You've got quite the sharp eye, I see." Clancy nodded. He lifted the lid of the bureau, closed up the writing flap, and turned to face her. "Most of the time, yes."

"Good, because now you'll have to find my Celtic hatchet too. That came from the same tranche as the Celtic torq which the police confiscated to save that idiotic councillor's blushes."

Eva flicked through the neatly written pages. The catalogue entries were thorough and detailed.

"You're welcome to borrow this catalogue, but you must bring it back. I catalogue everything I have and I only keep one catalogue for each category. This one is for my most special items, so guard it well."

"I'll do my best, Mr Clancy." Eva leafed through the book a little longer then slid it into her handbag and made a show of fastening the bag shut with care.

"Anything else you need?" said Clancy.

"One thing. This Celtic torq of yours. What is it exactly, and how did they get their hands on it?"

"My torq is essentially a large solid gold neck band with a bulb on either end. Look in the catalogue. There it is, see? Quite a piece it is, too. The thief must have taken it with all the rest, but he wasn't so careful as to keep hold of it. It was found on the beach this morning by some man walking his dog. Thankfully he was the honest type, or I'd have lost it twice over. Now the police have it and they won't release it to me, because of their inept confusion over the Saxon King pieces stolen from the councillor's house."

"And the torq has nothing in common with the Saxon King pieces?"

"No. And the loss of the Saxon King pieces is their problem, not mine. I only want my Celtic torq back. It's mine. But don't worry, I'll deal with that. Can you see what I've got to deal with – all this on top of running a business."

"It's certainly a mess, Mr Clancy."

"A mess of every kind," said Clancy. "And look, I'm grateful for you showing an interest in my son's missing friend Renton. Very kind of you. But the emphasis must be on finding my missing items something's happened to them. If that seems a little selfish then so be it. But Renton could well turn up in a few hours, whereas my precious items are definitely gone. Who can say what will happen to them if you don't find them soon? They could be long gone."

"I understand your urgency, Mr Clancy. But if we can look into Carl Renton as well we certainly will."

Clancy nodded and checked his watch. Gold, naturally. Noticing that Eva still lingered before him, the man scratched the back of his head.

"Is there anything else I can help you with, Miss Roberts?"

"Yes," said Eva, nodding. "Just one thing. Are you hiring us for the job, Mr Clancy? Or just sounding me out?"

"I'm hiring you. If you can find those things of mine, I'm sure your fee will be worth every penny."

"Yes, Mr Clancy. I'm sure it will…" Eva beamed brightly. Her smile was such that Clancy couldn't help beaming right back.

But Eva still saw the case as two jobs, no matter what Mr Clancy wanted. Finding the missing items from his collection was the headline but finding Carl Renton seemed to be his son's priority. Even Clancy Senior admitted the man was good people. And there were still others dependent on Carl Renton turning up alive and well, people who relied on his help to recover from their slavery to drug addiction.

Whether it paid the bills or not, finding Carl Renton had to be part of the job. And Eva reckoned they would have just enough time and capacity to do both, so long as the gold didn't elude them for long.

Five

After a strong coffee to fend off the lunchtime excesses Eva and Dan returned once more to Kings Road. As soon as the coffee was done Eva printed a contract, grabbed her jacket and they left the office. It was still hot outside, the traffic was slow, and most car windows were fully wound down, but playtime was over. It was time to get back to work and they arrived back at the Clancy residence within an hour of having left. Aaron Clancy's job was the only show in town, which meant they needed the man's signature on the dotted line before he had the chance to change his mind. Mark and Joanne had been left behind as placeholders to keep the door open and their seats warm. It helped no end that Mark knew Joe from school, and Eva saw them through the living room window talking quietly when they arrived. She rang the doorbell and got ready to wait but Joe Clancy opened the door almost immediately. The young man searched Eva's eyes as if there might be some news already but Eva shook her head in answer. There was nothing to say yet. Clancy Senior appeared at the back of the house, emerging from the stairwell into the hallway. Eva met his eye, conscious of the job contract burning a hole in her hand. She wanted it signed, pronto. Getting the job felt like a stroke of luck and she was determined to keep it.
"I'll need a word with you in a minute, Joe," said Eva, before turning her attention to Clancy Senior.
"Anything you need," said Joe, "just so long as it helps find Carl."
Eva smiled and walked down the hall with the freshly printed contract in hand.

"First and foremost a businesswoman, I see," said Clancy, his hands stuck into his pockets.

"A necessary evil in my line of work," said Eva. "Soon as the paperwork is done we can just get on with the job."

"Then we'd best sign it, hadn't we?" said Clancy. "Or it won't be long before those things are lost for good."

As Dan walked into the house he caught a glimpse of Eva schmoozing the client with the contract in hand. He watched her follow him up the stairs. Let the man have her to himself if he wanted, so long as he signed. Following Eva's lead, Dan had grabbed his own version of the private investigator uniform – his leather jacket to complete his white T-shirt and blue jeans look. But the heat was too much to wear the leather, so he draped it over the crook of his arm, walked inside and greeted them all with a nod. But the conversation in the front room seemed stilted and awkward and Dan felt hotter than ever. Beer and coffee had left him dehydrated.

"Any chance of a glass of water?" he asked. Joe shrugged and looked to Georgie to do the job. The girl gave a reluctant nod and walked out of the room.

"So… what have you lot been talking about?" said Dan.

"Carl Renton," said Joanne, flatly. "Sounds like a nice guy."

The room fell silent again. Joe didn't seem the most enthusiastic of hosts – he hadn't from the start. The closer Dan looked at him, the harder Joe worked to refuse his eyes. Dan noticed the sweat on his forehead and cheeks, the tired look in his eyes. Either the kid was still fretting about his missing friend, or he was unhealthier than they had realised. The boy looked like he was about to faint from the heat.

"Joe," said Dan.

Joe finally met his eye.

"You okay? You look like you need a drink yourself."

"I'll be okay. But I'd feel better if you were out there looking for him. That's what you're going to do, right?"
"We will be soon enough."
Georgie came back holding a glass of water. Dan shook his head and pointed to Joe. "I think you'd better give it to Joe. He looks like he needs it even more than I do."
Georgie looked at Joe with concerned eyes. She handed him the drink and Joe snapped. "Will you just stop fussing."
"But he's right, Joe," said Georgie. "They can see it too. You're not right, Joe. You need to see a doctor."
"Whatever," he said. He took the glass from her hand and poured the whole thing down his neck. "There you are. Satisfied? I don't need a doctor, all I need is rest. A rest from all your carping and all this stress." The young man rose from his chair and stalked out of the room. He climbed the stairs and they heard him slam a door upstairs.
"Sorry about that," said Georgie.
"You've got nothing to apologise for," said Joanne. "Is he always like this?"
"No," said Georgie. "Only when he's feeling bad. The stress of Carl going missing has made things worse."
"Worse?" said Dan. "Then he's been like this for a while? Ill, I mean?"
"I don't know. He just gets sick really easily," said Georgie. "He doesn't look after himself, no decent food, and he's always in the house. He's been so very down lately. That's where all this illness comes from. He needs somebody around him, somebody like Carl… I should go and see him."
"You do whatever you need to do," said Dan.
Georgie left the room and headed upstairs.

"Rather her than me," said Joanne. "He didn't seem grateful about you bringing back his wallet. He doesn't seem happy even that Eva's offered to look for Carl Renton. And he's really ungrateful whenever poor Georgie does anything to help him. That girl could do a lot better than him. If I was her I would be away like a shot."

"She doesn't seem the kind to leave him in the lurch," said Mark.

"Then she needs to toughen up. Boys like that don't get any better," said Joanne.

"Did you get anything else out of them while we were gone?" said Dan.

"Nothing but his mopey face and Georgie making excuses for him."

"Then I think it's time to go. But I still need that drink," said Dan. "I might have to go and help myself to a glass."

"Why not? I would if I were you," said Joanne.

Dan picked up the empty glass and walked out into the hallway. He passed the stairwell and caught the vaguest hint of voices upstairs then kept going until he reached the large white and black kitchen at the back of the house. He rinsed the glass and poured himself a water and downed it in one, then poured another. His eyes roamed over the black worktop and he saw a few rogue crumbs of broken glass beneath the windowsill. Remnants of the break-in left by the window fitter. Dan picked up one of the glass crumbs and rolled it in his hand. He picked up the other shards he could see then looked for the bin. There it was, attached to the back of a cupboard door. The lid lifted as he opened it and Dan dropped the broken glass inside. Beside some sweaty old salad, something else in the bin caught his eye. A paper screwed into a tight ball. The colours appealed to him and his natural curiosity did the rest. Dan pulled the screwed-up ball out of the bin, opened it and then flattened it on the worktop. It was a leaflet with an image of a young man sitting on a clifftop looking out to a misty sea. The words *But I Want To Be Happy!* Were emblazoned above the image. Dan pulled the leaflet open and found the kind of informal, preachy Christian advice which he remembered from the tables at the Refuge Food Bank, back in his year on skid row.

Like the other leaflets he remembered, this one said God could fill a hungry soul with goodness. But far as he saw, no one in the Clancy house was hungry in any sense of the word. The kitchen was awash with fancy food and posh drink labels. There was a Lexus on the driveway and gold on the walls. Clancy Senior clearly had money coming out of his ears. Dan knew the religious tract hadn't been intended for Clancy Senior. It must have been given to Joe Clancy by Carl Renton, and its position at the top of the bin said it was a recent acquisition. Which put a different kind of spin on their friendship. What Joe had implied as just a 'normal' friendship now seemed coloured by Renton's higher calling. Maybe Renton just couldn't help himself when it came to preaching. Dan recalled a few of the well-meaning folks at the foodbank had been exactly the same. They couldn't switch off from preaching no matter how hard they tried. But as Dan looked at the image on the front of the leaflet – the young man looking out to sea, Dan wondered if that was how Carl Renton had seen Joe Clancy. A kid lost and alone and hurting; in need of rescue. If so, Renton's offer had clearly been rejected – discarded as ruthlessly as the soggy old salad. Dan felt that the leaflet was telling him something about Carl Renton, and something else about young Joe Clancy too. For the leaflet to make it this far then Dan reckoned the kid must have read it. He wondered if the screwing-up signified something else. A rupture between the friends perhaps… a falling out? But a kid like Joe Clancy wasn't going to reveal anything lightly. Dan looked at the leaflet once more, making a few mental notes, before dropping it back into the waste bin. Whether the kid admitted it or not, something must have happened between him and Renton. Dan picked up a lonely slice of cucumber from the kitchen chopping board, stuffed it into his mouth and walked away.

Aaron Clancy sat at his bureau desk, hunching over Eva's contract, following the Ts and Cs with the nib of his fountain pen. The man was certainly thorough. She should have expected as much from a man who catalogued every precious item by hand. He flipped to the last page, and satisfied, he finally signed on the dotted line and handed it back. He pulled a cheque book from the bureau and started to write a crisp new cheque. Today was turning into the best day the week. Someone else's misfortune meant their happiness. But it was the way of the world. One man's manure fertilised another one's roses. Clancy tore the cheque free and handed it to Eva. A deposit of one thousand pounds was more than enough to draw a smile.

"There we are. It's official," said Clancy.

"So it is," said Eva, eyeing the cheque before slipping it into her handbag.

"And you'll start right away?" said Clancy.

"I'm already on it. I started the very moment you began to answer my questions."

"Well, that is prompt," said Clancy.

"And I've got one more question for you now," said Eva.

"But the answer is *out there*, Miss Roberts, not with me."

"Even so, this could be worth thinking on. It's about Carl Renton, Mr Clancy."

"As I said, this case isn't about him. This is about my collection."

"But what if there was a connection between them?"

"A connection?" said Clancy. He frowned in confusion.

"Yes. I'm sure you must have considered it already. That Carl Renton might have somehow been involved in you losing your special items?"

"Carl Renton, a thief? Come on. That man is the most unlikely thief you could imagine. He's far too straight, too safe, too churchy. People like him don't commit crimes so that they can always feel superior to the likes of you and me. The kind who run rehabs for their faith aren't likely to go robbing anyone. It'd ruin their standing forever."

"But crimes are often committed by the most unlikely people."

"I'll bow to your experience on that, but I still can't see it. Yes, I considered him of course, but not for long. As much as the man irked me, Carl had a track record of keeping an eye out for my son. He's been here many times across this last year… surely if he was going to rob me he would have done so as soon as he saw my collection. Which come to think of it, is precisely why I wasn't very hospitable when I first saw you and your friends in my house. After last night's burglary the last thing I wanted was the risk of new guests."

"I can understand that. But you're sure Carl Renton could have had nothing to do with the theft?"

"Carl Renton wouldn't have needed to break the window, would he? He was already in my house. He could have just said he needed the toilet and gone upstairs and emptied my study of everything he saw and left my son none the wiser. It's possible, but not likely."

"Maybe you should have used a key."

"Hindsight is wonderful, Miss Roberts. But my son was supposed to be my security."

Clancy squinted and looked past Eva to the door. Something had distracted him. He stood up and went out into the landing then Eva heard it too. Quiet talking from one of the neighbouring doors. Eva watched Clancy pause in the hallway, his head angled down towards his shoes while he tried to listen in. She watched him walk close to the door. He raised his hand to knock but then held back. The manoeuvre looked well practiced, as if Clancy had spent a fair share of his time eavesdropping outside his son's bedroom. A fraction later, Aaron Clancy seemed to remember Eva was watching him. He glanced at her and knocked. The chatter inside stopped and Georgie opened the door. Seeing it was him, Georgie pulled the door wide open. Eva noticed the girl's top was now on inside out. It had clearly been put on in a hurry. Georgie noticed Eva's eyes and her cheeks flushed.

"What are you doing up here, Joe? You've left guests among the collection. Come on, Joe! You know what happened here last night!"

Eva stood casually behind Clancy's shoulder and looked into his son's bedroom. Joe Clancy sat in a recliner chair not far from his bed. The young man looked a darn sight better than when Eva had last seen him downstairs. His eyes looked brighter, his face less anxious. Something told Eva Georgie had supplied some medicine, and Eva guessed it hadn't been dispensed from a bottle.

"You've hired them haven't you?" said Joe.

Aaron Clancy glanced back at Eva.

"Yes, I have. And Miss Roberts confirmed something for me. You put far too much trust in strangers, Joe. No matter what their backgrounds or religion, we mustn't trust anyone too easily. Not anyone. You know how valuable my collection is." Georgie looked wounded by the man's words, as if she was their target.

Eva frowned. "But I didn't say that."

"Not quite, but thereabouts," said Aaron Clancy. "Your questions reminded me. Carl Renton was a stranger here not so long ago. We only thought we knew him. Now look – he's run off and left his own rehab in the lurch and by coincidence I've lost the best items in my collection to a sudden robbery."

Joe Clancy gave Eva a look like daggers.

"That's hardly what I meant, Mr Clancy," said Eva. "Yes, you do have to consider everyone in a case like this, but that doesn't make everyone a suspect."

Joe's eyes stayed on Eva. "I thought you were going to help find Carl, not blame him," said Joe.

The boy's father replied on her behalf. "Miss Roberts' job is to find what was stolen from us, no matter *who* has taken it. Right, I have to make some business calls, and then I'll go and speak with Southend Museum. If the museum have any decency they'll vouch that my torq has nothing to do with their Saxon King."

The man went to fetch his jacket from the study. He returned with jacket in hand and shut the door behind him. Eva noticed there was a keyhole in the study door but Aaron Clancy didn't use it.

"Was that door locked last night, Mr Clancy?" said Eva.

"No. My son was at home. I didn't need to take such precautions. I suppose I was proven wrong on that count. Still, now at least you're here to help fix matters," he said. "Please excuse me. I've got to dash."

The man bowed his head. "I'll check in with you later to see what progress you've made."

"Fine," said Eva, watching as he headed down the steps. She waited until he was out of earshot before she spoke again. "We'll be going now as well," said Eva, looking around Joe's room. There was so sign of music posters on the walls. No sign of favourite movies. Just a stack of books on one shelf, a small music system, a TV on the wall, and a stack of neat, brand new clothes at the end of his bed, complete with card labels, wrapping and stickers. Several pairs of blue jeans looked like they'd never left the hanger, and some square-folded shirts were still packed in cellophane. There was a similar pile beside his chair and a few stacked on the floor. The young man looked at Eva as she studied his room, as if her eyes were unwelcome.

"You'll be making a start then? Looking for Carl I mean?"

Eva nodded. "We'll certainly try. Is there anything else we should know?"

They heard Clancy Senior's car start up on the driveway.

"I don't know what you mean."

"Helpful advice. Places we should look, for instance," said Eva.

"No. I told you all I could. Now please… I don't feel my best. If you don't mind, please see yourself out."

Conflict, insecurity, resistance, self-assertion. It was all there in the young man's eyes. His personality had more spikes than a hedgehog. Eva nodded and turned to close the door, but Georgie held it open, making a silent appeal with her eyes. Eva walked away and stopped at the top of the stairs and waited for her. Georgie moved past Eva and led her down the stairs and back into the front room with the others.

"You will help us, won't you?" she said.

"Don't worry. We'll do our best to find Carl Renton."

"Thank you," said Georgie. "Joe needs Carl more than he is willing to admit."

"But why exactly?" said Dan.

The girl hesitated then cut loose. "Carl always give more of a crap about Joe than his dad."

They saw sadness in the girl's eyes, but she blinked it away and forced a smile. "Thanks for helping."

"Joe should be grateful he has you," said Eva.

"He is grateful. I see it. He just shows it in his own way."

One by one they made their goodbyes and left the house, stepping out into the blazing sun. They closed the door behind them and slowly walked to Eva's car.

"There. I told you they had money," said Mark.

"And he does," said Dan. "But he's still not keeping up with the Joneses when it comes to cars."

"What about the Lexus?" said Eva.

"It's good enough, if you like that kind of thing. It's a safe saloon with all the standard luxuries. But it lacks style."

Eva shook her head as she started the engine of her less than luxurious Alfa Romeo.

"I'll tell you one thing," said Joanne. "Georgie and Joe Clancy are more of an item than Daddy Clancy realises."

Eva nodded. "Yes. They are very close, aren't they?" she said.

"And that's not all," said Joanne.

Eva looked at Joanne's big eyes in the rear-view mirror and waited for the punchline.

"She's sleeping with him. That girl is sleeping with Joe Clancy right there in that house."

"What? So you're a prude all of a sudden?" said Dan. It was common knowledge among them that Joanne had been staying around Mark's family home with or without his mother's say so. But Mark was the only one to squirm. Joanne met Dan's eyes without a hint of shame and continued to make her point.

"She went upstairs with Joe, right? Next time I saw her, her T-shirt was inside out and she looked all sheepish. Joe can't have been all that ill, that's all I'm saying. And pretty bold too, considering Clancy senior was at home."

Dan nodded, impressed. "Yeah. I caught that too."

"And I don't think she's going home, either," said Joanne. "I'm think she's staying there full time, sleeping in Joe Clancy's bed and Daddy Clancy doesn't seem to know it. There's nothing prudish about that. It's just what I saw."

"I think you may be right, Joanne," said Eva. "Which means she would have been there during the break-in. Even if it was possible that Joe Clancy is such a solid sleeper that he didn't hear the break in, how likely is it that Georgie didn't hear it either?"

"Not likely in the least," said Joanne.

"Which means we just might well have our first suspect," said Eva. "Did you see all their coded communications when we asked them about the burglary?"

"No," said Mark. "She didn't do it. I went to school with Georgie too. She was top of the class, just too quiet to get the recognition the head girls did. She would never ever do something like that. I think she was acting coy because you almost outed her as sleeping with Joe."

"That's another theory," said Dan. "But people change, Mark, and not always for the better."

Mark didn't look convinced, but he let it go.

"And what about Carl Renton?" said Joanne. "Which way do we go with this?"

"We don't know the full story, but we do know this," said Eva. "The break-in and robbery happened last night, not long after Carl Renton disappeared off the radar."

"It sounds like you're suggesting Carl Renton is a suspect as well," said Dan.

"It's possible he was involved. Maybe he had some kind of cash-flow issue with his rehab operation. Who knows? But I don't buy the idea that it's a coincidence that the theft happened the same night as he goes missing. When is it ever just a coincidence?"

"But I lived a year getting help from people like Carl Renton," said Dan. "It's hard for me to see someone like that behind a serious crime."

"Dan," said Eva. "You've told me a lot about what happened during that year. Was every single one of those people – the volunteers, the helpers at the foodbank – was every single one of them totally scrupulous and trustworthy?"

"No. But any place like that is going to have a few bad apples in it. A few of them were probably on the take for food freebies."

"And what about the Christian ones? Were they always pure as the driven snow?"

Dan blinked in thought. "No. Most of them were good people. But one or two… they seemed a little too intense. They seemed like they might have had an ulterior motive. Not all of them by any means."

"But that's what I mean. Nobody's a saint, not even the saints," said Eva. "This investigation is about finding Aaron Clancy's lost treasures, but I think it's also about finding one lost Renton too. Carl Renton might well be involved in this somehow. Find Carl Renton and we might well find Aaron Clancy's treasure too."

"Treasure?" said Dan. "I never thought of it as treasure. Just a load of shiny junk. It might be worth a fortune, but I'd never want it in my house. Keep it in a safe somewhere or sell it instead."

"I think Aaron Clancy is a different type of man. He clearly loves the stuff. It's certainly treasure to him."

"And there I was thinking we were going to have a good old-fashioned day out at the beach."

"The beach will have to wait." Eva turned to Joanne and Mark. "What about you? You were expecting a day off."

"Why? Where are you going now?" said Joanne.

"There's a good chance that Joe Clancy hasn't told us everything we need to know about Carl Renton. We need to learn a lot more about him if we're going to find him. I think the best place to start would be his rehab project."

Joanne's eyes gleamed at the prospect of another adventure. "We're coming with you," she said. "This day's just getting more and more interesting."

"We're going to a rehab," said Dan. "Interesting would be an understatement."

Eva pulled her phone from her jacket pocket and handed it over to Dan in the passenger seat. "Find me an address for the rehab, will you? Whatever it takes."
"Should be easy enough," said Dan.
Dan thumb-swiped the screen and typed in Eva's four digit pin. He knew it off by heart. He was about to thumb the web browser when he saw Eva had unopened messages waiting for her. Being on the nosey side of helpful, Dan dabbed the missed call button and saw the call had come in about an hour ago. Next he dabbed the message button and found a new unread message. His eyes scanned it in a few seconds.
Hey, Eva. I know we had some problems before, but I really hope that's all water under the bridge. I'm trying to get in touch with you because I really need your help. I'd like to patch things up too. Here's hoping you'll give me a chance. Call me back when you can. Lauren x.
If that wasn't a cry for help, Dan didn't know what was. He looked at Eva and she glanced back.
"What?" she said.
He was suddenly aware of Mark and Joanne in the back seat.
"Nothing," said Dan. "I'm just looking it up now."
"Okay. My guess is it'll be in central Southend."
"Coming right up," said Dan.
His eyes hung on the last couple of lines of the text. *...give me a chance. Call me back when you can.* Whatever had happened between them, he knew Eva was all about second chances. Eva had to call the girl back. If she didn't, her conscience would only plague her. Dan parked the thought, thumbed the web browser app on the screen and began to type in '*Renton...*'

Six

As soon as they arrived, Eva got the distinct impression that any lingering sense of taking the day off needed to stop right there. The rehab's houses looked lively, to say the least. Carl Renton had opened two rehab houses under the project name of Restore. No doubt a scriptural reference, as well as from the sentiment about restoring a person to health, second chances, and all that. One house specialised in drink rehabilitation and one in drug rehab. The houses were found on the same densely terraced Westcliff street, tucked away between Southend Hospital and the busy vein of West Road. Here, Westcliff was a grid of terraced houses, some of which had slipped into disrepair, and multiple occupancy properties. The pavements were busy and most of those walking around in the sunshine seemed to be people on the wrong side of the tracks. Eva's Alfa bounced over a few harsh speed bumps before she found a suitable space. She parked up and all four of them stared down the street. Further down, beneath the canopy of the trees lining the street, two guys and a young woman leaned against a wall outside one of the houses. Behind them, the front door was open, and another man leaned out, wearing a hoodie pulled up over his head on a hot summer's day. Eva didn't even need to check the house number. A place like that, people like that – it just had to be Renton's house. Eva glanced in her rear-view and saw a similar gathering further back up the street. If she hadn't known these houses were rehabs, Eva might have had them down as drug dens. The people looked the same ilk and had the same vibe.

"On second thoughts, maybe we should have dropped you home," said Eva. "This doesn't look like the kind of place we should take you," said Eva. "Either of you."

"But Mark's your apprentice," said Joanne. "Shouldn't he go with you? And if I'm going to be of any use I should go along too."

Mark sighed. He looked reluctant about Joanne's suggestion. "Sorry, Joanne," said Eva. "But you could still be of help."

"How?" said Joanne.

"Keep a look out," said Eva. "See if anyone is doing anything unusual around these two houses. If something has happened to Carl Renton, one of these people might have been involved."

Joanne's face turned into a dour frown and she sat back. "I get the picture," she said.

"We don't know what we're dealing with here," said Dan. "Eva's right. If Clancy's treasures have found their way into one in these houses, the thief really will fight tooth and nail to stop us getting near them. There's a lot of money at stake."

"I helped you at Clancy's didn't I? I might be able to help you again," she said.

"And you will. But not yet." Eva got out of the car before Joanne had the chance to hassle her again.

Dan followed suit, leaving Joanne and Mark alone in the backseat. Joanne folded her arms as Eva and Dan walked away. "Just when things were getting interesting," she said.

"There's interesting and there's dangerous, Joanne," said Mark. "We should do as they ask."

"Sometimes, Mark, I wonder how you ended up working for them in the first place." After a long moment, Joanne grinned. Mark looked at her with a quizzical eye. Joanne answered his unspoken question by reaching for the door handle.

"What are you doing, Jo?"

"There's two houses here, and two sets of us. Eva and Dan do need our help, they just don't know it. Come on. We can go and talk to the people at the other house. If we find something to help move the case on everyone will be happy."

"And if we get into trouble?" said Mark.

"Don't be such a spoilsport, Mark. You can loosen up when you want to."

Joanne got out into the bright sunshine as Eva and Dan began talking to the people standing around outside the house up the street. Mark clambered out after her and shut the car door behind him. Before he could protest, Joanne marched down the street towards the second house in the near distance. A couple of people in the distance had already turned to watch their approach. A pang of anxiety began to stab at Mark's chest. The rabble ahead were too far away to see well, but it was clear they were a different breed. Mark hoped the housemates were on the more reformed side of the rehab spectrum. Following in Joanne's wake, hoping was all he could do.

Eva pulled up short of the group standing by the front wall of the house. She checked the house number by the door, while Dan took in the faces, manner and potential threat level of those ranged before them. The group turned one by one to look at Eva and Dan. They didn't seem hostile, not yet, maybe just curious. But they didn't seem friendly either. Dan had them down as edgy. Twitchy even. This was the drinkers' house. He thought about the tract leaflet he'd seen at the Clancy residence, thought that it was designed for people who looked as desperate as these. He wondered whether any leaflet could ever penetrate the fog of their personal addictions.

"Hi," said Dan, attempting to break the ice only because it was there. Because they had questions to ask too.

The young woman of the group had an ashen, pinched look to her face, and her eyes were tired. Her hair looked extremely greasy. It was red like Eva's, only the woman was much thinner and hard living had given her pretty face a mean aspect. She wore a vest over a skeletal frame. There was a tattoo of radiant sun on her thin bicep. She looked at Dan with a faint sign of interest, while the men of the group spent all of their curiosity on looking at Eva. Compared to the women they were used to dealing with, Dan reckoned Eva must have looked close to a film star. It was amazing what an almost healthy diet and a tweed suit could do for a person. He ignored the girl and sized up the men. The man on the door looked to be in his forties, shaven headed, and shaky. He was sweating profusely. The two men leaning on the wall in front of the girl seemed more stable, and one was clearly posing to impress. He looked cocksure of himself, the type who wouldn't mind trading insults or slapping a weaker man to make himself look like the main guy. Dan knew the type well. And in the end, this was where that type always ended up. A drunk house, a drug den, or a prison cell. It was a logical progression of total jerkdom. Dan concentrated his attention on this guy, just in case something went wrong too soon. The man saw the readiness in Dan's eyes and shifted on the wall, but to make up for any sign of weakness, this guy made sure he was the first to respond.

"You here to tell us where he is then, are you?" he said, all cocky as hell. Dan felt his mood changing, his old stomach wound pulling tight around the scar. It still hadn't healed perfectly, but his gut was strong enough for most eventualities.

"Actually," said Eva, "We're here to ask where Mr Renton might be. Presuming we're talking about Carl Renton, that is."

The cocky guy's little eyes landed on Eva once again and lit up like a fruit machine jackpot. Meanwhile the rehab girl's eyes tracked back to Dan and with a swish of her hair, she tried to appeal for his gaze. He looked back at her once more and quickly moved on.

"It's the only thing worth talking about, ain't it?" said the guy on the door. His voice was a nasally whine. Like a human weasel. "Carl disappeared on us, right when we needed him the most. He bailed out on us but he said he'd always be here." The guy was a motormouth of panic. "He said we never had to worry about our meds, about our food, all we had to do was be here and we'd be okay. Fat lot of good that is when he doesn't bloody turn up, know what I mean?!"

"Shut it, Steve. You haven't stopped bitching and moaning since before sun up," said the girl.

"I've got a right to moan, haven't I?" said Steve. "We all have. We've been let down! What are we supposed to do now? Someone like me, I could start fitting if I don't get my pills sorted. I could go into full withdrawal. People die from that, you know!"

"Look. If you help us maybe we could help you," said Dan, keeping his voice level and calm. "We want to find Carl. We need to talk to him. It's urgent."

"What about?" said the girl. "You're not police, are you?" The woman eyed Eva. "She might be, but you, you're way too street to be a rozzer. Do I know you from somewhere?" she asked.

The girl took the opportunity to give Dan another look in the eye. Dan hoped she didn't say she remembered him from his fallow year at The Refuge foodbank. Too many of those types still hadn't moved on in the five years since he'd left it all behind.

"I don't think so," he said. "Just got one of those kinds of faces, that's all."

"He's probably just plain clothes, Sal," said Mr Cocksure. "Trying to fit in so he can get more information."

"It doesn't matter who you think we are," said Dan. "If we find Carl Renton then your problems still get solved, don't they?"

The man shook his head. "Their problems you mean, not mine. I'm virtually clean now. I don't need anyone's help."

"Then maybe you should move out and make way for someone else who does need the help," said Dan.

Eva gave Dan a sharp look. The girl smiled.

Cocksure tried to smile. "I don't see any hurry, do you? Especially now," said the guy. "People like big Carl Renton, they don't just drop everything and run off, do they? No, that's not him at all. Which means there's a problem. Carl would have told everyone long in advance exactly where he was going and who was going to cover for him. Which means he didn't plan this at all. Which means something bad must have happened to him."

"And you'd know something about that, would you?" said Dan.

"What are you implying?" said the man.

"Nothing at all. You made a statement," said Dan. "I asked a question. It's called a conversation."

"It's only a conversation if I want to talk back," said the man. "To you? No thanks. But to the lady here…"

"Careful," said Dan. "I don't want to make you look bad in front of your friends here."

"And think you could do that, do you?"

Dan took a breath and hit the pause button on his escalating mood.

"I know I could," said Dan. "Don't sweat it. We'll find him without your help. What about the rest of you? Does anyone else here know anything?"

The shaky guy on the doorstep nodded for Dan's attention.

"Robbo there," he said, nodding at the cocky guy, "I know he's not got the greatest bedside manner—"

"Shut your mouth, Steve," said the cocksure guy.

"But he's not far off the mark. Carl runs the whole show – that's both houses. He's always shown up on time and done the necessaries. Meds, counselling, paperwork, the lot. With him gone like this, you have to think something could have happened to him."

"And?" said Dan. "What do you think could have happened?"

"A car crash maybe? An accident of some kind…" The guy shrugged.

Both Eva and Dan saw some other speculation was there hiding behind the nervous man's eyes. He scratched his bald head before he carried on.

"And you know," he went on, "people can have all kinds of accidents, can't they? Genuine ones, and the not so genuine ones. Acts of God and all that and then there's the ones someone might have arranged."

"Arranged?" said Eva.

"Steve!" said the girl. "What are you on about now?"

"I'm just saying what you all think. Carl couldn't help himself, could he? The man didn't know when to stop. If Carl had just left it at going to church and giving money to the poor and running his rehab houses, he would have been alright. Everyone would still have loved him. But the way Carl spoke, he thought he was living in a war, didn't he? He thought he was a soldier."

"Steve?!" said the cocky man, sending him a hard look. "You've got verbal diarrhoea, son. Ignore him. That's just the withdrawal talking."

"No. I always spoke to him. You never did. Carl called it spiritual warfare. He said he was in a battle with the enemy for the souls of the people, for the soul of this town. I know what that sounds like, but he meant it. And he hated what those new class A's were doing to the kids. Those Uber things. Carl said that was the work of the devil, pure and simple. He said he was going to work non-stop to bring it to an end. He was even going out on these vigils down to the beach and to the docks to try and catch the people doing the importing. It was nuts. You think about it. These Ubers are big bucks, right?"

"Steve!" snapped the cocksure man. "You need to shut up before your mouth runs away and you get your arse kicked."

"You back off," barked Dan. A fierce look appeared in the cocky guy's eyes, but the look in Dan's dark eyes was fiercer still. Robbo folded his arms and the girl smirked in admiration.

"Steve can tell us whatever he likes," said Dan.

"I was just saying he should think of the consequences, that's all."

"But I like Carl," said Steve. "He looked after me. I just mean there might be more to it than it seems."

"Please go on," said Eva.

"These vigils of his. That's what he called them. Sometimes he used to go down the airport. Sometimes he used to drive down to Tilbury docks. Sometimes to the beach. He didn't tell me about all of it, but what if he was onto something. He thought they were fighting for God. He took risks. What if he got in someone's way…?"

"You mean the drug dealers?" said Eva.

"Yeah. Whoever ships 'em in. That would have been a very risky business."

Dan frowned. He looked at Eva and nodded his head. "That sounds like a possibility."

"Yeah?" said Robbo. "Well, you'd better hope you're wrong about that, Steve, or you just might have put your own head on the block."

"Only if one of you goes and snitches on him," said Dan. "At least he wants to help."

"Steve?! He's got no good in him," said Robbo, laughing. Even the woman with the eyes for Dan started snickering.

"He just needs his meds. You're lucky he didn't start spouting on about his other conspiracy theories as well. If he did, you'd still be here at midnight

"Does anyone else in there have any other ideas about what happened to Mr Renton?" said Eva.

"There is no one else in this gaff," said Robbo. "The cat's away so the mice and all that. We're the only hold-outs left."

"Then what about staff?" said Eva. "Does anyone else work here besides Carl Renton?"

"Yeah. Colin works here too," said Steve. "Colin Boyd. He'll have his work cut out with the smackheads up the road. They're harder to deal with than us lot."

"Harder than you, Steve?" said the girl, with a wicked smile.

"That lot?" said Steve. "They're shiftier than the forty thieves. Most of 'em are thieves an' all."

"That mouth of yours, Steve…" said Robbo, sucking his teeth.

"Then maybe we should speak to the people in the other house too," said Eva.

Robbo gave Eva a prolonged look then transferred his gaze to Dan.

"Yeah, maybe you should," said Robbo, with a smarmy grin.

"I'll be seeing you," said Dan. He winked at Robbo, confirming the added edge in his words were just for him.

As Eva and Dan turned away, the red-haired girl made an "ooooo-oooooh!" sound, and broke into a wheezy laugh.

"He doesn't frighten me," said Robbo.

"Yes he does," said Steve. Nervous Steve smiled and walked back into the house.

"What did you make of that?" said Dan as they walked away.

"That you wanted to knock that guy's head off," said Eva.

"That goes without saying. I met a ton of people like him back in the day. Nothing changes among those on the lowest rung of the ladder. But I meant that guy's story, about what could have happened to Carl Renton."

"Like you said," Eva replied. "I think it sounds plausible. The volunteer types – the Christians you knew at the foodbank. Some of them were like that, right?"

"Like…?"

"Sold out to the cause. Like they would have risked everything for their faith. Maybe even their lives."

"There were a few. For some it was a hobby, for others just a day job. That was plain to see. But for half of them, there was nowhere else they'd have rather been. Like old time Billy Grahams, or Victorian missionaries who would cry tears for the love of God. I had no idea those kind of people still existed until I saw it with my own eyes."

"I suppose it must have been heartening, in its way."

"It was, and yet at the same time I found it weird. Even so, you couldn't fault those people. They helped us because they believed it was the right thing to do. And yes, I think Carl Renton could have been exactly that type of person."

"Which means he's probably been putting his life at risk for weeks, maybe even years, trying to face down these drug dealers."

"Hmmm," said Dan. "Not smart, I agree. I saw volunteer guys do the very same thing at The Refuge. They tried to take on the dealers once or twice. I admired their guts, but I also thought they were dumb as hell. They had nothing to back them up but blind faith."

"You have to admire that, Dan."

"I know you do," said Dan.

"What does that mean?"

"Deep down you've got that same kind of hope, haven't you? That's where your tenacity comes from."

"And you don't?" said Eva.

"Not quite. I've got something. Whatever it is, it tells me I've got to fight like hell to see any kind of justice in this world."

"I know what you mean." She gave Dan a forlorn smile. "I think it goes with the job."

Dan's eyes landed on the Alfa as it came into view. The glare of the sunlight on the windscreen faded and he saw there was no one inside.

"Eva, they're not in the car."

"What?" said Eva.

"Mark and Joanne. They're gone."

Eva looked into the Alfa and saw Dan was right. Her half smile dropped right off her face.

Up ahead, where there had been a cluster of malingerers outside the other house, the street was now empty.

Eva's throat tightened. Dan started walking at a determined pace.

Joanne walked into the narrow front hallway of the compact terraced house, following the tight chicane of a corridor past the stairwell towards the back rooms. Mark followed close behind Joanne, as two large-eyed men who smelt of cigarette smoke and acrid body odour pushed up close behind him. He found both men frightening. They were almost animalistic. Their thoughts seemed to be written across their strained, electric eyes and one of them was sharper than the other. From the moment they had arrived at the house, the men only had eyes for Joanne, and one of them stared at her so much it felt vulgar. He looked her up and down, his eyes flicking between her face and her legs like he was watching a sporting spectacle. Joanne acted like she didn't notice. Either that or she was playing dumb. Mark guessed all women had to do that to some degree. Like every man was a potential sex pest in waiting. Ahead of her, two more led the way. A girl with a skull-like face, her hair tied back into a severe black and silver ponytail and another skeletal man who reminded Mark of a bygone Brazilian footballer way past his sell by date. They led the way deeper into the belly of the house. It felt like they were being escorted to the dungeon for terror and interrogation, and who knew? Perhaps they were. Mark's eyes flitted past the health and safety notices on the wall and the signs about not stealing food. He saw notices about house meetings and prayer groups and key worker appointments, and didn't like any of it. Even the house smelt odd. It smelt of cooking grease, baked beans, sweat and cheap disinfectant.

"So everyone here is in recovery?" said Joanne.

"Yeah," said the frail Brazilian lookalike, in a rough voice. "Recovery from crack, heroin, meth, you name it, we've all been on it in here."

"How far into your recovery are you?" said Mark. He knew the question sounded bad as soon as he'd said it. He felt one of the men behind him leaning over his shoulder and turned back to see the second lanky guy leering at Joanne's backside as she walked. The guy gave Mark a toothy yellow grin, as if to say, 'Can't blame me, can you?' Mark frowned but didn't say a word. They were outnumbered, and on unknown territory. He shifted his body to block the guy's view. The other man with the shifty eyes chuckled.

They walked into a small dining room decked with cheap brown carpet where a second-hand dining table had been turned into a meeting table. There was a flipchart arranged by the bay window and a garden door at the back. Mark was relieved to see a man with some kind of authority sitting with his legs crossed at the table, with an impish, sweaty fifty-something guy in a tracksuit sitting beside him. The rehab worker's authority was denoted by his clipboard and glasses. Other than that, he had little else to give them any hope of protection from the rehab clients. The man was blond haired, frail looking, and bespectacled with tension all over his face. The guy looked edgier than anyone else in the house.

"Who are these people, Ken?" said the man, looking up at Mark and Joanne with an expression of confusion and irritation.

The Brazilian guy answered. "Think they need to see you, Colin."

The guy sitting with Colin beamed at Joanne. "If she moves in can I move in with her?"

The others laughed.

"Sorry but my living arrangements are already sorted, thanks," said Joanne. She took Mark's arm by way of a statement. A second later and all the guys in the room were looking at him, and Joanne was oblivious but Mark felt himself beginning to sweat as much as the rest of them.

"I didn't know we were due any visitors today," said Colin, the man with the clipboard. He adjusted his spectacles on his thin nose. "Look. It's really not convenient. We're going to have an urgent house meeting in a minute. So, which agency are you from?"

Joanne misunderstood. "Agency?" she said.

"It doesn't matter. Wherever you're from, you still have to call ahead and arrange an appointment to see us."

"Yeah," said the Brazilian. "And by then this house probably won't even be here."

"Why did you say that?" said Joanne. She turned to look into the man's dark, glassy eyes. A faint twinkle appeared a moment later, like his brain was on a go slow.

"Don't worry. It'll still be here," said Colin, but he didn't sound convinced. Mark noticed the silver crucifix around his neck.

"Carl Renton, the man behind this outfit has gone walkies," said the woman.

"Vanished," said the Brazilian. "Which means this place will probably vanish soon too," he said.

"You don't know that," said Colin. "This is a charity. There are processes, procedures, the trustees too. The house can't just disappear. Don't panic."

"Oh yeah?" said the woman, with a hard edge in her voice. "Then why do you look so spooked, eh, Colin? Is it because you think you're out of a job?"

Colin sighed. His mouth twitched. "Don't be ridiculous. I'll be provided for no matter what happens."

"The Good Lord provides," said the Brazilian type. "Preach it, bruv." The men behind Mark laughed out loud. There was no way of knowing whether the man was being facetious or not. It seemed Colin couldn't tell either.

"Are you from the newspapers?" said Colin, studying Mark and Joanne anew. "I don't recognise you two from the mental health circuit."

"We're not on the mental health circuit," said Mark. Whatever that was… "We're from a private investigations agency."

There was a briefest silence followed by snorts of laughter and derision.

"You two? Private investigators," said one of the men behind them. "Do me a favour? You've read too many comics."

"No," said another, who nudged Mark in the back. "He's the one reading the comics," said one of the men behind them. "She looks capable of anything."

"Leave her alone," said Mark, wheeling round.

"Oooooooh!" said the shifty one. "The geek fancies a tussle."

"Eddie, stop it!" said Colin. "Okay. Emergency house meeting in two minutes. I'm sorry. I don't know who you are, but frankly, this isn't the time. I can't speak to anyone about the situation here until I've spoken to the trustees."

"So can I take it that you really don't know what's happened to Mr Renton?" said Joanne.

The man took off his glasses and rubbed his eyes. "No... no, I don't. I only wish I did. Now, please, I need to get this house in order. You'll have to leave. I mean it. I can barely get a hold of the clients as it is, without having any more problems to deal with."

"Okay. We're going. But just one thing," said Joanne. "What do you think could have happened to him? Where do you think he might be now, for instance?"

The man shook his head. "Sorry. I just don't know."

But a voice from behind Mark's shoulder caught their attention. The shifty looking one with the sharp eyes looked at them and there was an unpleasant smile on his face.

"I told Carl he was playing with fire. This rehab lark. This is a game for ex-junkies. Hard people who've been there and know how the cookie crumbles. Carl is just a big softy. I told him straight." The guy had two small little dark eyes set close together over a narrow nose.

"Eddie, stop talking!" snapped Colin. "Don't say another word until we've had our house meeting."

"Why not? The pretty one is asking all the questions. We're not going to see anything like her around here again." Eddie turned his sharp eyes back to Joanne. Mark felt the hackles rising on the back of his neck. If he was big enough, tough enough, Mark would have told them all where to go. In recovery or not, they were still rogues, one and all. The man kept talking, his eyes on Joanne the whole time.

"Carl asked me how I got switched onto brown. Heroin. I told him and Carl got all angry and said he wanted to meet these dealers face to face, to show them the harm they were doing. He said that at my interview when I joined the house. And I know he said the same to others. Did he say that to you, Ken?"

"Oh yeah," said the slow-witted one standing beside him. "He said it at every interview. He meant it too, like. It's like he had a death wish."

"A life wish," corrected Colin. "Carl wants to save lives."

"By risking his own? Now that is the dumbest thing I ever heard," said Eddie.

Colin stood up. "You'll have to leave now, please." He gestured to the housemates as if to say 'can you see what I have to deal with?' and Joanne nodded.

"Thanks. We might be back."

"By appointment only," said Colin.

"Or any time you like," wheezed Ken, to laughs all round.

Mark tugged Joanne's arm. "Come on. We learned something, didn't we?"

"Back to reading comics, eh?" said Eddie. Mark ignored him, but Joanne gave the man a sharp look as she passed him in the corridor. He didn't make it easy for her to slide past.

"Thanks again," she called. But the clipboard guy didn't respond. Instead, as they made their way along the corridor, they found the man with the sharp eyes, and the other man – the one who stared, following close behind. Mark turned back. "You've got a house meeting to go to," he said.

"It's a free country," said Eddie. "And Colin's really not worth listening to. Not when you two are here. You look much more fun."

The man called Ken laughed, but his eyes were all over Joanne now. Even Joanne seemed to notice, and Mark saw the revulsion on her face as she withdrew and pressed herself to his side.

"We're going now," she said.

"Oh, don't be like that. We don't get many visitors in here," said sharp-eyed Eddie. The other man was quiet. But Mark didn't like the hungry look in his eyes, nor the way he kept gulping and swallowing. Like a man starving for a good meal.
"We're still going," said Mark.
"You're going alright," said Eddie. "No trouble there at all. You can just turn around and walk out of that door and no one here will say a word. Get back to reading your comics, son."
The other man laughed out loud. Mark slid his arm around Joanne's shoulders and started to turn her away towards the front door.
"Come on. Let's go," he said.
As he spoke, a big bony hand landed on Joanne's other arm, and she was pulled back. It was Eddie. The man beside him was champing at the bit. A glimmer of panic showed in Joanne's eyes.
"Let her go!" said Mark. "You're making a big mistake."
"No, sunshine. You're making the mistake."
"If I call out – or if she screams, you'll be in trouble then," said Mark. "You'd get evicted. Lose your chance at getting clean, all because you couldn't keep your hands to yourself."
Eddie's grim smile widened and the man shook his head.
"See? That's where people like you… and those other idiots from the agencies don't understand people like me and Ken here…" The man leaned forward. The smell of his rotten, tobacco infused breath filled both their faces. For the first time, Mark noticed the small dot on his cheek wasn't a mole. It was a prison tattoo.

"Not all of us want help. You know the thing is with brown. Heroin, I mean… It's the best thing in the world. Seriously. It's so moreish. Once you pop you just can't stop, and I don't even want to. No one who's ever had that buzz ever really wants to stop, not deep down. They might be able to convince themselves for a bit, but really, all they want is the next hit. And me? I only live here because Renton offered me a bed. That's all. I'm not giving up anything. Get me?"

"Then you shouldn't be wasting their time," said Joanne.

"She's a sassy little mare, isn't she?" said Eddie, and squeezed her arm. "I'm not wasting anybody's time, darling. Carl Renton isn't coming back. Anyone with any common sense can see what happened. Dealers don't muck around because they can't afford to, sweetheart, and poor old Carl Renton thought he could take on anyone. Shame to say it, but he was wrong." Eddie squeezed her shoulder and Ken laughed like a drain.

"Get your hand off me or I'll scream," said Joanne.

"Think that'll work, do you? Colin is as weak as a mouse. He isn't going to do a damn thing whether you scream or not. The man's already quit. I can see it his eyes. So why don't you just come upstairs with me and my mate for a little while, and who knows, maybe I'll even show you why brown is so very, very nice."

"Get off her!" snapped Mark.

Eddie made a face. "Ken, get rid of him will you."

"No problem," said the other man. He stepped around Joanne as she tried to pull herself free, but Eddie's grip tightened on her.

"Mark!" she said in alarm.

"I'm not going without you," he said.

The leering Ken reached for him, palms out, hands flat, trying to push him outside and shut the door. Mark stood his ground as the first shove came. He watched the shifty one try to drag Joanne towards the stairs.

"Now, now, play nice," he said.

"Joanne!" called Mark. The leery man struck Mark in the chest and he stumbled back against the wall. Mark lost his balance and started to fall. Ken reached again to take advantage, shoving him falling towards the open front door out towards the messy front garden and the street outside. Mark knew he was going to get hurt, but there was no way he could leave. Seeing the panic on Mark's face, guessing what the men intended, Joanne growled with effort and yanked herself away from Eddie and made for the open door. Mark started to pull himself up on the doorframe as Ken turned to block Joanne's way. "Get out of my way!" she roared. But the guy laughed in her face. Mark snatched in a breath, took a moment to push past his panic. He picked a target. The only thing he could think of was to kick out at the man, to distract him to buy Joanne a chance at escape. As the guy reached for Joanne, he lashed out, kicking hard. The man's leg buckled and he stumbled forward into Joanne. He knocked her back towards Eddie, who seized her, his arms threading beneath hers. It was the worst possible outcome.

"Gotcha," he said.

"No, no, no!" shouted Mark. The leering man turned and stood up, more eager to shut him out than he was to get any revenge. Mark pushed himself at the door and shoved in hard. The door stayed wide open, slamming against the inside wall.

The leering man wiped his sweaty forehead and stepped forwards, ready to give Mark the beating he needed to send him packing. But as soon as he started towards him, the man stopped in his tracks once more. The light from the street was blotted out by a shadow.

"What the hell's going on here?" said Dan.

But even before he'd finished asking the question Dan saw it all. The shifty guy with his hands all over Joanne, the girl off balance but fighting hard as the man tried to pull her towards the stairs, and the guy blocking Mark from helping his girlfriend. The picture told a thousand words. Dan stepped into the narrow hallway and both men's faces changed. Eddie let go of Joanne. But it was too late for small gestures. Dan grabbed Ken by the throat and slammed him back against the wall, hard enough to wind him completely. Which left Dan free long enough to deal with the second threat. He reached for Joanne, tugging her free, letting her out into the open alongside Mark.

"I didn't mean any harm," said Eddie. "I just wanted to show her something."

But Dan didn't hesitate. He pushed the man against the bannisters and leaned into his face.

"I know your kind. I know exactly what harm you intended."

"You don't know anything about me," said the guy.

Dan looked between each of his dark, shifty eyes, and saw all he needed to know. The potted biography as well as his dark intentions. Dan grabbed his collar, thrust him back against the shaking bannisters, and smashed him once in the face. He let the guy go, dropping him to the floor, his back sliding against the bannister, and then Dan turned and nodded towards the sunshine.

"Let's go."

The rest of the house appeared in the chicane from the back room. The Brazilian lookalike, his girlfriend, and the bespectacled man Dan guessed had to be Colin Boyd.
"What's going on out here?" said the man, shaking.
"You're Colin Boyd?" said Dan.
The man seemed hesitant but nodded anyway.
"We're looking for Carl Renton. We want to help him. Do you have any idea where he might be? Any idea at all?"
The man shook his head and pushed his glasses back up his nose. "I told your friends the same."
Dan sighed and looked around at the rest of the murky, untrustworthy faces in the hallway.
"How long has this house been running?"
"This one? Just over a year," said Boyd.
Dan nodded. "Then take my advice. Get control of this place or close it now."
"I can't just close it. These people live here!"
"You'd better, Mr Boyd, because without Carl Renton around it's plain to see you're not running the show. You had no idea what was happening out here, did you?"
The man fell silent.
"I can't do this without Carl!" he said.
"There, you said it. So shape up or shut it down before something bad happens."
Dan gave them all a look of warning, then straightened himself up and turned away.
"If you find Carl, tell him to call me. Tell him it's urgent."
Boyd's words were a desperate appeal. They sounded like the last throw of the dice. Dan barely looked back. His attention was already on Joanne and Mark. They made sure they were a good way from the house before Eva started on them.
"What the hell did you think you were doing?"

"Trying to help," said Mark.

"Really?" said Eva. "Getting yourself into that predicament? Did you think that was going to help us?"

"We went in to ask them about Carl Renton," said Joanne. "None of that was supposed to happen."

"Damn right it wasn't," said Dan. "Just in case you need reminding, this business isn't a game. Or these people. I lived in their world, Joanne. It isn't like ours. It's cutthroat. Survival of the fittest. I'm not exaggerating. And before we're finished looking for Carl Renton we might well have to face people a darn sight more dangerous than those idiots in there. So, do us a favour, and do what you're told. At least until you know what you're doing."

"I knew what I was doing," said Joanne.

Dan opened his mouth but Eva cut in.

"And it almost went badly wrong, didn't it?"

Joanne sighed and nodded her head.

"Then learn from it," she said, turning away for the car. "What did you get from them?"

"Carl Renton really is missing," said Mark. "The rehab house manager was calling an emergency meeting about it. It was plain to see he was panicking. No one knows where Renton went, but that scumbag with the shifty eyes had a theory that Renton was trying to handle a local drug dealer all by himself."

Eva nodded and glanced at Dan.

"The same theory we heard at the alcoholics' house," she said.

"Then we know the man's missing, and we know the rumours, but we've still got no real leads," said Dan.

"Then you think the houses were a dead end?" said Joanne.

"Mostly," said Eva. "The rumours are instructive, but nothing more."

"So what do we do now?" said Joanne.

"What now?" said Dan. "You keep out of trouble, that's what."

"We try another angle," said Eva. "We could talk to the police about Aaron Clancy's missing items. The police might know if there's any link to Renton."

"It's a missing person case, Eva," said Dan. "The police won't be interested in a missing person case until forty-eight hours has elapsed. You know that as well as I do."

"But they'll have seen it was in the papers, so it'll be on their radar ahead of time. And Clancy's burglary is already on their radar. It's got to be worth a try…"

The silence between them was an answer in itself.

Seven

The journey to the office was quiet and any sense of a convivial happy day off had been replaced by the shock of their near miss. Wounds were being licked in the back seat. Dan was brooding too, though probably more because of the scumbags at the rehab than Mark and Joanne's mistakes. Glad to be out of the atmosphere in the car, Eva led the procession into the office beneath their apartment. Their agency office was an ex-shop space. An old-fashioned shop from the days before supermarkets. The interior had been redone at least twice in their time – once because of an arson attack – but the original shop bell was still mounted high on the wall and it still rang anytime the front door was opened. Mark took up his usual position at the front desk, where he manned phone and reception. Under normal circumstances, Joanne would have sat at his side, telling him what to do, but after her mistake at the rehab the girl raced past Eva to the kitchen at the rear. Eva saw the apology in her eyes.
"Coffee?" said Joanne.
Eva nodded back. "Please." She offered a smile but did no more to ease the girl's fears just yet. Best to let her have a short time to consider the consequences of her actions first.

Eva retreated to the desk behind reception. She picked up her mobile and scanned her contact list, then dabbed a name and number which she hadn't used for a good long while. Eva wondered how he would respond to her call. Hard to say. Most cops were cagey at the best of times, especially when dealing with private investigators, but Detective Inspector Joe Hogarth was a different prospect altogether. Sometimes an adversary, sometimes an ally, the man's moods seemed to blow with the wind.

Hogarth's phone rang for so long she became convinced the man was ignoring her. She pulled the phone away from her ear and was all set to try someone else when a gruff voice sounded from the phone in her hand.

"Miss Roberts. Long time no hear," said Hogarth.

Eva put the phone to her ear and summoned a smile to grease the call.

"We've been busy, Inspector. You too no doubt."

"There's always plenty to keep me on my toes in this town. There's even enough for private investigators too," said Hogarth. "Much as I'd love to chew the cud, my guess is that this isn't just a social call."

"I'm afraid you've called my bluff," said Eva.

"A habit of the job," said Hogarth.

"Okay. Well, I doubt this is on your list of priorities," said Eva. "But it has to do with the Saxon King exhibit. The one Councillor Audley borrowed from Southend Museum, and then promptly lost."

"Oh yes. That idiot," said Hogarth. "Pride before a fall and all that."

"*And* it has a little do to with a break-in incident at a house in Chalkwell. One which would have been reported by a Mr Aaron Clancy, a man who happens to be a client of ours. It might also involve a man by the name of Carl Renton. A name you may have seen in the press."

"That's a real dog's dinner of issues there, Miss Roberts. And none of them sound like they're in my line of work."

"But I think these could very well end up in your in-tray, Inspector. You might have heard that Mr Renton has gone missing."

"Yes, I've seen that nonsense in The Record. Looks like they've taken to manufacturing the news when they haven't got anything to report," said Hogarth.

"That's nothing new, believe me," said Eva.

"Renton's rehab houses are well known among the police here but I can't help you with Carl Renton himself. The man's nowhere near officially missing as yet and there's a whole queue of MisPers ahead of him in the pecking order. I did happen to hear about what our town's beloved councillor had done. Took Southend's new crown jewels back home to flash to his pals, and they got nicked right from under his nose. Now the councillor wants us to keep it under wraps for him so be doesn't cop the fall-out. Sounds like that little genie is already well out of the bottle. Shame. As for your house break-in, can't say I'm aware of it. And I've got no need to be, either. Not unless someone got themselves killed in the process. As they used to say in Woolworths, that's not my department. Burglary that is."

"But I really think it might all be connected, DI Hogarth. You'll likely hear about it soon enough."

"Come on then. What makes you think any of that mess could be connected?" said Hogarth.

"They overlap. If I explained it all to you in detail it probably wouldn't make much sense."

"It's hardly making much now to be honest, Miss Roberts."

"Nor to me either, but *it is* still connected... You've heard nothing at all about Carl Renton?"

"Another no, I'm afraid. I've seen The Record's front-page article, but it's been blown out of all proportion. A middle-aged man goes off the rails and disappears? He certainly isn't the first to do that. That's what I did when I packed in the Met."

"Going off the rails is hardly likely in this case. The man is a Christian activist."

"I know he runs the wet house and the drug house on Westerly Road because of his beliefs. Your Mr Renton does seem to believe in miracles but far as I know keeping the faith doesn't prohibit a man from taking a sudden holiday."

"But a holiday unannounced? With all his responsibilities? It's against the man's nature and his routine."

"Yeah, I've read the article, Miss Roberts and I picked up all the innuendo and the panic Alice Perry wants to create. But half the people she interviewed will be in withdrawal because they haven't seen any methadone since Thursday morning. It's called clucking, Miss Roberts. When a junkie starts clucking they'll say and do anything. Look, Mr Renton has barely been gone a day and The Record wants us to send out a search party. Alice Perry is off her head. That rag is always full of hyperbole and scandal, but she's really overcooked this one. If Carl Renton turns up tomorrow morning, Alice Perry is going to have egg all over her face. If you ask me, it couldn't happen to a nicer person."

"I think she ran with the piece as a gamble, Inspector. I know the girl. She's like a shark. She's smelt blood in the water and she's chasing it for all she's worth. I don't know how she smelt it, but she did. And I think she could be right too."

"Yes, she's a shark alright. Maybe you should be calling her for the inside track on this rather than me. None of us this end can do anything with it until it becomes a formal missing persons issue, and that'll take time."

"But informally, Inspector...?" said Eva.

"Why call me? Don't you normally cultivate PC Dawson to do your bidding?"

"That's a little harsh even if it is true," said Eva, hiding her embarrassment at the DI calling her out. "Dawson is a very helpful contact, but you work at a higher level. I was hoping you might see all the strands coming together from across the board."

"If you're right, maybe I soon will. But presently, I don't see it. Not even one of those strands."

Eva sighed, wondering if Hogarth was up to his old tricks of obfuscation, keeping the door closed and the investigation to himself. Eva's silence must have revealed her thinking.

"Miss Roberts. I don't always appreciate your methods and I especially don't appreciate your partner's approach to a great many things. But I know we've managed to fix a few things along the way."

"We have," said Eva. "Then you'll let me know if you hear anything?"

"Certainly. *If* it's appropriate to do so," said Hogarth.

"What does that mean?"

"Exactly what I said. I won't jeopardise an investigation for the sake of pooling information but that said, I'll see what I can do…"

Eva wasn't convinced. Hogarth was quiet at the other end before he offered a crumb of his thinking. The smallest symbol of his willingness to help.

"Your client. Aaron Clancy. This break-in…"

"Yes?"

"Lost something of value, has he?"

"Actually, a whole batch of very expensive things. But of those items, he's pretty hot and bothered about a Celtic torq band. He says the police are holding it because they suspect it could be part of the Saxon King haul which was stolen from Councillor Audley's home."

"Yes, all the council are on tenterhooks at the minute so they've gone overkill. They're pulling out all the stops to find what's missing before the proverbial hits the fan any worse than it has already. And what if they're right to do so?"

"What do you mean?" said Eva.

"Just an idea. You're looking for connections. What if both robberies were linked?"

Eva's eyes narrowed in thought. "Interesting. What do you know about the museum theft?"

"Two central pieces are missing, a gold buckle and a silver stick."

"They don't sound like my client's items, but it's a possibility, I suppose," said Eva. She picked up a pen and scribbled a note about the potential link between the museum loss and Clancy's.

"Is there anything else you can think of? Anything else that might help?"

"You know, you're beginning to sound like my gaffer, Miss Roberts. Nope. That's all I'm afraid. But don't you worry, if there is anything in this, we'll be all over it soon enough."
"And you'll let me know what you hear?"
"Yes. *If* it's appropriate to do so. Just so long as you plan to do the same."
"Of course," said Eva. "Just one last question, Inspector. How did the police get their hands on Aaron Clancy's Celtic torq?"
"Sorry, Celtic what?" said Hogarth.
"The piece being held by police in case it belongs to the Saxon King's collection?"
"Again, not my department. But I heard it was found by a man walking his dog on the beach. Which goes to prove there is still an honest man in Southend."
"Yes, I heard that part," said Eva. "I wondered where exactly."
"For someone on the ask, you drive a hard bargain, Miss Roberts. I have a job to do as well. Hold on. I'll ask our resident gossip expert if he knows anything."
Eva heard the DI pull the phone away from his mouth before he called out, "Simmons!"
DS Simmons. Eva had met the man on occasion and had been less than impressed. It seemed Hogarth held the man in similar esteem.
"Does anyone know where that big gold band was picked up?" said Hogarth.
There was a pause at the other end before a distant response. Hogarth returned on the line.

"The man said he found it near the Marine Activity Centre. Not far from the flash bistro with the palm tree mural. The museum have been chasing us ever since, as has someone else, who claims ownership. Your client I presume."

"Our client, yes."

Hogarth became distracted by chatter at the other end, followed by a laugh. He snorted a laugh in reply before explaining himself.

"Sounds like the guy who found it must have told a friend. Chinese whispers and all that. DS Simmons tells me that the beach down there is teeming with metal detector men and bucket and spade-carrying treasure hunters as we speak. Desperadoes, eh?"

"Really?" said Eva. She looked up as Joanne landed a steaming mug of coffee on her desk. The look in Eva's eyes caught the girl's attention.

"Chances are Alice Perry will be reporting on the great Southend Gold Rush tomorrow morning," said Hogarth.

"Let's hope that's all she has to write about," said Eva.

"That beach isn't too far from you, is it?" said Hogarth, dropping a motivating hint. "I guess we'll be speaking again soon, eh?"

Hogarth didn't waste any time on further pleasantries. The phone clicked as he hung up, and Eva shook her head. She had called Hogarth as an extra resource from her kitbag, and here he was turning the tables. The DI sounded as busy and wily as ever, but at least they knew where they stood with him. There was something to be said for that.

The smell of coffee had Dan looking up from his laptop. He looked at the spare mug of coffee in Joanne's hand.

"Is that coffee available for drinking, or are you just teasing?" said Dan.

"What? Oh," said Joanne. She walked the coffee mug towards Dan and he took it from her and held it in both hands. Reclining in his chair, he looked across at Eva.

"So what did Detective Inspector Hold-out tell you? From the look on your face I'd say Hogarth must have actually told you something."

"You've never warmed to him," said Eva.

"Or his predecessor. I've got good reason for that."

Eva sipped her coffee. She frowned as it scalded her mouth, but she took another sip anyway.

"He says that Aaron Clancy's Celtic gold piece was found by the Marine Activity Centre."

"And so?"

"That's the piece currently held in dispute with Aaron Clancy. The council are causing a fuss to ensure it isn't part of the Saxon Gold. Something Hogarth said about it made me think – two losses like that suggest we might have a serious thief on our hands. Someone who could have done both robberies."

"It's possible," said Dan. "But we weren't hired to catch a thief. We've been hired to track down the booty."

"But to find Clancy's artefacts, we may have to catch that thief."

"I'm still not convinced," said Dan. "It sounds like our thief has butter fingers if he's dropping these items on the beach. Hogarth's manipulating you."

Eva nodded. "I don't know about that, but that's not all Hogarth said. It turns out that half the town's metal detectorists are down there now, trying to find their own pot of gold. Dan, if there's anything else down there, we should be looking too."

"Hunting needles in a haystack?" said Dan.

"I suppose. But we might not even need to hunt for the needles themselves. We could just take a look at the people hunting for the gold."

"We really are scraping the barrel today."

"But it's possible that the person involved in that theft could be down there looking for what he left behind. And if that's true, we might be able to identify him and follow him to the rest of Clancy's missing artefacts."

Dan stood up. "So we do get to go down the beach after all. Should I bring a towel?"

"No. But a bucket and spade really wouldn't go amiss," said Eva.

She walked towards the door, passing Joanne and Mark on the way.

"So do we get to come?" said Joanne.

"Shall we let them?" said Dan. "Okay. But no ice cream. You've been naughty, remember."

Joanne shook her head. Her eyes suggested she was ready to cut loose with a quickfire reply. Dan waited for it, but thankfully she bit her lip.

***

The beach was busy. The road was packed with an impatient stream of parents driving back from the seaside, with accompanying wails of young children coming from more than a few open car windows. The pavement was packed with walkers, booze-breathing drinkers, cyclists and late afternoon joggers. As soon as they reached the sea wall, they stopped and looked at the frenetic activity on the other side. A couple of blue-hatted PCSOs were milling around watching, standing out in the crowd because of their high-viz jackets. Around them were a diverse group of people, from kids in swimming trunks, to old men in eyewatering speedos, to a fractious, shifting group of no less than thirty or forty people armed with metal detectors and shovels going hell for leather at the sand in the wide patch between the Marine Activity Centre and the Seascape Bistro.

"Look at all these people," said Dan. "It's like someone kicked an ants' nest. They're everywhere."

"Where do we start?" said Joanne.

"How do we start?" said Mark.

"We just go onto the sand and look around," said Eva. "Use your eyes and ears."

They took a collective pause for breath before climbing the steps of the sea wall to join the melee on the other side. They split up and began to scatter among different sections of the beach. A middle-aged guy with big black shades and a large pot belly bursting from beneath his vest walked past Dan aiming his metal detector low at the sand. He walked in a straight line like he was mowing the lawn. When the man came to a human obstacle standing in his path, the man looked at the person in his way and waited until they stood aside. About thirty seconds later, the guy turned at the bistro wall and came straight towards Dan. Having taken the measure of the man, Dan folded his arms and waited. The guy slowed to a halt as his detector reached Dan's boots. He looked at Dan's face over the top of his shades. He was the breathy type, the kind of man who breathed through his mouth rather than his nose.

"So what are you looking for?" said Dan.

The guy pulled one of his sizeable earphones away from his head. His voice was nasal and deep. As soon as he spoke, Dan wondered whether the guy was 'challenged' in some way.

"Someone found gold here. I'm here for the missing Saxon gold. Just like you and everyone else," said the man.

"You think you'll find it here?" said Dan.

"I've got the same chance as you, haven't I? Better even, if I work methodically. Better still, you don't have a detector."

"No. I don't," said Dan.

"Finders Keepers," said the man with a grin.

"You wish," said Dan.

The man's grin faltered and he nudged the metal detector towards Dan's toes, suggesting he clear out of the way. Dan couldn't help but smile. In more ways than one, the guy had a lot of guts.

"I don't have to wish," said the guy as Dan moved aside with deliberate slowness. "If it's here, I'm going to find it."

"How long have you been searching already?"

"Since I heard about it. Since the morning."

The man's answer left a doubtful look in Dan's eyes. The man had been searching a long time. Surely there was nothing else to find by now.

The man put his headphones back over his ears and ploughed on across the sand to the next obstacle along. Dan watched the guy's big butt move at a purposeful pace before he turned to scope the beach. He saw Joanne heading into the crowds near the bistro, Mark not far behind. Meanwhile, Eva was cutting along the side of the marine centre, stalking along the side of the building down towards the wooden platform at the back end of the jetty, the part which held racks of bright plastic kayaks and canoes. People watching. Dan could handle that. He set off down the beach, his leather jacket slung over his shoulder. Forget the bucket and spade or the metal detector. Dan only wished he'd brought a large bottle of water, and his shades..

Hogarth had said the Celtic torq was found near the marine centre. That was as specific as it got. The treasure hunters were mostly digging and scanning the shingle between the bistro and the marine centre, which suggested some inside knowledge on the location of more treasure. But there was also a good chance human nature had taken hold instead, the herd mentality shifting the main hunt to the beach between the two buildings. It didn't necessarily follow that the busiest patch was the place to be. Eva laid a hand on the edge of the wooden platform at the back of the marine centre and peered between the racks holding the kayaks and canoes. She stretched to get a look at the beach on the other side of the jetty, and from the limited view afforded her, Eva saw it looked almost empty. The emptier beach looked far more appealing. Not only because of the no-crowds aspect, but because it provided a good area to view the crowds from. Eva turned her head, and her gaze tracked down towards the end of the jetty, where it ended sharply in empty space and glistening mud. The tide was out, providing plenty more beach for the ambitious detectorists, and it also allowed Eva a means of escape to the sanctuary on the other side. She began to pick her way along the sand, weaving between the children joining in the search for fun, side-stepping the more territorial adults who were digging their patch. There was more than a hint of aggression on the air. The image of seagulls scrapping and pecking one another over a few chips came to mind. Any findings were likely to be just as meagre, but she guessed it wouldn't stop them from pecking one another's eyes out if the tension got any higher. Such human instincts were the very reason they had a business in the first place, but seen up close, Eva still didn't like it. She eyed the vastly outnumbered PCSO's and gave them a friendly nod.

The large female PCSO didn't respond but stared back at Eva as if she recognised her but couldn't recall where from. Eva moved on. She picked her way down the beach, past another mass of people. Soon the shingle was replaced by firm soft sand and soon after it turned to sea mud – wet, boggy and thick. Eva looked at her shoes, looked at the mud, and glanced back at the sea wall. It was a long way back to take the pavement route. She shrugged, slipped off her shoes and pinched them together in one hand. She set off, her feet squelching into the soft, cold, oozing mud. Her lip curled at the sensation. She strived to keep her balance, ignoring the threat of the small solid objects deep in the mud. Eva reached the end of the jetty and reaching for the top edge of the wood for support. Her hand traced the edge of the jetty feeling the cold smooth galvanised metal hook and plate where small vessels would be able to tie off. She looked across at a wide grassy beach full of space. It wasn't devoid of treasure hunters. She saw a few detectorists roving around, and a group of teenagers with shovels midway up the beach, but compared to what she had left behind, it was almost serene. Following the line of the jetty, she started to pick her way back along the emptier beach, her feet smothered in sand like a stinking clay. There was no way she would be able to put her shoes on until her feet were clean again. "Stupid," she muttered. She looked around again. People-watching, was the aim of the game. There was a chance one of them was their thief. She scanned the loud teens and the few busy detectorists but felt uninspired by any of them. None seemed to be looking at a particular place. If the true thief was among them, then surely he would have been working a single area – the places he remembered he had walked when he dropped the torq. But there was no

such person in sight. Maybe Hogarth's idea wasn't so bright after all. Would the thief come back or would he know they would be looking for him there? It all depended how smart he was. A smart man might give up the lost treasures and move on. A desperate man, well, that was a different story.
Eva's phone buzzed in her bag. Her eyes narrowed. Maybe they had found something on the other side. But Eva had another feeling about the message and with it came a whole lot of frustration that had been simmering beneath the surface for most of the day. She pulled her phone free and saw a voicemail reminder. She had ignored it once already, but there was no way of knowing without checking. She sighed, dialled 901, and put the phone to her ear. When the voice came on the line it was still almost shocking. Her heart sped up and she was plunged deep into a host of memories and sensations, recalling Lauren's young face, her smile, and the better times.
"Hi, Eva. It's me again. Please, please, listen before you delete this message. I know, I honestly know you have plenty of reason to avoid speaking to me…"
Eva's eyes widened as they roved the beach. The sun beat down on her as she listened and took in the panoramic view of the pale sands all the way to the white masts of City Beach, the pier and Pirate Dan's theme park. The seafront was awash with people as far as the eye could see. And yet here she was, alone, feeling again like an awkward teenage girl listening to the friend who had betrayed her all those years ago. Eva wanted to end the call, to stop the feelings, but she kept on listening and endured the message along with the heat.

"…I acted like trash. I know it, and I'm so sorry. But I really hope you won't hold that against me right now because I really, really need your help. If I could call anyone else to help me, if I knew of anyone else who knew what to do, I'd be doing that instead. Not because I don't want to speak to you, but because I know you don't want to speak to me…"
"You didn't speak to me, Lauren!" spat Eva to the unhearing message. "You cut me dead!"
But the message rambled on, and Lauren's words grew quieter, until soon her voice cracked altogether. Eva heard her sobbing as she spoke.
"I'm in trouble, Eva. And by trouble, I mean danger. He's out to hurt me. Yes, it's a guy. He's been trying to ruin my life and he won't stop… and now it's turned into threats and I really don't know how it will end unless I get help. Real help. Not just words. I've tried all the usual channels. I've done what people always say to do, but it's just not working. He's got me trapped. But you, Eva… I heard what you do for a living these days. You were always so smart. You were the one who always knew what to do. So please… Please call me back. Say you'll help me. I think you might be the only one who can."
The message ended there and Eva found herself swallowing a host of unwelcome emotions. Her throat ached. She pushed the thoughts away as best she could, her eyes glancing back at the teenagers digging in the sand. Eva felt the prickle of tears trying to force their way out, but she frowned and fought their advance. There was no way she was going to let Lauren hurt her again.. She needed to be tough, at least as tough as the girl had been with her. And yet…

"Jeez, Eva. That was almost twenty years ago," she told herself. "Half your life…"

She watched one of the teenagers start to mess about with one of the old wooden dinghies used by the fishermen and yacht owners to row out to the boats anchored in the estuary. There was a line of upturned dinghies, running along the sand near the sea wall. The teenager toed one of the boats, then waved for his friend to join him. The boat lay close to the wall of the marine centre. Playing with those boats, the teens were going to cause a problem for someone, but Eva wasn't in the mood to play the policewoman.

"What about second chances and forgiveness, Eva?" she muttered, shaking her head, still caught in two minds. She looked at her phone screen. She saw the missed call and thumbed the screen once. Then thumbed it again to return the call.

As soon as the call tone kicked in Eva shook her head and frowned. "Damn it. What the hell am I doing? She dumped you. Let her wait."

Three rings in, Eva cut the call. She pursed her lips and then, at the sound of an excited shout, she glanced up the beach. The young teen was still playing with one of the wooden dinghies and he was shouting for his other friends to join him. Eva's brow dropped over her eyes. He sounded excited. Maybe a little too excited. *They'd found something.* Had he found the stash? But surely the treasure hunt couldn't end here? It didn't make sense. Eva started to stalk her way barefoot across the sand, the pebbles and shells painfully biting into her heels as she moved. She tried tiptoe, moving faster with every step. The teenagers gathering around the empty boat were turning into a wild frenzy. They must have found more gold. The nearest of the metal detector men had stopped his work to watch. In a matter of a minute, Eva knew the whole beach would gravitate to their noise. She gritted her teeth and broke into a kind of loping run. A shoe fell from her hand and she scraped it up, almost falling in the process. The detector man looked at her as she passed. "Have they found it?" one asked her. She didn't reply. She pushed on until the young men heard her coming and the ones at the back turned to watch. She saw a wild-eyed look to them, as if they'd been caught red-handed in some lurid act. Eva didn't understand it. They should have been celebrating.

"We were looking for the gold…" said one, an apology in his voice. "The Saxon gold like in the museum, that's all, like what they found," said the nearest floppy-haired youth. "It wasn't Saxon, it was Celtic," said Eva. But she saw her words weren't going in at all. Something was wrong.

The teenager's young companion dragged a hand down his face. "He's telling the truth. We didn't know this was here. This has got nothing to do with us…"

The way he said it… the look in his eyes… a sudden chill rushed over her skin. "What is it?" she asked. The boy stood aside from the dinghy and Eva's eyes dropped onto the thin ankle protruding from beneath the edge of the upturned boat. The other youth lifted the boat as if he wanted her to see – needed her to see what he had seen. He lifted the hull and there it was. The body of a man who looked like he had almost been turned into rock. Sandstone to be precise. Hunched and rolled up in a catatonic position lay the body of a small man encrusted in sand. His clothes were covered in it. Small dunes had gathered in the smallest folds and had covered parts of his body and legs. Sand covered some of his face, like a sea wave frozen as it lapped the shore. Eva blinked. "Oh my…" She frowned grimly. She'd seen death before many times, and it was never easy. And this was certainly not a natural death. There was no evidence of a wound, but beyond the thin cover of the sand there were hints of bruises, welts and contusions. The man had been badly beaten. And then what? Where was the fatal wound? Where was the congealed, sand-pooled stain of blood?
"I swear this had nothing to do with us," said the youth by the boat. "We saw the boat, so we lifted it up to see what was there. Just in case…"
He was rambling and apologetic, but Eva's mind was already whirring. She wanted the teenager's panicking to stop.
"It's okay," she said firmly. "I know you didn't do it. I saw you find the body. Now… there are some police on the other side of the jetty. Two policewomen. Go and get them. Be discreet, be calm, don't shout your mouth off, or there'll be chaos. Just be calm and quiet and tell them you're one hundred per cent serious about what you've found."

The young man gulped and turned grave. "Serious," he repeated..

Eva nodded at him as an instruction, and the young man and some of his companions tore off for the nearby pavement, their adrenaline helping them to vault over the concrete sea wall. The hawk-eyed detector men noticed and were already beginning to turn her way. The vulture-like human instinct at work.. Eva seemed to have found something of interest, and they hadn't. They wanted a piece of the action.

"Help me keep the body covered by this boat, will you?" she said to the remaining two teenagers. They nodded dumbly and stood by as Eva started to shift the boat back into position as a shelter above the body. She hardened her voice. "Help me, will you?"

One of them snapped out of it and started to move and the other followed suit. They stared at the body as they tilted the boat and slid it back over. Eva heard their light, panicked breathing.

"What happened to him?" said one of them.

"He... I think... I think someone killed him," said the other.

Eva didn't say a word. She looked up and saw some of the treasure scavengers looking their way, talking with hands on hips. She met their staring eyes willing them to look elsewhere. But their gaze was fixed. It was only a matter of seconds before one of them started walking. And then they did, both at the same time. A tall, older man with wispy hair and an old-fashioned metal detector, alongside a younger nerdy type with a newer, shinier piece of kit. Eva stood up and started to move towards them, using her body to block their way. The gesture annoyed the taller man. From the look of him, Eva guessed he was the type who wasn't going to be the one to back down. Especially not from a woman.

She glanced back across her shoulder. The PCSOs had not yet arrived and the weaker of the teens were still guarding the boat. Just. Eva stopped walking and the two men arrived before her.

"Found something, have you?" said the tall old man, a wild wisp of grey hair floating up from his scalp in the breeze.

"It's not something you'd be interested in."

The man gave her a cynical look and arched an eyebrow. He looked at his companion.

"It'd be good to take a look anyway, wouldn't it?" he said. The other man nodded.

Eva shook her head. "It's not what you think it is. Wait. The police will be there in a second."

"Police? It's part of the Saxon gold, ain't it," said the man, almost smacking his wrinkled old lips. He started to circle around Eva, but she moved across and blocked his way.

"The whole beach is a public area," he barked. "I'm a citizen and a resident. I can take a look if I please."

The man smelt of sausage and onions and sweat. Eva turned her head back again to see a glimpse of a big PCSO uniform arrive at the near street corner of the marine centre. She breathed one last hint of fermented sausage and gladly stepped aside.

"If you must," she said.

The man smiled as if he'd won the day. Eva folded her arms and walked on behind them, knowing the man's victory would be short lived. The lumpy figure of PCSO Gill Penner stepped down to the beach, her eyes betraying her doubts as she looked at the upturned hull of the boat guarded by the teens. She saw Eva walking her way behind the two detector men. The teens led her to the boat and they pointed into the shadows beneath it.

"What is it?" called the old man, too excited to wait until he got nearer. "You found the gold, didn't you?"

"It's not gold," said one of the boys, but his eyes and attention were on the big PCSO. "It's definitely not gold."

"Mind out of the way then," said PCSO Penner. Her face was almost a scowl. She moved to the side of the boat and dropped to an uncomfortable crouch. She lifted her hat to get the peak out of her eyes and then she lifted the rim of the boat and looked beneath. Eva watched her eyes widen. She looked up at the boys, the old man with the wispy hair, and then at Eva. The shocked look on her face was like a cry for help. Eva nodded calmly.

"He was injured before he died, PCSO Penner. Beaten. Take a close look at his face," said Eva.

"Oh my God," said the old man, bending to peer beneath the hull. He froze as he saw the sand-covered feet. The younger detectorist backed away as if it would save him from the horror. PCSO Penner stood up and pulled the whole boat up and away from the sand so she could get a good look. One of the teens turned pale and jerked away. Behind her. Eva felt more people starting to gather. At the sea end of the jetty, Dan appeared with a few others who had noticed the fuss. As soon as he saw the huddle near the building, Dan started to accelerate ahead of the pack. He broke into a jog. Eva looked down at the dead man's face. It was familiar somehow, even through the covering of sand. She squinted and racked her brains to remember why she knew that face. Carl Renton, maybe? No. She'd seen his photograph, but this guy was the wrong build, far smaller and skinny too. The dead man's build was more like that of the men in Renton's houses. Lithe and skeletal and small. Dan pushed through the throng until he was at Eva's side, he saw the boat in Penner's hand and saw the body on the sand beneath it.

"I know that guy," said Dan.

Eva and Gill Penner looked up at him. Penner held her police radio by her mouth.

"He was the man on the Broadway," said Dan. "Remember?"

"What man on the Broadway," said Eva.

"When I went to buy the newspaper. This was the guy who almost threw himself in front of a bus."

Eva's eyes widened and Dan looked at PCSO Penner. "This afternoon, just before lunchtime. This guy walked out in front of a bus on the Leigh Broadway. He was being followed."

It took a second before Dan's meaning registered, then PCSO Penner pressed the button on the side of her radio transceiver. The radio crackled into life. She called it in.

"But why? Why this man?" said Eva.

Dan shook his head. He knelt down to peer at the body and saw something glinting from the sand close beside the man's back. Something metallic. Dan stole a glance up at Eva and Penner. Penner was busy on her radio and most of the crowd seem transfixed by the dead man's body. Dan slid his hand into the sand in one fast, fluid move. His fingers grazed a cool metal surface, finding a small cold tin. And beside it, closer to the body, his fingers scraped past a far smaller lump, one wrapped in plastic and grains of sand. Dan snatched both items into his hand and closed his fingers around them. He flipped his hand to hide them and stepped away. He looked around but no one had seen him except Eva. The look on her face said she didn't approve but neither was she about to complain.

Dan opened his hand and ran his finger over both pieces. The silvery tin was the eye-catching piece. The tin was old and ornate and engraved with old fashioned patterns, a style from an old era. But old as it was, there was no way it was Saxon, Celtic, or anything ancient. He decided it had to be a tobacco tin of some kind, which placed it in a far more modern era. Value wise, it was no treasure. It looked more like a charity shop curiosity than a precious item.

"What is it?" said Eva.

"A tobacco tin?" Dan rolled the other lump into his spare hand and picked at the wrapped surface. It was very well wrapped and it was hard to see what was inside.

Eva shook her head. "It's too small for tobacco…"

"Then what is it?"

Dan flipped the lid and found the box just as neat and shiny inside. It was well kept without a trace of dirt or old tobacco. "An old snuff tin, maybe?" said Dan. "It's more the size for snuff. But it's certainly not being used for snuff anymore…" Dan smelt the tin. The only thing he smelt was the metal itself. But then he saw a trace of plastic film snagged to the inside. Clingfilm. Dan narrowed his eyes and brought the other tiny package from his pocket. He lifted it up so Eva was able to see it but shielded it from those nearby. He started to pick at the seams with a fingernail. Gradually he unwrapped it, until he found the solid white tablets at the core. Each bore the imprint of a big capital letter U.
"Ubers," said Dan.
"And you just took them from a dead man. That's evidence, Dan," said Eva, quietly. Penner stopped speaking into her radio. She turned around to face the crowd. Eva kept her face blank and Dan did likewise, slipping the small silver tin and the tiny drug package into his small jeans pocket. PCSO Penner slid the dinghy back down the wall over the body to block any further rubberneckers, then used her bulky figure as a barrier, stepping around the boat towards the people nearby.
"There's nothing to see here, folks, and more police are on their way. So please keep your distance and go about your business."
But no one paid any attention, so Penner raised her voice. "Off you go now. Chop chop. Move along."

The teenagers seemed more than glad of the excuse to leave, as did the first layer of nosey parkers. But Dan and Eva stayed. Their minds whirred as they took in the details of the body, the location, the clothes and shoes, recalling their briefest encounter with the dead man as he darted across the Broadway in Leigh. But what did it mean? There was no doubt in Eva's mind that Carl Renton was in trouble, but was it possible that Renton was linked to the dead man with three Uber tablets in his pocket? It didn't seem likely, but the Ubers made it possible. And what of the silver tin? Penner's young PCSO colleague appeared in a hurry at the sea wall. She was a nervous looking girl with olive skin and dark hair tied up under her PCSO cap with its distinctive blue band. From past experience Eva and Dan knew PCSO Gill Penner was not the must dutiful of coppers. She had once accepted money for passing on sensitive information to a compromised council employee – but she had somehow gotten away with a mere suspension. And as they now dealt with the discovery of a likely murder, alongside Penner was the greenest PCSO in town. In terms of skills and expertise, Eva and Dan outranked them ten times over. Trouble was they didn't have a badge or title, which meant they had precisely no influence whatsoever – and if anyone would flaunt the fact, PCSO Penner would. So they stayed back to keep her at arm's length as they worked out their next move. A new crowd was closing in around the boat, faces filling in the gaps left by those who had backed away.
"Tell them to back off, Kaplan," said Penner, as she stood by the boat.

The young PCSO sighed as she looked at the crowd. Eva saw trepidation in her eyes. "Everybody," called the girl. "Please listen." But her voice was too soft to be heard by more than a few. Penner told her so and she tried again. "Listen up!" she called. "Back away and give us some room. Other police will be here soon. This is a crime scene. Please step back."

A better effort. She was louder, but her voice was still too soft. Eva felt like pitching in to help shoo the crowds away but she guessed the gesture wouldn't have been welcomed by either woman. In the end, Eva didn't need to do anything, as another police officer appeared. A uniformed copper with a round face, doorknob chin and bright, smarmy cold eyes.

"PC Orton," said the new girl, looking relieved.

"Okay. Come on you lot," said the PC, clapping his hands. "Move along, the lot of you," he called. "This is a crime scene. Off you go now!"

The policeman didn't have much in the way of charm, but he made up for it in decibels. The crowd started to shrink as he waved his hands at them like a farmhand with a flock of sheep. But as the more obedient treasure hunters peeled away, two men weaved through them towards the boat. Orton didn't see them. The PC had lifted the old dinghy to get a look at the body beneath. The two men closed in purposefully. Eva watched them, the shorter, stockier man leaned in to snatch a look before the taller, thinner man behind him snuck in for a look of his own. Both men turned away looking pale and wide eyed. Eva kept her eye on them. The men looked at one another in shock.

Eva saw their flitting, fearful eyes. It wasn't just morbid curiosity she'd seen on these men. It was something else. Eva stepped close to Dan, whispering in his ear.

"Do you see those two?"

Dan's eyes were already on the men, absorbing the details of their pale, grainy faces, and their fraught looks. The PC finally noticed them.

"You two. Sod off," said Orton. "This isn't a bloody peep show, it's a crime scene."

Dan looked at their faces, and one of the men caught his eye.. Tall, weaselly, and dark eyed. Something about the man reminded of him of the scumbag man at the drug rehab. And that wasn't all. For a moment, Dan couldn't place the him. And then the penny dropped. "That guy. The taller one… he was on there on the Broadway too. He's the guy who was following the dead man under that boat… I'm sure of it."

Eva looked again. The two men had moved off away from the boat. They were talking, but neither of them could hear what was said. "You're sure about that?" said Eva.

"You know I am," said Dan. "Didn't you see him before?"

"He was a blur. You got a better look than I did."

"Trust me. It's him," said Dan.

Eva looked. "If they know something, we can't let them get away," she said.

Some way back, the two men stopped walking. They joined the rest of the pack, arms folded, worried looks on their faces. They were muttering something between them.

"I'd like to know who they are, what they are talking about too."

"So long as they stay put, that shouldn't be much of a problem," said Dan.

He left Eva's side and weaved between the shoulders of the people until he reached the new young PCSO. She looked at him and stood her ground.

"Step back please, sir."

"Officer, I'm a private investigator. I've worked with your colleagues before. My name is Dan Bradley." PCSO Penner saw their conversation and moved in fast.

"I know who you are," said Gill Penner. "I know the woman you're with as well. But this is a police matter, none of your concern."

"My partner is the one who found the body," said Dan.

"And like I said, it's a police matter now," she said, firmly. The constable noticed their minor stand-off and stepped away from the boat to face Dan himself. He looked Dan up and down with sharp eyes.

"You heard my colleague. Off you go now. We don't need any drama here."

"Listen to me for a second, constable," said Dan. "See those men back there? The tall one and the stocky one. See them?" Dan nodded into the crowd, past Eva, trying not to look too obvious about it.

Orton saw the men then gave Dan a deeply sceptical eye. "What about them?"

"I saw that tall guy following the dead man. He was after the guy in Leigh about lunchtime. The dead guy was panicking and the tall guy was after him."

"You saw that?" said Orton.

Dan nodded. "It's true."

"He's a private detective?" said Orton, looking at Penner.

Penner frowned and nodded, like their presence wasn't good news.

Dan nodded.

"Be that as it may, this is a police matter now."

"Whatever you say, constable. But you still need to talk to those men."

"On *your* say so?" said Orton.

"No, of course not. But just as a precaution, because it's a good idea, that's all. They acted weird when they saw the body. What if they were involved in this?"

But Dan saw he was talking to a brick wall. He needed to get past the jobsworth to reach the self-interest lying just beyond.

"And think, if they are involved, you'll have identified them in advance. It could save a lot of police time later, don't you think?"

The man processed Dan's words and glanced at the two men.

"I could take their names, I suppose."

The stout PC stepped around Dan, a fresh version of the same smarmy smile on his face. Dan tagged on behind, and Eva followed suit. The PC reached the patch of sand in front of the two men and made a show of clearing his throat.

From somewhere far off came the sound of police sirens. They rose and fell on their air as faint as perfume on the breeze.

"Excuse me gentlemen… but I'm told you might have known the deceased," said the PC.

"What? Who told you that?" said the taller man.

The shorter, stockier man paused before he nodded. The guy reminded Dan of Roger Daltry from The Who. A boyish face gone craggy with age. He seemed wiser than his friend.

"Yes, it's true, Norman was a friend of ours… I can't believe what's happened here. How did he…?"

"That's not for me to say, sir. Norman, you say? How exactly did you know the man?"

"He… *was* a friend. A colleague too. A fellow market trader. We worked on all the markets together over the years."

"The markets?" said the PC.

"Yeah. Southend, Basildon, Romford, Wembley. We've been everywhere as market traders."

"Does that include your tall friend here too?" said Dan.

The shorter, stockier man shot Dan a look and didn't answer. But Orton nodded, signalling for him to answer the question.

"Yes. I do," said the tall man in a gruff voice. "I help out on the stalls. Norman had his own stall. I worked mostly with Tommy here."

"And his name was Norman, you say?"

"Norman Peters," said the stockier man.

"Norman Peters," said Orton. This time the cop took out a notepad and pen from his pocket to write it down, but then seemed to think better of it. Instead he called over his shoulder. "PCSO Kaplan. Come here please!".

The young woman with the olive skin appeared beside Orton.

"I'll need you to make some notes, Kaplan," said the constable. "The name of the deceased is Norman Peters."

The girl recited the name as she hurriedly took out her pad and pen and started to scrawl as fast as she could.

"What can you tell us about Mr Peters?" said the policeman.

"What do you want to know?" said the stocky man, Tommy. "He dealt in clothes. Fashion at discount prices. He wasn't exactly the brightest spark you'd ever meet in your life, but he was a decent bloke. He was one of us."

"How old was he?"

"Forty-eight, forty-nine. I can't remember," said the taller man. Tommy shrugged.

Dan shot the taller man a look. The man met his eye for a moment before he looked at the sand. "He was a good friend," he said, but his voice was flat, and disingenuous.

"Bloody right. Poor Norm didn't deserve that…" said Tommy.

"I'll need both your names, of course," said the PC.

"Of course. Thomas Pink. People call me Tommy."

PCSO Kaplan started scribbling for all her worth.

"Clive Grace," said the taller man.

"Kaplan," said the PC. "You take down these men's details and anything else they can tell us about Norman Peters. I'll deal with CID when they arrive. Gentlemen, please be sure to tell PCSO Kaplan here all you can."

The men nodded and the PC started to move back towards the boat and the body still under PCSO Penner's care. Dan looked at Eva, irritation etched over his face. They followed the PC.

"You did hear what I said, didn't you, constable?" said Dan. "I saw the taller man – Clive Grace – I saw him pursuing Norman Peters through Leigh. Next thing he ends up dead here on the beach."

The PC stopped walking. He turned slowly and looked into Dan's eyes.

"I heard what you said, Mr…?"

"Bradley."

"Mr Bradley, yes, yes, that's right. I heard it alright. But as I told you before, several times as I recall, this really isn't your case. You've done your part.. You've reported the matter, and now we'll be dealing with it from here."

"But that man could be—"

"He could be a witness. A suspect. Or nobody at all. And all of that will be determined in due course as a matter for the police. Now, if you don't mind, I've got a job to do even if you haven't."

The PC turned away and forced himself through the last wall of people surrounding the upturned dinghy, giving them a loud reprimand as he passed by.

"Will you all now please back away! I said back away!"

"Can you believe that pig-headed idiot?" said Dan.

"Unfortunately, yes," said Eva.

"So then, you tell me. What the hell is going on here?" said Dan. "So far we've got one dead market trader, his body half buried under a wooden boat, a missing vigilante Christian, and a stack of missing gold treasures."

"And on top of that you've given us a new problem to deal with."

"You mean the silver tin?" said Dan, reading Eva's eyes. He took the tin from his pocket. "That was supposed to help us, Eva. I had to see what it was. It was there right beside him on the sand."

"It had fallen out of his pocket, at best. It's evidence," said Eva.

"Yeah. And one of those kids might have nicked it just as easily if I'd left it there."

"By then the body was already in police hands."

"Hey. If I didn't grab it, we wouldn't have the clue. It's something, Eva. We have it now."

"But what does it tell us?" said Eva. "Apart from that dead market trader liked to dabble in Ubers?"

"Exactly the thing that Carl Renton wanted to stop. That's how this could be linked," said Dan. "Ubers."

"But Ubers are everywhere at the moment," said Eva. "This man Norman Peters had a silver tin and an Uber or two. It doesn't prove anything?"

"Three Ubers actually," said Dan.

"Okay, three. And for all Carl Renton's efforts, he was failing. It was Mission Impossible. Ubers are everywhere, killing people just like the papers are saying, For all we know it could be Ubers that killed this guy too," said Eva.

"You saw the marks on that guy's face. Norman Peters didn't die from taking any kind of Ecstasy. Not unless these Ubers beat you up as well as make you high."

"It doesn't matter. The link is superficial, Dan. It doesn't take us nearer to finding Clancy's missing treasures and it doesn't explain what happened to Renton either. For all we know, this death could be a completely separate crime. In many ways, that'd be easier to believe than the alternative."

"You said they could be linked."

"It's tempting to believe it. But I don't want to follow the wrong path. We've got to find Clancy's collection before it gets sold off and that could happen any time at all."

"Face it, Eva, it could have already happened. If not, finding that stuff is going to be a big ask. Aaron Clancy is dreaming if he thinks we're going to find his loot easily. It could be anywhere by now. The last place it'd be is on this damn beach."

"But the Celtic torq band was found here," said Eva. "His missing items were here."

"One dropped gold band is careless. But dropping the whole treasure chest? That was never going to happen. We have to look somewhere else."

"But look what we found instead…" said Eva, her voice trailing off as they both looked at the old boat guarded by the police.

Eva sighed. "We need something, alright. Okay, maybe DI Hogarth was wrong on this one. We didn't find the thief or the treasures."

"He wasted our time so he didn't have to waste his. But maybe we should take a closer look at this tin. A guy like that, who sells cheapo trendy fashions on a market stall – this tin doesn't fit a man like that. The tin is telling us something, Eva."

"It tells me we're going to have problems with Hogarth when he finds out."

"I found it on the sand."

"Yeah. You can try that on him if you like," said Eva.

As the sirens drew closer, Eva headed for the sea wall to clean the mud off her feet. Dan tried to get one last look at the body, but PC Orton faced him down with a hard-eyed stare. Dan took a final glance back at the two market men being interviewed by the young PCSO before he gave it up. He followed Eva over the sea wall to find a new crowd gathering on the pavement to watch the fuss on the beach.

Eight

Dan laid the silver tin on Eva's desk and the four of them gathered around it, inspecting the intricate detail of the patterned engraving. The tin lid was decorated with a patterned border, and within the border were flowers and laurel wreaths, then another internal border, and inside that was a detailed central design. Some of it had faded and been smoothed away by use and time.
"It looks like an antique," said Eva. "Certainly a period piece and almost certainly a snuff box."
"Which would make it at least mid-twentieth century, right?" said Dan.
"From that design, I'd say it's a lot older. There's too much detail for the austere fifties. And it looks like real silver to me. I'd say its Victorian, at least turn of the century."
"So maybe it *could* be part of Clancy's collection?"
"It's not in his catalogue, and he didn't mention anything like it," she replied. Eva teased the lid open with a fingernail. Dan had certainly left fingerprints all over it, but she had no intention of joining him.
"It's been well looked after," she said. "But no, this isn't from any special high value collection. This is purely a domestic piece. A curiosity."
"So how does it fit into the scheme of things?" said Dan.
"Well, it could simply belong to the dead man, Norman Peters. A collector's item. A keepsake."
Dan's face stayed blank. He didn't feel it. Eva was clutching at straws.

Eva shrugged. "Yes, I know. The guy we saw running in Leigh wouldn't own a piece like this. Though he might have if he owned it to sell it. Market traders are traders first and foremost. They buy and sell all kinds of things. Maybe he bought it as an investment," said Eva.

"Wait a minute," said Mark. He leaned over the tin and squinted at the design. "What's that in the central pattern — right on the front."

"Where?" said Dan.

"There," said Mark.

Joanne leaned in close and stared hard at the centre of the tin lid.

"I see it," she said. Eva strained her eye at the central emblem. There in the middle of a wreath was a simple cross. A crucifix central to the whole design, part smoothed away by time. Eva blinked, and looked at Dan.

"It's almost worn away, but it's still just there."

Dan flipped the tin in the light until it was clear. The faint lines showed clear and fine as silk thread.

"It's a cross," said Dan.

"A crucifix," said Eva. "A coincidence, you think?"

"Because of Renton's Christian background. You know what I think about coincidences," said Dan. "It's possible. Though the cross isn't exactly a rare symbol."

"We could check with Joe," said Mark, looking excited. "He might know whether this box belonged to Carl or not."

"As a last resort, yes. But he's not exactly the most stable of people is he?" said Eva.

Mark gave her a questioning look.

"If we give him reason to think that Carl Renton has been harmed in any way, I'm worried he might do something stupid."

"You mean he might try to kill himself?" said Mark.
Joanne seemed to agree. "He does seem fragile."
Mark chewed his lip. "But if Renton is alive, then asking might help you find him."
Eva nodded. "We need to be sure."
"Then, we've got another link," said Dan. "A tenuous one maybe. You decide," said Dan. He plucked the half-unwrapped Uber tablets from the desk. Mark and Joanne leaned in out of fascination. Joanne's eyes gleamed.
"So these are the killer Es which are doing the rounds…" said Joanne.
Dan folded his arms. "Looks like it. Norman Peters had a silver tin with a crucifix on it, and three deadly Uber pills all wrapped up in clingfilm. It looks to me like he'd stored those pills inside the tin. There's a hint of clingfilm snagged inside the rim of the tin. The pills might have fallen out of the tin when he died and fallen on the beach."
"Or when he was dragged underneath that boat," said Eva.
"I didn't see any sign of dragging left on the sand. I'd say the boat was lifted and dumped over him," said Dan.
"Though any trail might have been hard to spot, what with all those treasure hunters out and about."
"True," said Dan. He shrugged. "With all those people on the beach we're bound to have missed something. Maybe we should go back."
Eva shook her head. "Not yet. First we need to look at what we have. So far we have the tin with the cross, and the Ubers. Both found on the dead man, Norman Peters. What does that tell us?"
Dan scratched his chin and tried to read the spark in Eva's eyes.

"Peters liked keeping his drugs in a fancy tin? What does it tell you?"

"Those links could be tenuous if there was only one of them. But there isn't. We have the tin and the Ubers. Both of those cross over into Carl Renton's work. The cross is the man's mission. The key part of that mission was to stop the drugs coming into Southend, specifically the Ubers, just like these. And both of these things, the cross and the Ubers, turn up in Norman Peter's pocket."

"A dead market trader in bad clothes," said Dan.

"The chances of coincidence aren't likely," said Eva.

"Not when you look closely," said Dan.

"You know the police will need these for their investigation," said Eva.

"I know. But I'm glad we got our hands on them first. And before we hand it over, we still need to find out whether this tin belonged to Carl Renton."

"Fine," said Eva. "But let me deal with it. Joe Clancy is on the edge. We need to handle him with tact and caution."

Eva opened her handbag and pulled out the folded contract signed by Aaron Clancy. She read the paperwork, looking for Clancy's contact details.

"What?" said Dan. "You think I have no tact or diplomacy?"

"I'm saying they're not your best skills."

"Now that was diplomatic," said Joanne.

Eva picked up her phone and dialled. She put the phone to her ear and walked to the kitchen. As she waited for the call to connect she pulled the coffee and filter papers from the cupboard and flicked on the filter machine.

The call was connected and a strangely hesitant female voice came on the line.

"He-hello?" said the voice.

"Georgie?" said Eva.

"Yes. Who is this?"

"Eva Roberts, the private investigator. We met earlier."

"Of course," said the girl, the relief audible in her voice.

"Listen. I need to speak with Mr Clancy. Is he in?"

"Aaron you mean? No. He's out at the council, still talking about his Celtic band."

"Aaron Clancy didn't know Carl Renton all that well, did he?"

"No. Carl was mostly here when Aaron wasn't around. That's how it worked."

"Hmmm," said Eva, struggling. She didn't see another way around it. Despite the risks she was going to have to talk to Joe about what they'd found.

"Can I speak to Joe, Georgie. I need to ask him something."

"No, you can't, Miss Roberts. I'm sorry."

"Why not?"

"Hmmm. We argued and he's not really talking right now."

"What did you argue about?"

"He won't eat again. He needs to eat, I told him over and over, but he won't – he told me to stop interfering."

"Georgie, if you don't mind me saying this, what exactly is his problem? Sometimes he seems argumentative and unpleasant, sometimes he seems frail and sick. What's going on with him?"

The girl paused before she spoke.

"The truth? I think that Joe may be just a little bit spoiled…" Her words sounded like a grand understatement. But Georgie wasn't finished. "But these days, it's not just that. Something's wrong with him, Miss Roberts. He shuts me out. I think he's more ill than he lets on, but he won't talk to me about it."

"That's not good at all," said Eva.

"Why? What is it?" said Georgie.

"We think we found something which might belong to Carl Renton. I wanted to confirm whether Joe recognised it or not."

Eva held back on the how and where aspect of the discovery.

The girl's tone brightened. "That's good news, isn't it? Maybe I could help you? I knew Carl pretty well, not as close as Joe, of course, but we met plenty of times."

"Okay, let's see," said Eva. "Do you know if Carl Renton used to own a small silver tin. Not much bigger than a matchbox?"

"Silver? A silver tin?" said Georgie. Eva pinched the phone between her ear and shoulder as she scooped several great heaps of ground coffee into the paper cone in the machine. "Yes. I know it. He used to keep these little tiny scraps of paper in that tin. He'd written Bible passages on each one. He told me that he used to give them out to people in the street. People who looked like they were having a bad day. They were all handwritten things. Just a couple of lines a piece, all folded in half. I thought that was sweet of him. Like he had a little box full of good wishes for people in need. I know Mr Renton thought it was a bit deeper than that."

Eva stopped scooping coffee and slammed the lid down on the machine.

"That tin… it's not very big," said Eva. "It has a detailed floral design, laurel wreaths set inside an engraved border."

"And in the middle was a tiny cross," said Georgie. "Yeah that's it. That's Mr Renton's box of Bible quotes."

Eva's mouth flickered. The discovery was an advance, and yet she instinctively knew it wasn't good news either. Eva waited a moment too long and Georgie asked a question.
"Where did you find it, Miss Roberts?"
"On the beach," said Eva, flatly. "I'll tell you more when I can, okay?"
"I'll tell Joe. That should cheer him up."
"I hope so," said Eva. "We'll keep on looking."
She ended the call as a cold wall of apprehension hit her chest. It seemed they had the scale of the matter at hand all wrong. The investigation seemed to be widening, taking them elsewhere. But Eva didn't know where they were headed, and she didn't like it one bit.

Now they knew the origin of the tin, there was no further need to keep hold of it. It was best put back to use in the police investigation, forming the body of evidence towards an eventual prosecution. Dan took a breath and made the call. He was put through to DS Simmons instead of Hogarth, no doubt because the DI wanted to avoid dealing with him. But as soon as Dan revealed what they had, Simmons covered the phone with his hand and shared the news around his office. DI Hogarth couldn't have been more than ten feet away, because Dan heard the explosion in full Dolby surround sound.
"I'll bring it in. You can have it now, if you want," said Dan.
"DI Hogarth says not to bother. He's already on his way."
Dan knew full well that wasn't all Hogarth had said. DS Simmons was too polite to repeat the rest.
Dan hung up the call.

"Get your tin hats on," he said. Eva glanced up from her laptop where she was busily scanning The Record's latest reports on the spate of Uber deaths.

"Tin hats?" she said.

"Hogarth's coming to collect his dues: the tin and the tablets."

"Oh..." said Eva.

Ten minutes later, the front door shuddered open and the bell on the wall announced their visitor with a long shrill ring. Hogarth slammed the door behind him and raised a pointing finger at Dan.

"What the hell do you think you're playing at? You took evidence from a crime scene, man! And unlike the great unwashed out there, you don't have any excuse, or any right to claim ignorance. I know what you were thinking. You thought that was part of your client's missing loot. It doesn't wash with me either way. You had an obligation to inform us as soon as you saw it."

"I saw it," said Dan. "But I didn't know what it was, or how it was related until after I picked it up."

Dan's tone was calm, his voice even, but everyone in the room knew he was playing fast and loose with the truth. Eva closed her laptop and sipped the dregs of her coffee.

"Afternoon, Inspector," she said. "Your investigation must be taking shape by now."

"And you're not much better, Miss Roberts. You certainly knew to call me. That was what we agreed."

"The items had barely been in our possession longer than half an hour when we called you. And here you are," she said.

Hogarth jabbed his finger at her but said no more, saving his anger for Dan. He looked back at Dan and his face returned to a healthy shade of puce.

"You damn well should have left it where it was. Crime Scene and forensics have set up around that body, and if not for you, they would have had an uncontaminated crime scene and probably a very easy collar. There would have been prints on that tin, and now the only prints we'll find on it are yours."

"Contaminated the crime scene? Us?" said Dan. "Half of the town contaminated your crime scene before I did. There were treasure hunters and desperadoes all over the place, marching in packs like jackals. You never had a clean crime scene in the first place.

"But you still took it."

"They weren't found on the body. They were near it. I made a judgment call that it was safe to borrow them."

"Borrow them?!" said Hogarth.

"Maybe I made the wrong call," said Dan with a shrug, "It happens. Don't tell me you've never made the wrong call, because I've seen you at work."

"Don't you dare push your bloody luck with me, Bradley. You've given me about three reasons why I could nick you here and now. Including perverting the course of justice. Don't think you'd like to hear those words in court again, would you, eh?"

"Steady on, Inspector," said Eva "We called you to ensure you got the evidence – and the information as well."

"Information?" said Hogarth. He took a breath.

Eva nodded and stood up from her desk. She held up an empty coffee cup as a symbol and a peace offering. "Coffee, Inspector?"

"You'll need more than coffee to win me around after this incident."

"Coffee is a start," said Eva.

Hogarth fell silent and looked around the office, as if he was suddenly aware of his outburst. Eva received the hint and looked at Mark and Joanne.

"You two… we need to talk to the inspector. Would you mind taking a break?"

Joanne didn't look impressed, but she quickly gathered her things. "Come on, Mark."

"Thank you," said Eva. As soon as Mark and Joanne had left the office, Hogarth walked to the empty reception desk and took hold of Mark's chair. He spun it round to face Eva, plonked himself down on it and dragged himself towards her with his feet.

"When our Crime Scene Manager hears about this, he's going to have someone's guts for garters. And this time it won't be mine," said Hogarth.

Dan sighed. "He'll get over it."

Hogarth shook his head. "Okay then. Information. So what have you got? And after these shenanigans it had better be information, and not more bloody questions. There's a dead body on that beach with a severely battered face, and you can bet The Record will be milking this one for a week. Which means I'll be under the cosh from day one."

"You had PCSOs on site," said Eva.

"Because of the treasure hunters," said Hogarth.

Eva nodded. "The PCSOs were barely able to protect the body from the vultures on the beach. It's likely if Dan hadn't taken those items someone else would have done and you wouldn't have them at all."

"So you were both helping me out, only I never realised. Show me how lucky I am."

"Here," said Dan, laying the silver case carefully on his desk. "We think it's a Victorian snuff tin," said Eva, "but it hasn't been used for that purpose in a very long time."

Hogarth's chin crumpled in thought. He stared at it, then leaned over the top, squinting to look at the detail.

"And you found this on the body?" said Hogarth.

"Beside it, like I said," said Dan.

"Whatever. But it was with the body?" said Hogarth.

"Yes, it was," said Eva.

"And?"

Eva moved close to the desk and Hogarth looked up. She pointed an unpainted nail at the fine details on top of the case.

"Do you see the crucifix at the centre of the design?" she said.

"Yes," said Hogarth. "And?"

"This tin is what you might call Victorian Christian paraphernalia. It's silver. A Christian keepsake, for an old time snuff taker."

Hogarth folded his arms and waited for the next detail to be imparted. But there were no more words. Instead, Eva gave Dan a look, and his eyes widened a little with the equivalent of a shrug. Hogarth read their nuanced looks but couldn't fathom the meaning. Dan sighed and pulled out the little clingfilm bundle from his jeans pocket. He laid the half-unwrapped tablets beside the tin and one spilled out, rolling to settle right in front of Hogarth's nose.

"An Uber, Mr Bradley? I always knew you were a bit of a rogue, but I never had you down as an Uber man."

"That's because I'm not.."

"Wait. Don't tell me. You found these on the sand too. Right next to the dead body with the caved in head."
"You're smarter than you look," said Dan.
"I'm twice as smart as you think you are, Bradley," said Hogarth. "But I'd still like to hear whatever theory you've come up with. It's always good to find a starting point."
"Then your starting point is this, Inspector," said Eva. "This tin belongs to Carl Renton."
"What? Because of the cross?" said Hogarth. "I know the man is a committed Christian, but that's still a bit of a leap in the dark isn't it?"
"It's not a leap in the dark. Renton was seen using this tin. He didn't keep snuff in it. He used to keep handwritten Bible quotes in there. When he saw someone in need of a lift, he would take one out and give it to them. Like a kind of lucky dip of Bible quotes."
Hogarth hesitated. "How do you know all that?"
"Carl Renton used to visit our client, Aaron Clancy's son. He's a bit of a confused rebel-rebel type, just a teenager really, but the father hasn't got much of a relationship with him. I guess Carl Renton saw the boy as another lost soul who needed saving."
Hogarth nodded. "People like that are always trying to save the bloody world. Do they stop to think what happens when everyone's saved? What then? We all sit down together, eat humus, wear sandals and sing Kumbaya? You know as well as I do, there's people in this town who don't want saving. They'd punch you in the face for trying."
"That's not the way Carl Renton saw it," said Eva.
Hogarth rubbed his chin. "No. I suppose not."
"What?" she said.

"You spoke of him in the past tense. Why, Miss Roberts. What else do you think you know?"

"Only what you see here," said Dan. "Your dead man Norman Peters had Carl Renton's Bible quote tin and three Uber pills when he died. Read into that what you like."

"You admit that you took evidence then?" said Hogarth.

"No. I only meant it's reasonable to assume they were his."

"Very reasonable," said Hogarth, sounding less sure.

"It's very unlikely that Norman Peters would have been able to buy that tin from Mr Renton. And it's even more unlikely he would have given it to Peters. It had special meaning for him, and all we know about Norman Peters is that he was a market trader who sold cheap, garish fashion – and that he worked with other market traders Clive Grace and Tom Pink."

Hogarth maintained a frown as he listened.

"Grace and Pink turned up with the crowds when we found Peters' body," said Eva. "They came along and had a look, and both looked pig sick afterwards."

"They were friends, then?" said Hogarth.

"So they said," said Eva. "But I saw those two muttering a fair bit in the crowd afterwards. I'd like to know what they were talking about."

"Hmmmm," said Hogarth.

"Did PC Orton pass any of that on to you?" said Dan.

Hogarth's jaw jutted and tensed. "Not as yet. Why?"

"We asked him to tell you about the market traders. Instead, he got a PCSO to take notes for him."

Hogarth looked instantly irritated again.

"What do you make of it?" he asked.

"As a starting point?" said Dan, with a hint of irony.
Hogarth refused to bite. Dan continued. "The dead market trader doesn't look like a junkie to me. He looked like, what did you call me? A bit of a rogue. I've seen plenty of junkies up close. Norman Peters wasn't one."
"You said you saw him alive? When?"
"Just this afternoon," said Dan. "I saw him walk out in front of a bus on the Leigh Broadway. He was nearly turned into a pancake."
"We thought he'd had a lucky escape until we found him on the beach," said Eva. "Turns out his luck didn't last."
Hogarth frowned. "Then you're saying he must have been killed this afternoon. In daylight hours...?"
"It seems that way," said Eva. "And that's not all."
Hogarth's eyes gleamed. "What?"
"He walked out in front of that bus because someone was following him."
Hogarth shook his head, confused. Dan explained. "He was being followed by one of the other market men who was there later when we found the body. Specifically, a man called Clive Grace."
"Can you see why we wanted PC Orton to interview the man?"
Hogarth bared his teeth. "Yes. I think I do," he said.
"Now maybe you'll be glad we took the silver snuff tin," said Dan.
"Oh, you only did that out of self-interest, Bradley. That's easy to see."

DI Hogarth stood up and, producing a tissue from his pocket, he covered his hand and picked up the silver tin and wrapped it up. He repeated the trick with the cling film and tablets. He hesitated before putting the pills into his pocket; he looked at Dan and said, "presuming you don't want them, of course."

"No. You can have all the fun," said Dan.

"Oh, I'll be having lots of fun without those, I can assure you. Think I might be having a little word with PC Orton when I get back to the station. Just to see what else he picked up, of course."

"Of course," said Eva. Hogarth turned for the door, leaving them with a curt nod. At least he was a little friendlier than when he'd arrived.

"There's one thing I'd ask you to think on, Inspector," said Eva. Hogarth turned his head. "Norman Peters was killed with Carl Renton's tin in his pocket, and thee Uber pills, which were probably inside the tin. Carl Renton spent his whole life devoted to fighting drugs for his faith. What conclusions would you draw about his disappearance now?"

Hogarth thrust his hands deep into his trouser pockets. "Maybe the same as you. But I still won't go there yet. It's far too early to say. The man's not officially missing as yet."

"Not officially. But officially is just a word. Carl Renton has gone all the same."

"People aren't always what they seem, Miss Roberts. Maybe Renton saw his chance to cash in and swiped the loot while your client was away buying some more shiny stuff over in Bahrain or whatever. Think about all of those US TV evangelists on the take. It does happen, doesn't it? That's the power of temptation."

"Carl Renton had been fighting temptation all his life."

"But the question is, did he win, Miss Roberts?"
"In the end, I'm not so sure he did. But I don't think he lost like that."
Hogarth caught her meaning and gave a nod.
"If you're right, we'll soon find out. But I still don't know what's happened to your man's treasure, do you?"
Eva shook her head.
"Makes you wonder about Renton, doesn't it?"
"Missing persons, thieves, and murder. That combination makes me think all kinds of things, Inspector."
"Join the club," said Hogarth. He opened the glass front door to find Mark and Joanne hanging around like urchins on the street outside. Eva called Hogarth back once more. He poked his head in the door.
"Have you heard back on the cause of death yet?" she asked.
Hogarth shook his head. "Too early. But having his head smashed in might have had something to do with it."
"But there was no stab wound? No obvious cause."
"No. But the verdict will come soon enough. If you hear anything else, remember to share. Just like we agreed, eh?"
Eva nodded. "That's a two-way street."
Hogarth gave Eva a grim smile and shut the door behind him.
"He's such a nice guy," said Dan. "I've missed him."
"I think he loves you too," said Eva.
"So what's next?"
"Hogarth was playing it cool about Renton going missing, but he's too smart for that," said Eva. "He sees what we see."
"Which is?"
"It's not definite. Either he fled with Clancy's special things and went against everything he stood for, or…"

"Or he became a victim because he got in the way once too often."

"I'd say."

"Which means?"

"Which means we need to…" Eva's mobile phone started buzzing. She paused, pulled the phone from her bag and checked the screen. Her face flickered and she thumbed the call reject button. "…which means we need to go and have a word with Joe. From what we know already, Renton was at the Clancy's house not long before those things went missing. Hard as it seems, we can't treat him with kid gloves forever. The police certainly won't."

"Fine then," said Dan. "We'll speak to Joe Clancy." His eyes dipped to Eva's phone. "You ever gonna answer that call, by the way?"

"What? Now's not really the time, is it?"

But put on the spot, Eva looked awkward.

"You should just call her, Eva. Get it over with," said Dan.

"Call who?" said Mark.

"Oh. No one. Just an old friend. She says she needs my help," said Eva.

"Then that's a good reason to call," said Dan. "It could mean another paying case. We could do with the business."

"It could mean any number of things," said Eva. "Including some I may not like."

"She's asking for your help. Since when do you turn down a request for help?"

Eva sighed. "This might have to be an exception."

"Do yourself a favour. Call her. It'll only eat at you otherwise – you know I'm right."

"Not now," said Eva, rising from her chair. "Come on. Let's go and see if young Mr Clancy is accepting visitors yet."

"I should go with you. I know him best," said Mark.
"Not this time, Mark. You should both go home. We can start again fresh tomorrow."
Mark looked at Joanne and she nodded her head.
"Come on, Mark. I can take a hint."
Eva smiled at them. "See you tomorrow."
Dan watched them go. He picked up his leather jacket from habit more than any need. It was after hours, but the day was still warm and bright.
"Why did you send them home? Mark might be right. We could use him."
"Sometimes the hired help aren't always good for getting things done. Besides, if I am going to call my old friend Lauren, the last thing I want is Joanne listening in. You know how much of a snoop she is."
"That I do. But she's gone now. So call her," said Dan.
Eva picked up her jacket and bag. She rolled her eyes and sighed. "Fine. But if I'm calling, you're driving."
Dan picked up the keys to his blue Chrysler Crossfire and Eva locked the door behind them.

They got into the two-seater and slammed the doors. Dan gunned the engine as Eva looked at her phone and hesitated.
"You shouldn't put it off any longer. Even if you don't want to help her, you need to give her a chance to get help elsewhere."
"She didn't give me any chance at all, Dan. She dropped me like a dead weight."
Eva didn't like the sound of her own self-pitying words and it showed. Dan shot her a look across the driver's seat.
"Okay, okay. I'll call her. But this isn't going to be easy for me."

"It probably wasn't for her."

Eva hit the 'return call' button and her phone started to dial. The Egomobile dived down the hill from Southchuch library and Dan's old boxing club. By the time they reached the foot of the hill, the call connected.

"Eva?" A single word. But it was a voice which brought back a cascade of memories and emotions. Eva was surprised. One word, and Eva found herself smiling. The bitterness, the acrimony, it was all still there. But the biggest sensation of all was one of pure relief. The dam of time had been finally broken.

"Lauren?"

"My God, Eva. It is you! You actually called me. I honestly thought you were never going to call me back. I couldn't blame you, of course I couldn't. I had to hope. And here you are. Here we are!"

"Here we are, Lauren."

"How are you?! Are you okay? Are you still with that boxing guy, solving crimes and having adventures like an Essex Starsky and Hutch…"

"Hmmm. I can't say I ever thought of us as Starsky or Hutch…"

There was a pause. Dan shot Eva a look from the driver's seat. Lauren's voice became guarded.

"That was supposed to be a joke, Eva. I'm trying to break the ice here."

"Break the ice?" said Eva. Her smile slipped, and a lump of unwelcome feelings surged to the surface "Is that the ice you created when you stopped returning my calls, and had the audacity to blank me in the street? I was a sensitive person, Lauren. I was a teenage girl, and you treated me like a leper, all for no discernible reason We were best friends. Least, I thought we were."

"Eva, please, I was a teenager too. Teenagers make mistakes. Don't forget that."

"That was a mistake? A mistake that lasted twenty years. Do you have any idea what that kind of treatment could have done to me? You see cases like that these days, it's termed abuse, Lauren. Mental cruelty."

"Eva... like you said, it was twenty years ago. I made a mistake. I thought... I thought we could get past that."

"Hey. Don't sweat it, Lauren, it only really hurt for the first few years. After that, I guess I toughened up. The part of me you hurt has turned into a kind of callus."

"A callus?"

"Yes, as in a toughened scar left by an old wound."

"I was a girl too, Eva. I was trying to act cool. I decided I needed to move on, aim for a new life, new people."

"You thought that was cool? Dumping your closest friend like I was a bin bag?"

"Eva..." the woman sighed, and Eva heard more than a hint of upset in her voice. "You're talking as if we're still fifteen or sixteen years old. But you don't understand what's happening in my life now. So many things have happened since then... not all of them good..."

"It's not easy to get over what you did. I'm still the same person, Lauren."

"Yeah? Well, good for you, Eva. Because I'm not. Damn it, I wish I was. Sorry, Eva. For what it's worth, sorry."

"Lauren—" But before Eva had finished speaking, the line went dead. She looked at the phone screen. Hot faced and red cheeked, she looked at Dan.

"Way to go," said Dan, his voice full of irony. "So, did that make you feel any better? Because it really doesn't look like it."

"*You're* telling me off for being impulsive and emotional? *Seriously?*" said Eva.

"Nope. I'm reminding you that she called you for help. Did you even find out what help she needed?"

"Not quite," said Eva. "I was going to ask, but then she ended the call."

"And now you'll probably never hear from her again."

Eva looked out of the window as the seafront loomed ahead. Lifstan Way took them virtually all the way from their office down towards the very patch of Southchurch seafront where Norman Peters' body had been found. The treasure hunters were all gone, bar the last few die-hard detectorists, who weren't going to let the small issue of a dead body get in their way. Dan turned left and they both scanned the beach beside the Marine Activity Centre. A white police tent had been erected around the entire left-hand edge of the building, stretching right across to where the upturned dinghy had hidden the body. There was a plain white van and a police squad car parked alongside it on the sand.

"Forensics will be hard at work," said Dan, changing the subject for Eva's sake.

Eva nodded, and her eyes returned to the present.

"Yes," she said, quietly. "They'll come up with something. I only wish they would put the same forensic effort into helping the living as much as the dead. No matter what anyone says, Carl Renton is in serious trouble."

Dan said nothing. They both knew the stats. The odds of Renton being found alive worsened with every second he was unaccounted for.

"Do you think she really needed our help?"

Dan looked over at Eva.

"Lauren, I mean."

Dan shrugged "She waited twenty years before she called you. That's got to tell you something. Either she called you to make a pitch for forgiveness. If not you take it at face value. The woman told you she was in trouble. Subtract your personal history from the situation and that's all you've got to go on."

"It's easier said than done."

"You're the sensible one here, Eva. Forget about the past for a second. Would you help her if she asked you outright?"

"You know the answer to that."

"Then you'd better call her back. She's in trouble. You don't need any more regrets hanging over your life."

Eva nodded and stared straight ahead before taking the plunge. She dialled the last number with bated breath. The ringtone came on. But then the voicemail clicked in and took control.

"Hi. This is Lauren. Sorry I can't take your call right now. Just leave a message and your number and I'll call you back soon as I can… BEEEEEEEEP."

"Lauren. It's Eva. Look. I'm sorry. It's just that I never got a chance to say what I felt before, but I shouldn't have done that. If you still want my help, I'll be waiting for your call.."

Eva ended it there and took a breath. The rest of the journey passed in silence as they waited for a call that didn't come. Dan had been right. Eva didn't need any regrets. She was already pretty busy in that department. Now she had to hope there weren't any more to come.

***

Aaron Clancy's Lexus saloon was absent from his drive when they arrived at Kings Road. It was six forty-five, heading for seven. The day was hanging on, as was the heat, and the first of the city commuters had already arrived back from London, padding up the hill from Chalkwell station with their briefcases and handbags at their sides, sleeves rolled up, jackets slung over their shoulders. Eva rang the doorbell and waited as the chime subsided inside the house.
"I know it's not late yet," said Dan, "but isn't Aaron Clancy supposed to be on a break from all his golden holidays?"
"Yes. That's why he was here to hire us."
"But look. He must have been out all day. He's not here now."
"Probably because he's still chasing down his missing collection," said Eva.
"But didn't he hire us to do that for him?"
"True. But he seems pretty attached to those things, desperate to get them back. Maybe he's the type who can't help looking for himself."
Dan nodded. "Or he just doesn't like being at home. I know that kid gets on my nerves. I think Joe Clancy is a whiny and self-pitying little scroat… but maybe he has his reasons for that. Daddy Clancy's behaviour suggests he cares more about his gold than he does about his son."

Eva nodded. She watched a blurry silhouette heading their way through the glass in the front door.

"And you said his mother isn't in his life either?" said Dan.

"Not much, according to Mr Clancy."

"Makes you wonder why some people bother to have kids," said Dan.

"People get drunk and do stupid things."

"*You* get drunk…" said Dan.

"If we had children, the business would be gone inside a year."

"You think I couldn't run it by myself?" said Dan.

Eva pursed her lips to stop herself from replying.

"I think we like working more than we let on. Besides, I can't stay at home all day. I'd go nuts."

The shadow reached for the door handle. Eva raised an eyebrow at Dan. "Can we do this another time, please?"

Dan smirked, and Eva shook her hair straight to cleanse her mind of troubling thoughts. When the door opened they saw it wasn't Joe.

"Georgie," said Eva.

"Do you ever go home?" said Dan.

The girl blushed. "Not very often, if I'm honest."

"Does Clancy Senior know?" asked Dan.

The girl made a face and gave a little shrug.

"Can we come in?" said Eva.

"Sure." The girl stepped back to make way and Dan closed the door behind them.

"You said you found something. I should get Joe. He should hear about it," she said.

"Thank you," said Eva.

They waited in the lounge. Eva stalked around the room, perusing a bookshelf beside the big black fireplace. Dan stared out of the window towards the shining estuary far beyond. A moment later, Joe Clancy appeared at the door, he looked pale as ever, but perhaps a little brighter from expecting good news.

"Georgie said you found something? Something belonging to Carl? I was starting to think I was never going to hear from him again."

Eva saw a gloss of tears in the young man's eyes. But it was too late to hold back now

"You really liked Carl, didn't you?" she said.

"I did. But Carl liked me. That was more to the point. I wasn't a disappointment to him, well… hardly ever. He always saw the best in me, no matter what."

"I'm sure you're not a disappointment to anyone, you mustn't think that, Joe. Thinking like that can bring you down."

"When you've walked in my shoes, then we can talk about that. Anyway. What did you find?"

Eva nodded.

"The police have it now."

"The police? Why?" said Joe.

Eva carried on without giving an answer. "It's a small silver tin. It was engraved with laurel wreaths inside a rectangular border. In the centre of the design was a cross."

"Carl's tin? You found that?" The young man looked perplexed, and his eyes flashed with concern. "But Carl wouldn't have ever let go of that, I know he wouldn't. That tin was almost a part of him."

Eva nodded. "Hmmmm."

"So where did you find it?"

She looked at Dan and hesitated for a moment before she told the truth.

"We found a body on the beach. But don't go jumping to the wrong conclusion."

"A body?!" Now the young man's mouth dropped open. He looked aghast, and shook his head slowly as if to say, 'don't say it'.

"Joe, it wasn't Carl. I promise you that."

"What? Then who…? I don't understand."

"Turns out it was a market trader by the name of Norman Peters. Does that ring any bells to you?"

The young man remained perplexed. A furrow appeared in his brow. He looked down and shook his head. "No. Not at all. Should it?"

"He was found with Carl's silver tin. The dead man also had a few Uber pills in his pocket when he died, too."

"Ubers? Drugs, you mean? Carl hated all of that stuff. Oh no!"

"Don't jump to any conclusions, Joe. We don't know anything else yet. There could be any number of reasons why that man might have had the tin."

"Really? I can't think of any good ones, can you?" said Joe. Georgie began to look upset too.

"I can't *stand* to think what might have happened to him." Eva watched the young man's eyes fill with tears. He wiped them away with the back of his arm.

"You saw Carl shortly before he disappeared, didn't you?"

"I saw him on Thursday night. Last night. The last night he was around, yes."

"How did he seem?" said Eva. The boy seemed to be drifting away from her. Probably his emotions.

"Same as ever. Caring. Helpful. Maybe a little more fired up than usual," said Joe.

"Fired up?" said Dan.

"Yes. He told me he was going out on another one of his vigils. He'd heard that some of the really bad drugs could have been coming in via the beach at Southchurch. It was a just a rumour, but Carl had narrowed it down to a couple of places, and he was keeping watch."

"What did he hope to achieve?" said Eva.

"First, he said he wanted to reach out to the dealers. To tell them they were wrong. Tell them the harm they were doing and get them to change their ways."

"To repent?" said Eva.

"Yeah, but Carl didn't use language like that. He was a modern man. A modern Christian. He used to pray for people to change. Pray for the evil in them to be turned to good."

"Praying?" said Dan.

"I know how it sounds, but Carl said it worked. And they didn't just pray. Carl liked being a man of action. He said if nobody else stopped these people – the dealers and traffickers – then he would."

Eva and Dan exchanged a glance. "Did you get the impression he was going to do anything dangerous last night? Was he planning a confrontation?"

"Carl said he was ready for that. But he was a good talker, a nice guy. Carl could always talk himself out of trouble."

Dan nodded, but the scepticism showed in his eyes.

"But not all people like talking," he said. "Some people strike first and think later."

Eva winced at Dan's words and kept her eyes on the young man. She watched his Adam's apple bob up in his throat.

"Did anything else happen that night, Joe? Your dad was out. You saw Carl Renton, before he disappeared. Then you went to bed…" Eva changed tack and softened her voice. "And… Georgie was here?"

The girl glanced at Joe and tugged a lock of hair from her eyes. Joe sighed. He looked like a guilty schoolboy as he nodded his head.

"Yeah. I think you guessed it already. Georgie stayed the night." He stared down at the floor before he looked up to meet their eyes. "The truth is that Georgie stays here a lot of nights. She worries about me, like Carl does."

"And why does everyone worry about you, Joe?" said Dan.

"Because I'm a loner. Because I get kind of depressed. Because I get left alone and my dad really doesn't give a shit. Something along those lines, take your pick. People seem to treat me like a long lost puppy. But I don't mind too much. At least some of them care."

"Was Georgie here when you saw Carl?" said Eva.

"Not really. Georgie knows to give me space when Carl is here, don't you, Georgie? Carl likes praying for people, so Georgie gets out of the way in case Carl wants to pray with me."

"And did he?"

"No. Not last night."

"Then what did you talk about? Did he seem okay?"

"Carl is level headed. He's always okay. But I was tired last night. I wasn't at my best, and unfortunately, Carl chose that night to give me one of his special lectures."

"Lectures?" said Dan.

The boy paused and took a breath. "About not letting my dad shape my life in a bad way. About not being self-pitying. As if it's my fault he doesn't care. Sometimes I tolerated all that holy righteous crap because I liked Carl's company or because I was lonely and I needed it. But last night, I was really down. I felt ill. I wanted to go to bed. I wasn't in a good place for a lecture. I wasn't very friendly to Carl.. But now…" his voice drifted. "Now I might always regret it. It looks like I might never get the chance to make things right."

It was Eva's turn to swallow on some unpleasant feelings "Don't make such predictions, Joe," said Eva. "He might be out there somewhere, lost or in trouble."

"But you don't believe that, do you?"

"I haven't given up," said Eva. "And neither should you."

The young man nodded and his eyes glazed.

"But there is one thing I still don't get," said Dan. "That night, you had a break-in, and the best of your father's collection went missing."

Joe Clancy nodded.

"The way I hear it, you didn't even hear a sound. Not even the sound of the glass breaking. You were upstairs in bed sleeping as sound as church mice. I assume you were both in the same room…?" he said, looking at them.

The coy look on their faces told Dan they were definitely in the same room and in the same bed. "And *neither* of you heard anything?"

"Georgie was fast asleep… but I wasn't," said Joe. "I heard the glass break. I was in the toilet, taking a pee. When I heard the glass breaking I just panicked."

"And?" said Eva.

"I didn't know what to do. I started freaking out. What if they had a knife or maybe even a gun? I wasn't going to stand in their way. Not over taking some of my dad's stupid artefacts… I ran back to bed and I pushed my chair against the door and I stayed with Georgie until it was over."

Dan and Eva looked at the girl.

"When Joe came back, I woke up and saw he was scared. It was so frightening," she said.

"I bet," said Eva. "But why didn't you admit this before?"

"Because of my father. I'm supposed to be his insurance policy, his cheap homemade security guard. But when the chips were down, I failed, didn't I? How could I ever admit that to him? You must have seen how he is. He'd probably disown me…"

"He wouldn't disown you, surely?" said Dan.

"Maybe not literally speaking. But he wouldn't let me ever forget about it. Not ever."

"The burglary then. You heard it all?" said Eva.

Joe nodded. "They were quiet. Very quiet. Professional, I guess," said Joe. "We just stayed up in my bedroom until it was all over with."

Eva nodded. "And Georgie – you're here with Joe every night?"

"Almost every night. To make sure he's okay."

"She lets me off for good behaviour every now and then," said the boy. Georgie gave him a look, but Joe softened his words with a smile.

"It's good to hear you'll be here if he needs you," said Eva. "We'll get back out there looking for what was stolen. And for Carl too."

"Thank you," said Joe. "I'd like to apologise to him face to face for everything I said. I know he was trying to help me, just like he always did."

Eva nodded. "We'll do our best." They turned to leave.

"And thank you," said Georgie, as she followed them to the door.

"For what?" said Eva.

"For not judging Joe, or me. He's only like this because his dad made him that way."

Dan raised an eyebrow but Eva nodded. "I know. Take care, Georgie."

The door closed behind them, and they walked down the driveway towards Dan's Crossfire convertible parked right across the street.

"That's one messed up family," said Dan. "Maybe we'd better not start messing up one of our own just yet."

Eva raised her eyebrow.

"You changed your mind fast enough," she said.

"This job. It teaches me new lessons every hour of the day."

"That's for certain," said Eva.

Nine

Saturday morning.

Dan slumped to rest over Eva's soft warm body, collapsing with a moan, pressing his lips against her shoulder as he succumbed, entirely spent. Eva smiled and closed her eyes. She held him close, the warm and hazy feeling still flowing through her senses, making her feel as though everything else could wait, that everything would be alright just so long as they could stay like this and forget about the world. How long had they been together now? Most of that same twenty years Eva had thrown in Lauren Jaeger's face when they spoke on the phone. Twenty years?! and still no children to show for it. No child apart from their business, the neediest child of all. But then children would never work anyway… would they? There was childcare responsibilities, finances, and upbringing to think of, let alone the danger they would continue to bring into their lives, day in and day out, just to bring home the bacon. So… maybe they would have to change careers too. Get something safer. Something which still paid enough to hold everything together. A nine to five job – one each – paying enough cash for the money-suck of childcare too. That alternative version of life sounded so safe, so ordinary, so boring. Eva knew it wasn't for her at all. As the slow glow of passion started to fade, reality sank in once more. Eva was a private investigator and life had made her that way. The years had shaped her, sculpted her into what she was, and for all the trouble it brought her, she loved the job too. Leaving the investigation business would be like having a limb cut off, maybe two. Thoughts sailed on through her mind as Dan rolled away from her and blinked as she started to get up. He admired her body as Eva stood up to gather his discarded T-shirt from the floor. Dan looked at Eva's eyes and frowned for a moment. But then the penny dropped.

"You thought about it, didn't you?" said Dan. "*You did.*"
"Thought about what?" she said, looking sheepish.
She pulled his T-shirt down over her head and body and cast a knowing, sleepy eye down at him.
"Kids," he said.
"You need to put that idea back in Pandora's box right now, Dan."
"But you still thought about it."
"As if *you* could read anyone's mind," she said.
Dan rolled his head back onto his folded arms. "Not anyone's… but I can read yours."
"Fine," said Eva. "Maybe I might have thought about it for a second. But it wouldn't work. And I know you. The minute life got hard, you'd run off and re-join The Company so you could set off on another crazy mission just to avoid changing a nappy."
Dan frowned but Eva stared down at him and maintained her grin.
"You got me there," said Dan.
"I have, haven't I? The truth is I already have the only child I'll ever need."
Before she reached the door Eva glanced at her phone on the bedside chest of drawers and saw it was lit up with a fresh missed call.
"You're right there," said Dan. Eva walked over to the drawers and picked up her phone. Dan reached out from the bed and tried to snatch her wrists, but she pulled away.
"What's up? No time left for a little more fun with your favourite PI?"
"Afraid not," said Eva. "That ship has already sailed." Eva dabbed her phone screen and started to read the message.

"Does that have anything to do with all this talk about nappies and children?"

"Possibly. But it's more to do with Lauren. She called again before."

"And we didn't hear it? The earth really must have been moving."

"Don't flatter yourself," said Eva. "My phone is on silent." Eva turned away for the door.

"Where are you going now?" said Dan.

"To try again. To make the phone call you said I should make. Then I want a shower."

"It's still early, Eva. And it's the weekend. Take it easy."

"It is the weekend, yes. But the clock is ticking on the Clancy job. The longer Carl Renton is missing, the worse it gets. Same applies to Clancy's treasures too. Tell you what, why don't you do something useful like get the coffee started?"

As the door shut and Eva disappeared, Dan dropped his head back on the pillow and shut his sleepy eyes.

"Something useful? *Come on…*"

Eva walked into their lounge-cum-dining room and pulled up a chair at the dining table. She tweaked the blind to distract herself, peering out through the slats at the street below. But there was nothing to see apart from a paperboy cycling along with his neon orange satchel, and a late staggering drunk meandering his way home. Eva breathed to calm herself, and then she hit dial. This time, Lauren picked up the call inside two rings.

"Lauren," said Eva.

"Eva," she replied. Her voice flat and defensive.

"Look…" said Eva.

"Eva, you really don't need to explain… or apologise. Everything you said before was justified. I just didn't expect you to come out and say it so quickly."

"To be honest, neither did I," said Eva.

They both took a breath. "Well, listen to us talking to each other like we're both thirty-something women," said Lauren.

"Ridiculous. Don't say it. It'll never happen," said Eva.

"No. I thought it wouldn't, either. But when I look at the face in the mirror, you know, I really think it might be true."

"Never look at a mirror too long, Lauren. That's my tip for success and happiness."

"So you're a guru as well as a private investigator now?" said Lauren, adding in a defensive laugh.

"I could never be a guru, Lauren. All I do is help people get solutions to their problems. Sometimes it's closure on a missing person case, or a lost possession, say." Their current case was both, but Lauren didn't need to know the details.

"What about helping someone when they think they might be beyond help."

"Nobody's beyond help, Lauren. And you wouldn't have called me unless you thought I could do something."

Lauren sighed and attempted a laugh. It still wasn't convincing. "You know, even after all these years you seem to be able to cut straight to the point."

"In this profession you have to," said Eva. "Anyway, what did you end up doing for a job? You were supposed to hit the catwalk, remember?"

"Another arrogant pipedream that went up in smoke, I'm afraid. Nope. I never did make it to any catwalk. I did end up working in fashion for a while, I worked for a trade publication. That was hard work, with the merest hint of glamour, but nothing like the real thing. Then I grew up and realised I needed to make some actual money to pay a mortgage and buy a car. I was twenty-nine but still living like a nineteen year old."

"So what happened after the trade press?"

"I turned my hand to recruitment. In other words, I sold out. But hey, I was good at it. So good I became Blane's top agent in the South East for twenty fourteen and twenty fifteen, and then I started dating Mr Blane Junior himself."

"As in Blane – the high street recruitment agency?"

"The one and only."

"Wow," said Eva.

"Yes," said Lauren. "Back then life finally looked like it was going to work out well, and I could wave goodbye to all those other fashionista wannabes. And the years between twenty fifteen and seventeen were a really great time. I worked hard and played hard and fell in love with a totally remarkable guy."

"Blane Junior. Why can I hear the but coming, Lauren?" said Eva.

"Because fairy tales aren't real, are they? Not even when they last for two years or more, you don't always get your happy ending."

"I've never even been close to living the fairy tale, Lauren. In fact, I've lived through everything but."

"Being a PI, huh?"

"And being with Dan too. But it's been an adventure, at least."

"After twenty seventeen I can't call my life an adventure. It's something closer to a horror movie. You see, my original happiness came from Jamie Blane's tragedy. I didn't think about it until later but I guess I should have seen trouble coming right at the start. Jamie never grieved. It had to come out somehow, didn't it?"

"You've lost me, Lauren."

"Jamie Blane is the son and heir of Blane Recruitment. I was their best earner. It was a match made in heaven, except that Jamie was married when we first met, and when we first started taking lunch together. I think I already knew there was a thing between us then. We both knew. But so long as neither of us said anything, didn't admit it to each other, those cosy lunches were able to go on. So they did. And then in late twenty fifteen, Suzanna Blane died. It was a car accident. She was involved in a crash with a drunk driver on the A12; it was horrible. Jamie and I waited a little while, but maybe not long enough. I'm pretty sure tongues were wagging. But it didn't matter. We lived together in a kind of insular cocoon for about two years. We were happy, but I guess, deep down, Jamie wasn't. I thought he was finally grieving when it first started happening. The mood swings. The fiery tempers. They were brand new to me. I guessed he'd supressed his grief for me, and then, bang, there it was, coming out in one big ugly hit. But really I was just making excuses for him. Jamie turned controlling overnight. Monstrously controlling.

I went along with it for a few weeks but he didn't get better. He got worse. His anger turned to threats, and not long after that, became violence."

"Did you get help? Did you leave him?" said Eva.

"Oh yeah, I tried all of that. But that only works if the man realises it's over. It requires acceptance. Or if you disappear, and I tried that too, believe me. But when Jamie found me he told me these words. I'll never forget what he said. It went like this… If you ever bail on me ever again, I'll ensure you lose every penny you've ever earned from me. We'll find a way to do it. We'll cook up a fraud. I'll prove you embezzled money from the firm, and you'll never work again. And that's just the start. If you try it again, I won't just come for you. I'll come for your family. First, I'll come for your sister. And if I can't find her, I'll come for your mother too."

Eva took in a sharp breath.

"He actually said those words? Your boyfriend?"

"He didn't just say the words, Eva. He meant it. Every single word. After two years in paradise I ended up living with the man from hell, and how I endured it, I just don't know. But seriously, I can't take it anymore. I want out, but Jamie's smart and he's dangerous. I'm frightened of what he might do if I went to the police or the women's refuge. Eva… I've thought about this for so long, but I just can't see a way out. I even thought about killing myself – that's how bad it got. But then I remembered you. You always had a solution and I heard what you do for a living. It made sense to call you. You're my last roll of the dice, Eva. I can't try all the usual routes because they're not just a dead end, for me they're dangerous. And he will follow through on those threats, I know he will. You always knew what to do. And there's no one else in the world who understands me like you. And with the skills you've got…"

"Lauren, there are plenty of people with my skills, I assure you."

"But, Eva, I can trust you. Who else could I turn to? You will help me, won't you…?"

Eva blinked and closed her eyes tight shut. She remembered Lauren as she was before the acrimony and the years of silence. She remembered spring schooldays, the long summers, riding bikes around Basildon's Victoria Park, kicking around talking about music and boys.

Eva took a deep breath and closed her eyes.

"Of course I'll help you, Lauren. What else are friends for?"

"You will? You will!"

"Yes, but you have to hold on – not long – just another day or two, that's all. Can you do that?"

"Hold on?"

"Yes, I'm in the middle of a missing persons case, and we've just uncovered a dead body. This investigation looks set to take a turn for the worse. I have to get this done."

"Just a couple of days?" said Lauren.

"Two, maybe three tops," said Eva.

"Okay, Eva. I've held on this long, I don't see a couple more days being too much. You won't change your mind, will you? Jamie is really scaring me, Eva. I think he's lost it, I really do."

"Be strong, don't let him break you, and please, don't you dare do anything stupid. I'll be there for you as soon as I can."

"Like I should have been there for you all along. Thank you, Eva. You've given me some hope."

The call ended and Eva put the tip of her mobile to her lips. Shaking her head, she stood up, stretched and set off in search of coffee.

"Eva," she muttered. "I hope you just made the right call…"

Only time would tell.

But time told all too soon.

By the time Eva had drunk her second coffee of the day, her phone started buzzing again.. Instead of watching Saturday Kitchen with the rest of the world, they were downstairs in the office, scanning the local news sites to see if any of Clancy's other missing treasures had been found. In the time it took to read Lauren's name on the screen Eva's newfound peace with the world was all but gone. She picked up the phone and stood up from her chair. At that very moment, Mark and Joanne walked into the office. Eva saw their breezy weekend smiles and abruptly turned away. She stalked into the kitchen and slid the door shut.

Joanne's face dropped. She looked at Dan.

"What's the matter? Did we do anything wrong?"

But all Dan could do was shrug and wait until the call was over.

"Lauren? What's happened?"

Eva leaned over the sink and stared out into their neglected backyard. A large fat ginger tabby cat stared down at her from the side wall.

"It's Jamie. He knows I've spoken to someone about him. I don't know how, but I'm telling you, he knows. He totally lost his shit at me again. Eva, I can't deal with this. I've told him I need a break. I have to go out for a few hours to calm down. He made me swear all oaths and all other kinds of other crazy things, and then he threatened me again, but I have to get out of here. I know you can't help me yet, but I really need to talk to you. Can I come down and see you?"

"Lauren... it's not a good time, like I told you before..."

"Eva, Please. I don't have a choice. I have to get out of here just for an hour or two. Let me meet you. I'll buy you lunch. I told him I was going out for a walk, which means I can't take the car, because then he'll know I was lying."
"What? But that's crazy," said Eva.
"I know it is. Which means I'll be coming to Southend by train. I'll be at Southend Central at around eleven. Do you think you can meet me?"
Eva frowned and stared back at the cat until he looked away.
"I'll meet you," she said. "But it'll have to be lunch on the go. We need to keep pushing before we lose any hope of finding our missing person."
"I understand, Eva. I'm sorry to do this to you. I owe you one."
"Okay, Lauren. I'll see you at eleven," said Eva. She ended the call, blew out a deep breath and looked at the clock on her mobile phone.
Eleven am gave her no more than one hour. Factoring in getting ready and driving time, Eva saw she barely had any time at all. She rubbed a hand across her forehead. Unless something broke on Clancy's missing artefacts and Carl Renton, Eva reckoned they would be empty handed by the time the weekend was up. Surely Clancy wouldn't want to pay a bean if they had nothing to show him for their work. But they would have to roll with it and hope for the best. Eva walked out of the kitchen and grabbed her tweed jacket from the back of her chair.
"Morning," said Eva, shooting a glance at Joanne and Mark. They lingered near the shop doorway, like party guests who didn't feel entirely welcome.
"Is everything okay? We just popped in to help. Seeing as Mark knows Joe, we thought you could do with our help."

"And we probably could," said Eva. "Especially since I've just been landed with an unwanted meeting with my ex-friend Lauren. She kicked me to the kerb like a dirty old can, but now she's in trouble she can't wait to meet up. As much as I am all for peace and love, I'm thinking this meet-up might be more than awkward."

"You're meeting with her?" said Joanne.

"If I want a clean conscience I have to. The woman's in some fix with a trashy, violent partner."

"Can't you put her off?" said Dan.

"Tried that, and the answer's no. Hopefully meeting her will put her off for a few days until we finish up with Clancy."

"Where are you meeting her?" said Joanne.

"Southend Central. In about an hour."

"You're going now?" said Joanne.

"If there's any time left I was planning to take a quick look at the pawnbrokers, first. Just in case anything from Clancy's catalogue has ended up there. It's worth a look.."

"That's an idea. Can I come with you?"

"To the pawnbrokers? I don't see why not. But I'll need to do the meeting on my own."

"That's okay. I'll could try the cheque cashing shops while you're busy."

"Okay, fine," said Eva.

"I'll call the head office for Renton's rehab charity to see if they've heard from him. Then I'll head down to Warrior Square, maybe to the tower blocks too," said Dan.

"Old habits, eh?" said Eva.

"One of the crowd must have heard something," said Dan. "Do-gooders like Carl Renton are like minor celebrities on the down-and-out circuit. Every street drinker and crackhead in a ten mile radius will know who Carl Renton is."

"And you think they'd tell you if they knew anything?"
"We'll see," said Dan with a shrug. Eva turned for the front door but Dan called her back. "Eva?"
Eva turned back.
"Look on the bright side," said Dan.
"Which is"
"At least she's not ignoring you anymore."
Eva frowned, shook her head and turned away without another word. Joanne grinned at Dan before she followed Eva out into the street.

Ten

The pawnbrokers on Alexander Street was one of the most notable in town. Eva and Joanne perused the abandoned heirlooms and jewellery in the shop window, Eva flicking through the entries of Aaron Clancy's homemade catalogue as she ruled them out. Truly special pieces like Clancy's were few and far between. They went into the shop to double-check but the woman behind the security glass shook her head at each of the catalogue entries. The next most notable pawnbroker happened to be on Clifton Road, not far from the entrance to Southend Central station. The place, a narrow black shop front, sandwiched between a betting shop and a Chinese restaurant. The immense hulk of the Last Post pub was part of the same block – and stretching from one side of the block to the other, it housed almost all of the town's low-budget drinkers throughout the day. Eva made a mental note – the pub was certainly another place they could question people.

The second pawnbroker seemed to be the man who owned the shop. He was grey haired and sharp eyed, wearing a pair of spectacles perched up his head like a man who needed to check for the smallest details on a regular basis. Eva took her catalogue to the counter and asked the same question, page by page. The man glanced at each item, before he looked at Eva with his silver-grey eyes.

"Is this about the museum robbery?" he said.

"No, but why do you ask?" said Eva.

"Because all of those are one-off pieces. Some of them look very, very old and therefore hard to value."

"That would be true," said Eva. "You say you haven't seen them, but what about anybody else? Has anyone come in asking you about pieces like this?"

"No way. Not in here. Pieces like that stand out a country mile. It'd set the alarm bells ringing in my brain before I ever shelled out a penny. Look around, love. All you'll see in here are the same old family heirlooms, jewellery and watches. I deal in that kind of family stuff."

"You don't move any big ticket items?"

"Oh, we do. Cars, yes. Porsches, Ferraris, that kind of thing. It comes through the same business but gets dealt with at my home office."

"But where would stuff like this go?"

"That stuff?" The man scratched his nose in thought. "In this town?" The man thought hard. "Well, you've got two avenues. Black market and export, and I mean immediate export to somewhere with no connect to our legal system. That's the only way to get rid of stuff like that, and you'd be taking a serious hit on the real value. Russia's an obvious choice. China too. Big, ostentatious buyers and money, with no qualms. But there's a worse option. They disappear altogether. They get scrapped and smelted for reuse like a cheap old motorcar."

"Then you don't think these could have come through a pawn shop."

"Certainly not a reputable one. Not owned by anyone who wants to stay in business for very long."

"Interesting," said Eva, glancing at Joanne. "And are there any businesses like that around?"

The man hesitated. "Not mine, that's all that I can tell you. You're Old Bill, are you?"

"No," said Eva. "But it's a common question."

"Doesn't matter either way, love. My answer's still the same. Any established pawnbroker wouldn't touch anything like that. Not unless he's the one with the foreign connections."

"You said established?" said Joanne. "What does that mean?"

"It means that those who need to make cash quickly might take the risk. But I don't associate with that kind. We're a regulated firm and proud of it. The kind you're looking for probably wouldn't even have a shopfront. It would all be sleight of hand and word of mouth."

Eva nodded. The message was clear enough. There were rogues around who would shift stolen items, maybe even loan money against them. But they wouldn't be found in a town centre shop.

"Oh well. It was worth a shot though, eh?" said Eva.

"Course it was. But missing pieces like that need to be found fast. How long have they been missing?" said the man.

"About two days."

"Then you'd better get your skates on, or they'll be on a slow boat to China before you know it. Or smelted. Give it a few weeks, and the idiots will be wearing it as a recycled bog chain necklace."

Eva didn't need reminding. "Thanks," she said. She gave him a thin smile and turned away for her meeting with Lauren Jaeger.

"Do you think he was right?" said Joanne, as soon as they closed the door behind them. Eva hadn't noticed before, but taking in Joanne's outfit, she saw the girl had come to work dressed as Eva junior. She wore a smart suit but with a youthful cut, and the skirt cut higher than Eva would have liked for herself. Tweed was nowhere to be seen. But black suited Joanne just fine.

"He obviously knows the pawnbroking business better than we do," said Eva. "And unless he's the man with the foreign contacts – then you'd have to assume he's right. Which means we're running out of time on both fronts. Tomorrow Carl Renton will have been missing forty-eight hours, which makes him police business. But as Missing Persons are ten a penny, whether they'll act on it is another story. Though the press attention from The Record might help. Hogarth must see the connection by now."

Eva glanced at Joanne and saw she'd lost her. The nuances of their relationship with Hogarth and the technicalities of police procedure were above her paygrade. Mostly because her paygrade didn't exist. Joanne was still no more than a tenacious volunteer with a boring day job working for the council at Civic Centre. She'd stumbled into their lives because of her relationship with Mark, and they'd been unable to shake her since. Not even when they wanted to, which happened from time to time.

"What happens when it goes official?" she asked.

"Officially? The police will take over the hunt, but hope rests mostly on Hogarth and his team, and only if he takes it seriously. Which means they might fare about as well as we will. But we've shown we're willing to cooperate, hopefully he'll do the same."

"And Clancy's missing items?"

"For the police, it's a simple theft case, one man's missing loot, versus the council museum's prestigious missing items from the Saxon King's tomb. He's got an incident number, who knows if he'll get anything more. Clancy can shout all he likes, but one man versus the council? The police will focus on the council theft every time. They've lost some ancient artefacts which have been on national news before, which makes it a PR case with lots of profile. They have to be seen to come out on top. They'll make Clancy wait as long as they like. Which means we're still Mr Clancy's best hope of finding the rest of his collection before they get smuggled out or smelted."

"But it's not been easy so far, has it?" said Joanne.

"No. Especially not when I have to deal with sudden demands, like Lauren's request for a meeting…"

Eva realised Joanne was still with her. They had climbed the station's wide entrance steps, heading for the ticket booth windows and the steel ticket barriers. "Sorry, Joanne. I'll have to take it from here."

"But she's not here, is she?" said Joanne. "When's the train due?"

Eva checked the blue screen and saw they had almost ten minutes to wait before the next London train was due in. Looking around, Eva saw there was nowhere good to wait. Getting through to the platform seats required a ticket, and she certainly wasn't going to waste money just to meet Lauren. Nor was she inclined to stand around in a busy ticket hall with no space and no comfort. Joanne read her mind. "There's a bar next door. We could wait in there. You can see out across the platforms from there, and I could keep you company with a drink."

"It's a little early for drinking."

"They serve coffee too," said Joanne.

Eva relented. Some company to kill time wouldn't hurt and Joanne's enthusiasm for learning the arts of the PI always made for a little entertainment. They walked into a dark-walled pub, with a wide window which overlooked the brightly coloured interior of the station, providing a decent view across several platforms. There was also an exit door leading directly to the platforms, but Eva didn't even bother trying it. The rail company wouldn't have let the pub keep it open. It would be an invitation for fare bunking.

She ordered the drinks, and they took two seats overlooking the platform-facing window. Six minutes to go.

"Where's next in the hunt for the loot?" said Joanne.

The pub was dark and empty but for a young, fidgety looking guy with cropped brown hair. He was idly flicking through a copy of The Sun newspaper as he bounced his knee and picked at a beermat with a fingernail. Occasionally he looked up and Eva saw his eyes flick to Joanne. Having been caught looking, he turned back to his newspaper and his half finished morning beer. Eva guessed he was waiting for someone. In a train station bar everybody was playing the waiting game.

"Well, we've tried the main pawn shops. We could try the less scrupulous ones next, so now we have to go the next rung down the ladder. The cheque cashing firms is a good idea. If the thief doesn't know how to trade, he might even start with those outlets. It's a bad move to make money, but in this town anything is possible. If we draw a blank there then the next rung down is the pub trade. But by the time we get that low, I'm guessing the slow boat would have sailed. By that point we may as well start walking around with metal detectors ourselves."

"Not your style," said Joanne. "But if you need one, Mark has one in his shed."

"He has?"

"He said it was his dad's."

"Thanks for the tip, but it's definitely not my style. Norman Peters, the body we found on the beach, that's our way in… I still think our best bet might not be to chase Clancy's treasure directly, but to look at the murder itself. It has to be related."

"Why?"

"The beach location. It's come up a few times now."

"Since when?"

"Clancy's torq was found there. Then Norman Peters' body was found there, under the hull of a boat. And he had the silver tin which belonged to Carl Renton."

"That's certainly a link."

"Yes, and we knew about that link. But then we learned that Mr Renton went out on his regular night time vigils, including at the beach. Now, what if that beach was the very same one where Clancy's torq was found – where Norman Peters' battered body turned up hidden under a wooden boat…"

"But that's just a what if… isn't it?"

"Yes, but look at it logically… Renton's drug traffickers could land at any beach if they were coming in by boat. Southend has at least six miles of coastline. That's a lot of opportunity."

"I suppose Southchurch narrows it down," said Joanne. "But only if Carl Renton was at the right spot."

"Carl Renton had been doing this a long time," said Eva. "We have to assume he knew the right place to be. But here's the thing. We can probably pinpoint the kind of beach he would have gone to. A row boat can land on any beach. But it's unlikely the traffickers would use a wooden dinghy to row ashore. It would be far too slow for an operation like that. Too much risk. They'd have no chance of evading the authorities if they were caught."

"So they must have a motor boat of some kind." Joanne nodded, but her bright eyes betrayed her confusion. She couldn't see where Eva was leading her.

"Much better. But a decent high-powered motorboat simply can't land on the beach. It would damage the motor, the propeller at the back, and probably the hull itself. A speedboat would have to find a safe place to load and unload from the water. And that means finding an access point where a boat can tie up."

"You mean like at the Marine Activity Centre?" said Joanne.

"Exactly. I walked along by the end of the jetty there, and I found the metal hooks where a small vessel could tie up and get down to business. I don't think there's any other safe places to tie off a boat along the whole of that area."

"What about the yacht clubs? Or the Marbella Club?"

"They're in the wrong area, and far too visible from the road."

They heard the squeal of train wheels grinding to a halt as a long blue train slid into the station. Eva lifted her cup to finish the dregs. This had to be Lauren's train.

"That's three times. It's connected, Joanne. It has to be. We're not going to find Aaron Clancy's treasures by hunting for them directly. We'll only find them by solving the whole case. Including Norman Peters' murder.. Time for me to go. What will you do now?" said Eva, as she stood up and grabbed her handbag.

"I don't mind doing a little more legwork yet. Maybe I'll try those other pawnbrokers, just in case."

"Fine. But don't push too hard and don't put yourself at risk again."

"Of course not," said Joanne. She raised her glass. "I think I may as well finish this before I leave."

Outside the train doors beeped and slid open to let loose a rush of new arrivals who pushed and hurried en masse towards the ticket gates. Eva gave a final goodbye smile and rushed out towards the street, determined to meet Lauren before she got lost and wasted more of her time. Joanne watched Eva go. Out of sheer curiosity, she stood up and took her glass with her to the opposite window. The young man reading The Sun watched Joanne walk across the pub until she reached another window seat, this time overlooking the station car park and the busy street beyond. Joanne sat down, sipped and watched. The young man took a moment to admire her profile, then checked his phone for the time. As Joanne watched the crowds pour out of the station, she saw Eva and another woman of roughly the same age and build slowly walking down the railway station steps. Eva's visitor had pale brown hair with streaks of blonde, and she wore a nervous smile on her pretty face. While Eva's body language was the same as ever, friendly, open, and impersonal, the other woman seemed to be the touchy-feely type. Joanne watched her reach for Eva's arm, claiming her attention as they talked. There was something about her body language... about her eyes... The woman looked needy. As she watched Eva and her visitor walking away, another man scooted up the station steps, passing through Joanne's line of sight. Joanne's eyes instantly gravitated towards his narrow face and they stayed there. For a second she couldn't fathom why, but she felt she recognised him. His face jolted her. For a moment she thought he was the awful man from the rehab house, but that wasn't it. Instead, taking the train station entrance, the thin man turned along by Joanne's window, passing her again. He was coming into the pub. The door opened and the man walked in. Tall, dark eyed, and slightly stoop shouldered, the man looked around and his eyes met hers. Joanne's chest turned cold, but the man looked away, dismissing her immediately. It was then that she truly recognised him. He was the man from the Leigh Broadway. The man who had chased Norman Peters in the hours before his death. Joanne tensed up, aware the young man with the newspaper had been watching her on and off for some time. She swallowed, hoping he hadn't been listening to her conversation with Eva. Joanne kept her body facing the bright window, her eyes front as if she was purely people-watching. To prove she wasn't listening in, she picked up her mobile phone, opened the web browser and started to read whatever she could find. But her ears were fully tuned to the men as they greeted one another.

"Watcha," said the older man.

"Alright?" said the younger one.

She watched from the corners of her eyes as the older man slid a rucksack from his shoulder. He laid it on the table with quiet purpose, as if the bag was significant. Then there was a silence before the fidgety young man coughed and started to stand up.

"You want a drink before you go?"

The man turned his head towards Joanne. She kept still and felt the thin man's gaze on her shoulder. She worked to keep her expression blank and calm and sipped her drink.

"No, best not," said the man gruffly. "Things to do and all that. How about we have a little word outside, instead, eh?"

"Suit yourself," said the younger man. The tall man stood up and passed the bar. Joanne almost turned her head as he stopped and greeted the barman. She noted the slightest informal gesture between them, nothing more than quick handshake between two friends and a quiet word. Something about the barman 'getting himself a drink'. The barman nodded back and gave the thin man a wink. And then the tall man and his younger contact left the pub, leaving an unfinished pint and The Sun newspaper on the table. Joanne kept her eyes down on her phone as they passed by her window. But as soon as they reached the main steps, Joanne looked around at the barman. He eyed her as he dried a pint glass and set it on a rack beneath the bar, then turned away, uninterested, and picked up another glass. Joanne moved as close to the front window as she could, until she finally caught a tight-angled glimpse of the two very different men, the young man and the taller, sinewy figure, now standing on the steps. By now the older man was doing all the talking while the younger man nodded his head as he listened dutifully. The guy handed him the rucksack, a cheap unbranded black bag which looked a little more than half full. The younger man strapped it on his back and they shook hands. And like that, they were done. The taller man turned away down the steps to the street and made off briskly for the high street, while the younger man disappeared back into the station. Joanne moved back to the opposite pub window, and gazing over the train platforms, she saw the young man rushing towards a London train whose doors were already beeping and about to close. He leapt on board the train just in time. There was a click and a hum as the train began to pull away., Joanne watched the young man settle into his seat, fastidiously clutching the rucksack to his body.

"Clancy's gold, Eva," she whispered to herself. *"It's already gone…"*

Joanne shook her head and turned for the exit. She swept out of the pub and skipped down the station steps but the man had already turned the distant corner onto the high street, and Eva was nowhere in sight.

Eva walked side by side with Lauren, a woman she hadn't been friends with for twenty years. The same old bright eyes were there, the same cheeky smile, the same striking looks, but much else had changed. There was a sadness behind the brightness, and those eyes were far more tired than she remembered. There were new age lines too, lines set into her brow and around her mouth. The Lauren she knew was still there, but the new Lauren was a fuller, battle-hardened beauty than the girl Eva remembered. Every time she looked at Lauren, she found herself searching for traces of the girl she remembered and found herself being shocked at how much life had already left its mark. Lauren must have been feeling the same.

"It's so good to see you, it really is," said Lauren. She squeezed Eva's arm the way she used to when they were fourteen and fifteen, trying to act like the coolest girls in school, when the truth was they were anything but. Lauren had always tried harder to fit in with the *it girls*. Eva pretended she wanted to fit in with them, but deep down she knew she never had a chance, and to be honest, she didn't mind that much. Not even then. Looking back, she knew the it girls were the ones who had mostly screwed around with older men when they were far too young. The men should have been rounded up by the police and prosecuted, but then it was a different era. And most of those girls got married before they reached nineteen. Life was funny like that, and not always in a good way. Some of those girls would be women now, lives filled with regret. Eva's early naivety – some called it childhood innocence – had protected her from wanting to grow up too fast. Lauren hadn't always felt the same.

"It's good to see you too," said Eva, her smile wavering on her face.

"You don't sound so sure," said Lauren. "But I can understand why."

Eva winced and forced herself to smile a little brighter. Despite their past she had no intention of being mean to the woman. Even a stage-managed rapprochement meant compromising and at least trying to play along.

"No, I am glad to see you, Lauren. I'll be happier still when we can put the past behind us."

But only Eva's second statement was true and Lauren seemed to sense it. Lauren blinked and her voice changed as she looked around the busy high street as they walked along. "I haven't been here for so long," said Lauren.

"This town is changing. But then we weren't from round here, were we?"

"No. Basildon was the epicentre of our lives. Back then Southend seemed glamorous!"

"Well I guarantee that glamour fades once you've seen what we've seen," said Eva. "I take it you don't live in Basildon anymore?"

"No. I was doing well, so I moved on. Brentwood appealed, you know, *The Only Way Is Essex* and all that, but when I got with Jamie I moved in with him. In Loughton."

Eva nodded along, but small talk wasn't going to pay the bills and friendship wasn't on the menu. The Clancy case was eating into her peace of mind. It was time to get down to business.

"I feel for you, and your situation, but I'm not sure what a private investigator can do to help, let alone a friend."

"You *are* changing your mind?"

"No. I didn't say that. But it is something to think about. How do you think I could help?"

"Don't worry, I have thought about that. I spent a little time reading some of your web profile, and I've seen some old news clippings about you," she said.

Eva gave Lauren a sideward glance. She couldn't help a defensive narrowing of the eyes. "You read up on us? Why?"

"Eva, it wasn't the first time I've followed what you do from afar."

"But you made it sound like you'd only just found out what we do for a living," said Eva.

"I suppose I was trying to play it cool again. Play it down. Funny how playing it cool always seems to backfire when I'm the one doing it. Come on. We were friends. I know I blew it. But I was always interested in you, and I always wished you well. A while back you started making some big waves, something to do with a London criminal network, and then there was a terrorist incident. Didn't you two help prevent a major attack?"

"Things get overblown," said Eva. "That's the modern media for you."

"No, they didn't. I read about those things when they happened. You were always smart, and you're tougher than I ever gave you credit for, but I had no idea what you were really capable of."

"I don't feel tough, Lauren. Never did. But life makes us what we are."

Lauren sighed. "I guess it does." She gave Eva a thin smile and glanced across the street towards a busy coffee shop. "Coffee?"

"No thanks," said Eva. "I think I'm all coffeed out. Another one and I'll end up bouncing off the walls like a pinball."

"I'm glad you said that, because I need a proper drink. What about that wine bar – the downstairs cellar one back on the corner there?"

Eva narrowed her eyes. "I'm a little pushed for time, Lauren."

"It won't take long. I need a drink, and I think it might help thaw the ice between us."

"It's still a little early for drinks, Lauren."

"It's almost twelve. Maybe they'll take pity on us."

Eva thought of Clancy and Renton. The case was calling, and Eva wasn't sure how much she wanted the ice to thaw. Keeping her distance from people was a trick Lauren had taught her very well. But it was hard to say no. They took two minutes to double back along the high street, then hooked a left down the road which cut through the centre of the precinct. Right on the corner was the door of the basement wine bar. Eva was surprised to see the door open. They walked into the twilight of the doorway and descended the steps into aromas of cooked meats and the wood of oaky wine barrels. They took their seats, and a grey-haired man with a shiny red face came to take their order. They ordered wine and nothing more and the man nodded with a drinker's approval. Lauren scanned the wine list while she kicked idly at the pieces of straw scattered over the wine bar floor. She supposed it gave the place a rustic, French kind of air.

"Lauren," said Eva. "If you're stuck in a rut with a violent man, you need to grab your things and walk away. You make your preparations, you shift your cash, get your belongings together and just go. I don't see how you could need me for that."

"Then maybe you didn't hear what I said. Jamie Blane is never going to let that happen."

"Lauren, I've heard it all. Guys talk trash. And those kinds of men, the violent ones, they talk more trash than most. It's bluster, Lauren. You need to see through that and you need to walk away."

Lauren stared at Eva with frustration in her eyes. Their glasses of wine arrived, and Lauren took a long slow sip.

"Jamie isn't going to let that happen. I've seen him ruin ex-colleagues just for fun, Eva. *For fun.* And he's threatened to ruin me, maybe even get me jailed. And that's not all. If I leave him he *will* go for my family. He's met them. They think he's great, because he's got money, and I've never told any of them how much of a bastard he really is. He's hurt me, Eva. Next he'll ruin me, and then he'll go for my family. This is not your average domestic breakdown."

"But they're lies surely," said Eva, taking a sip.

"No. I know Jamie now. He'll do exactly what he says because he always does."

"Then what did you ever see in this man, Lauren?"

"He's not the same man I met. It took two years for me to see it, but it's like he's got two different personalities. He's a closet psycho. I mean it."

Eva nodded. "Okay, okay, I believe you. But you're still going to have to show me how I can help you. Because, to be frank, I don't see how I can."

"Eva. I know what you do. I'm sure you could come up with any number of ways to get me out of this. You wouldn't be afraid of whatever Jamie did."

"But what's your end aim?" said Eva. "Running away? Keeping your family safe? What's your happily ever after?"

"Running away doesn't fit with who I am. None of this is my fault. I got with a guy and he's turned into totally different man. Why should I run? Why should I lose everything because of him? I worked hard for what I have."

"Then what is it that you want?"

"I want Jamie put back in his place. I want to walk away with my share of the money, everything that I put into the relationship. I want to be safe and free."

"Sounds to me like you should be talking to a solicitor, not a PI."

"Eva, we are so far away from legal proceedings. Jamie wouldn't let it get that far. He would rather see me dead first. He'd strike against me and my family before it came to that. I can't risk it."

Eva's mouth crumpled as she thought it over.

"Lauren, you need to spell it out. What do you want me to do?"

"I want you to make him see that I will take the same kind of action against him that he's threatening against me. *That's* what I want. I want him to see that unless he lets me go – on my terms – equal and free without any comeback – then he's the one who'll be facing consequences, not me. He needs to understand that when he moves against me, he moves against himself."

"Like mutually assured destruction?"

"Kind of," said Lauren, taking another gulp of wine. "But this idea could only ever be carried out by someone who I can trust. And by someone who I know can handle scumbags and put a man in his place."

"Sounds like an eye for an eye kind of situation… I'm not sure I'm the person you need. I don't' do intimidation or threats. I'm a private investigator. I've never been a thug."

"I'm not asking you to be a thug, Eva. I'm asking you to be who you are. Smart and tough, able to outwit a scoundrel and beat him at his own game. I want you to help me leave him in a strong position with a smile on my face and my own money in my purse. My own cash. I want to be untouchable. *Checkmate*. That's what I want."

"Then you're not seeking violence? Or retribution?" said Eva. She sipped her wine.

Lauren took a moment before she shook her head. She ran a finger around the rim of her glass.

"Good," said Eva reading the woman's face. "Because for a moment it sounded as if you were asking me to hurt him because he hurt you."

"Eva, I would never ask you to compromise yourself," said Lauren firmly.

Eva nodded. "Then how would I play something like that…? I'd investigate him until I was able to build a file of proof of his threats against you, and any other methods of control. If he was having an affair with another woman, I'd also get evidence of that as collateral for any negotiation on your exit strategy. You're not married to this Jamie guy?"

Lauren held up her ringless finger. "Nope."

"Then any side affair would have no legal standing, but if it ever went to a court case, it would show that the guy had been a thorough scumbag and prove he was the one in the wrong."

"This one is never going to go to court, trust me."

Eva frowned. "You sound very sure about that."

"I know Jamie, that's all."

"Fine. But can you see how I work now?"

Lauren nodded. "Yeah. You're smart, I knew that much already. And I know if something goes wrong, I know you'll be able to deal with it."

"Goes wrong?" said Eva. "What could go wrong? I'll be careful."

"I don't know. Things happen. Jamie's unpredictable, Eva. That's half the reason I'm sitting here now. Like I wasn't expecting this to happen this morning…"

Lauren slipped up the sleeve of her summer jacket and exposed a long red and black bruise. It looked fresh and painful.

"What did he do?" said Eva, scowling.

"Shut my arm in a door. I'm lucky he didn't break it. The other reason I'm here is that I know you've kicked the backsides of some seriously bad people when the chips were down. I'm certain you could do it again."

"But those situations were never planned, Lauren. They happened when I was fighting for my life. Or trying to save someone from getting killed. I don't ever plan to get into a situation like that by choice. Lauren… is there something you haven't told me yet?"

Lauren sipped her wine. "Eva. I've told you what he's done and what he'll do to me and my family if I run. Anything else you need to know about this guy, it's out there in the public domain. Jamie Blane has a high profile. He's a success story in the recruitment business, and he's a total braggart."

"Then you're happy with how I'd play it? And you're happy with the limits of what I will and won't do?" said Eva.

Lauren nodded and summoned a smile.

"I'm here because I need your help to save my life."

Eva felt the barb in the woman's comments, and it managed to slip past her defences. Eva's eyes flashed with anger.

"I said I'd help you, Lauren. But I also said I'm not going to hurt anyone, no matter how much they might want me to. If you want a different kind of help, I know a few names who might—"

"I'm not interested, Eva. I need you. Please. And I'm prepared to pay you. I'll sign a contract if needs be, I'll pay an advance, whatever it takes. Please don't make me take this to a stranger. I know you're angry with me. But you're angry with the old me. The cold little sixteen-year-old bitch who blew you off for a shiny new set of friends. I can say sorry for that as many times as you want me to if it will help, but even if it doesn't, I'm still here because I'm in deep trouble."
"You're offering me money?" said Eva, eyes wide with surprise. They needed money coming in, they always did, but Eva knew she couldn't accept it on a matter of principle.
Lauren nodded. "That's how much this matters."
"I can't take your money, Lauren."
"Of course you can. You do this for a living. Or you can't because you're still angry with me, is that it?"
"That's not it. You said he's controlling your finances."
"And he is, but like you said, I needed to get some cash together. So I squirrelled away a little here and a little there. I had a well-paid job, Eva. I can afford to do this. I want to hire you to execute the plan."
"Plan?"
"Your plan to get me free."
"That was a sketch of an idea."
"It doesn't matter, Eva. I know you can do this. Let me hire you."
Eva looked at her wine and weighed up her options. Lauren had once been a friend. If not for the bad blood, she would have done the job for free. But the past did exist. The cold shoulder and the distance of near on twenty years between them. Lauren had chosen to make herself a stranger.
"You're serious? You want me to investigate your partner."

Lauren nodded. "I do. And I want you to help me get away from him without any further trouble."

"I can't give guarantees. You'll be paying me for the investigation, not for protection, not for any kind of revenge scheme."

"I know all that. But I also know what you can do – if necessary."

Eva took a sip of wine and thought hard for a long moment before her business brain won the day.

"You'll still have to wait a day or two before I can start. Think you can manage that?"

The woman nodded. "I have ways and means of putting him off. Maybe I can persuade him to go on one of his so-called golf trips."

"Golf trips?" said Eva, with a spark in her eye. "How long does he go for? How frequently?"

"See?" said Lauren, breaking into a smile. "You're on the case already. He's tried to break me so many times. But with your help, I know he'll be the one who ends up broken."

Eva raised her glass but stopped at Lauren's last words. The woman saw the look on Eva's face and rolled her eyes.

"Figure of speech, Eva! Come on. Jamie's an evil son of a bitch. You can at least allow me a little fantasy, right? You always were a little too serious."

"Yes," said Eva. "And being serious has helped me solve more cases than I can remember."

Lauren's mouth flickered before she raised her glass. "Then I'll drink to that," she said.

Eva saw a glint in the woman's eyes which made her feel uncomfortable. She put the feeling down to the past, because where else could it have come from? Unlike Dan, Eva had rarely been one for hunches and gut feelings. She preferred cold hard facts. They had shared a bad past, and one glass of wine could thaw that. As she sipped her wine, Lauren dipped her hand into her handbag and she produced a white envelope and laid it on the table.

Eva glanced at the envelope and at Lauren's eyes. She had the look of a woman who had just played a winning hand.

"What's this?" said Eva.

"There was no pricing on your website," said Lauren. "But from what you've achieved, I guess hiring you can't be cheap. That's a thousand to get us started."

"Lauren, we're still just talking."

"But I need you on board. Now, is that enough?"

Eva looked at the envelope. "We'd need to fill out some paperwork. To make it official. I'll need to know *everything* there is to know."

"Fine. You've got my email somewhere. Email me back and tell me exactly what you need."

Eva swallowed and looked at the crisp white envelope..

"Take it," said Lauren. "You're going to earn it anyway, so you may as well take it. Please."

Eva left the envelope where it was a moment longer before she looked up and saw the imploring look in Lauren's eyes. She took it off the table and slid it into her handbag to take back to the office safe. As soon as Eva took it, Lauren's eyes gleamed. Eva pursed her lips and nodded by way of thanks. From the look in Lauren's eyes, it seemed her hope had been restored. But Eva sensed there was something else in those eyes too. She was now beholden to the friend who had cut her dead and that ancient history was still there between them. The sensation chilled

Eva, and she felt a pang of regret at taking the advance, but told herself it was just the past intruding on the present. The past was gone.

"Two or three days," Eva repeated, keeping what little control she had left. But money had changed hands, and services were owed. Lauren smiled and drank her wine.

"I can hardly wait," she replied.

Eleven

Dan parked the Egomobile at the side of Warrior Square's large tree-edged green. Tucked just behind the high street, Warrior Square was a place the junkies and the alkies liked to pass their idle hours in the hot sunshine. The beach was just a half mile away yet the green was always busy. The reason was simple enough. Whatever they needed, booze, heroin or crack, it was always just around the corner. Bliss on tap at low, low prices. And what was convenient for the addicts of Warrior Square was convenient for Dan too. The busy tower blocks and the food bank weren't far away, making the area a key hotspot for finding people who might have known about Clancy's missing treasures, Renton's whereabouts, or about one dead market trader known as Norman Peters.

Dan stopped and looked across the green. He recognised a few of the distant ne'er-do-wells who lounged in their circle at the high street end of the square. One was the big bodied awkward-squaddie known as Suitcase. Dan knew he had to be careful with that one. Suitcase was much smarter than he let on and seemed to remember Dan from his time on the street five years back. At the time, Dan had operated under the alias of Craig, partly because he never wanted it widely known how low he had sunk and partly so he could carry on a street level investigation without being found out. It was all a long, long time ago, and Dan had moved on, but guys like Suitcase had long memories. So instead, Dan opted for the easy route. It was Saturday and the sun was shining. There was a case on, one with a payday on the end of it which depended on fast action in a rapidly closing window of opportunity. The information he wanted was likely going to cost him, but expense couldn't be avoided. The case needed a shot in the arm, and Eva had been distracted by her friend. Dan turned away from the square, walking away at a pace so the gang on the green wouldn't have time to bother him. He turned the corner onto Southchurch Road and headed in the direction of the Sutland Arms. It was early yet, but there were already a couple of cockroach types standing on the corner saloon doorstep, smoking eagerly after their first drink of the day. They soaked up the morning rays with a 'this is the life' look written on their faces. As soon as they realised a strong young guy in a leather jacket was headed their way their faces changed.

"Morning, gents," said Dan.

"Morning," said one. The bigger man just stared.

The guys were dressed in leathers that had seen far better days. The bigger one with a grey beard wore full leather trousers. His smaller, wiry, buddy was dressed in jeans and a leather waistcoat over his scrawny bare torso. It wasn't even hot yet, but the heat was coming. You could feel it in the air.
"I wondered if you guys have heard of a man called Norman Peters," said Dan.
"Peters?" said the smaller one, like it meant something. The bearded one stayed silent and shook his head.
"Yeah. Peters. You heard of him?"
"I used to know a Steve Peters," said the small man, babbling. "Great on the bass guitar, he was. Used to play at all the pubs in Basildon, he did. What a man."
Dan shook his head. "That's really good. But I'm asking about a man called Norman Peters. This Peters was found dead yesterday afternoon. On the seafront. His body had been left under a boat."
"You mean the body found by the treasure hunters? The silly fools looking for lost gold on Southend Beach. Well, some people will believe anything, won't they?" said the little man, laughing.
Dan's face tightened a degree. "Yeah. Some will. So you don't know the man?"
"No. Not Norman Peters. The man I knew was Steve Peters. The bass player."
Dan narrowed his eyes.
"Clive Grace, what about him?"
"Err... that rings a bell," said the little man. The man's big bearded friend shot him a look and blew a tendril of smoke over his head. The big man started talking.
"We don't know him," he said with a cough.

"You seem remarkably sure of that. And you're his spokesperson, are you?"

"When I'm sure, I'm sure," said the guy with a shrug.

"What about Tommy Pink?" said Dan.

The guy with the beard shook his head again. But the small guy snapped his fingers as if he'd just remembered something crucial to mankind.

"Tommy Pink! I know Tommy Pink. And Clive Grace too. What was the other guy's name?"

"Norman Peters," said Dan.

"No you don't. You're getting confused," said the grey beard. "You're always confused."

"No, I know them. They're the boys who do the markets. Tommy Pink has run a clothes stall down Southend Market every Thursday for years. Does the circuit, he does, Romford, Basildon, Southend. Wembley, everywhere him."

"That's the guy," said Dan "And Clive Grace?"

"Clive's the lanky one. Clive's not so friendly. Hasn't got Tommy's patter either, no gift of the gab. But he does the markets too. Norman… little Norm. Normski. He was the smaller one, wasn't he? Very friendly, he was. Always knocking out clothes on the cheap. Cheap as chips. Not my style mind, just all the stuff the young 'uns wear, that's him."

The bearded man tutted and shook his head.

"Did Norm ever sell anything else?"

The bearded man's eyes narrowed and he leaned forward. "Alfie here talks too much. You shouldn't try to take advantage of him," said the man with a half scowl.

"No one's taking advantage of anyone here, pal. I'm making conversation, that's all," said Dan. "Nothing wrong with a little chat now, is there?".

The little guy shrugged with an airy grin. "No. Nothing wrong at all far as I can see. Now, I can't say I remember Norm Peters selling anything apart from clothes. Not to me anyway."

Dan looked the little old man up and down. No, he didn't look like the type for Ubers. He looked the type for drinking too much and sleeping it off in doorways. But he was chatty enough.

"What about Tommy Pink and Clive Grace. What do they sell?"

"Tommy? Tommy's a businessman. An entrepreneur. Sporty too, loves the water he does. Tommy sells all kinds of clothes, but before that it used to be mini TVs years back. Then computers. These days clothes. But he sells whatever's current that's Tommy."

"And Clive Grace?"

"Oh, him. He follows Tommy's lead, as far as I know. I don't know the fellas well, like. But Tommy used to come hawking around the pubs, selling things out of a bin bag. Not these days though. He's above all that now."

Dan grinned and nodded, seeing the bearded man's discomfort mounting with every passing word.

"Tommy Pink doesn't sell anything in the pubs anymore. But what about Clive or Norman...?"

The big bearded man flicked his cigarette butt into the gutter and stepped down from the pub doorstep. He moved close into Dan's personal space and looked him in the eye. The guy was about the same height, but maybe ten years older and at least thirty pounds heavier, the extra weight mostly composed of blubber and fermenting beer.

"This conversation is over," said the man. Hot, rancid, smoker's breath poured over Dan's face and made him blink in disgust. He screwed up his nose and shoved the guy stumbling back onto the steps.

"Actually, I think Alfie here was just warming up," said Dan.

"Alfie's a halfwit!" said the man.

"Oi!" said Alfie.

"He doesn't know what you're asking him," said the bearded man. "But I do."

"Then maybe I should be asking you all the questions instead."

"Or, maybe you should turn around and get lost. What are you? A cop? You don't look like a copper."

Dan ignored the question and concentrated on Alfie. "Has anyone tried to shift any shiny ornaments in there lately? Any very old silver or gold?"

"You're not one of those stupid treasure hunters as well, are you?" said Alfie.

"You know, I suppose I am," said Dan.

The old man chuckled, but the bearded man shook his head and put a hand across his friend's chest and steered him towards the saloon doors..

"There's been no gold or silver or anything like that coming through here," said the big man, as he pushed Alfie back into the pub. The small man complained the whole way.

"Now I know you're lying," said Dan. "A man can buy anything he likes in the Sutland Arms, half the town know that."

"Well you can't buy what you're looking for. Not any of it."

The man's eyes glinted at him angrily.

"What are you saying?" said Dan.

"I know what you're looking for. We heard about the Saxon King stuff and that Celtic band as much as anybody else in this town."

"It's not just the Saxon King stuff though, is it?"

The big man's eyes narrowed. He turned quiet.

"How do you know about it?" said Dan.

"It was in the paper. That councillor got mugged off. But it didn't come through here."

"The Saxon stuff? What about anything else? Similar, but mostly old gold."

The man frowned. His confusion looked genuine. "Anything else? What else could be like that?"

"Okay then, what about Tommy Pink, Clive Grace and Norm Peters. What have they been selling?"

"Listen to me and listen good. *I don't know what you're talking about.* They're market traders. It's Saturday right? Maybe you should go down Basildon Market and see how they make their money for yourself."

The guy's eyes were busy and his body language said he wanted to get away. He turned for the door.

"Looks to me like you know more than you're letting on."

"Why don't you piss off!" said the man, shoving the pub doors open. Dan seized the man's shoulder and yanked him around hard, so the guy almost fell over before he righted himself to look into Dan's eyes.

"No need to be rude, my friend. You know Tommy Pink, you know Clive Grave, you knew Norm Peters. So maybe you also know why Norm Peters ended up dead on the beach yesterday afternoon."

The man swept Dan's hand off his shoulder and stood back.

"The only thing I ever knew about those men is that Tommy is a market trader, and Clive works with him. Norm was a trader too. I didn't know them. They weren't my mates, just like they weren't Alfie's mates. They were just faces. Tommy and Norman especially."

"But not Clive?" said Dan.

The man blinked at Dan and held his tongue.

"You're asking the wrong people the wrong questions. Alfie doesn't understand you might be putting him in danger. He doesn't deserve it."

"Danger? How could having a conversation out in the sunshine put anyone in danger?"

"If you want to know any more you'd better ask Tommy yourself."

"I'm not sure that's such a good idea, seeing as one of his mates ended up dead on the beach."

The man shook his head and shot Dan a look of disgust.

"You think Tommy Pink would do something like that? I don't know the man too well, but I know that he wouldn't do that. The fella's stand-up. A lot more stand-up than some scallywag casting aspersions about him outside the Sutland Arms.."

"Right. So Tommy's a drug dealer who doesn't harm anyone. Now there's a first."

The big man's eyes flared and his mouth opened in shock. But the shock Dan saw wasn't from surprise. It came from Dan being direct. The big man stepped away, shaking his head. He stepped inside the pub."

"You're a liar and a troublemaker. You better keep away from me and keep away from Alfie. We don't want no trouble. And if you've got half a brain, neither will you."

Dan wasn't done. He followed them into the pub and the guy with the grey beard looked at him. Now Dan reckoned he saw a glint of fear in the man's eyes.

"Don't worry. I'm not after you. I'm looking for him." Dan nodded across the empty dark wooden pub towards Vic Norton, the weasel-faced old man sitting at an empty table at the back, as calm and lordly as the master of all he surveyed. Norton was dressed in one of his favourite charity shop shell suits, the sleeves rolled up to his elbows. As usual there was a folded newspaper and a dark pint of soupy bitter in front of him. The newspaper revealed the horse racing pages. Norton had thin and overly long wispy grey hair set around a pale pink and grey face and looked at him with big watery eyes. He felt the old man had been watching him for a while.

"Trying to get your information for free these days, I see," said Norton in his trademark rasping voice, as Dan arrived at his table.

"It's wise to spend money only when I need to."

"Then you need to. Listening to people like little Alfie is a waste of time. Talking to Alfie is like talking to the man in the mirror. He only tells you what you think you want to hear."

"He told me a few things."

"I heard. You're never very subtle, are you? You were asking about Tommy Pink and his crew. You've always had a big mouth, Bradley. One day that's going to get you into serious trouble."

"Not for the first time," said Dan.

Norton's voice dropped to a whisper, his eyes hard.

"If you want anything about them from me you'll be quiet about it and you'll pay cash. In advance. That would be very sensitive information."

Dan pulled up a chair and sat down. "You heard what I was after."

"Sounds like you're chasing something but you don't know what. Something about some gold. And you're after Tommy Pink and Clive Grace. Why?"

"I'm not after them. Those two are just stepping stones."

"Funny to be making allegations about people who you say are just stepping stones."

"But I'm not wrong, am I?"

"That counts as a question, Mr Bradley. If you want the answer, it'll cost you."

"I think I know the answer to that one already."

Dan pulled his wallet from his pocket and pulled out a twenty pound note.

"I told you, it'll cost you," said Vic with a sneery, yellow toothed smile.

Dan thumped the twenty down on the table top. "We'll start with twenty." Norton's eyes flitted to the distant side of the pub across the dark bar. Dan looked back too and saw the grey-bearded man look away.

"See," said Vic. "You shooting your mouth off to all and sundry makes it difficult to help you."

"Then let's try another subject."

"What subject?" said Vic.

"Carl Renton, the missing rehab worker."

Vic's eyes gleamed and he nodded like a toy dog. He slid the twenty pound note under his hand and claimed it. "The Christian on a mission to save the world," said Vic.

"You heard what happened to him?"

"Yes. He disappeared," said Vic.

Dan put an empty hand out on the table to ask for his money back. Norton grinned.

"He was playing with fire. What happened to him, bound to happen sometime, wouldn't you say? Shouting his mouth off about the drug dealing in the town and turning up wherever he thought the stash was about to land. Carl Renton was only lucky he didn't start on the Somalis first. Disappearing would be preferable to what those Somali boys would have done to him."

"I'm after facts, Vic. Not stories. Is Carl Renton still alive?"

"I'd wager he won't be coming back."

Dan shook his head and thought of the effect on Joe Clancy. "Do you know who did it?"

"No. And even if I did, I wouldn't tell you for a measly twenty quid, now would I?"

"Then you owe me some more information for that money."

"Such as?"

"You haven't told me anything more than Alfie did."

"Then ask me another question. Try me," said Vic.

"You heard anything about any missing treasures?"

Norton's eyes glimmered. "Ah, your gold. Why? Should I have?"

"Maybe. Who's been shifting anything like that. Stuff that looks like heirlooms, rare stuff. The kind of things Indiana Jones brought home in the movies."

Norton pursed his lips and narrowed his eyes. "I heard about the museum robbery. And I heard about that Celtic band found near the marine centre."

"Did anything like that come through here? The Saxon stuff or anything else?"

Norton shook his head. "There you go again. Anything else. What does that mean, Bradley? Is something else out there?"

"I'll be asking the questions, Vic."

Their eyes jousted in silence for a moment.

"No," said Norton. "I'm afraid not."

"Then what have you heard?"

"That's the thing. Nothing. That Saxon King stuff, the belt buckle, the silver stick, none of it has been shifted through any of the pubs I know of. I would have heard about it if it did."

Dan frowned. "You're telling the truth?"

"Yes. I would have heard. That Saxon treasure never reached the circuit." Norton leaned closer and his eyes shone. "And that means it could be an inside job."

Dan shook his head. "I don't think so. But it still doesn't make sense. One of you would have heard of it. What about the market traders? Could they have been involved in the robbery somehow? Norman Peters certainly ended up dead over something."

"Same answer. It can't have been the treasure you're after. I would have heard if Tommy Pink and his crew had got hold of it. Those boys would have definitely put the feelers out to try and sell it."

"Is that how it works?" said Dan. "They put the feelers out?"

"Are you still asking about your missing treasure or about Tommy Pink, Mr Bradley?"

Dan's eyes gleamed. "I'm asking you about everything they *sell*."

Norton drew back in his chair. His eyes gleamed brighter than ever. "I don't know what you mean."

"Yes you do. But I'm not paying for *that* information, because I think I know enough already. I asked you about Carl Renton and you didn't give me anything. I asked you about the stolen treasure and you tell me no one's seen it."

"Actually, you asked me about two different sets of gold, didn't you? Care to tell me anymore?"

"Leave it, Vic. Leave well alone," said Dan. "Then you didn't want to tell me anything about the market men either. Seems the supergrass is losing his touch. I guess you'd better give me my money back."

Dan proffered an empty hand.

"I'll never lose my touch," said Norton. He didn't move a muscle and ignored Dan's hand. "I can't help it if you don't like it when I answer in the negative. It's all still information, Bradley.

"You owe me some info, Vic," Dan said, standing up.

"But I told you all there is to know," said Norton. Dan scanned the old man's eyes once more before he stood up. He sensed the old scoundrel was telling the truth.

"Until next time, then," said Norton.

"I guess so," said Dan, turning away. He walked past the grey-beard and little Alfie. The grey-beard scowled and turned his back, but Alfie raised a hand and waved goodbye. Dan nodded back and walked out into the sunshine, still grappling with his problem. Clancy's Celtic torq, his other treasures, and the council's Saxon King items had been stolen, yet no one had heard of them on the black market ever since. And the pub black market was like one big network, an all-seeing-eye of underworld opportunities. And if the Sutland Arms hadn't seen it, then it wasn't for sale. On top of that, from Vic Norton's words he now had to presume Carl Renton was dead, and yet no one knew what had actually happened to him and there was no body. That seemed unlikely too. But Vic Norton was the man who would have known either way. If Vic Norton didn't know – or wouldn't tell – something was seriously wrong. The only proven link they'd found to Carl Renton was a dead man with his silver tin, and poor old Norman Peters couldn't tell them a damn thing no matter how much fuss Dan caused. Dan looked up to the sky in appeal and folded his hands behind his head. It felt like the case was finally beyond them, every door was shutting, every angle blocked. Without a lucky break, a very loose tongue, or a new discovery, Dan didn't see how they were ever going to get Clancy's treasures back to earn their fee.

But in his moment of impasse Dan found he had an insight. Two, in fact, because one followed the other.

The first came from experience. A dead man couldn't talk, but his body could still tell them something. The police pathologist must have learned something, though Dan knew it would be difficult to prise the information from Hogarth, no matter what he'd promised Eva.

And then came another realisation. They had no idea when Norm Peters came into possession of Renton's silver snuff box – a detail which mattered a lot. If Renton had lost his snuff tin a day or two back, Peters might easily have found it long before he died. Which took them back to the realm of pure coincidence between the Peters' murder and Renton's disappearance. But if Carl Renton did have the snuff tin when he left the Clancy house just before he went missing, it had serious implications about the nature of their disappearance... and who might have been responsible.
The thought struck Dan like a needle-shot of adrenaline in the chest. He *had* to know for sure. He darted across the street, heading back towards his car parked at the corner on Warrior Square. And when he was only halfway across the street, a familiar voice called out his name. He turned to see Joanne waving at him wildly from across the street. The girl broke into a jog to reach him. When he saw the excitement in her eyes he wasn't sure if he was ready for Joanne's drama. But it didn't look like he had any choice in the matter.
"Dan! I'm so glad—"
"Are you okay?" said Dan.
"Yes."
"Good. Then whatever else it is, Joanne, hold your fire. I've got something I need to discuss with Inspector Hogarth."
"But this is urgent, Dan."
"So's this." Dan led the way to the car leaving Joanne in his wake.
But in the end, Dan wasn't able to hold back the flood. As soon as they were in the Egomobile, Joanne cut loose on what she had seen. And only when she was done was Dan allowed to make his call.

Twelve

Detective Inspector Joe Hogarth wasn't exactly one of Dan's all-time favourite policemen, but seeing as the case needed a shake-up, and Eva was busy dealing with her ex-friend problem, Dan had no choice but to put in the call. In the end, it only took one rejected call and a follow up before Hogarth eventually relented and took the call. "Hogarth. It's Bradley," said Dan.
"I know. The wonders of modern technology and all that. But you're not the one who normally calls. Has Miss Roberts finally put you to work for a change?"
"I'm always working, Inspector. I just don't like wading through red tape like you guys."
"Neither do I. But it's called procedure, Bradley. Helps a prosecution case last beyond the first session. Did you actually want something from me, because you may have heard I've got a murder investigation to be getting on with?"
"So it was murder?"
"I'd say so," said Hogarth. "Norman Vincent Peters suffered a broken jaw from multiple impacts with a heavy implement. We know that much. I'm told there's still more to come on the toxicology side of things, but that's not in yet."
"And you're seriously expecting something from toxicology?"
"Our pathologist seems to think so."
"Ubers," said Dan. "He had a pocketful of them as well as that tin."

"Possibly more than that too. We found a scrap of a plastic bag snagged in the wood underneath the seat of the boat – the boat that Peters' body was found under. The plastic had traces of MDMA on it in levels consistent with these Ubers."

"The boat? You're saying the boat was used to stash the stuff before Peters died?"

"Could be. But if so any sign of a stash was long gone. Who knows where, eh? In this town it's probably already down the junkies' necks."

"But that's interesting, anyway. It means the boat might not have been a random pick."

"It doesn't mean anything yet. Toxicology might give us something."

"Have you heard anything on Carl Renton as yet?"

"The Record's missing missionary? No. Nothing yet. It's not even a MisPer case yet."

"We went to Renton's rehab operation yesterday. The staff are in a flap, and the rehab clients, the junkies and the alcoholics share the same theory that something bad must have happened to him. The rest of the local grapevine agrees."

"The bad little grapes always seem to agree with one another," Hogarth observed.

"According to the people who know him best, Carl Renton had taken to staking out several areas in the town – known hotspots for drug importing."

"A dangerous move for a lone wolf. And what was his plan then? To gather evidence for police?"

"Possibly, but I doubt it. I've rubbed shoulders with guys like Carl Renton before at The Refuge foodbank. He's what I think of as a true believer. His kind of stake-outs would have involved a lot of praying for divine intervention, for something to happen to turn back the drugs."

"For a miracle, in other words."

"A true believer, like I said. But Carl Renton was also an action man. I heard that too. He might well have tried to intervene."

"Which means he was naïve on all fronts."

"People like him are different to you and me, Hogarth. We've been kicked around one too many times. But Renton was one of the eternal optimists. The world still needs them whether we get it or not."

"If Carl Renton got himself killed because of believing in fairy tales then he's only added to my workload."

"Either way, it seems Renton's rehab clients knew what he was up to – and a lot of other people did – which means there's a fair chance that the traffickers could have been warned about him in advance."

Hogarth sighed. "Bloody hell," he muttered. "Then it was a damned risky business from the start."

"I know. But it sheds some light on Renton's disappearance, don't you think?"

"That forty-eight hours isn't quite up yet, Bradley. I'll concentrate my fire on Norman Peters' case until then."

"Making any progress there?"

"Anything else you want to know? My shoe size? What I had for breakfast perhaps? Give us a chance, Bradley. If I'd had the evidence you held back, it might have been easier."

"Peters was a dodgy market trader with Uber pills in his pocket and a silver tin which belonged to Carl Renton. You've just said there was a trace of another package in that old boat…"

"And? What are you saying? We already know the man sold cheap fashion items at Southend and Basildon Markets."

"People like him sell everything. I just heard Peters used to sell stuff at the pubs too. You tried that circuit?"

"To be clear, you're suggesting Norman Peters was selling Ubers?"

"It's possible."

"It's far more likely he was a user. A lot of fools are, and Norman Peters strikes me more as a fool than a mastermind."

"Fine, stick with that opinion for now if you must. But Peters did have the silver case, Hogarth. He's linked to Carl Renton somehow… what if he was involved in what happened?"

"To Carl Renton? But so far nothing has happened, has it? Officially, he's not even missing."

"You shouldn't hide behind that red tape, Hogarth."

"This red tape means I can concentrate on one crime at a time and get them solved. If Carl Renton really has disappeared, we'll look at the meaning behind the silver tin then. Be satisfied you've put the link on my radar."

"Bully for me," said Dan. "When the forty-eight hours is up you really need to think about what part Norman Peters might have played in the man's disappearance. He was there, Hogarth, I'm sure of it.

"Have you seen Carl Renton's photo in the paper?" said Hogarth. "He was a very big man."

"I've seen it."

"You have seen Norman Peters, haven't you?" said Hogarth. "He made Pee Wee Herman look like Arnold Schwarzenegger.

"I saw him," said Dan.

"Then you'll know Peters was a short-arsed market trader in clown clothes. Not exactly your classic giant-killing psycho if you ask me."

"I didn't ask. Like you said, I just put another link on your radar. Catch you soon, Inspector."

"You can certainly try," said Hogarth. Hogarth ended the call first. Dan shook his head as he looked at his phone screen.

"That guy," he said to Joanne, who was sitting in the front passenger seat – Eva's usual place. It was strange to see a different female face riding shotgun. "Why didn't you tell him about what I saw? About the rucksack and the hand-over in the pub at Southend Central?"

"Because Hogarth wouldn't have heard it. He barely listened to me as it was. He's got a one-track mind, and all of it is focused on Norman Peters – the body under the boat at the beach. He couldn't deal with talking about Carl Renton let alone anything else. Besides, you only know what you *think* you saw."

"I saw that skinny market trader handing a half-full rucksack to a young guy who boarded the train to London. That could easily have been Clancy's gold."

"Hmmmm," said Dan, his brow dipping low over his dark eyes. They were still parked at the side of Warrior Square. Dan stared vacantly across the green as he was lost in thought.

"We can check it out. But first, there's something I need to talk to Joe about. But it might be handy you're with me."

"Why?" said Joanne, as Dan started the engine.

"Joe Clancy likes to play the closed book. But his girlfriend, Georgie, she isn't so shut down. Maybe you could try chatting a little more information out of her."

Joanne nodded, and Dan saw the hint of pride showing on her face. Even though the girl could be a nuisance sometimes, Joanne was enthusiastic enough to be an asset. Every now and again, she came in handy. Dan turned the Egomobile out onto the street. The engine roared as they headed down along Southchurch Road.

Joe Clancy looked pale again. Dan saw the patch of sweat above his lip and he didn't look altogether happy to see them. Joe looked at each of them and kept the door held close to the frame until Georgie appeared at his shoulder and pulled it wide open.

"So, where are the others?" said Joe, his eyes flicking around the street behind them.

"Busy looking for your father's missing treasure, like half the rest of town."

"And what about Carl?" he said. Georgie patted Joe on the back, her face full of sympathy.

"Still missing, I'm afraid. Though there are some things I'd like to discuss with you about him."

The young man frowned and stepped away from the door. "You'd best come in then."

Dan and Joanne nodded and walked in. Dan watched Joanne mouth something to the girl, asking if the young Clancy was okay. Georgie shrugged. Dan followed Joe into the living room and they sat down in the deep leather armchairs. Joe regarded him cautiously.

"You've found something, haven't you…? You found something and you want to break it to me gently."

"Why would you think that?"

"I suppose I'm worried, that's all," said the young man.

Dan picked through the ways to ask his questions without causing the kid to suffer an emotional breakdown. He took a breath and slowly began.

"You heard about the death at Southchurch seafront. At the marine centre."

Joe Clancy nodded, "You told me already," he said. He wiped his brow and stared at Dan as if it was a feat of concentration.

"You really need to get a doctor, Joe," said Dan.

"It's okay. Carry on, please."

"Whatever you say. The guy was called Norman Peters. This is important. I need to know if you've ever heard that name anywhere before?"

Joe shook his head and pursed his lips. His eyes were still fixed on Dan's. There was something about the look in his eyes, something odd. Dan couldn't place it, so he moved on. Joe was a weird kid alright, unwell too, but definitely weird and maybe even more awkward than Mark. Which was something of a feat for anyone.

"Norman Peters was a market trader. He sold cheap fashion at the local markets. We found the silver snuff tin – Carl Renton's tin, in his pocket."

"I know. You told me that already."

"Yes, we did. But we didn't actually ask you any questions about it."

"Such as?" said Joe, with a hint of impatience.

"How do you think Norman Peters might have gotten hold of that tin? And when?"

"Why are you asking me?"

"Because you were close to Mr Renton. And you remembered the tin."

Joe nodded again. Joanne's eyes were on him too. Joe sweated some more and wiped his brow. Georgie pulled a tissue from a pocket and handed it to him.

"The tin," said Joe. "He always had that tin on him."

"And you can confirm that Carl came here on the night he disappeared. Yes?"

"Yes," he said. "Unfortunately, that's true."

"Why unfortunately?" said Dan.

"Unfortunate because it was the last I saw of him. And because we rowed."

"You had a row with him?" said Dan. He shifted in his chair and shot a glance at Georgie.

"Yes, I actually dropped a big hint about it before. Carl was pushy when it came to his faith, and I wasn't very forthcoming with him on the religious front. I think sometimes Carl saw me as potential convert, and other times, I wasn't so close as he would have liked."

Dan recalled the tract in the kitchen bin. "Did you ever come close to joining Carl's faith?"

"I liked Carl, and I'll admit, I was lonely. Sometimes I might have played along or seemed more enthusiastic than I actually was. I valued him as a friend. But that night I began to feel more like a scalp in the Christian conversion game – more like a trophy than a friend."

"Hey," said Georgie. "That's not fair. You weren't well that night, you were in a bad mood, so you treated him badly. I think that's all that happened."

"You were there? Did you see their row?" asked Dan. Georgie blushed, like she had overstepped her mark..

"To be honest, no. Their little chats were mostly always private. Joe and Carl seemed to like it that way. Carl was always friendly to me, don't get me wrong, but Joe was his project. The one he was looking after because Joe was alone so often."

Dan turned his attention back to Joe. "Okay… so you rowed because Carl was trying to convert you – at least that's how you saw it. And then he left."

Joe gave a grudging nod. "I told him to go."

"Really?" said Georgie. "But I thought I heard him say he was leaving."

The young man gave Georgie an irritated look. "What? No, I told him to go…"

Georgie looked doubtful but nodded regardless.

"And you regret that row?" said Dan.

"Yes. Of course. Maybe if I had been friendly, Carl might have stayed longer… and things could have turned out differently." The young man's eyes misted with tears. Dan felt his regret was genuine and he changed tack. Their row could have been significant, but it wasn't obviously so. It was something to be logged for consideration.

"The silver tin… do you remember if Carl had the tin on him when he was here?" said Dan.

"Well, he must have done," said Joe.

"That's not an answer, Joe. Did you see the tin at any point that evening before Carl left this house?"

"I can't remember. I don't think so."

Georgie shot a sideward glance at young Clancy and both of them saw it. Joe either didn't notice or didn't want to.

"Okay," said Dan. "This is an important one. Do you think there could be any kind of connection between the murder of Norman Peters and the disappearance of Carl Renton?"

"What? A market trader and Carl? What could they have in common? No, I don't see it."
"Norman Peters had Carl's tin. I was the one who found it."
Joe shrugged. "Then maybe Norm Peters found it too."
"Can you remember for certain the last time you saw that tin?" said Dan.
Joe struggled, biting his lip as he searched his memory banks. Georgie watched, and couldn't hold back any longer.
"Joe, there has to be a connection between that market trader and Carl going missing, there has to be!" said Georgie. "I know Carl had that tin on him the other night."
Joe shot the girl a hard look.
"How do you know? I can't remember for certain, so how can you?"
"Because Carl smiled at me and gave me one of his little Bible quotes as he walked out of the door. I thought it was a bit odd as he'd never done that to me before. But he did. This one's for you, he said."
"He did?" said Joe. "What quote did he give you?"
"It said something like 'God is With You Gideon'. But that's not the important part. The important thing is that he had the tin, don't you think?"
Joe frowned, a furrow appearing over his brow.
"You're sure he gave it to you on the last night?" said Joe.
"I'm sure," she said.
Joe swallowed and looked away.
"I still don't see how that means Carl could be connected to any murder."

"Then I'll spell it out for you," said Dan. "By the time Norman Peters' body was found, he was the one with that tin, not Carl Renton," said Dan. "Somehow, in the short time between the last time you saw Carl and when Norman Peters was killed, Peters somehow got hold of that tin. Not only that, but emptied out all of those Bible quotes, and then found time to get himself killed. I saw him alive and kicking yesterday afternoon. So, how and when did he get hold of that tin? Do you see the connection now? Do you see how serious it is?"

The young man's face turned ashen. He leaned back in his chair, shaking his head.

"It's too much… You're not saying… are you?"

But Dan thought the kid knew exactly what he was saying. He just didn't want to face it.

"Please," said Joe. "I think I need a minute to myself. I'll feel better soon." He pulled himself up out of the chair and staggered to the doorway. Georgie offered to help him up the stairs, but he scolded her as soon as she approached. "Just leave it," he said. "Sometimes you help too much." The girl stepped back and let him make his way out of the room. They stood in awkward silence as Joe slowly climbed the stairs and shut his door.

"I guess we should go," said Dan, looking at Joanne. But Dan lingered, seeing something uncertain in the girl's eyes. "Do you have something to tell us, Georgie?" said Dan.

The girl's eyes flitted between them, her lips open as if she was about to speak but the words never came. Instead, they heard a car roll up the kerb onto the driveway outside. The engine shut off, and they heard the clunk of a car door. They saw Aaron Clancy through the window, tall and purposeful, his eyes already passing over their faces through the bay window. Dan and Joanne saw Georgie clam up before their very eyes.

"I should go and see if Joe is okay. Do you mind?"

"Then you didn't have anything to tell us?" said Dan as the girl walked away.

"I told you already," she muttered, tucking her hair behind her ear. "I should see if Joe is okay…" she said and walked away, climbing the stairs quickly as the front door opened in the hallway.

"That's weird," muttered Joanne.

Dan nodded. "That girl knows something, and did you hear the way she contradicted Joe about the way Carl Renton left this house Thursday night? That really needs clearing up."

Aaron Clancy appeared in the living room doorway. He looked them over and offered the briefest of smiles, but the smile couldn't cover his obvious mood. The man looked surly and stressed. Dan rose from his seat, as did Joanne.

"Now there's only two of you," he said. "Have you come with news?"

"News of a kind. There was a crowd with metal detectors at the beach this afternoon. News about the man finding your Celtic torq there must have spread. People seem to think it's part of the stolen Saxon King exhibit."

"That's only natural. Why would they think two sets of ancient treasures are on the loose? I take it nothing was found?"

"No. Nothing from your collection. But we did find a body…"

Aaron Clancy's eyes widened. "Bloody heck. And that was on the same beach? Any idea who it was?"

"A market trader by the name of Norman Peters."

Clancy frowned and shook his head. He looked perplexed.

"Then the name doesn't mean anything to you?" asked Dan.

Clancy Senior shook his head, firm and definite. It was a much clearer response than given by his son.

"Not at all," he added. "And what about my collection?"

"I don't think anyone there found anything. But I'm sorry to say we haven't found anything either, not yet. But don't worry, my partner, Miss Roberts is still out there, and we've been looking all day."

"Looking is one thing – but I hired you to find them," said Clancy. "You'd better get a move on before they disappear altogether.."

"We're working on it, I promise you. But this case is looking a lot more complicated than we first thought. Your missing gold is just one part of it, Mr Clancy."

"It's not for me," said Clancy.

"I know you'd like it to be, but it's not that simple. Carl Renton was here on Thursday night, and he went missing."

"Here we go again. We agreed that Carl Renton wasn't a priority. Whether he turns up or not, it's a side issue."

"One of Mr Renton's prized possessions, a small silver snuff tin, ended up in that dead man's pocket."

Clancy frowned and then shrugged.

"A silver snuff tin? But that isn't mine. It's a red herring, man, forget it. Move on and look for my belongings. That dead body has nothing to do with it."

"But it might, Mr Clancy. On Thursday night your items were stolen, Carl Renton was here, then he disappeared, you had a break-in and then your treasures disappeared. It was a very busy night. I need you to tell us what went on from your angle. Blow by blow."

The man made an exasperated expression and dragged a hand down his face – so hard it left pink marks behind. "Very well, if we must. But let's just get this over with, before this investigation drags on until I have no chance of getting my treasures back."

Clancy walked into the room and opened a cabinet beside the fireplace. He pulled out a decanter with pale amber liquid in it. He raised the glass to check how much was left. There was a single tumbler in the cupboard beside the decanter. Aaron Clancy poured himself a sizeable measure and put the decanter away.

"Forgive me if I don't offer it around but this stuff costs more than a hundred per bottle. It's pricey but it's worth it."

"Single malt?" said Dan, sniffing the air.

"The best there is. I've found myself needing one or two over the last few days." Clancy took a sip and they watched him savour it before he swallowed. "Fire away."

"Just tell us what happened," said Dan.

"Like I told you, I went out with a lady friend of mine. I was expecting to come home that evening but things got a little, how shall I say…" He glanced at Joanne and picked his words carefully. "*Friendlier,* than I anticipated. I stayed there that night. When I came home the next morning I noticed a few of my pieces were missing from the cabinet in my study, and then I looked closer and realised the very best things had been stolen. I went into the kitchen and saw the back window had been broken. There was glass everywhere. That's when I questioned Joe and Georgie and found them to be no use at all. My son had been asleep the whole time and hadn't even stirred when the break-in occurred. It sounded a bit rich to me, but like I told you people before, Joe is a teenager so I suppose, technically, it is possible."

"Do you think your son lied to you?"

The man frowned. "No. I think the best of him… I think he might have been drinking lately. A drunken man can sleep through almost anything."

"That's possible," said Dan. "You think he drinks, then?"

"He's a teenager, isn't he? Thankfully, he's not yet resorted to drinking any of my best stuff. There'd be trouble if he did."

Dan nodded. "Take a step back, Mr Clancy. What about when you left here that night. What time was that? How were things left?"

"I'd already been out at teatime. About five-ish. I'd been working on some ideas for future business trips. I got a little carried away in my work and stayed late, until around eight pm. I stopped to grab a spot of shopping and came home. By the time I got back it was nine and I had to hurry to get ready for my date."

"Who was at home then?"

"In the house? Joe was here. Georgie was here too, but she was getting ready to leave."

"Like she always does?" said Dan. Joanne kept her mouth firmly shut.

"Yes. I insist on it. Joe can have a girlfriend, but she can't stay here."

"Okay," said Dan. He moved on without passing comment. "And you saw Georgie leave?"

"No, I was busy getting ready. But the girl's nothing if not meek and obedient. I knew she had gone because I heard Joe had stopped talking by then."

"Was Carl Renton still here when you arrived?"

"No. I'd missed him, thankfully."

"And your treasures and other collection items were still here?"

"I didn't check on them specifically but I would have noticed if any of the display pieces were missing. They would have been quite obvious, but I didn't notice, so I guess not. They were stolen in the break-in during the night."

Dan nodded, and moved on again.

"Your son. How did he seem to you that night?"

"Rotten, moody, objectionable, and a little under the weather again. He was upset from his little meeting with Carl Renton, which was something of a novelty. But I found it quite an annoyance actually. If Renton is of any use, it's to make my son happy. But he was in an awful mood. He seemed annoyed with me for working late and annoyed at me for intending to go out again. But then I'm well used to that. These mood swings, maybe it's drink, or maybe it's to do with that girl of his. That's another reason I won't let her stay. Sometimes I'm not so sure she's such a good influence on him after all. You don't suppose she had anything to do with the theft do you?"

"Anything's possible, Mr Clancy," said Dan. "But I doubt it."

"But anything is possible. I wanted to warn Joe to keep an eye on her, but I knew how he'd take it, so I refrained. Now I wish I had." He sipped his whisky again. "I'm not sure about anyone anymore."

"And what happened after that?" said Dan.

"I showered, changed and made myself look presentable. I was running late, so I had to hurry, of course. Then I began to worry something was wrong with Joe, as a father does, so when I was ready, I went to see him before I left. I took him up a glass of water, asked if he was okay but the boy spurned me as usual, so I left him up there falling asleep."

"And then?"

"And then I left for my little evening of fun, and the rest, as they say, is history. As you know, Joe failed to hear the break-in, and the finest of my personal belongings were stolen from right under his nose. But with your help, not for long. Does that help you at all?"

"It may," said Dan.

"Good then. And you've seen my son, I take it?"
Dan nodded.
"How is he?" said Aaron Clancy.
"Same as ever, Mr Clancy."
"That bad, eh? Then I suppose I'd better go and see him now." Clancy shook his head and downed the rest of his whisky, sluicing it around his mouth before he walked out of the room.
"Is there anything else?" he said, looking back.
"Nothing else," said Dan.
"Very good. Then please see yourselves out. Let me know when you find something, won't you?"
Dan and Joanne listened to the man as he climbed the stairs. They left the Clancy house and walked slowly down the driveway.
"What did you think of all that?" said Joanne.
"The only one who doesn't seem to be holding back is Clancy Senior, the client. Funny thing is, I like him least of all."
"But he owns the missing items and he's paying the fee."
"And that's why I kept my mouth shut."
"You didn't tell him about what I saw in the pub at the station, either."
"To use a word from the Eva Roberts' lexicon, that's because what you saw was inconclusive. There's no way to be sure that you saw Clancy's treasure winging its way to London in that rucksack. Besides, if I tell him we saw his items board a fast train to London and we didn't stop it, I don't think he's going to thank us very much, do you?"
"Probably not," said Joanne.

"Private investigation can be a messy business. Sometimes the only thing to do is watch, listen and keep your mouth shut."

"That doesn't sound very you, Dan."

"It isn't. But when I've learned all I need to know, that's when I can cut loose again. There's a lot going on in that house. Somehow we need to drill down to see what's happening beneath the surface."

Behind them, up on the first floor of the Clancy house, two pale shadows watched Dan and Joanne walk away from behind net curtains.

Thirteen

"Georgie was there all night," said Eva. "Clancy still doesn't know that."
Eva looked a little frazzled by her meeting with Lauren. Dan could see there were things on her mind, but with Joanne around he would have to hold back from asking.
"So, do we think she was involved in the theft?" said Eva. "Maybe as a go-between or even the one who set it up?"
They walked as a trio, heading for the beach between the marine centre and the Seascape bistro. The police tent at the side of the marine centre was still in place. There was a blue and white "Do Not Cross – Crime Scene" tape around the entrance gap through the sea wall, and there was a separate small taped barrier coned off around the tent. A small police presence was still in place, guarding the now empty crime scene.
"Georgie was there, but I don't think she was involved in it. I still buy the cowering-in-fear theory Joe Clancy gave us. It matches his sweaty demeanour. Sounds harsh to say it, but the kid's weak."
"So it wasn't Georgie," said Eva.
"No. She's too soft for that," said Joanne.
"So what else happened that night?" said Eva.

"They rowed – Joe and Carl Renton. Joe confessed to that himself. It could have been about the kid's reluctance to join the faith. I found a screwed-up Bible tract in the kitchen waste bin, which kind of backs up his story. If Carl was the conversion type, the kid would have been a big disappointment to him. But it could have been something else. Georgie said she heard him say he was leaving, but Joe says he argued with Carl and told him to go. Which is a big difference. If she's right it changes the dynamic. Joe paints it like he had the power and Carl was dismissed on his say so... But if Carl said he was leaving – perhaps leaving for good – it suggests he had the power in some way."

"Power? I don't follow," said Eva.

"It was just the way she described how Carl left the house. Joe explained it differently – That he told Carl Renton to leave. That seemed important to him. I don't know why, but we'll work it out. But if Carl was leaving for good, then that gives me a sense that Carl Renton had had enough of their relationship."

"It's still the same thing. Joe refused to come to the faith," said Eva.

"The conversion theory. But what if it was something else? The ornaments, artefacts, treasure, whatever Clancy calls his shiny things. They could have been involved as an issue between them. Maybe Renton's charity was insolvent and needed saving. Maybe Renton had secretly abandoned the holy life and wanted a more material life and the kid wasn't delivering as promised, so he walked out and took matters into his own hands."

"Now that started out sounding like a sensible theory, until you gave Carl Renton a personality transplant," said Eva. "Theories like that tell me we're no nearer to finding Clancy's missing treasures than we were at the beginning."

"I don't know," said Joanne. "I saw that handover at the station after you'd left with Lauren."

"Okay," said Eva. "Assuming that was part of Clancy's hoard then we know some of it has already left town – for sale in London, I assume. The city's only an hour away."

"Even if we don't recover it all, we'll still uncover the culprit. We can close the case and earn our fee," said Dan.

"Let's hope Clancy sees it that way, but that's not what I was focusing on. If Clive Grace is shifting stolen gold, it puts another question mark over the motive for Norman Peters' death. Peters was killed the day after the robbery. So he could have been involved in it… but why would he have Carl Renton's silver case in his pocket?"

"Which Carl had on him the night he disappeared. He gave Georgie a Bible quote from it as he left them."

"Which suggests to me Carl was still very strong in the faith. No personality change there, so him being involved in the robbery still seems highly unlikely. This case is a mess. What is it? Is it a robbery gone wrong? A conspiracy, with one thief killing off the other thieves so only he can benefit from the proceeds? How does Renton fit in?"

"Joe knows more than he's letting on," said Joanne. "I think Georgie could be the best way in. She always talks about honesty. If she had the opportunity to be honest with us, I think she would."

"Perhaps. But this is where the murder happened, right here. And this is where Clancy's Celtic band was found," said Eva. They paused by the sea wall and looked out to the blue water lapping on the glistening shore near the end of the marine centre jetty. The smarmy-faced constable was one of two PCs guarding the white crime scene tent, and he looked ready to bark at them as soon as they came near. Eva didn't want to give him the satisfaction. They kept a safe distance. There was still plenty of signs of past treasure-scavenging and raked sand higher up the beach, but further down the tide had done its job and washed all footprints and spade marks clean away.

"From the outside it seems complicated, but most motives are usually grimly predictable. If there's a way into this case, we'll find it. You spoke to Hogarth," said Eva. "How'd that go?"

"Better than you'd think, but he didn't want to talk about Carl Renton. Not yet. He's still working the Norman Peters' murder like it's an entirely separate thing."

Eva nodded. "To be expected. Any news on Peters' body?"

"Beyond Peters having a broken jaw? If there was, Hogarth wasn't sharing. He says he's waiting for the toxicology report."

"Toxicology? And will he share the results?" said Eva.

"If *you* call him, maybe."

Eva nodded. Dan started to climb the steps over the sea wall but Eva tugged him back. "Not here. That awful PC is just itching for a confrontation. Let's take the next steps along." Dan eyed the PC and backed off. "Uh. That guy again," he said, with a sigh. "Fine. Let's go."

They walked no more than fifty yards on and took the next set of steps. Here they stepped down alongside a volleyball net which seemed to be a permanent feature, but Eva couldn't remember ever seeing it in use. The marine centre was a way to their left on the other side of the net. The sand here looked barely touched compared to the rest. Clumps of natural grasses poked through in random areas, and the line of scruffy old wooden dinghies continued, all turned upside down on the sand, left by the side of the wall, some with names messily daubed on their sides. But a cursory glance confirmed no sign of any motor boat which might have been used for a run to the jetty.
"We're moving too far from the marine centre, too far towards the town," said Eva. "The marine centre is the focal point in this business. Let's take a careful walk back but keep away from that cop. I'm not in the mood for any more awkward encounters today."
"It didn't go well with Lauren then, I take it?" said Dan.
Eva met his eyes. "She's trapped in a seriously toxic relationship, emotionally and physically abusive."
"It happens," said Dan. "Shame it's happening to a friend."
"That's the thing. Lauren's not a friend, is she? She was once, twenty years back but we're different people. All the same, I'm having trouble forgiving her."
"Why did she want to meet up? For advice?."
"More than that," said Eva. "She's hired us to help her. She's even given me an advance."
"An advance? To do what?"
"To investigate her partner and dig up some leverage on the guy so he'll let her go without carrying out any of his threats."

"Most of those types are weak little scumbags. That should be a cinch."

"Hmmmm," said Eva. "I'm still not sure if I've done the right thing."

"Because you've taken her money? But you said it, Eva, she *was* a friend. She's not now. Now she's just another client who pays actual money. Well done. You turned a problem into a paying job. We'll get stuck into the evil boyfriend case right after we solve this one…" Dan started to walk towards the marine centre.

"It's not about the money, Dan. It's about her. It's about the case. Maybe I should pass it on to someone else. Someone totally independent."

"Why?" said Dan, looking back.

"I don't know but I have some reservations."

"Yeah. So what are they?"

"I can't explain it. Not yet."

"Keep the case, Eva. I'll work it if you don't want to."

Eva shook her head. "No. She wants me to do it, I know she does. That was the whole reason she came down here."

"It's a job, Eva. Sometimes we don't like the client. Just like this case. In fact I don't like the Clancys much at all, but we've got to get the case done to get paid. The same goes for this Lauren woman."

Joanne gave Eva a sympathetic look, but it didn't do much to soothe her. Even if she was being precious and judgmental, Eva couldn't do much about it. She watched Dan cut across the grassy dunes back towards the marine centre jetty. Joanne began to follow, walking further down towards the muddy tideline, her eyes searching the sand along the way. Eva decided to split the difference and walked a line halfway between them, both cases churning through her mind as she paced along the sand.

Stolen treasures or deadly drugs… what was the heart of the matter? The case seemed to have no beginning and no end, no up and no down. Without proof of who had the treasures, or a motive for the Peters' murder, or a sign of the missing man, they were stuck. Eva's face was set in a tight frown, her eyes tracking toward the sun as it tried to burst through a haze of summer cloud. She was so caught up with her distracted thoughts she almost trod in it. But her shoe landed beside a clump of grasses growing from a patch of soil instead of sand. Odd. And then Eva saw the dark area wasn't soil at all. It was sand just the same as all the rest. Discoloured sand, stained dark reddish-brown in a blotch which had spread beyond the tufts of tall grass, fading at the edges where fresh clean sand had been kicked over it.

"What's this…?" muttered Eva. With grim caution, she prodded the edge of the sand with her fingernail. A clot of sticky, half-dried sand substance came away on her nail. She took a close-up look and then a reluctant sniff. Hard to be sure… but she reckoned that if blood had been spilt on the sand in sufficient quantities, it might have looked a lot like this. The majority of the treasure hunters had been on the other side on the beach between the bistro and the marine centre, but there had been a few detector men hunting on this side. But those must have been so busy hunting for gold they'd not noticed the blood. And the police crime scene people were centred around the dinghy further up the beach. They'd ignored the wider beach. The possibilities flashed through Eva's mind. A street fight spilling onto the beach from one of the neighbourhood pubs... An injury from a broken bottle. But Eva had taken her fill of supposition. The blood had to be related to the other crime. But she needed certainty.

"Dan! Come here," she called. He turned back, saw Eva's face and broke into a jog. Joanne came too.

"What is it?" said Joanne, looking at the sand.

"Blood," said Eva. "It has to be blood. And again, it's close to the jetty. Not far from where we found Norman Peters' body."

A way off, at the white tent, the PC and accompanying PCSO watched them with interest but stayed put by the tent.

"Do you think the blood belonged to the market trader?" said Joanne.

Dan looked at Eva and shook his head. "No, I don't. From what we saw, that guy had been beaten around the head."

"Hogarth confirmed it," said Dan. "A blunt trauma."

Eva nodded. "There were no big cuts. Nothing to make this much blood. So where did it come from?"

She peered at the marine centre building and at the long wooden jetty as the sea began to lap at its furthest struts. "The proximity of Peters, now this blood. That jetty has got something to do with all this. We need to know who uses that jetty... someone must have seen something..."

Eva narrowed her eyes. "This is getting out of hand. If you think Joe Clancy is holding back on us in any way we need to know what it is now. The same applies to Georgie too. More lives could be at stake. They've got to tell us what they know before someone else gets hurt."

"Aaron Clancy was at the house," said Dan. "If we go back there now, he'll see us grilling them."

Eva pondered for a second. "True. He'll only pressure us about his missing collection. We need to talk to them in private."

"And the way Joe was trying to play it, all those half-truths and correcting Georgie when she tried to tell us more, I'm not sure we want Joe at all. It's Georgie we need to speak to at this point."

Eva nodded. "Good idea. But how do we get her attention without alerting Joe and his father?"

Dan took his phone from his pocket. "Easy. Georgie and Joe are always there. We'll call the house. It's fifty-fifty that she's the one to pick up the call. Joe didn't bother last time, and Daddy Clancy is probably out by now."

Eva prodded at the bloodied sand. "We need to know who this blood belongs to. You'd better call Hogarth as well."

"You'd be better for that job," said Dan.

"Okay," said Eva. "I'll call it in – after we've arranged to meet Georgie."

Eva took Dan's phone. He'd used the Clancy number before. Eva dabbed at the screen and put the phone to her ear. Fifty-fifty, just like Dan had said. But when the phone was picked up, Eva found she had the wrong end of the fifty-fifty. Aaron Clancy's deep voice answered the call.
"Mr Clancy?" she said..
"Hello," said Clancy. "Miss Roberts. Have you called to tell me you've found my collection?"
"Not yet, I'm afraid. But I do have some questions for Georgie. Is she there at all?"
"Questions for Georgie? Whatever for?"
"She's a bright girl. It's a simple thing."
Clancy fell silent, and Eva wondered if she'd have to blag her way past the man. But Clancy stayed quiet. She heard him pull the phone from his ear and call out the girl's name.
"Georgie! Phone call for you."
"For me?" came a little voice.
She heard the girl's feet descending the stairs, then the phone being picked up.
"Georgie. This is Eva Roberts."
"Yes, Miss Roberts?"
"I need to speak to you. Alone. It's urgent. Do you know anywhere we could meet?"
"Umm," the girl's voice turned quiet. "Chalkwell Park is near here. We could meet there… or wherever…"
As they spoke, a new sound came on the line. A small click, and then a hint of an echo – just the merest change in the quality of the call. Eva narrowed her eyes. The girl was dithering but now Eva couldn't wait for that. In fact she knew neither of them could say another word without being overheard. "See you there in ten, Georgie."
"In ten? Where?" said Georgie.

But Eva hung up. She hoped the girl was smart enough to work out the reason for it. And if Georgie was smart enough for that, she would be smart enough to avoid telling the others where she was going.

"What was that about?" said Dan, reading Eva's eyes.

"There's another phone at the Clancy house and someone else picked up. They didn't say a word, so they were trying to listen in."

"Who? The boy or the golden goose?" said Dan.

"Aaron Clancy seemed curious about why I wanted to speak to Georgie. But after what you said about Joe, it could be either of them. Come on. Time to go," said Eva.

Under the watchful gaze of the PC and the PCSO they climbed the steps through the sea wall. By the time she set foot on concrete Eva already had her mobile phone to her ear. "Inspector Hogarth? This is Eva Roberts. Brace yourself, Inspector. I think we've found another one for your to-do list…"

Fourteen

They drove at a pace, sweeping along the wide hill of Kings Road. The steep incline afforded a decent view of the houses on the other side of the dip where they rose up towards Leigh and the busyness of the glamorous Broadway shops just a mile beyond. Their perspective meant they caught a glimpse of the dark car on the driveway. Clancy's car. Which meant he was still home. They scanned along the pavement, but Georgie was nowhere in sight, which meant she was either still at the house or already in Chalkwell Park. If anyone had followed her, they would be there too by now. Eva and Dan had come separately, Joanne opting to travel with Eva in her Alfa. They parked both cars across the street from the entrance to Chalkwell Park, and well out of sight of the Clancy house. Across the street a black signboard beside a black wrought iron fence marked the entrance to the park. Behind the gate a steep tree-covered path climbed towards the back field of the park, which itself was set on an exaggerated slope.

"Let's hope she's in there," said Eva.

They walked through the gate and shut it behind them. Dan looked into the tall conifers which darkened and cooled their surroundings the further they walked up the slope. Ahead, the canopy formed an archway, which opened out into bright summer light. Reaching the top of the path they looked out over the bottom sweep of the great green field as it rose to join the rest of the vast park. On their immediate left was a children's playground, with mothers and children buzzing around the swings and the roundabout, many noisy and emotional from too much sun. On the field groups of teens were kicking balls around and frisbees flew. Shouts came from the tennis and basketball courts up ahead.
"Chalkwell Park in summertime. It's a busy place," said Joanne.
"Yeah. Which gives shady types plenty of places to hide," said Dan. He studied the most obvious of the people ranged around, both near and far. A few noticed Dan watching and looked right back, but Dan couldn't see anyone who looked suspicious.
"There she is!" said Eva, sounding relieved. She pointed to a small isolated figure sitting alone on the grass like a pixie. Her long hair and shy demeanour marked her out. As soon as she saw them the girl stood up and gave them a little wave, a curtailed flick of the hand which seemed extremely self-conscious. Georgie stuck her hands deep into her pockets as they left the path and climbed up the rolling field. Dan's eyes tracked from the dark trees towards the cluster of leafy green trees by the pond at the top of the field. He couldn't see anyone watching, but it was impossible to be sure.
"Thanks for coming, Georgie," said Eva

The girl offered a wavering smile. "No problem," she said. "But what is this about?"

"Do you think anyone followed you here?" said Eva.

"Uh… no. I don't think so. Did you seriously think they would?"

"Someone was listening to our call," said Eva. "There's another telephone in that house.

"Yes, there's one upstairs in Aaron's study."

"Then he eavesdropped on you," said Dan.

Georgie frowned. "You think so?" she said. "But the door's rarely locked. Joe uses that phone too sometimes. I'm a bit confused. Why did you want to see me, Miss Roberts?"

"I'm going to risk speaking out of turn, Georgie," said Eva. "If I offend you, you'll have to forgive me. But we've asked you here because we think you might be the most trustworthy person in that house."

"I'll take that as a compliment," said the girl. "I think it's easier to be honest."

"It always is," said Dan. "If you've got nothing to hide."

"I haven't got anything to hide from anyone. Nothing except that Aaron doesn't know that I err… well, stay around the house overnight sometimes."

"Sometimes?" said Eva.

The girl's face turned a shade of pink. "Well… most of the time, to be honest. Most nights most weeks. My mum stopped complaining about it. She knows that Joe's father is well off. I told her all about it, all about what he does, about his jewellery business, his treasure and all that so she stopped complaining. I think she hopes I'll end up marrying Joe and get access to the money. She doesn't know how it really is."

"It's okay, Georgie. We're not here to discuss your private life," said Dan.

"Our concern is with what really happened to Carl Renton, because we think it could be connected to the dead man on the beach."

"Because of the silver tin," said the girl, wide eyed and solemn. "Yes. You know, I've thought long and hard about this," she said, slowly.

"Yes…?" said Eva.

"There are a couple of things you should know. The man you found on the beach. Norman Peters…"

Dan frowned. Eva kept her face calm and open, but she felt her heart start to beat a little faster. She nodded at the girl for encouragement.

"I didn't know that man's name at all, not until I heard it on the radio, and then I saw his face on the news…" The girl's face flickered with emotion. She gulped and shook her head.

"You *knew* Norman Peters?" said Dan.

. She looked at him before she gave a slow nod.

"Kind of, but I didn't really know him at all. I recognised his face only because he came around the house a few times."

"The Clancy house?" said Dan.

The girl nodded.

"But why?"

Thoughts began to race through Eva's mind. As Georgie spoke, the piles of unopened new clothes on Joe's floor flashed through her mind.

"That's the weird thing… He came because Joe used to buy clothes from him. Designer clothes at cheap prices. That's how come he has so many clothes in his room."

"He got them from the market trader?" said Dan.

"Why would a rich kid buy clothes from a market trader?" said Joanne.

"And why would a market trader sell knock-off clothes direct to Joe's front door?" said Eva.

"I don't think I have all the answers," said the girl. "But I saw it happen more than once. Joe paid most of his allowance to that man. I used to think it was funny, because I didn't think the clothes really suited Joe that much. And he didn't even wear many of them. But he's like his dad – he's a hoarder. He just couldn't help getting more of them."

"You're sure this guy was the same Norman Peters?" said Eva. "We need to be certain about this."

"Yes. But I knew him as Norm. That was what Joe called him. Norm. The man was a bit rough and ready but he seemed friendly enough, and he was very straightforward on the door. He didn't like to linger. The clothes were always packaged up in the right sizes and he handed them over and Joe paid for them, cash. I knew there was something a little bit odd about it all, but I didn't think about it much because Joe seemed happier for buying them. And what with him being so ill all the time, and what with his dad always being away, I didn't mind so long as it brightened him up."

Dan frowned.

"Peters sold him a lot of clothes… on a regular basis?"

"Yes. That's how I recognised him."

"You saw his photograph on television?" said Eva.

The girl nodded. "Yes, but I checked it on the net too. I knew it was him. Norman Peters was the same Norm who came knocking with the clothes. The news said he was a market trader who sold fashion clothing and I already knew that. It totally freaked me out. Why would anybody have any reason to kill a man like that? He didn't seem a bad man."

"We're still trying to work that out, Georgie," said Dan. "But why would Peters sell door to door like that? He was a market trader. Last I heard, Peters didn't even bother with the pub trade these days. It doesn't make sense…"

"But more to the point, why would Joe deny that he knew him," said Eva.

Georgie took a deep breath. It seemed Eva had hit a pressure point, and Georgie looked suddenly troubled. "I spoke to Joe about it after I saw Norm's face on the local news, after they said his body had been found. He acted totally odd about it. He went into denial. Like he was making out that I had made a mistake. Like I was mad and the man who came round the house was a completely different person. At one point he pretended it hadn't even happened. But I asked him about it again and then he got really angry with me. He's still being cold with me now. I care about Joe… He's so mixed up and upset, and now he's probably frightened too… His dad doesn't really give a toss about him, either. But this thing with the market trader, Joe should have told you the truth."

"But why didn't he?" said Dan.

"Because he's mixed up, scared," said Georgie with a shrug. "And… I think it might be worse than that."

"Worse?" said Eva.

"I wondered before but I put to the back of my mind. Joe doesn't have much money. Much less than you might think and his dad isn't exactly generous. I knew Norm sold him stuff on the cheap, but even so, Joe seemed to be buying far more than he could really afford. The more I think about it, there was no way he could have gotten all those clothes on the allowance he gets from his dad."

"Then how was he paying for all those clothes, Georgie?" said Eva.

There was a silence. The girl's eyes dropped to the grass, while Eva, Dan and Joanne looked at her.

"Before the burglary, a few other things went missing from the house."

Eva looked at Dan. She guessed the rest and ventured to say it.

"Joe was paying for these things with his father's belongings?"

The girl looked sad. "I don't know for certain, but I think so. His dad complained about little things going missing. Not his treasures of course, but a few electronics, his camera, his voice recorder, and a mobile phone one time… I don't want to get Joe in trouble. I want him to be in the clear. That's the only reason I'm telling you this. With everything that's happened, and losing his friends as well, I'm afraid Joe might snap. And Joe doesn't realise how bad it looks."

"How bad does it look, Georgie?" said Dan.

"I know what you think. He's a thief. That he might be involved somehow in that man's murder. Joe's innocent and foolish sometimes but he's not like that, not in a million years. You believe me, don't you?"

Dan sighed. Eva nodded. "I know it's been hard for you, Georgie, but you've done the right thing. Joe should have told us this himself."

"He won't get into trouble, will he? With the police I mean?"

"I'm sorry," said Eva. "I can't make any guarantees."

"Why not?" said the girl with tears in her eyes.

"Because that depends," said Eva, "on what else Joe knows. And what else he's done…"

Fifteen

When they reached the Clancy household they found Clancy Senior was on the living room phone. He watched them advance along the driveway, and his eyes widened a degree when he saw Georgie among their number. He held up the handset to show them he was busy and raised a single finger in a 'one minute' gesture.
"Maybe he's eavesdropping again," said Dan.
"We don't know for sure that it was him," said Eva.
Before the promised minute was up, the door opened and Joe let them in.
"And we didn't even press the doorbell," said Dan.
"I saw you coming," said Joe. Seeing Georgie was with them he looked stressed, his eyes flitting between each of their faces, but landing most often on hers.
"You'd better come in. But keep it down. My father's still chasing everyone in Southend about his Celtic band."
"He's still on that?"
"He's still on everything," said Joe. "You don't know what he's like."
"Oh, I think we're beginning to build a fair picture," said Eva.
"About everyone in this house," muttered Dan.
The young man let them in and they passed the door of the living room. Joe led them left into a second reception room. There were armchairs as well as an oval dining table. The kid chose one of the corner armchairs and left them standing. He fidgeted around in the chair as Dan's eyes fixed on his. Joe saw the look and tried to stop fidgeting, but the effort showed on his face.

"What is it? Why are you here again?" said Joe, his temper fraying. "I can see you met with Georgie, and now you come here looking at me like judge and jury. What am I supposed to have done?"

"You knew Norman Peters," said Dan. "But when I asked you about him you denied it."

Joe's eyes flicked towards Georgie. His face turned dark and he shook his head. Georgie shifted on her feet. Dan expected the girl to beg for forgiveness, to apologise, to play the meek little girl to the ungrateful brat, same as ever. But apparently she'd had enough of that.

"I told them, Joe. And I'm not sorry I did. All these secrets you keep – I think they are what make you ill. You can't keep burying everything and expecting there not to be consequences."

Joe shook his head in horror and disbelief. "Georgie, what are you talking about?! What have you said?"

"The clothes, Joe. You kept buying clothes from that man. The man they found dead on the beach. He came here every week, and then he came every few days and you kept buying clothes from him when you didn't even need them."

"The clothes…? You shouldn't have told them, Georgie. That was *my* business…"

"It didn't matter who told us, Joe. We were getting closer to finding out," said Eva. "And it's not you we're after here, is it?" Eva let the question hang in the air. "If you want us to be able to find your friend Carl Renton – and if you want us to help your father rescue his collection before it gets lost forever, then you need to level with us. Starting right now."

The kid coughed and wiped his brow. He was sweating as badly as Dan had ever seen him, but how much was down to a fever, and how much was down to his guilty conscience was impossible to say

"Level with you? About what?"

"About how well you knew Noman Peters," said Eva. "And about what you think happened to Carl Renton And about your father's collection for that matter. You've held out on us about one thing after another. What else are you hiding?"

"Nothing... You don't understand," said Joe.

"Then help us understand," said Dan. "Starting with Norman Peters."

The kid coughed and looked at the door, like he was concerned that his father might come in at any time. The door stayed shut. Joe began to speak with a quiet but faltering voice. "It was like a credit arrangement at first. I first met Norm – Norman Peters, that is –- when we went to Southend market. I was with Georgie, but she won't remember it. She was too busy looking at the make-up stall. I started looking at the clothes on Norm's stall and we got talking. I bought a few little things and I went back the next week. The next time I bought a pair of jeans but there were a few other pieces I liked but couldn't afford to pay for there and then. We got talking and that's when he told me about the clothes he sold away from the stall. He said he sold all these other fashion lines, exclusive lines... and he offered to let me look at them, maybe take some on credit. I said yes. I never had much money and never had any access to credit either. I liked the clothes he sold, so I went for it. I went to the market to get them a couple more times... but then he said he could bring them around to me instead, said it would save me traipsing down to the market to find him."

"Clothes? You got into a credit arrangement with Norman Peters for clothes?" said Dan.

"Yes. It was like having free money. I'd never had anything like it. I live here but it's never felt like my house. I've guarded all my dad's stuff like a guard dog… all his treasures, all over the house everywhere but I've never had anything of my own. In the end I couldn't help it. Norm's credit made things too easy. And Norm didn't seem to mind extending the credit… except in the end, he said he wanted what I owed him. He said he wanted all of it. By then I was in hock to him for almost six hundred pounds. There was nothing else I could do but offer him other things instead of cash. First to go was my Xbox and my old 3DS. Then my stereo. After that, I had to look elsewhere."

"Elsewhere?" said Eva.

"I started with the kit my dad hardly ever used. I knew he wouldn't miss it. Techie stuff. Gadgets he'd bought on a whim. Norm took those as well, but it didn't last long before that stuff ran out."

"Then what?"

"Then I started scouring for other things. It was Norm who suggested taking one of the ornaments which he'd seen from the window. I panicked and grabbed the least important one, just a tasteless old ivory carving. It took my dad nearly a month to notice that one. But he noticed the African bracelet going almost straight away."

"So what did you tell him?"

"Nothing. He hadn't catalogued everything, only the really valuable stuff. So he blamed himself for being reckless. He looked at me funny when he discovered his pewter bowls missing, and I'm sure he would have cottoned on sooner or later... look, I'm sorry to say it, but I'm almost glad they found Norm dead when they did. If not, I was going to get found out for sure."

Dan stared at Joe with narrowed eyes. "All that risk. All that trouble. That whole credit arrangement con for just a pile of clothes you don't even wear?"

"It's a bad habit, I know. I did the same once with a book club. One of those online ones. I ordered a ton of books but never read them. I got into trouble with dad because I put everything on his card. He was angry for a good while, but he stopped complaining because they were books. He figured books were good. But I only liked the covers."

"Pretty much like the clothes you never wear," said Georgie. Joe shrugged. Dan narrowed his eyes.

"It's the truth," he said.

"The burglaries," said Dan. "You said you heard the glass break and were too scared to challenge the burglars. Any reason for that? Did you have any prior knowledge that someone might be coming?"

"What do you take me for?! Of course not," said Joe, angry and indignant.

"You don't know who broke in for your father's collection?" said Dan.

"No, I don't," he said.

"Carl Renton," said Eva, changing tack. "I know Carl's more important to you than your father's pieces. We're starting again, resetting the whole case. So I'll ask you again. Do you have any idea what might have happened to him? Is there any connection between Carl Renton and Norman Peters?" Dan glanced at Eva, but she didn't engage.

"I have no idea what happened to him, none at all. If I knew I wouldn't have asked you to look for him. I want you to find him. I want the chance to apologise to him for being such a jerk the last time I saw him."

"You argued about Carl pushing his faith on you," said Dan. "And that's all?"

Joe coughed into his fist and looked at Eva and Dan. Now the truth was out he looked thoroughly spent. "That's all," he said.

Georgie forced a smile and walked to his side. "Things will be much better now you've told them everything, Joe. You'll see. With everything out in the open, there's nothing for you to worry about apart from getting better." Georgie slid an arm around his back. The young man looked far from convinced but nodded lamely and accepted her comfort without complaint.

The door opened and Clancy Senior walked in, shooting glances all around.

"What's the big drama all about?" he said, eying each in turn. Joe stayed quiet, a guilty child awaiting his medicine. Dan was the first to speak. "No drama, Mr Clancy. Just ironing out a few kinks in our understanding of events, that's all."

"Is that all you people do? Ask the same questions over and over again? What about my missing collection? I've just been on the phone to the police and the council again. Those bloody bureaucrats are still holding up the release of my Celtic torq. I could do with some good news from you."

"We're working on it, Mr Clancy," said Eva. "Every grain of information takes us closer."

It was Clancy's turn to look unconvinced. "You people need to get a bloody move on. Those are precious items."

"And we're getting a move on, Mr Clancy," said Eva. "I think I know where to concentrate our efforts from here on in."

"Oh?" said Clancy.

"Time will tell," replied Eva. She gave a nod to Joe and Georgie and led the way past Clancy out into the hallway. Clancy simmered behind her. A moment later Eva, Dan and Joanne were back on Kings Road, walking away from the Clancy house in the late afternoon sun.

Dan spoke as soon as they were clear of the house. "Have you spotted what connects Norman Peters and Carl Renton? You have, haven't you?" said Dan.

Eva nodded. "Joe Clancy," she said.

"Yes and what's more, he's the only connection I see. He's admitted it. He lied to us about not knowing Norm Peters, and he would have stuck to that lie if not for Georgie. What's to say he's not lying about his parting row with Carl Renton too? Or anything else for that matter? He's already admitted to a bunch of petty thefts to pay off a debt to Norman Peters. And do you buy the idea of him buying clothing from the guy?"

"Norman Peters used to sell in the pubs as well as at the market," said Eva. "So it's possible he would sell door to door for compulsive types like Joe. But he's shown himself to be a liar, so we may never know for sure."

"Peters liked selling clothes, yes," said Dan. "But he also liked silver snuff tins and class A drugs. Here's an idea. What if Joe Clancy is the one who gave Norman Peters the tin?"

Joanne and Eva looked at Dan as they neared the cars.

"How would that work?" said Eva.

"It would work if Joe isn't as weak and sickly as he seems. At least not physically sick. What if Joe was angry with Carl… what if he struck out against him… what if he stole the tin and gave it to Peters himself? He denied seeing that tin on the last night he saw Carl Renton, but he could have been lying about that too."

"Too much speculation, Dan, and not enough facts. Joe Clancy is a proven liar, but I don't see him killing his only real friend in the world, no matter how many lies he's told us."

"Not just lies, Eva. He's stealing too. What else is he capable of?"

"We'll see. Everyone tells lies, Dan. Especially to themselves. We'd best stick to finding the truth before we get lost again."

"And how do we do that exactly?" said Dan.

"Now we know there is a connection between Peters and Renton we need to get back to the marine centre jetty."

"Why? Hogarth will take care of the blood on the beach."

"I'm sure he will, but that's not what I'm after, Dan. Clancy's Celtic band was found there. Peters was found dead there, with Ubers in his pocket. The Ubers Carl Renton wanted to stop. We have blood on the sand, and we know Carl Renton was on a mission to stop drug smuggling on the beaches. And almost any kind of seaborne smuggling into Southend requires a drop-off by motor boat. Join all of those dots and what does it tell you?"

"The marine centre jetty is the centre of the case," said Dan. "It has to be. Plot it all on a map and what would you see? The whole case swirls around it."

"But what about the transaction I saw at the train station pub?" said Joanne.

"If that was Clancy's missing gold, then we've already lost it. But we haven't lost the case. Before we're done, we'll still nail every villain in this mess. But before that we'll need more than statements and denials. We need to see the cause of this grief and bloodshed and see it with our own eyes."

Eva and Joanne got into the Alfa and Dan leaned down towards Eva's side window. She slid it down.

"You want to go to the marine centre now?" said Dan. "The police will be there. DI Hogarth will most likely be there looking at the blood on the sand."

"The public will be watching too," said Eva. "No. There's no point heading there now."

"Then when do we go?" said Dan.

"Tonight. We'll go at the time Carl Renton would have.""

"If those drug smugglers have half a brain, they'll keep well away."

"But where else can they land in this town? If they want to keep earning money they have to go back to the jetty, whether they like it or not."

Dan thought about it and didn't answer. He leaned away from her car door as Eva started the engine.

Eva gave him a goodbye nod and pulled away. Dan watched Eva and Joanne drive off before walking to the Crossfire. By the time he started his car engine, Eva had crossed the distant traffic lights at the foot of the hill and her Alfa Romeo was a streak of red surging up the slope of the faraway hill heading back towards Southend.

Sixteen

Night time at the marine centre beach. The wide volleyball net flapped in the night breeze, most of it invisible, lost to the darkness. Further down, sparkling black water lapped noisily at the shore. On their right, Southend Pier reached out into the water, seeming no more than a long string of Christmas lights pulled to a tight straight line. From their position inside a Victorian seaside shelter, Eva and Dan watched the two white police tents flapping in the breeze. The shelters had been renovated by the council, tarted up with modern paints to cover the old navy-blue gloss, but the seats in the shelters were just as uncomfortable as ever. They shifted every few minutes, but their backs remained sore and their buttocks stiff and cold no matter how they sat. A second white tent had been erected over the blood patch in the centre of the beach, but the forensics people were long since moved on. Both tents were guarded by a single duo of equally stiff, bored looking uniformed police officers. Thankfully, the smarmy constable from the afternoon shift had gone, replaced by some old stick who looked well past his best, and a young slip of a PC who looked like he should have been tucked up in bed after cocoa and a bedtime story. Neither man looked alert or comfortable, but they were present nonetheless, which posed a challenge for any smuggling mission coming their way.
"It's not going to happen," said Dan. He looked through his binoculars at a yawning policeman and watched the other one stretching out his back. "No one's coming here tonight."
"If the traffickers were using this for a drugs drop-off, then they'll have to come back here soon. It's worth a go."

Dan checked his phone. It was one am and time was creeping along.

"And it's too early," said Dan. "Those cops seem tired, but they look alert enough to see whatever's coming. We should presume the traffickers have seen them too. Which is another reason we need to stay well out of sight. If they see us here waiting, we'll be one more factor to put them off.

"But they'll still have to unload their haul somehow, won't they?" said Eva. "Otherwise there'll be a bunch of unhappy drug users, and someone else presumably very unhappy further up the chain. If the traffickers don't fulfil their part of the bargain, I should think they'd quickly lose their place in the chain. They'll be under pressure to deliver. Maybe they'll be under even more pressure now that someone in possession of Ubers has been killed."

"Or maybe they'll be scared stiff of the same thing happening to them, and they'll have packed it in."

Eva looked at Dan. "Since when does risk put villains off from making their money."

"Fair point," said Dan, shrugging. "Then the least we've got is a wait on our hands."

"Then let's dig in and keep quiet…"

They dug in. The seaside shelter was nice and dark and did a good job of keeping them hidden from the occasional passing car. They were equally hidden from the police and the shoreline. The only way they could have been detected was if someone shone a torch directly at their faces from the beach. But that was unlikely. And even then, the sea wall mostly hid their bodies. They would have to rely on their wits for the rest. A flask of coffee and some supermarket sandwiches kept them going until three am. By four am the esplanade was dead from end to end, with not even the sound of a car on the air. Dan's head was thick with tiredness, and Eva was edgy from drinking too much coffee. A fresh breeze came in off the water, and the police sentries stood huddled in quiet conversation on the sand, shooting banter between their posts to pass the rest of their shifts.
"They're losing concentration," said Eva.
"Like I am," muttered Dan. "Bound to happen sometime…"
They watched as the wider cop laughed at an unheard joke, before he started to trudge away up the sand. They watched the man as he produced a key from his pocket. It jangled in the breeze.
"He must have a key for the marine centre… I think he's off to use the toilet or something," said Eva.
"Which presents an opportunity for someone… Wait… Look… It's getting better. The younger cop has started playing with his phone. He's on the net or he's texting someone…"

A moment later there was a noise somewhere out on the water. The faintest whining engine noise, but it was so far off even the young cop didn't look up. It was hard to hear at all. And the police officer carried right on tapping at his phone screen.

Dan took a pair of binoculars from the seat and stared out into the blackness over the distant water. It felt like a waste of time. He saw no lit vessel, no movement, nothing to be seen. Of course there wasn't. But the noise seemed to be getting louder. The whine sounded like a mosquito at first. Before long it sounded like a distant motorcycle. Soon it sounded like a larger motorbike, and the policeman stopped texting and looked to the road, checking both ways before turning to the sea. Dan and Eva stiffened and dipped lower in the shelter. A short time later and the sound was definitely coming from the water. The sound of an outboard motor could be discerned from typical engine noise. A propeller churning water, and the rush and splash of the propelled water being cast behind it. Dan put the binoculars back to his eyes. This time he saw a faint arc of white water pale against the darkness. The jet of water was accompanied by a glint of light shining on the side of a hull and then it was gone again. Dan's view blocked by the end of the jetty.

"It's got to be them," said Dan, whispering with excitement. The young cop was still and stared out towards the water. He left his post beside the smaller tent in the middle of the sand and walked a few steps towards the sea. "That motor sounds pretty powerful. Maybe it's a bigger boat than we thought," whispered Eva. Dan's eyes were on the cop.

"Either way, if it docks here, they're going to be seen, end of story," said Dan. As his words trailed away, a loud shout came from the other side of the marine centre. The cop wheeled around and almost fell down on the sand.
"Jordan!" called the voice. It had to be the other cop. They turned their heads to see the other policeman leaning over the sea wall from the pavement. "Jordan, over here now!"
"Something's happening over the other side of the building," said Eva.
Dan leaned up from his position as the policeman called Jordan, ran back across the sand towards the sea wall.
"And I think I know what that something is about," said Dan. "Come on. Here's our opportunity." They clambered over the concrete wall in front of them and landed on the soft sand beneath. Ahead of them was an exposed diagonal run of beach towards the jetty. As soon as they made a move they would be exposed on all sides. But there was no decision to be made. It was happening. Dan broke into a gentle run, keeping his pace fast and his footsteps soft, opting to land in the clumps of grass wherever he could. Eva followed close behind. Dan paused for a moment and looked at the sky. He listened.
"That motor sound has stopped," he said.
"Damn it," said Eva. "False alarm you think?""
Dan shook his head. They heard some rowdy shouts and a few barked police warnings came from the other side of the marine centre building. "What's going on over there?" said Eva.
"It's a distraction. Got to be," said Dan. "It's just the way I would have played it. If they wanted to use the jetty, they had no choice. Quick, before we're seen…"

They passed the small white police tent as it billowed in the breeze. From halfway down the beach Eva fancied she could see something of a murky shape out in the blackness, the merest hint of movement on the nearby water. But it was almost silent. Eva and Dan moved on. They reached the edge of the canoe and kayak storage area, the wide platform behind the long narrow arm of the jetty. Between the shouts and swear words heard from the other side of the jetty, Eva heard fractional sounds from the nearby water. There was a gentle bump and a scrape which seemed to reverberate softly through the structure. Eva leaned away and looked down the length of the jetty. There, at the far end, she saw a shadowy figure crouched and skulking on the very end of the platform. He had a long spidery body. And there, just at the corner of the jetty, she saw where a small wooden vessel had nudged alongside the structure. The spidery shape reached out as a rope was tossed up to his hand, and Eva watched as he tied off the rope on the hook at the top end.

"It's happening," whispered Eva. "They're here."

"I see them," murmured Dan. He reached up for the top of the jetty, and quietly hauled himself up. He scrambled up quietly, and then half-hunched over, began to pick along the width of the platform, deftly jinking between the boat racks for cover. A moment later he returned, crouching above Eva just like the man at the farthest end. Dan's eyes were bright with adrenaline. "I've seen what's going on over there. You won't believe it, but it's the guy from the rehab. The one who tried to drag Joanne upstairs with him. He's arguing with the cops on the other side there. He looks out of it, too."

"But surely that'll only bring more police?" said Eva.

"By the time they arrive all of this will be over. We'll stay down there," said Dan, "Try and get close to the water. It's the best way to stay out of sight."

Dan jumped down beside her and landed cat-like on the sand. Keen and tense, they started to advance along the sand, staying close in the shadows of the jetty. When they neared the edge of the water, they had to strain their ears. But the waters were calm, and the nearest sounds soon became clear.

The man reaching up from the boat was little more than a silhouette. He thrust up a thick arm, his head appearing over the edge of the jetty. They watched as he handed up one black bag and then another bag. As they were lifted, the bags became visible in the light of the moon and the street lamps. They were rucksacks, black, the kind hikers used, with lots of zips and pockets. The bags didn't look completely full but were certainly bulky enough. As soon as the second bag was up and in hand, the man on the water asked a question.

"Still all clear up there?"

Eva and Dan looked at one another. The voice was familiar. They watched the skulking man glance back across his shoulder, and the same pale light illuminated his face. They saw his thin narrow face, mean little eyes and sour mouth. It was him. Clive Grace.

"Bloody hell," whispered Dan.

"We've got them," said Eva. She took a risk and leaned back as the man in the boat clunked his oar against the wood to push off. As the boat gained distance from the jetty, they saw the stocky figure of Tommy Pink dressed from head to toe in black, but his pale face was as bright as a miniature moon. He plunged his oars into the waters, then settled into his boat and started to make off on the water. As he worked to settle into his rhythm, his face turned towards Eva. She saw his face full on, and for an instant his eyes seemed to latch onto hers. The man stopped rowing and stared. Tommy Pink leaned left and right in the shadows and continued to stare their way.

"He's seen us!" hissed Eva.

"Under the jetty now," hissed Dan. He ducked under the wooden platform as the row on the other side of the jetty began to die down.

A mobile phone buzzed above them on the jetty. It was answered by the end of the second buzz. Clive Grace's rough voice carried faintly on the air.

"What? By the jetty? You sure?" They heard Grace's footsteps scrape across the wood above them, the gentle thudding moving sideways, and Eva imagined him glancing down, scanning between the slats to find them where they stood. The man took a couple of moments before he made a breathy reply. "No one there, Tommy. The police are good and busy on the other side… Okay, okay. I'll take a look…"

The call seemed to end there. They heard the thin man's body drop to the wooden deck and saw his legs dangle over the edge, a couple of feet from their faces. Eva and Dan froze, both of them staring at the cold black water not far ahead of them. It was invisible beneath the jetty, but they could both smell its cool saline fragrance, both a threat and a promise.

Grace dropped to the sand, and Dan yanked Eva tight to his side as he slid behind a set of struts with a zig-zagging set of cross bars between them. They watched Grace turn around and stare into the shadows beneath the jetty. His narrow eyes searched all around them, not yet adjusted to the blackness beneath the jetty. They saw the old-fashioned cosh in the man's hand, a dark wooden stick with a bulb at one end, a strap wrapped around the man's fist. He held the cosh tight as he stared into the darkness around them. Dan and Eva held their breath and stared right back. Grace shook his head and a smile slipped over his face. He chuckled to himself and dropped one of the rucksacks from his back down to the sand. He opened the top, and dipped a hand inside, snatching at something within. Grace pulled his hand out and poked at the item in his palm. Satisfied, he stuffed the thing into his pocket – a package wrapped in clear plastic, and then he pulled out another. He stuck a few into his pocket, then closed the top of the bag and slung it on his back..

With a cocky grin set on his miserable face, the man skulked away.

"He didn't see us," said Eva, the relief clear in her voice. "He barely even tried to look. If he'd looked closer, he would have seen us."

"But he's not our only problem," said Eva.

They listened and found the sound of the argument gone. The show was over.

"Now *we've* got to get away from here without being seen by those cops."

"That's easy enough. We'll use the distraction side of the jetty," said Dan. They picked through the struts, ducking beneath some, edging around others in the clammy darkness, until they reached the other side – the wide patch of sand between the marine centre and the Seascape bistro. Eva stopped sharply, and Dan bumped into her back. He drew alongside her to see what she had seen. There, standing beside another distant seaside shelter she saw Clive Grace slipping something into the hand of another man of much the same skinny build..

"Generous to a tee, our Mr Grace," whispered Dan. "He's giving the man his reward for creating the distraction."

"They'll all get what they deserve soon enough." Eva nodded at the man from the rehab as he slinked away along the street, head down, no doubt looking at the pills in his hand. Clive Grace walked off in the opposite direction back towards the town.

"Those two could be twins," said Dan.

"They could be related. And there it is – the heart of the matter. The Uber business," said Eva, turning to Dan. "How Clancy's gold collection got caught up in this mess, I don't know."

"As it happens, I've got an idea or two about that," muttered Dan.

Eva gave him a curious look. "Either way, it's safe to say Norman Peters' death wasn't about ancient gold. This is about modern gold. The kind of gold that kills…"

But even if they never found Clancy's lost collection Dan had an inkling about what had happened to those missing treasures. Certainly no more than an inkling. But with each new detail they uncovered, the stronger it got.

Seventeen

Sunday.

The next morning came around all too soon. There had barely been time for any sleep, and what there had been was fitful at best. Despite a ridiculously short rest, at seven am Eva was showered, dressed and topped up with coffee. The permutations of what they had seen spun through her head. As she put it to paper, the case clearly coalesced around the Clancy house and the marine centre beach. The Clancy house was a home of bad vibes, doubtful relationships, and dodgy deceits – while the beach was a place of spilled blood, double crossing and drug smuggling. Clancy's treasures were still missing, stolen in one way or another. Norman Peters was dead, perhaps even *because* of his involvement with Joe Clancy and Carl Renton. Or because of upsetting his drug trafficking colleagues, Tom Pink and Clive Grace. The cosh in Grace's hand told its own story. Joe Clancy's lies seemed trivial in comparison. Then there was Carl Renton himself. Still missing. It was a mystery, yet the more Eva looked, the elements seemed to be more connected than ever. Eva wondered whether they could be simply connected as linear events, one domino falling to knock down the next. If only she could have lined them up in the right combination, Eva felt the rest would fall into place in just the same way. Dan emerged from the door to their apartment holding a fresh cup of coffee. His hair was sleek and wet from the shower. He sipped from his cup before using it to point at Eva.

"Call Hogarth. That's what we need to do next."

"At seven thirty?" said Eva. "I don't think so."

Dan took another sip and made a face. "If he's worth his salt as a police detective, he'll already be hard at work. He's got a murder case on. This is what guys like him live for."

"But why call him?" said Eva. "To tell him about Tommy Pink and Clive Grace?"

"Hold fire on that. I think we need to be absolutely sure on those two before we hand them over. He'll only have our word for what we saw."

"But we saw it all, Dan. A tip-off should do it."

"But without evidence the police could bodge the case. It happens. What we need to know is what happened to Norman Peters. That blood on the sand couldn't have come from his head. How did Peters die? And whose blood was it?"

"It'd be better to have some info to trade with Hogarth. That's how he likes it."

"So tell him you've got some news on the way."

Eva frowned, but Dan was right. If Peters' cause of death was clear it would fill in one more blank – one more domino in the line of cause and effect. Eva took a gulp of coffee, popped an Ibuprofen in her mouth to fend off the onset of a headache, and started to dial.

The first sound that greeted her ears was rushing traffic, followed by the man clearing his throat. "Miss Roberts. You're keen this morning. Got something for me, have you?"

Eva raised an eyebrow, feeling almost caught out by Hogarth's ESP. Then her tired mind realised it was just his sense of humour.

"Actually, it's a follow-up call, Inspector. Did you get anything back from the post-mortem on Norman Peters?"

"Oh, that. Must have slipped my mind to call you back. Yes, we got something alright. The little fella was smashed to a pulp right there on the beach. Bloody aggressive it was. I saw a couple of bruises from punching, so put it down to a beating, but our pathologist says it was worse than that. The culprit knocked his front teeth out, broke his jaw, and fractured his skull. He tells me Peters was struck five times with a heavy weapon. The blow which fractured his skull is likely to have knocked him out."

"Knocked him out?"

"Looks that way, because his head hit the sea wall on his way down. There's a graze on his head which corresponds to some evidence found on the wall."

"You're saying the beating didn't kill him?"

"No. The Ubers did that. Toxicology says Peters must have ingested three, or maybe even four pills before he died. They were only partially digested too. Looks like they were taken either just before or just after he took his beating."

"Three or four Ubers?"

"I know, Miss Roberts. That's far too much. These ecstasy pills are very potent, and the mix isn't always safe either. If you take two of these at once, it's a gamble. Three or more, that's Russian roulette with a fully loaded gun."

"What do you make of it?" said Eva, her eyes on Dan as he listened in.

"Same as you do, Miss Roberts. Not even the wildest raver in town would drop three of those things whilst alone on Southend beach, and certainly not after a beating. Norman Peters either decided to top himself, or someone did it for him. But the beating he sustained had to be part of it."

"Interesting. Tell me, do you have any suspects in the frame?"

"We'll be looking at some possibles this morning. No one's been ruled out. Not his market trader mates, or anyone else. But when it comes down to the Uber business, this murder could be down to anyone in the trade. It's a big business lately."

Eva swallowed. She felt the temptation to share what she knew but decided Dan's decision to wait was for the best.

"What is it? I can almost hear that mind of yours whirring," said Hogarth.

"Can you?" she said.

"Yes, so before you ask, no, I haven't had anything back on that patch of blood. Crime Scene and forensics have been working on it as a precaution, though I think we could be overdoing it. Blood on Southend beach at the weekend? It could have been from any set of drunken pub brawlers you care to choose."

"It's the location and the timing, Inspector. I feel it has to be connected in some way."

"Then we'll find out soon enough. Okay. I'm almost at the station now. It's time to hang up before my gaffer sees me driving while on the phone."

"You should get a hands-free, Inspector," said Eva.

"There's a lot of things I should do, Miss Roberts. I'll add that to the list."

The call finished and Eva turned her chair to face Dan. He blinked at her. "I got the gist. Norman Peters was beaten to a pulp with a weapon not unlike the one we saw in Clive Grace's hand and then he was topped by someone forcing a bunch of super-strength Ubers down his neck. Makes you wonder what the poor fool had done to warrant that…"

"Makes me wonder what kind of scumbag you'd have to be to do it. But then I think we might have seen a few candidates already, don't you?"

"Yeah. Tom Pink and Clive Grace fit the bill nicely. And then there's Joe Clancy himself. The little guy wouldn't know an honest word if it bit him on the backside, and he was effectively being blackmailed for cash by Norman Peters. That clothes credit story is for the birds. Georgie might believe it, but do you?"

"The clothes don't lie. And how could he be responsible for beating up Norman Peters, Dan? The boy's in such a bad way. And Georgie will no doubt provide him with an alibi."

"I hear you. But we still need to check him out, big time."

"We've checked him out already. Georgie has told us everything she knows. So has his father."

"I only wish we could have spoken to Carl Renton about him, seen him the way Carl saw him. We need to watch him, Eva, just like we did with the jetty last night. That worked, didn't it? We need to catch him unawares."

Eva sipped her coffee as the ache in her temples began to fade. The Ibuprofen was starting to kick in.

"Okay. But Aaron Clancy won't like it at all if he finds out."

"Then we'll avoid him like the plague."

They finished their coffees and got ready. When Mark came in, Joanne was with him. They looked keen and ready for the battle, but the grim, haggard look on Eva and Dan's faces soon had their smiles waning.

"What happened to you guys?" said Joanne.

"A stake-out, that's what happened," said Dan.

"We took a leaf out of Carl Renton's book and took up a vigil on the marine centre jetty."

"Did you see anything?" said Mark.

"We saw something alright, and my bet is that Carl Renton saw it too," said Dan. "And we're back out this morning."
"Don't you want any help?" said Joanne, pushing.
Eva shook her head. "Not this morning. It's Sunday. You two should go home and put your feet up. This one is going to be another sit-and-wait job. But don't worry, we'll keep you in the loop."
They made their goodbyes and left the office, weary but ready for the battle without Joanne's questions and pushing.

***

They watched Aaron Clancy drive away from Kings Road at just before nine am. As with DI Hogarth, Clancy seemed equally happy to flout the law against using a mobile phone while driving. They could see Clancy ranting into his mobile as he started the engine and reversed the car off the drive. He slapped his steering wheel and was still shouting to himself as he drove away.
"The council, maybe?" said Dan.
"Not on a Sunday. The police maybe," said Eva, "And unless we find his things it'll be us next."
They sat in Eva's Alfa Romeo. The small red hatchback was far less conspicuous than Dan's metallic blue Chrysler convertible. With Clancy gone, Eva started the engine and pulled forward until they had a good line of sight into the big front windows of the Clancy house from their position, angled across the street.

The upstairs windows bore net curtains, but they were see-through enough to reveal movement like shadows within. They caught a glimpse of a young female silhouette, the shape and outline suggesting she was naked. Georgie, of course. It seemed the young couple were taking full advantage of Clancy Senior's recent departure.

"Looks like we're in for a wait," said Dan.

"Maybe," said Eva, glancing at the dashboard clock. "Anyway – I told you, Joe's not as ill as he claims."

A short ten minutes later the movement shifted downstairs. They watched the door to the living room open, and in came Georgie. She was now was fully dressed, a tall glass of water in one hand. Joe walked in behind her, and right away they saw his demeanour was different. His face was less pale, his eyes big and bright. He seemed sharper, maybe a little edgy too. Once again he was telling the girl what to do.

"That was quick work," said Dan.

"Young people do everything fast," said Eva. "Didn't you know?"

"And is he telling her off again? What now?" said Dan.

They watched. They saw Georgie nodding back as Joe talked at her. The girl swished her hair, downed her glass of water and left the room. Joe followed and they disappeared from sight. They waited another full minute, and then a blurred shadow filled the window of the front door. The door opened and out came Georgie. She walked out onto the doorstep, and Eva and Dan stiffened and wished they'd parked further away. It was too late to move now. If they were seen they would have to come up with a very good excuse.

Georgie was carrying an empty tote bag. It floated by her ankles on the breeze. She turned to face Joe as he held the door and gave her another set of firm instructions. Eva dabbed the window button and the glass slid down an inch to give them a better chance of hearing. If either of them looked across the street to the right, they would be seen. All they could do was listen.

"Anything else?" she said.

"Oh, yeah. And some fizzy water. The good stuff, not the cheapo own brand. Oh, and get me some of those bacon Frazzles. And a multi-pack of Mars bars… and some orange juice with the bits in it. You know that always makes me feel better."

"I could have picked it up yesterday, you know. I was out then."

"Yeah. But I forgot. Come on. It's not that far, it won't take you long."

Dan kept his voice to a whisper. "Looks as if his father's 'how to be an arse' lessons are really paying off," he muttered.

Georgie turned away down the step, her lank hair flapping in the breeze, covering her face. Eva felt her heart beating hard with the fear of being caught out. But by the time Georgie pulled the hair from her eyes she was already walking away up the steep sloping street towards the shops of Leigh Road, and Joe Clancy had already shut the door.

"They didn't see us," said Dan.

"A spot of luck where Georgie was concerned," said Eva. "But Joe closed that door in a real hurry…"

"Now that you mention it…" said Dan. "Let's go and see what we can see."

They got out of the Alfa, closed the doors and and walked across the street. Kings Road, a template Neighbourhood Watch zone, well-to-do and concerned with keeping its desirable status. If they were going to spy into the property through the front, they certainly couldn't do so for long without someone intervening. As soon as they reached the house front, Dan walked to the left to the window of the cluttered living room, while Eva turned right towards the second reception room – the dining room with the recliner armchairs in each corner. She reached the edge of the window and peered in to see Joe Clancy walk into the room. Immediately, Eva pulled back, then slowly edged forward again. With bated breath, she watched Clancy sit down at the table. He set down a small baby-blue plastic chopping board, along with a small sharp kitchen knife. The kind used to peel potatoes and chop apples.

"Dan!" whispered Eva. He glanced across and she waved him over. Dan joined her side, poking his head around the edge of the window frame before pulling away again.

"What's he doing?" said Dan.

But Joe answered the question himself. He reached deep into his jeans pocket and pulled out a tight-wrapped brown manila paper bundle and laid it on the table. With a shaking hand, he peeled the torn, crumpled paper back, dipped his fingers inside and pulled a small white tablet free. He laid the tablet on the chopping board with great care. With the air of a craftsman, he took the knife and artfully pressed it to the tablet, pushing down only when he seemed certain of where to make the cut. He cut the tablet with a last second thrust, and repeated the manoeuvre, then laid the knife aside. He picked up three of the tablet pieces, dropped them back into the shabby parcel and screwed it up tight, returning it to his pocket. He picked up the last fragment of tablet and eyed it once before depositing it onto his tongue. After swallowing it down, he lifted the cutting board, wiped the crumbs to one corner, and swept them down into his mouth with his finger.

"I knew it," said Dan, pulling away. "The clothing arrangement was a front. The credit story a blag."

Eva pulled away too. "He's taking Ubers…"

"And he's been taking them all along. That's why he looks so ill. He's hooked on the damn things."

"So why's he cutting them into pieces?" said Eva.

"Probably a good idea when you're as weak as he is. And an even better idea when your drug dealer delivery man has been murdered and you don't know where your next fix is coming from. His supply line has been cut off. Maybe that's why he seems jittery as hell. He's using small doses to get by and pretty soon he won't have any at all."

"Then Carl Renton…" said Eva. "Do you think he knew Joe was using?"

"Joe being hooked on those damned pills changes everything. But from now on we've got him cold. Any questions we've got, Joe Clancy is going to give us a straight answer to every single one."

"He's never helped us before," said Eva.

"Trust me," said Dan. "We know too much for him to refuse. This whole thing has had us chasing our tails, now we know why. But I think things might be about to change…"

When they reached the other side of the road, Eva's mobile started to buzz. A queasy feeling hit her stomach and she thought of Lauren. Eva sighed and plucked the phone from her handbag. Thankfully it wasn't Lauren. Hogarth's name was on the screen. The queasiness subsided a little.

"Miss Roberts," said Hogarth.

"Inspector?"

"I've just had little chat with my DCI. The drugs boys have told him there's a been a delivery somewhere on our patch, and he's adding the problem to my in-tray. The drugs squad have noticed another surge in Ubers coming into the local black market only last night," said Hogarth, building up a head of steam. "Have you heard anything on this?" Hogarth let his question hang in the air but Eva stayed quiet.

"Norman Peters," Hogarth continued. "There were Ubers in his pocket and pathology told us there were Ubers in his blood, traces of them on that dinghy too. These bloody pills are already a menace but now it looks like I've got another problem I need to solve, pronto."

"Sounds like you've been handed a hot potato, Inspector."

"Put it this way. When the music stops, I'm always the one holding the bloody parcel. We spoke about favours and information sharing as I recall. I don't suppose you've heard anything that can help us?"

"Why ask me, Inspector?"

"Because I noticed that you turned coy on me this morning. And because you two always seem to be in the loop."

Dan shook his head. Eva frowned back at him.

"You're under pressure to get some kind of result here?" said Eva, saying the words for Dan's benefit.

"Always. That's how the game works at this end," said Hogarth.

Dan shook his head again and drew a line across his neck to tell her to cut the call.

"At this point, Inspector, all I can say is to look at the people you already know about."

"We're dropping hints now are we?" said Hogarth, the anger showing in his voice. "The people we know. Such as?" said Hogarth.

Eva hesitated, then said it out loud. "The market traders might be a good bet. Selling clothes down the market might earn them a living, but who knows what else they've been up to, eh?"

"What do you know, Miss Roberts?"

"I'm not sure, yet. But we're working on it," said Eva.

Dan winced and looked away.

"Of course you are," said Hogarth. "Thanks for the tip. Your better half wouldn't have given me a bean."

"He's not that bad," said Eva.

"I'll take your word for it."

The call was over. Beside Eva, Dan was frowning.

"What did you tell him that for?" said Dan. "He'll be all over them now. What if we can't get close enough to them now to finish the job?"

"I gave him a hint, that's all. A big hint."

"A hint? You virtually told him."

"He shared with us, and he asked me to share back. Unless you want him to stonewall us in every future job we get, you'd better just accept it and move on. He has a list of suspects. If we get moving, we'll still get what we need before the police move in.

"Great," said Dan. "We're under even more pressure than before."

"We were always under pressure. You have met Aaron Clancy, haven't you?"

They climbed back into the Alfa and Eva started the engine. From high up in the Clancy house, a shadow looked out from the upper window. As the car pulled away, Joe Clancy lifted the net curtain and looked out to the street. His newly bright eyes happened upon the roof of the gleaming red car as it accelerated away. The young man turned his eyes towards the top of the hill, waiting for Georgie's return. He felt better, but still not good. Only a quarter of an Uber pill couldn't dull the sharp anxiety inside.

They were almost back to the office when Eva's phone started to buzz again. She slid the phone from her pocket and handed it to Dan without checking the screen. If Lauren was calling he would have to put her off. At least she wouldn't have to do it. But it wasn't Lauren calling.
"Eva?"
"No, Mark. It's Dan. Eva's driving. What's the matter?"
"We went home just like you said. Then Joanne decided to go back down to the marine centre beach, just to see what was happening. But when she got down to the seafront she saw a commotion a bit further on."
"A commotion?" said Dan. Eva looked across at him.
"Yes. Joanne said there was a group of people standing around on the beach. She said she thought she heard a scream. She went to see what was happening—"
"Cut to the chase, Mark" said Dan. "What's going on down there?"
Eva looked at him from the driver's side.
"They found another body."
Dan's brow dipped low over his eyes. He shook his head and met Eva's eyes.
"Where?"
"The beach, not far from the jet ski shop and the Chinese restaurant. Do you know it? Joanne's there now."
"Why didn't Joanne call this in?"
"She wanted to tell me first, now she's people-watching – just like you asked us to do before."
"That girl just can't help herself, can she?" said Dan. "Okay. We'll head over now."
Dan cut the call and put the phone on the dash. He looked at Eva. "You hear all that?"

"Another body?" said Eva.

Dan nodded.

"Oh no," she said. "Where?"

"Down on the seafront near the jet ski shop. We'll need to get there before the police close off the area."

Eva grimaced. Her headache was coming back, biting through the relief given by the painkillers. Instead of heading for the office, she ran a red light and took a sharp left turn down Lifstan Way. The road ahead was clear. She hit the accelerator and had the speedometer hitting forty in the space of a few seconds. Somewhere on the air they heard sirens. Hogarth was chasing the same case as they were, and the body count was rising. It seemed they were in a race on all fronts. For all kinds of reasons, money the least of them, it mattered that they won. By the time they passed the side of Southchurch Park, with the estuary in sight, Eva's Alfa was nudging fifty in a thirty zone. She hit the brakes hard before she took the left to join the seafront traffic. As yet there were no flashing blue lights in sight. Eva drove fast and pushed up close behind the camper van ahead of them. She willed it to move faster. It didn't. A few minutes later, she pulled up on yellow lines outside the Golden Dragon and the jet ski shop. They opened the doors and jumped out of the car, Eva ignoring the oncoming traffic which swerved to avoid her car door. She found a gap in the traffic and broke across the street. Dan slammed his door and ran after her. They saw a fuss of stressed grim-faced people standing by the sea wall, and a glimpse of others standing in clutches on the beach side. Eva eavesdropped on them as she ran past and stepped through the gap in the sea wall.

"Terrible, it really is…"

"…must be that poor missing man from the newspaper…"

Eva's heart thudded hard in her chest. She tried running on the sand, kicking up a mess as she struggled towards the middle of the beach, losing her breath as she went. She slowed and snatched in deep breaths as she reached them. A group of people stood around a half-hidden heap lying splayed across the sand, close to the black line of seaweed and detritus from the water. Joanne turned, her face appearing from the crowd on the sand.

"Is it him?" said Eva. "Is it him?" But she didn't wait for an answer. Still gasping for breath Eva moved past the edge of the pack until she had a clear view. There was an old man kneeling beside the sand-covered body. He looked up at Eva as she leaned in from the crowd. His spectacles glinted in the morning sun.

"Are you a doctor?" said the man.

Eva shook her head and looked down at the body. Dan appeared at Eva's side.

"I don't think a doctor can help this one anymore," said Dan. The large body lay face up to the world, his big arms splayed left and right, the face bloated and grey and pitted from contact with the sea. Thankfully, the sand had crusted over him to hide most of the gore. But it couldn't hide the awful pallor of his skin, nor the evidence left on his limbs. A shredded, knotted rope had been tied around both ankles and rope dangled from his left wrist, while the right wrist was free. Eva looked closely and saw some grazing type damage to the bare wrist, as if a rope had been there too. The long blue sand-crusted rope stretched away like a tail reaching for the water and mud.

"They tied him up," said Eva. "They tied him up and threw him out to sea… He was a good man." A good man, and yet his life was cheap.

Eva dropped to her knees and her eyes followed the trailing blue rope. Near the water she noticed the end of the rope had been knotted into two empty loops, side by side. Dan saw it too. "Looks like the body had been weighted down. But whatever they used didn't work for long enough. Just a few more weeks and all there would have been was bones in the mud."

Eva nodded, but she was only half listening because she had noticed something else. Details. The head had been injured and bruised. Bludgeoned, no doubt, much like Norman Peters. Now Eva's eyes trailed across an unnatural pit in the big man's stomach, a wound like a crevasse encrusted in thick sand. "Dan," she said in a whisper. "His stomach…"

"The blood on the sand…" muttered Dan.

"It belonged to Carl Renton," said Eva. A gathering had formed behind them. By the sea wall, Eva's eyes caught sight of the small, nattily dressed blonde heading their way. Joanne had seen her as well and moved close behind Eva.

"Just a heads-up. Alice Perry from The Record has arrived. She's on her way over."

"Ugh. I'd rather not deal with her. Come on. We've seen what we needed to see. Poor Carl Renton isn't missing anymore."

"So we're back looking for Clancy's treasures," said Dan.

"And the killer, Dan, and the killer. From what we know about him, Carl Renton only ever tried to do good. He didn't deserve this. We're going to get the evidence to put the killer behind bars. One way or another, someone's got to pay.".

Alice Perry eyed Eva with a sharp bright smile as she passed them by, her blonde hair blowing in the breeze. There was a glint in her eye, of victory and menace. Even after everything she'd done, everything they had on her, Perry seemed to have no fear and no shame.

"Are you two leaving so soon? And there I was hoping for a quote. This is going to be quite the front page. Missing Hero Murdered in Uber Drug Crisis."

"I've got a quote for you, Alice," said Dan. "I've even got an exclusive photograph of your kitchen to go with it."

"Maybe you and I can talk about that another time, eh?" said Perry, shooting a different kind of look at Dan.

"You knew this was going to happen!" said Eva, calling out. "That's why you ran the Missing Person article so soon. How did you know?"

Alice Perry stopped, looked back, and grinned at Eva.

"Now you just sound jealous," said Perry. She kept her voice even and walked a way back towards them. She stopped a safe distance from Eva's fiery eyes.

"How did you know this was going to happen?" said Eva.

"Because I'm good at my job. Because I have a nose for these things. Carl Renton had been playing with fire for a long time, Eva," said the girl, being overly familiar. "He was going to end up as a news story sooner or later."

Eva's eyes narrowed. *"How did you know?"*

"I had a contact at the rehab. But I have contacts everywhere. My contact called me and told me Mr Renton didn't come back, told me they were in a panic, told me what he thought had happened." Perry smiled again and shrugged. "It made sense to me, so I contacted his church, they confirmed he hadn't showed up, and I ran with it. I'm so glad I did. This story could run for weeks, and I was in at the start."

Eva thought about the people they'd met at the rehab. Of them all, she could only imagine the thin, small eyed scoundrel as a man who might definitely seek to profit from another man's death. "You know, Alice, you are one *cold little—*"

"Hold that thought, Miss Roberts. Surely you of all people know that a girl's gotta do what a girl's gotta do." Perry added the briefest wink as insult to injury. "And I see that Dan's still keeping hold of his little private souvenir snap of our time together. Have you ever stopped to wonder why?"

"You're the worst, Alice."

"Now, now. All that hate's not good for you, Miss Roberts. I hear it's very ageing. Now remember, if you'd like to provide a quote about Mr Renton, you know where to find me."

"Yes. Right at the bottom of the trash," said Eva.

Alice Perry arched an eyebrow, turned on her heels and walked away.

Dan appeared at Eva's side. To Eva's mind he looked a little defensive.,

"I told you," said Eva, "that photograph would only keep her in check for so long. She doesn't care anymore. Which means she's dangerous again."

"She's not dangerous. She's got nothing on us," said Dan.

Eva looked back towards the road. There, stepping over the sea wall, was the lanky figure of Clive Grace, accompanied by the stockier Tommy Pink. Pink clambered over the wall after him. Both men advanced past Eva, oblivious to her watching them. They walked purposefully across the sand. When they got nearer, they held back, and stood side by side muttering to one another. Grace nodded. Pink muttered behind a hand raised in front of his mouth. Eva turned, tempted to confront the men with what she suspected, even though it wasn't wise to do so. As she set off towards them, Dan read her mind and tried to call her back, but Eva kept walking. But before Eva got there, somebody else beat her to it. A small silver-haired woman wearing an expensive purple jacket stormed up to Tommy Pink and Clive Grace. The woman looked upset. She trembled as she stared at them.

"You know what happened, don't you?!" she said.

"What? What are you talking about?" said Pink, looking around. Clive Grace took a step back, moving out of the old woman's line of fire.

"Dear God, I know you do. I was there at the marine centre on the day Carl disappeared. I saw you with him, having some kind of argument with him. I saw it. So don't you dare deny it!"

"Now now, lady," said Pink. "You're just confused. I don't know anyone called Carl"

"Yes, you do. That is Carl Renton, lying down there on the sand, killed only because he wanted to help people." The woman sobbed. "I knew Carl very, very well. He was a good man. He was trying to stop the drugs killing the young people. I saw you arguing with him last Thursday – *I saw it!*"

"You're mistaken – now why don't you go and shout at somebody else?"

Eva saw Alice Perry was watching too.

The old woman shook her head in disgust and stormed off. The wail of police sirens which had been growing louder for minutes fell abruptly silent as the police cars finally arrived on the road behind them. Eva's mouth dropped open as she considered what she'd heard. Tommy Pink had been spotted rowing with Carl Renton on the very day he disappeared. Why would a market trader be standing on the beach by the marine centre? At that moment, the old woman who had confronted Tommy Pink passed by Eva's shoulder.

"Excuse me," said Eva. The woman didn't seem to hear her, so she called again. The woman heard her this time and stopped. She gave a thin smile, but Eva saw there were tears in her eyes.

"Sorry to bother you, madam. My name is Eva Roberts. I'm a private investigator."

The woman blinked at Eva, her teary eyes widened. "I see…"

Eva nodded. "I heard what you said to that man just now. The one you saw arguing with Carl Renton. Do you mind if I ask you about that?"

The woman shook her head. "I don't mind at all. I want everybody to know. I was in the same Christians Against Crime prayer group as Carl. Carl was the one who started it, actually. We used to meet and pray together about the issues in the town. Carl was a real strong man of the faith. What happened to him is terrible, it really is…"

"Yes, it is," said Eva. "So, Carl used to come down here to pray against the drugs coming into the town? Is that right?"

The woman sniffed and nodded. "I'm sorry. This is a terrible shock."

"Of course it is," said Eva.

"Carl liked to play detective. He said he thought the drug gangs were bringing stuff in on the seafront, and he suggested the places our group might go and pray against it. He suggested the Marine Activity Centre because of the jetty. We did go there as a group once or twice but Carl always wanted action as well as prayer. He said he'd been there at night and seen something. Well, you can see how old I am. Most of us are in our sixties and more. We weren't really interested in late night vigils and hunting for villains in the cold. We said we would continue to pray, but Carl wanted to stop what was happening. He said it was up to people like us to act. But poor Carl, it looks like he's paid the ultimate price. It's a word people should never use lightly, but it really feels like he's been martyred for the cause… and that awful man over there knows something about it, I'm sure!"

The woman glared at Tommy Pink's broad back.

"You really think that man had something to do with it?"

"Carl patrolled that beach more times than we'll ever know. But the other morning, Thursday I think, when I saw them for the last time, I saw Carl arguing with him. I was driving along the seafront. I had my window down because of the heat, and I heard it. That man has a terrible temper, he was shouting and telling Carl where to go. That was the very last I ever saw of Carl Renton, until now."

Eva crumpled her chin. "Did you hear the substance of the argument?"

"How could I? I was driving. But I knew it was heated alright. I said a little prayer in my car and drove on."

"I think you should speak to the police. Tell them what you saw."

"Yes, yes... I will. My name? Rosie Crimper. But please, before I speak to the police, I just need a little walk first – to clear my head – if you don't mind."

The old woman bowed her head and started to walk away. The woman's raw emotion had stirred the anger in Eva's chest. She frowned and marched across the sand before she could be stopped and tapped Tommy Pink on his muscular shoulder. Clive Grace saw her first, his mean, narrow face turning quizzical as his eyes took in her anger. Pink turned around and frowned.

"Yes?" he said.

"You saw Carl Renton on the day he died."

"Did I?" said the man. Pink looked at Grace whose eyes narrowed.

"I hear he was a popular man," said Grace. "I bet he saw a lot of people that day."

"But you argued with the man. You were seen."

"Hey. I'm a chatterbox. I like to have a debate now and then," said Pink, with a shrug. He folded his thick hairy arms. "I'm a market trader, see. I like to chat. Gift of the gab and all that. Sometimes I say things without thinking which cause offence. That's probably what happened there. I don't remember things like that. They happen all the time."

"You don't remember what you argued about? Seriously?" said Eva.

"What's it to you, anyway?" said Pink, tilting his head at Eva. "You old bill or something?"

"No, I'm—"

"No? Then you're another nosey bloody Parker like that old dear just now. People like you shouldn't go around casting aspersions. You should mind your own bloody business before you go and offend someone."

Pink turned to Grace and flicked his head away from the crowd. They turned away together and walked off slowly, as if they didn't intend to walk far. Eva shook her head and stalked away.

Dan watched the whole encounter.

"What did you say to him?" he said.

"I wanted him to know someone was onto him," she said, as she passed.

"Why?"

"Because I want them sweating," said Eva.

"Do you think that was wise?"

"Times like these I don't always feel like being wise," said Eva. She walked on and left Dan standing on the beach as she approached the police cars parked up by the sea wall.

"Eva!" called Dan, but she carried on walking.

As she reached the sea wall, the newly arrived police were already dividing duties among themselves as one officer jumped over the wall heading for the crowd. Eva recognised PC Dawson among the busy pack. She knew Dawson well. He had helped them through a good few scrapes in their time. As soon as Dawson saw the serious edge in Eva's eyes, he excused himself from the group and walked across to meet her.

"Eva? What is it?"

"That body over there belongs to Carl Renton, the missing drug rehab man. The one The Record have been banging on about. It looks like he was beaten around the head and there's also a terrible gash to his stomach. That might have been the wound that killed him. The ropes around his wrists and ankles suggests he was probably weighed down and thrown into the estuary, but it looks as if the ropes didn't hold, so he was washed ashore."

"Bloody hell," said another policeman who had been listening in.

Dawson nodded and got ready to move past Eva for the beach, but she stopped him with another word.

"PC Dawson, do you see those two men over there?" Dawson moved to her side and she carefully pointed out the figures of Clive Grace and Tom Pink at the edge of the crowd. "Those two men are market traders. They worked with the other murder victim, Norman Peters, and they were there on the beach when we found his body."

Dawson frowned. "And they're here again?"

"Coincidence don't you think…? And I just overhead a woman ranting at Tommy Pink about how she'd seen him arguing with Carl Renton on the day he disappeared. She swears Tommy Pink must have had something to do with it, and I've got good reason to believe that she's right."

"Reason to believe…?" said Dawson.

Dan had drawn up at Eva's side and heard most of the exchange. Eva looked at him and he nodded. It was time to share what they knew.

"Last night we kept the marine centre jetty under watch, and we saw those two men bringing in a shipment of what I'm sure were class A drugs. Specifically, we think they are importing the Ubers your drug squad and everybody else in the town are in a flap about."

"Those two?" said Dawson. "How can two market traders be responsible for all that."

"Not all of it, Rob," said Dan. "Just the local trade. From what we saw, I think they are picking up a small haul from a larger delivery vessel out in the water." Dan's eyes flicked across the street and caught sight of the jet ski shop on the corner. He narrowed his eyes in thought.

"Okay," said Dawson. "We'll talk to them, soon as we get this site under control."

"You need to speak to that witness too. She's over there," said Eva. "Her name is Rosie Crimper."

"Rosie Crimper," said Dawson. "Fine. I'd best get on. Thanks for the tip-off."

"They're involved, Rob," said Eva. "Pink and Grace have got serious questions to answer."

Eva nodded at Dawson as he pushed on, nudging through the crowds to the body at the centre. Now Dan was the one walking away. He climbed over the sea wall and headed for the street. Eva called after him. "Dan. Where are you going?"

Dan nodded to the shop across the street. "To the jet ski shop."

"But why?" said Eva.

"Something I need to check out, that's all…"

Eva watched him cross the street as Joanne drew up at her shoulder.

"I can't believe the nerve of that Alice Perry. I heard every word of it. All the front, after everything she put both of you through."

"Oh, I can believe it," said Eva. "A leopard never changes its spots. Especially a nasty one like that."

"Should you be worried?" said Joanne.

Eva shook her head. "No. She should be worried. If she tries anything like that again, she won't know what hits her."

Joanne nodded. "I'd like to be there when it happens."

"I wouldn't. Come on. I think I need more coffee. And more painkillers."

Eva turned to stared at Tom Pink's back while Joanne frowned at Alice Perry in the middle of the pack. The journalist was all smiles, working the crowd and chatting up the male police officers, milking everyone for her next big story.

"Come on," said Eva. "Let's go before I drop to the sand." As Eva and Joanne started to trudge away, Dan walked into the jet ski shop across the street.

When Dan walked inside, the lean silver-haired guy behind the counter looked up from his glossy marine sports magazine. He looked tanned and healthy, and his hair was close cropped. There were sea sports toys of all kinds cramming every nook, cranny and wall space. The place was a feast for the eyes. Dan noticed an open folder of abandoned paperwork beside shopkeeper's magazine, along with a messy stack of receipts and an equally abandoned laptop. Even the way the man was reading his magazine seem half hearted. Dan guessed he'd been looking across the street to work out what was going on, just like all the rubberneckers slowing the seaside traffic. Human nature. Dan watched the man's eyes drift over his shoulder back towards the beach before a lazy smile appeared on his face.

"Awful business," said Dan.

The guy's eyes latched onto Dan like iron filings to a magnet. "What is it? What's going on over there?"

"A body has washed up on the beach – so they tell me," said Dan.

"Is it that missing Christian rehab guy?"

Dan's eyes caught sight of the bright red masthead of The Record newspaper sticking out of a pile of papers and magazines behind the counter. The shopkeeper was a reader of Southend's sensational newspaper.

"Probably, yes," said Dan. With a corpse across the street, the conversation about the body took the place of standard pleasantries. Gossip over, it was time to get down to business.

"So, I was wondering," said Dan. "about a couple of things actually. About jet skis…"

"Jet skis?" said the guy. Dan watched his demeanour change back into business mode. "Great. Okay, so what are you into? Performance? If you like a bit of power and performance then we've got a GTR 230 over there. It's a bit of a beast, but you strike me as the kind who could handle it…"

Dan glanced across at the gleaming black and blue machine at the side of the shop. It was angled at the window in car showroom style, and Dan quietly acknowledged the thing looked good. A powerful jet ski looked as good as a performance motorbike."

"Yes, it looks good," said Dan. "But it's not—"

"Not the one for you? Okay. So, if you're just starting out, maybe you'd want to consider a Spark. But I really think you'd do better with a GTi…"

Dan raised his hands to stop the flow of words. "Thanks, but I'm not in the market yet. I'm just looking around."

"Looking? Fine. You can look as much as you like, but if you want some serious thrills, you need to try one of them. After that, you'll be hooked, I'm telling you."

Dan nodded and cast a glance of appreciation around the shiny jet skis taking up the floor space all around him. The walls were full of sea sports' equipment – kayaks, body boards, stand-up paddleboards and small surfboards. But the main part of the shop was all about the jet skis.

"So, how long have you guys been here?" said Dan.

"The shop? Near on forty years. Not me personally, of course. But that's how long this shop's been going."

"Okay… and you?"

"Thirteen years, give or take," said the man, grinning. "Long enough to be an expert, I suppose." Dan turned idly towards a rail full of wetsuits.

"I've got a deal on C-Skins wetsuits, if you're interested."

"Thanks," said Dan, but he turned his gaze back on the shopkeeper. "Listen. I've got a question about jet skis. It'll probably sound pretty dumb to you but hear me out."

"No question is too dumb. Fire away," said the man.

"I saw this one jet ski the other day. At least I think it was a jet ski. It was really dark, you know. Still very, very early. First, it sounded like a speedboat engine, but then I saw this arc of water spray coming from the back of the thing. Shooting up and back in an arc as the jet ski moved…"

The man behind the counter nodded. "Sounds like a jet ski. They roar like a motorbike. Especially the big ones. Was it like that?"

"Yeah… it did sound like that. Do they all shoot an arc of water like that?"

"Pretty much. But not all shoot the water out the same way."

"The one I'm thinking of shot out a *lot* of water in like a big curve. I saw that clearly."

"Hmmm. And it sounded like a beast?"

"Yeah. I think the guy was trying to keep it quiet too. He didn't seem to be pushing too hard."

"Not pushing? But where's the fun in that? Where did you see this thing anyway?"

"Up past the Marine Activity Centre."

The guy nodded but it looked like the information didn't help him. "It could have been a Waverunner. A Kawasaki model. They're pretty solid and beefy. We don't actually stock those. The kind of thing you need is the GRT. They're full-on. You'd love it."

"Maybe I would but listen. Those Waverunners – how far can you go in one of those?"

"It all depends on your comfort zone and how much fuel you've got. In theory you could go all over the estuary twenty times over. If you were crazy enough, you could push it out of the estuary and into the North Sea. But I wouldn't recommend that if you want to keep safe. Bottom line, you could do a ton of sea miles on a jet ski, but anything more than an hour, especially for a beginner, is too much."

"An hour would suit me fine. Another question. Have these things got much storage space."

"Again, think motorbike. With a big bike you get a storage box and you can add panniers. With a jet ski you get a front compartment, like a small car boot. You can fit in drinks, fishing gear whatever. But not much. The bigger the jet ski, the more storage you get."

"How much storage?"

"A few bags and a spare wetsuit maybe. We're not talking your holiday luggage. It sounds to me like you're thinking of finding one second hand?"

Dan's eyes lit up. "Now there's an idea," he said. "I don't suppose you know of anyone who has a jet ski like that? Someone capable of it in the dark? It was dark when I saw this guy."

"Did he have his nightlights on?"

"Nope."

"Then the guy was a dumbass or likes living on the edge. I happen to know a few guys like that. They mainly come in for accessories and for a coffee from time to time."

"And do any of those guys have a jet ski like the one I saw?"

"And dumb enough to ride in the dark without nightlights? Yeah. I can think of a couple. Danny Madison. He's been in enough scrapes to prove he's got a death wish."

"And the other guy?"

"The market trader called Tommy Pink. He comes in from time to time, always looking for a discount on anything he buys. He forgets we haven't all got low overheads like he does. Tommy's got a Waverunner. But don't bother making him an offer on it, he'll never sell and never upgrade. He's a one-car for life type of man. Rather than pay for the GTR I told you about, he just had his one painted black to match it, as if a paint job does anything."

Dan looked at the sleek black and blue beast of a jet ski in the centre of the shop.

"This Tommy Pink had his painted like this?"

The man nodded, laughing. "That's how much of a skinflint he is. I'm telling you, he'll never sell it. If you're sticking with second hand, then your best bet is Danny Madison. If you buy that thing off him you'll be doing everyone a favour…"

"Thanks for the tip," said Dan.

"But do yourself a favour, forget the Waverunner. The beast you're looking for is right here."

"I hear you," said Dan. "And you never know, one of these days, I just might take you up on that…"

Dan eyed the big black and blue jet ski one more time before he smiled and headed for the door.

So Tommy Pink had a jet ski – a model with ample storage and the capability to travel distances. Pink had also painted his machine black and was competent at riding by night without lights. It sounded like Mr Pink had turned his jet ski into a complete black-op machine and had the skills to conduct a night time smuggling operation. Dan headed to Eva's red Alfa with a quiet smile on his face. Eva was already behind the wheel, adjusting her seatbelt. The esplanade was rammed and the traffic had been reduced to a crawl. Dan guessed they would soon have to close the road off altogether. He opened the front passenger door and found Joanne was already there. She smiled and made no effort to move, Dan grunted in complaint, opened the back door and crunched himself into the back seat.

"You'll have to reverse and take the side turning or we'll never get out of here," he said.

Eva looked in the rear-view mirror and saw the turning behind them. She started the engine and slipped into reverse gear.

"What was that all about?" said Eva.

"It's Tommy Pink. Last night Tommy Pink was riding a jet ski, Eva. Not a boat. The guy in there even knows all about how Tommy Pink rides without lights on, told me how the man has just painted his machine black and knows Tommy Pink is experienced enough to ride the thing all over this waterfront. He's owned that jet ski for years. Think about it. If Pink meets his drug supplier on a boat out beyond the estuary, he could ride out there, pick up whatever's been delivered and bring it to the jetty by stealth. Apart from the noise of the engine, it's almost perfect. Pink is the mastermind of the local Uber operation. And I bet he makes a fair bit more than he ever did by selling clothes at Basildon market. Selling Ubers could be his retirement plan."

"A retirement paid for with dead bodies," said Eva. She reversed up over the corner of the kerb until the Alfa bumped back down onto the side street as she started a three-point turn. Dan looked at the rear-view mirror and saw Eva frowning in thought.

"Problem?" he asked.

She met his eye. "Our theory is that Pink had Norman Peters and Carl Renton killed to protect the drug import operation."

"Probably. Norman Peters must have posed a risk somehow. And Carl Renton was clearly onto him."

"But, in having them both killed Pink almost ruined his whole operation and put himself in the frame."

"Maybe it was worth the risk. The operation was back on last night. The only part that changed was that Pink switched from a jet ski to a boat when he got close to the jetty. To minimise the engine noise problem, I guess."

Eva's eyes misted in thought as she drove away down the side street, leaving the seafront chaos behind them.

"Pink and Grace are in this up to their necks," said Eva.
"Progress at last," said Dan.
"But we still haven't got anything to give Aaron Clancy."
"Yeah. Shame about that," said Dan. "It's the only hiccup in this whole case."
"It's a very big hiccup. That *is* the case. We're not getting paid for solving murders. Only for locating Clancy's missing treasures."
"I told you what I saw," said Joanne. "That man Grace gave a rucksack to some guy at Southend Central train station."
"A rucksack?" said Dan, leaning forward in his seat and resting his arms over the backs of the front seats. "They were using rucksacks last night at the jetty. Black hiking rucksacks – all straps and strings."
Joanne nodded. "Clive Grace brought one of those into the bar and gave it to his contact."
"Then I don't think you saw any gold being moved at all. What you saw was a sack full of Ubers heading out for London."
"Which fits with what Hogarth told us about a new Uber influx," said Eva.
"We just found the source of that local influx – Pink and Grace," said Dan. "Which could be good news as far as Clancy's case is concerned…"
"Good news how?" said Joanne.
"If you saw Clive Grace giving his courier a rucksack full of Ubers, then Clancy's gold could still be here in town…"

Eighteen

Eva's phone buzzed again. The odds said this call had to be from either Lauren Jaeger or Aaron Clancy. Lauren and Clancy were their current meal tickets but Eva really didn't want to deal with either of them. She was almost relieved to see Hogarth's name was on the screen. They had just arrived back at the office when the call came in. Eva's head was screaming for more painkillers, a glass of water and a cup of coffee. As she took the call she struggled to find her friendly voice.

"Inspector."

"Miss Roberts. Thanks for the heads-up on the market traders. We were due to interview them about Norman Peters anyway – to see if they knew what Norman had been up to. A nasty death like his was a definite message. Peters had to be involved in dealing Ubers."

Eva sat down at her desk and Joanne made a coffee cup gesture at her. Eva nodded and the girl went off to the kitchen. Dan signalled for one too as he tried to eavesdrop Eva's call.

"Peters was dealing Ubers?" said Eva. "There's a surprise." Dan grinned.

"Did you ask Tommy Pink why he was arguing with Carl Renton last Thursday?"

"Of course I did. Though Pink says it wasn't an argument. At least not from his perspective."

"I'm sure it wasn't," said Eva. "From his perspective."

"Pink says he was getting ready to go out on his jet ski – turns out he's a water sports enthusiast. I'm not surprised. All that lot are flash Harrys. When Carl Renton approached him at the marine centre Pink was almost ready to set off. Pink says Carl Renton said that he'd seen him on the water a number of times and asked him if he was aware of any criminal behaviour on the estuary. Pink readily admitted that he didn't give Renton the time of day because, he says, Renton was a troublemaker. He told Renton he hadn't seen a thing and would keep shtum even if he did. I reckon most other people would say the same. Apart from Carl Renton, who wants to take on a bunch of drug traffickers by himself?"

"It might be a convincing answer, but that doesn't make it true," said Eva.

"Maybe not. But then I also checked out Pink's story. He does have a jet ski and goes out on it regularly. And it turns out there were others who thought Renton was a nuisance. The local beach café owners agreed, as did some of the council beach cleaning crew. Renton was twisting the arm of everyone he could think of, trying to enlist them as his eyes and ears for the estuary."

"Renton was only trying to help."

"And maybe he was, but he was also rubbing a lot of people up the wrong way."

Eva shook her head. "Carl Renton was treading on the toes of drug dealers. Inspector, do you seriously believe what Pink told you?"

"In respect of the argument seen by that old dear Rosie Crimper, yes. Pink's story stacks up. Rosie Crimper is one of the local tea and biscuit brigade. People like her usually think of the likes of Tommy Pink and Clive Grace as the enemy. To her they'd be working class ruffians while Carl Renton was a middle class hero with time on his hands."

"Come on. That's hardly a fair description of the man," said Eva.

"Fair? Maybe not. But is it accurate? Probably, yes. Pink said Carl Renton got uppity and demanded Pink tell him what he'd seen – Pink replied that Renton should leave matters to the police. After that, Tommy Pink said Renton had lost it. Tommy told Carl Renton where to go, and that was the end of it. That's what old Rosie Crimper must have seen. The final flare-up. Whatever else Pink gets up to for either money or for kicks, I don't get the impression he would want to ruin his life by killing a Christian like Carl Renton. As for importing drugs, Pink says he has no time outside of his work. He says he works markets at all kinds of hours. We can check on that – but if he's telling the truth I don't see how the man could be running a drug trafficking operation and a full-time market business."

"Where the big money is concerned, Inspector, most people don't mind losing sleep. Pink is a very good talker. Please don't let the man hoodwink you."

"Hoodwink me? I'm the hoodwinker here, Miss Roberts. No one ever gets past me for long."

Eva was tempted to say that she'd seen Tommy Pink in action, smuggling with her own eyes, and that Joanne had potentially uncovered a drug running operation on the train line to London, but she knew Hogarth wouldn't act on their say so. And she didn't want to give the man the satisfaction of throwing the report back in their faces. When the time came, Eva intended to hand Hogarth the whole thing packaged up with a ribbon tied around the middle. The DI would almost certainly resent them for it, but Eva's priority was seeing the villains dealt with. If Hogarth posed a risk to that aim, Eva would work around him.

"You say Peters was dealing Ubers," said Eva. "And you think Tommy Pink knew nothing of what Peters was doing?"

"Norman Peters was a small fry, but he was his own man, with his own supply lines. He sold cheap fashion clothes to young people which means he had access to the right market for Ubers; it's not impossible he was targeted to sell Ubers by a bigger fish because of that access. Unlike Pink, Norm Peters had the perfect opportunity to cash in on drugs. You can't shift Ubers at Southend market, Miss Roberts. People would soon twig. I really don't think Pink is your man."

"Then what about Grace?"

"Same deal as Pink. Clive Grace is your snivelling hanger-on type. Looks like a miserable sod, doesn't he? Clive Grace follows Pink everywhere. He's Pink's assistant on market days. I don't see how he'd be any different to Pink. The same lack of time and opportunity applies to both men."

"But, Inspector… we *saw* Clive Grace following Norman Peters just hours before he was killed. You know what Peters had on him – those Ubers and Carl Renton's snuff tin. Why won't you see the link?"

"In my job I see the potential for links everywhere, but I have to deal in reality. Norman Peters was a colourful little scamp who went his own way. Who knows how he might have upset Clive Grace when you saw him on the Leigh Broadway? They're all rogues, Miss Roberts. But being a rogue doesn't make a man a killer, even if old Rosie Crimper thinks it does."

"Forgive me for saying this, Inspector, but I think you're being a little myopic on this."

Hogarth sighed. "I get it, believe me, I do. There's no smoke without fire and all that, but with this there's barely any smoke either. Look. I'll keep an eye on Grace and Pink for a day or two, but If I don't see any evidence of wrongdoing, then I'll move on down the list. We have blood but no weapon. We have a dead market trader but no witnesses. The same goes for Carl Renton. We'll find out what happened to them soon enough, but I think that could mean a big sting operation targeting the real drug dealers higher up the chain, not a couple of two-bit rogues from down the market. They're not killers, Miss Roberts. They're convenient, but that's all they are. I think Carl Renton came unstuck because he finally got what he wanted. A face to face meeting with the real traffickers. The big money people. Those kinds of villains don't mess around. As for Norman Peters. He was a small time guy in a big bad world and I think he got turned over in a bad way."

"But Carl Renton's silver tin, Inspector? What about that?"

"I think you're getting blinded by all the bling. That tin is just a small matter of timing, Miss Roberts. And in the grand scheme of things, that little tin may not mean much at all."

Eva groaned as a coffee landed on her desk. She picked it up and sipped.

"Then what about the blood on the sand? I assume you've had it checked?"

"It was a couple of days old, and the sand itself has caused a problem for the tests. Forensics are working on it, but I'm told they haven't got a match yet."

"But what about matching it to Carl Renton? You saw the state of his body? His wounds were terrible."

"Agreed. More blunt trauma and a major stomach wound. Not exactly pretty. Okay. I can ask if they've run a check on Carl Renton's blood, but I already know what they'll say. No match means no match, Renton included. We'll try CCTV next, of course, but those cameras only work so well at night on the beaches. No street light means no footage."

"Hogarth, I'm sorry, but you're in danger of getting this one wrong," said Eva. "Don't close your eyes to Pink and Grace. They're up to something – I know they are."

"I'm getting it wrong, eh? So how's your case with Aaron Clancy going? Because the way I hear it, you haven't found any of his missing loot, either. The thing is, Miss Roberts, we all get it wrong – until the moment we get it right."

Eva winced. "I hope that means you're keeping an open mind," she said.

"This work tends to keep your mind very open, which is the reason I called in the first place. I called to ask if you had anything else for me. Anything conclusive. But I think you've already answered that question. Good luck with your treasure hunt."

Hogarth hung up the call and Eva grimaced at her mobile. "Sometimes that man can be too obstinate for his own good," said Eva. "He interviewed Pink and Grace and somehow he doesn't see them in the frame for the Renton murder."

"And he could be right," said Dan with a shrug. "Renton was chasing hardcore villains. Maybe he got burned that way. Peters, though, that looks like a revenge crime. Or a message."

"Which fits what he thinks of Peters. A small man playing a hard man's game, making himself a target for rivals. Either way, Hogarth's telling himself what he wants to hear. That's not how you solve a case, is it? Which means we need to give him sufficient reason to see things our way."

"Sufficient reason?" said Dan.

"I mean evidence. Pink and Grace are in this up to their necks. Hogarth needs us to prove it."

Dan blinked at Eva and didn't say a word. She hardened her tone and pushed on. "We saw them importing, Dan. We saw them."

"Or are they just two more idiots playing a hard-man's game?"

"No. Idiots they may be, but they're not playing. They risked arrest to bring in that last drug haul. And they did it right under the nose of the police. Clive Grace was ready to use that cosh if he found us. They're involved in the murders, Dan. They have to be. And now we're going to prove it."

"Fine, but by the time we've finished with those two scumbags, Clancy's gold will be long gone. Looks like we'll be needing your Lauren Jaeger case more than we thought."

The very idea made Eva's frown deepen. She sipped her coffee and opened her desk drawer to dredge it for painkillers.

Nineteen

Eva and Dan travelled back to Kings Road alone. By the time Georgie opened the front door to them, Eva's painkillers were beginning to kick in. Behind Georgie they saw the hallway was empty. There was no sign of Joe or Clancy Senior anywhere. Next, Eva noticed a look of concern on the girl's face, but in spite of it, she saw Georgie was relieved to see them.

"You okay?" said Dan. The girl nodded and tucked her usual rogue lock of hair back behind her ear.

"It's Joe," she said. "He's been so odd with me today. I mean even stranger than usual."

Dan and Eva shared a momentary glance. It figured.

"You mean he's ill again?" said Eva.

"Yes, he's ill. And on top of that he's gone all moody and quiet with me. The thing is, I really don't know what I've done to deserve it this time."

"Trust me," said Dan. "It's not you, it's him. What about Aaron Clancy. Is he here?"

"Uh. No. He's out again. Either another meeting or he's with his girlfriend."

"I see. Do you mind if we come in?" said Eva.

Georgie let the door hang open and backed away inside the house. "Actually, it'd be nice to have some company. It's been deathly quiet here today." She led them into the busy room with the treasure clutter on the shelves and the walls. Georgie dropped her backside into a seat. Eva and Dan took the unspoken invitation to do the same.

Eva did her best to read between the lines. Joe was giving her the cold shoulder – probably fretting about his private Uber supply running out. But there could have been other reasons for his mood change. Had he known all along what had happened to Carl Renton? It was impossible to find out without playing their hand and asking the young man outright. Instead, Eva decided to bide her time to work towards the question.

"How long has Joe been like this?"

"A few hours, so far.

"No, I meant, in general. Unwell. Pale. Sweating all the time. How many days or weeks has he been like this?"

"Oh, he's been like this for months now. And I feel sorry for him, I really do. We used to be really good together. I mean, he was so much more fun before this phase started. I know it's not his fault that he's like this. I have to make allowances."

"Did you ever find out why he lost his wallet over in Southchurch?" said Eva. "That park where Mark found it is a rough part of town. Not Joe's kind of place."

"It isn't, I know. But Joe didn't tell me. He's a lot more secretive these days. But I think that's part of his being tired and moody – to do with this illness."

"So, has he ever been checked out by a doctor?" said Dan.

"No. He's really dead against that. His dad tried to force him to go once or twice, but he's so stubborn."

"Yeah. That figures too," said Dan.

The girl looked perplexed by Dan's words and Eva shot him a glance to warn him not to reveal any more.

"Joe's clothes-buying habit. Do you remember when that started?"

"Hmmmm," said the girl, thinking it over. "Two or three months ago, maybe more. He got really obsessed with it about six weeks back, and he's still hoarding them now."
"Maybe he lost his wallet when he was out buying clothes," said Dan.
"Maybe," said the girl, her eyes narrowing. "Wait. Do you think his moods and illness are connected to his clothes hoarding? Like a psychological thing. A physical manifestation of his mental health or something?"
"It's certainly possible," said Eva.
"It crossed my mind too," said Dan.
Eva took a breath before pushing on as far as she dared. "I was wondering something else." Georgie nodded for her to go on.
"You said Joe had resorted to paying for the clothes using some of his father's belongings…"
The girl looked suddenly strained. Her eyes darted to the stairwell and she licked her lips.
"Please don't say that too loudly," she said. "He'll only start again."
Eva nodded. "Have you ever thought about the burglary, Georgie? How it might be related?"
"To what?" said Georgie. She frowned as she read Eva's eyes closely. Eva said nothing more. She waited for the penny to drop.
"Please, you can't be suggesting that…"
"I'm not suggesting anything," said Eva. "It's just a question, that's all."

"A question about what?" The door creaked open and in walked Joe Clancy. The young man looked a good deal better than he had in the morning. Less pale, less peaky, but strain showed on his face, like he was working hard to hold himself together. The young man looked like he'd taken enough of his chosen poison to take the edge off, but also like it wasn't quite doing the job. He was eking out the last of what he had to stave off the coming crisis when it all dried up.

"Uh… they were just asking how long you've been feeling like this. You know, unwell."

"Were they now?" said Joe, shooting each of them a hard look before he calmed himself down again. "And what did you tell them, Georgie?"

Georgie suddenly looked under pressure. "I said a couple of months or more. You know, they wondered if it had anything to do with you buying all those clothes…" The girl spoke hesitantly before faltering altogether.

Joe Clancy's eyes flared. "That's none of their business."

"They only want to help you, Joe. I see that. They only want to help you get to the bottom of your problem. Like I do."

"That's not the kind of help I need. And it's not the kind of help anyone here asked for. If they're going to stick their noses into any other of my business without asking, maybe you should tell them to clear off." Joe cast a glance at Eva and Dan. "Have you even found a single piece of my father's collection yet?"

"Now hold on," said Dan. "You made it clear finding Renton was your particular priority. You didn't give a damn about your father's gold."

"Answer the question. Well, have you?" said Joe.

"No," said Eva.

"There you are then. Maybe they're not up to the task, Georgie. Perhaps we should tell him."

"Or maybe there's good reason we can't find those things. A reason you might know of," said Dan. Eva shot him another look of warning, Georgie followed her eyes, perplexed. The wind fell from from Joe's sails.

"No. I don't know any reason. In fact, I'd be very happy if you found them. Maybe happier than my old man. But If I had to choose one over the other, then I'd be happier if you found Carl... even if it meant everything else stayed lost."

Eva closed her eyes and took in a sharp breath, an involuntary gesture. So. Joe didn't know. And Eva felt he was sincere, not faking it. They'd pushed him to see where it would lead, and it had led them here. Joe didn't know Carl was gone for good.

"Then you haven't heard?" said Eva.

Joe Clancy shook his head, and a fresh line appeared in his forehead. "Heard what?"

Eva looked at Dan, but all he could do was nod. It was time to break the news.

"A body was found washed up on Southchurch beach, not far from where Norman Peters was found. A few hundred yards further on."

"A body?" said Joe. His eyes misted immediately. He shook his head.

"No. That can't be right. Carl is a good man, a godly man. There's no reason anyone would ever want to hurt him. He only ever sees the best in people. He only ever wants to help. I know I let him down, we argued, I just wanted to make it up to him!" The tears spilled down his face.

"Joe," said Eva. "I'm sorry. But it was Carl. His body was recognised by one of his Christian friends."

Georgie moved quickly to Joe's side and wrapped him in her arms. The boy seemed to hang there, as if Georgie was holding him up.

"But I don't get it," he whimpered. "Why?! First Norm, now this… both dead on the beach?!"

"Actually, we were hoping you might be able to give us some kind of insight there, Joe," said Eva.

"What? *Me?* Why?"

"Carl Renton's silver snuff tin. The Bible quote tin. We told you, Norman Peters had it. And you knew Norman Peters just like you knew Carl Renton. You were the only link between them we could find."

"You *seriously* think that I would have had anything to do with that? As if I would!" Hot tears of indignation coursed down the young man's face. "Carl looked after me. He was my friend! I let him down, but I would *never, ever* have deliberately hurt him."

"Maybe not deliberately, then," said Dan.

The words silenced the boy for a moment before his mouth cut loose again.

"You people! You call yourselves private investigators, but all you do is upset and blame the victims! You were supposed to help us!"

"Joe, come on. let's not pretend you're a saint here," said Dan.

"Not helpful," said Eva.

"I'm no saint, no, but I'm certainly no killer," said Joe. "I don't know who killed Norman Peters and I don't know why anyone would hurt Carl Renton. He treated me better than my father ever did."

"I think we have a reason why it might have happened," said Eva.

"Why?!" demanded the young man.

"Because of Carl's mission to find the people who were trafficking that awful Uber drug into the town. Because he was getting closer to the truth. But before we can say anymore, we're going to need to prove it."

The boy's eyes gleamed with anger and distress. "Then just prove it. Damn them. Find out who did it, get my father's gold back and then leave us alone."

"That's the thing, Joe. The trail's gone stone cold on your father's stolen gold," said Dan.

The boy looked at Dan. Dan held him in his gaze.

"I don't suppose you have any idea why?"

The silence lasted a little too long before Joe shook his head. "I'm sorry. No. I have no idea." Joe Clancy had every right to be upset, but Eva wondered if his sadness was connected to his father's treasures as well as his grief.

They heard the final growl of a car engine outside as it pulled up onto the driveway. The engine died and they looked out to find themselves face to face with Aaron Clancy through the windscreen of his Lexus. The man got out, looked at them through the glass, then walked slowly to the door. Eva wasn't relishing the thought of another dressing down for a total lack of progress. She was almost resigned to losing the case. The front door slammed.

"Back again, I see," said Clancy Senior, when he made it through the door.

"Yes," said Eva. "There are always more questions – and more developments to throw into the mix."

"Developments, yes," said Clancy. He cast the merest of looks at his son without seeming to notice his tear-filled eyes. "And here's a development for you. Councillor Audley, the man who first suggested that my Celtic torq was a part of the Saxon King's hoard, has finally intervened to make the police release it back to me. I'll finally get it back in a day or two. And I've got it in writing, so they can't wriggle out of it. So the question is, how are you getting on with finding the rest?"

Clancy's face dropped as soon as he'd spent a moment reading their faces.

"The trail's gone cold, I'm afraid," said Eva.

"Stone cold," said Dan. "The pawnbrokers and cheque cashing stores don't have it and the local black market is quiet about it."

"Of course they're quiet about it! We're talking about stolen goods for heaven's sake!"

Dan shook his head. "It's too quiet. My sources haven't heard any rumours, let alone seen anything. It's as if they vanished as soon as they were stolen."

"What? What good is that to me? That stuff is worth an absolute fortune, but to me it's priceless. I could never risk losing it under any circumstances. Surely if you work harder, speak to different people, you'll be able to find it? You can't just give up now, can you? What was the point in me hiring you?"

"Oh, we never give up, Mr Clancy. That's not our way," said Eva. "But we might have to take a more *unconventional* route to find it, than up to now."

"Unconventional?" said Clancy Senior. "I don't follow you at all."

"Carl Renton, Mr Clancy. Sadly, his body was found on the beach today. It had washed up on the tide."

Clancy shook his head. "What? That's terrible!"

"He was murdered, Mr Clancy. And that comes after Norman Peters was murdered in similar fashion just the other day."

"I'm afraid I don't understand. Not any of it."

"Neither do we," said Eva. "But we think it's possible that your stolen property could be related to these recent deaths."

"I don't see how. Can you explain?" said Clancy, looking perplexed.

Joe ran out of the room and flew up the stairs.

"And I think you're going to need to keep a closer eye on your son from now on, Mr Clancy," said Eva. "He needs you."

Clancy grimaced. "You can spare me any moralising lectures. I look after my son alright. You'd better just concentrate on finding my collection. I hired you because of a solid reputation. I'm a success in business because I can't abide failure. If you think you can't help me, you should quit the case now so I can find someone who can."

"I told you," said Eva, calmly. "We never give up. That's how we earned that solid reputation you mentioned."

Clancy shook his head and marched out of the room in disgust. Georgie offered Eva and Dan a meek look of apology and escorted them to the door. They said their goodbyes quietly and left.

"It's beginning to look like awkward cases are the new norm," said Eva.

"Never mind awkward, it's the unsolvable ones I don't like. You heard what that man said just now. He's already trying to wriggle out of paying the fee. That's what he means by us quitting. He doesn't want to pay."

"And like I said, we're not giving up," said Eva. "You saw Joe Clancy in there. You couldn't fake that reaction. When it comes to Carl Renton's death Joe Clancy is on the level. He had nothing to do with killing Renton or Norman Peters. And after that, I think we owe it to him to find out who did."

"We owe it to ourselves to get paid," said Dan.

"Don't worry. We're going to do that too. This case isn't getting away from us."

From the look in Eva's eyes, Dan could see that she meant every word.

Twenty

Sunday evening drinks usually sounded like a good idea after another day's work. And the day had certainly been hard enough. The night before had left them exhausted, and then there was Carl Renton's body on the beach. From there the day had become a barrage of frustration, from Hogarth to the Clancys. A drink in those circumstances would have always been wise, but tonight it was absolutely essential. The pub at Southend Central station had been used as a handover point for either stolen gold or illegal drugs. And with Hogarth refusing to act without any evidence, and Clancy putting them under more pressure than ever, Eva wanted to be sure about every aspect of the case. Joanne still believed the witnessed handover was about stolen gold. Dan was more inclined to think the handover was a part of a traditional drugs deal. The truth was either could have been right. By asking the landlord a few subtle questions, Eva hoped she would be able to decide which. But with Dan as a drinking partner, subtle was never guaranteed to last too long.

Dan ordered the drinks, and they sat at a table near the bar. A table just right for striking up a casual conversation with the bar staff. Five minutes after their first sip, the street entrance doors opened again, and another happy couple came in for an early evening drink. Mark and Joanne, as planned. They took another table nearer the door. The two couples dutifully ignored one another. When Joanne placed her order, Eva noticed the landlord gave her a lingering look. The big haggard man seemed to recognise her. Which probably wasn't hard because the pub was mostly empty.

"Not busy tonight then?" said Dan.

"See for yourself," said the barman curtly.

Dan raised an eyebrow. This guy was going to be hard work. He glanced towards Joanne at the other side of the pub, but she was busy talking to Mark. Putting on her act. Eva decided she was best for making the approach.

"It must be hard with the Last Post pub being so close," said Eva, nodding across the street in the general direction of the hangar-sized pub which stretched through an entire block, one street to another.

The man shrugged.

"It's not really competition though, is it? That's the cheap pub for the masses on giro day. This here is a train station pub. A watering hole for people on the move or nabbing a drink on the way home." The man looked at them like he didn't think they were either.

"I suppose," said Eva. "Which means you must see a lot of characters through here. All kinds of people."

The man nodded and put on a thin grin as he polished a pint pot.

"That's true. All kinds. Though I can't work out what some of 'em are about." He glanced towards Joanne just as she pretended to laugh at one of Mark's lame jokes.

"Keeps it interesting though," said Eva. "You must get a snapshot of people's lives in a train station. You see them as they are, what they're doing, what they're going through. Like that old black and white movie, *Strangers on a Train*."

"What?" said the barman. The man wasn't getting any easier.

"It's an old movie," said Eva, struggling. "About a love affair conducted on a train platform, in a station a bit like this."

The man snorted. "Yeah. I've seen a few affairs going on in my time. Not here mind. In my last boozer, up in Grays—"

Eva interrupted carefully, aiming to keep the man to the intended topic.

"In Grays? But come on. You must see some funny things here too. This is Southend, after all. Anything goes around here."

Dan gave her a look, like she was pushing too hard. Thankfully the guy seemed oblivious.

"A few things, maybe."

"Like what?"

"The oddballs. Nutters talking to themselves. And the gangs fresh off the train from London. Tooled-up teenagers looking for trouble with the locals. Oh, and the football hooligans too."

"Gangs?" said Dan.

"Yeah. Teen gangs coming to hit up the seaside for kicks."

Dan looked back at his beer. They weren't the type of gangs he was interested in.

"I bet you've seen it all happen," said Eva, "like a real-life thriller right in front of your face."

"Sometimes."

"Because people do all kinds of things in pubs, don't they? They arrange things. Make deals. Sell cars. Sell drugs, even…"

The man stopped towel-drying the glass in his hands. He froze and his eyes narrowed.

"And here…" Eva ploughed on, her heartbeat picking up. "…right next to the station too…"

She felt Dan freeze as the man looked her in the eye.

"What do you mean?" said the guy.

"Nothing," said Eva. "I only meant that your pub is right by the station. Some people must try some sort of dodgy dealing."

Eva tried to look neutral and natural, but she knew she'd pushed too hard and overplayed her hand. So she did what she could to rebalance the situation. She tried to look innocent, and when she felt embarrassed, she went with it. "I'm sorry, I didn't mean to offend, or imply—"
She kept her eyes on his.

"Yes, sorry, mister, no offence," said Dan. "This one's always being nosey, putting her foot in her mouth."

"Yeah?" said the man, looking unconvinced. "Well, just for the record – just in case anyone else tells you different… this pub is one hundred per cent clean. Because I'm clean. I don't tolerate drugs here. And I don't let any deals or anything go on in my pub. You know how? Because I can always tell if a punter is kosher or not. Always."

Dan nodded. "Good for you." He raised his glass and took a long sip.

"I think it's best if I leave you to enjoy your drinks, what do you say?"

"Sure," said Dan. He forced a smile, and Eva met the landlord's eyes a final time. And something passed between them. A hint of anger, and something else. Eva knew it was the truth the man didn't want them to know. It wasn't in his body language, only in the eyes, but Eva knew for sure. The barman was guilty. He knew every deal that went on under his roof, his jurisdiction, and in all likelihood he profited from every one of them. Five minutes later, they downed their drinks and left. Joanne and Mark were not long after them.

"Think he worked us out, don't you?" said Mark.

"It doesn't matter either way," said Eva. "What matters is that we've worked him out. He was in on that deal."

"Absolutely," said Joanne. "The tall, skinny man gave him what he called 'a drink'."

"A bung. A payoff for hosting the transaction," Dan explained.

"So, what was it? Drugs or the gold?" said Joanne.

"It was drugs," said Eva. "That man's face changed the moment I mentioned drugs."

"Then where has Clancy's gold gone?" said Joanne.

Eva shook her head. "That's not in our hands. All we can do is keep plugging away. If we can just unwind this grisly little mess, maybe we'll find the gold to boot."

"And if we don't?" said Dan.

"Then we'll still have done the right thing. Clancy's gold is mere vanity. This Uber business is killing people."

"But Clancy's vanity is paying our bills, Eva. We can plug away all we like but have to find that gold too."

They walked on together a way.

"Now we know the Ubers are at the heart of this," said Eva, "I think we should use that knowledge to force a mistake from our friends Pink and Grace."

"A mistake? How do you mean?" said Dan.

"They must think they're in the clear. DI Hogarth took them at their word. Hopefully that means they're feeling nice and safe and complacent. I think it's time to rattle their cages to see what falls out."

"Rattling cages is fine with me. How do you want to play it?" said Dan.

"What if each man thought the other had sold him out?"

"Sold him out how?" said Dan.

"We can work on that," said Eva.

Dan thought about it before a thin smile appeared on his face. "Sounds like a plan."

"I'll go and see Clive Grace," said Eva. "That man's so slippery I think he's good and ripe for tripping himself up."

"Watch yourself. You know he's armed."

"I think I know how to play him," said Eva.

"If you're sure, fine. Then I'll see if I can make Tommy Pink squirm."

Twenty-one

Monday. 8am. Basildon.
The market was busy with the noise and banter of the traders gearing up for another day's trade. The jokes were coarse, and the smell of cheap coffee and bacon butties filled the air along with the rumble of the buses departing the Eastgate shopping centre. Eva and Dan headed across the street towards the market, a fresh buzz of adrenaline fast-flowing through their veins. Sleep had repaired most of the previous day's damage. Hogarth's intransigence was still a sore point, and the issue of the Lauren case was a worry for another day.
"You see them?" said Dan. They waited for the traffic lights to turn to red allowing them to cross the street. The market was already serving the first keen shoppers. But most of the traders were out of sight, busy setting up their stalls.
"Not yet. We'll have to track around the stalls, find them, and pick our moment," said Eva.
"Then we'd better stay unseen until we start. They won't forget your face too easy," said Dan.
"I'll take that as a compliment," said Eva.
They walked the lines of metal-framed market stalls side by side. Stalls selling mobile phone cases, stalls selling magazines ranging from *The Lady* and *People's Friend* all the way to the top shelf material. They glanced at the clothing stalls as they passed.
"Norman Peters would have been here a week or two back," said Eva.
"But now we know clothing sales was probably only his official means of income."

As they looked around they recognised the lithe figure of Clive Grace crossing between the lanes, dead ahead. The man whistled as he walked, pushing an empty sack trolley ahead of him. He disappeared from view.

"He's headed for the car park," said Eva.

"That should buy you some time. I'll see if I can find Pink."

"Good luck," said Eva. "Just make sure he believes you."

Dan nodded. They gave each other looks of encouragement and set off on their separate ways. Eva moved down a line of street food sellers and sweet stalls until she stepped out into a parking area reserved for deliveries and drop-offs. There were cars, vans and lorries of all kinds parked around, their doors open, and hazard lights on. The vehicles were still being unloaded, but most of the unloading was done, and the majority of traders were back at their stalls. Dead ahead, leaning on his sack trolley, was Clive Grace. The man wasn't wasting any energy. He was rolling a cigarette. He put the roll-up in his mouth and lit up before he noticed Eva approaching.

"Mr Grace," said Eva.

Grace looked at her. He looked groggy and slow and it took him a moment to recognise her.

"You? You were at the beach," he said.

"Yes, That's right. That awful business when Mr Renton's body got washed up on the beach. So tragic, really. From what I've heard, he was a very good man. There are so few of those around."

Clive Grace sucked on his cigarette and narrowed his eyes.

"What do you want, lady? I'm busy."

"I want to talk to you about your little sideline."

"Sideline?" said Grace, his eyes flashing.

"Yes. You know the one. It's at risk, Mr Grace."

Grace's eyes flickered with something bright and unreadable. He tried to put on a smile, but it didn't wash, and he seemed to know it. So he dropped it and gripped the handle of his sack trolley pushing it towards Eva so she was forced to step aside. "I don't know what you're talking about. I thought Tommy put you in your place back on Southend seafront."

"Tommy Pink put on a front for prying eyes, yes," said Eva. "But what he says in public – for show – and what he says in private are two very different things"

"Said in private? What are you on about?" said Grace. He turned and shot her a vindictive look.

Eva nodded slowly. "I spoke to you on the beach just after Renton's body washed in. But you were also interviewed by the police."

"You're having a laugh. Tommy said that interview wasn't a problem. Said it went sweet as a nut."

"Again, what Tommy Pink says to you and says to police are two different things. Makes you wonder why, doesn't it?"

"Why would I believe a single word you say? I don't even know who you are. A busy body. A dumb troublemaker, like Carl Renton, no doubt. Just like him, you should mind your own bloody business."

"And is that the same warning you gave to Carl Renton when he got close to disturbing your little sideline?"

Grace's face twisted with hate and defiance. "I don't know what you're talking about."

"Really? Because Tommy does. He knew enough to tell my police colleagues all about it."

"Bullshit," said Grace, spittle flying from his thin mouth. He took an aggressive step into Eva's space. Eva held her ground.

"I wouldn't try anything if I were you. I work closely with Detective Inspector Hogarth. If you threaten me, or get violent, your situation just gets worse and worse."

She saw Grace had to work hard to hold himself back. "Who are you?"

"Don't you remember? My, my, Mr Grace. It must be all that night work schedule addling your brain. Tommy told us about that too. Maybe you should stop the moonlighting and get some sleep, Mr Grace. My name is Eva Roberts and I'm a private detective."

Grace's face tensed. "You better spit it out. It's all lies, but I may as well hear it anyway."

"Yes, you should," said Eva. "Tommy's the one with the brains, isn't he? He's the organ grinder, and you're just the monkey. Which is why Tommy agreed to do a deal as soon as he saw the way the wind was blowing. This Uber business has to end soon, Mr Grace. The press are all over it. Which means the police have to be all over it too. Things are about to come to a head, Mr Grace. And that means you boys would be the first to go down. The police will make examples of you, because their backs will be to the wall. Tommy was the smart one. He knew that. Which is why he was prepared to agree terms. Damage limitation and all that. I'm sorry to say you were a part of that damage limitation, Mr Grace. You're going to be the fall guy for the whole rotten thing."

The man gnashed his teeth at Eva. "Lies! All of it, fabricated!"

"Is it? Then how would I know about your little night operation at the marine centre. How else would I know that you wait on the jetty, while Tommy rides in with the goods on his jet ski and you take it from him."

Grace narrowed his eyes. He smacked his lips as he searched for the right words but couldn't find them. "It's not true."
"But it is, though, isn't it?" Eva took a gamble. "And Norman Peters used to help you too… until you fell out with him."
Grace narrowed his eyes further still and shook his head. "What?"
"Tommy's the smart one, remember. That's why this is happening, Clive. Tommy's taken action to keep himself on top. Tommy Pink knew those murders were about to cause your sideline even more problems. Which is why he's so content to let you take the blame."
"What?"
"Mr Grace. Do you think Tommy Pink would ever want to go down for murder? For life? Not him."
"We didn't kill anyone. Not him and not me."
"Such a shame that he's left you in the frame then, isn't it?"
"If I killed that bloody Bible-basher, why was Tommy the one seen arguing tooth and nail with that Renton man, eh? You tell me!"
"Funny," said Eva. "Tommy said that argument was just a little debate."
"Yeah. Well Tommy can say what he likes…"
"Yes he can, Mr Grace. Now if I were you, I'd think about getting your story in first. Before the noose gets any tighter."
Grace lurched towards her, seething. She faced the man and stared hard and evenly into the man's vicious little eyes.

"Now, now, Mr Grace. You've got your future to consider. It's in your hands right now." Eva waited a long moment, before she turned away and left the man seething. Eva walked away and a thin smile slowly appeared on her lips. Hogarth would never approve. But she hoped the end would justify the means.

***

"Tommy Pink," said Dan.
The stocky market trader was busy laying out his stall. It looked good, as in ten times better than most of the neighbouring stalls. There were clothes which looked like real Armani and there were sunglasses which looked like Police and Ray Ban and there were handbags which looked like Mulberry. But the prices said they weren't.
Pink turned around from the stall with its nifty layout putting the others to shame. He clapped his hands. "Yes, my friend. What can I get you?"
"I was just admiring the stock. Surely this can't be genuine?" Dan prodded the winged Armani badge on the back of a pair of blue jeans.
"Oh yeah. This is all genuine. I mean, it's not genuine Armani. Look a bit closer. Those are Arvani jeans. See? It's there on the belt label. You see it? As good as Armani, but it's Arvani. And that bag is a Marlwood bag. No, the names aren't the same but the quality is just as good. You want a brand name, then the high street can charge you ten times as much. With me you can look good and save your money."

He looked Dan up and down and thought for a moment before he said something else: "Or, if you really want to wear the right label, I might be able to do something for you later. After hours."

"Really?"

"Yeah. I can get stuff which looks as good, if not better, than the real deal. They smell real. They look real. They have the right names on them, the right badges. If you want that, it'll cost a little more. But you get to look the part, one hundred per cent."

"After hours?" said Dan.

"Yeah," said Pink. He looked at Dan and his face pinched into a frown.

"How's that possible?" said Dan. "Because I thought you were already pretty busy after hours."

Pink's frown deepened. He shook his head and turned away. "Friend, I'm too busy to piss around having my time wasted by a joker. I've got a business to run. Now, if you're looking to try and shake me down for something, please, don't even bother. I'm not easily intimidated, and you'll definitely regret it."

Pink ignored Dan and began piling up pairs of blue jeans from a box.

"You're already giving people a lot of regret, Mr Pink. You're making lives hard, and those are just the lucky ones. Let's talk about Ubers. Those Ubers you're shipping in are killing people left right and centre. And then there's Norman Peters. Dead as a doornail. Nasty business. Then Carl Renton, bludgeoned and hacked to death. He fared worse than Peters. Those mysterious deaths happened right beside the very place where you bring those Ubers in on your old Waverunner jet ski."

Tommy Pink dropped the pair of jeans he was holding. He turned slowly and looked at every face around him. He nodded at a lady shopper eyeing his rack of sunglasses. The nearby market men were all busy. Oblivious. And then he met Dan's eyes.

"Whatever you think you know, friend, you're wrong. *Dead wrong*. And you should know it's very dangerous to go throwing around allegations like that. I'm no killer. I didn't want Little Norm dead. I liked the silly bugger. And Carl Renton? I wouldn't kill him. I wouldn't kill anyone…"

"Really. That's not the impression your chum Clive gave to the police."

"What?"

"Your friend. Good old reliable Mr Grace. He told the police all about your little night operation at the marine centre. He told them every detail, right down to the type of jet ski you ride. About how you had it painted black for the night runs. How you collect those Ubers in those rucksacks, and hand them over at the jetty, smooth and easy. But that wasn't all he told them. He told them about Norman Peters. Explained why Norman had those pills in his pocket when he died. Why there was a package of Ubers taped inside the hull of the boat where his body was found. Grace even told them why Norman had Carl Renton's silver snuff tin in his pocket too…"

Dan watched Pink's eyes open wide. The man snatched in a deep breath and shook his head. Dan carried right on talking.

"Grace was only too happy to let you carry the can so long as he didn't get tarred with the same brush. Acting as an accessory to a drug trafficking business, and being a cold blooded murderer are two very different things. Or at least Grace was prepared to take the gamble that the court would see it that way. But that little gamble meant he had to hang you out to dry."

Pink's face flushed dark red. "Then why am I still out here, working? Why did the police let me go?"

Dan took a moment to think of an answer but played it like he was just being dramatic.

"Because they think they can get more from you yet. You're going to hang yourself out to dry."

"As if Clive would tell them that. He'd ruin his own life. And as if you'd even tell me this. Who are you? What do you want?"

"I'm a just concerned citizen with a few special contacts, Mr Pink. I don't like what you do. I don't like what you've done or who you represent. And now you're going to get what's coming to you. I just wanted to see your face when you found out. I guess I just couldn't resist."

Pink's face flashed with anger as he leapt past his stall almost knocking a rack of sunglasses onto the floor. He tried to grab Dan's jacket, but Dan flicked his hand away and took one step back.

"Now you listen to me, you son of a bitch…" said Pink, under his breath. "No matter what you think you know…"

"Tommy. As you can see, your friend Grace told the police an awful lot. What are the odds he gets a slap on the wrist and you go down hard?"

Pink growled and shook his head. "I didn't kill anyone."

Dan swiped his hands away and shoved the man back onto his stall.

"No, I forgot. You're a total saint, Tommy. But if I were you, just in case, I'd think of selling my jet ski so I could afford a decent solicitor. But then again, I reckon you might have a fair old stash put away already. All those Ubers must have been good to you, right? But not anymore, Tommy. Not anymore."

Dan picked up a pair of Arvani jeans and hurled them at Pink. They landed against the man's chest. He held them against his body as he watched Dan walk away. Around them, a few market traders and customers looked on. Job done.

"How did it go?" said Eva. Dan had arrived at the brown glass wall which marked the side entrance of the Eastgate shopping centre. He'd found Eva clutching two coffees. She handed him a cup and tried to read his face.

"About as well as I could have hoped," said Dan. "But I don't think I've made any new best friends. You?"

"The same. I think Mr Grace would like to have throttled me, or worse, until I reminded him of the extra jail time involved. So we did it. We've lit the blue touchpaper. I think it's time to stand back and see what happens."

"Better stay close. The mood Pink was in, I don't think it'll take long," said Dan. They sipped their coffees and wandered in the busy town centre sunshine, milling around the bus depot where the characters of Basildon mooched, waited and chatted. As soon as they'd finished their coffees they meandered slowly back towards the market square where, as they reached the edge of the market, a loud voice cut across the rest of the market noise. An angry shout, something like a grunt. Eva and Dan looked at one another. "It's happening," said Dan. "Come on." He led the way, jogging across the street into the market stalls. Eva followed. The noise got louder as they made it through the market lanes to the car park where the delivery vans and lorries were parked. But the source of the commotion was still hidden from view. Dan pointed to the boxy, ugly, two-storey pub that sat by itself on the edge of the market. The pub was called The Target. A bad name for a pub in a rough area. It seemed to be the source of the commotion.

"It's coming from around there," said Dan. They hurried on towards the pub, rounding the entire building until they reached a rough concrete storage area at the side, marked off by a tall grey wooden gate. The gate was open. Dan poked his head around the corner, and looking past a stack of metal beer kegs, he saw Pink slamming Grace back against the wall. "This is your evidence. We have to record this," said Dan in a whisper..

Eva showed him her mobile phone, already in hand. She thumbed the voice memo app and tapped the red button to start recording. They moved to the corner of the wall and aimed the phone as close as they dared.

"What the hell were you thinking?" roared Tommy Pink. A few passers-by lingered near the gate and tried to get a view into the yard before they went on their way. Dan waved them on. "You snitched on me. You snitched on us all. And that's hardly the worst of it!"

"Snitched!" roared Grace, ready to have his say, but Tommy Pink was too incensed to listen. He clattered the taller man back against the wall and grabbed Grace's jaw between his fingers..

"You bastard. How long were you creaming pills off the top? Eh? How long? You and Norm jeopardised the whole operation, and now you want to pin it on me. They found the merchandise in his pocket! There was a batch of them hidden in that boat!"

"No there wasn't!" said Grace. "I made sure there wasn't. I found it! I didn't stash it there, Norman did. He double-crossed both of us!"

"You told the cops about the whole operation right down to my bloody jet ski. As if I could believe a word you told me!"

"You put me in the frame!" said Grace. "You're the one who sold us out!"

"Don't you dare try and pin this on me. How long had you been robbing me, the pair of you?!"

"What? Come on, Tommy! There was more than enough to go around. You must have been doing the same, making some money on the side. I did a bit, but Norm screwed the both of us."

"You stupid bastard. It all had to be accounted for. I never took a bean!"

"But it was okay, Tommy, until Norman started getting greedy. I knew he was up to something. He turned cagey on me, acted afraid. When I saw what he was up to, I knew I had to do something to stop him. Tommy. I only tried to protect you…"

"You killed Norm? For me? No way – you did it for yourself because you were going to get found out! You killed him to save yourself. Scum!" Dan leaned around the corner to watch the two men struggling and trading blows. Pink was stocky and strong, but Grace was wiry and fast. The men looked evenly matched. "I think we've got enough," Eva said and stopped the recording.

"Suits me," said Dan. He waited a moment more, letting the two men sap each other's strength before he threw the gate open and waded in. Dan ran into the yard. He grabbed Grace and pulled him off of Pink. Both men's faces were bleeding but they were still savage and angry, like fighting dogs in the middle of a bloody frenzy. Dan hurled Grace back before he could swing again. Pink came at Dan instead so Dan let loose a couple of short, neat punches to the man's jaw. Tommy staggered back. The shock snapped him out of it.

"That's enough!" said Dan. "The show's over."

Tommy Pink tried to break past Dan towards the gate. Eva got ready to block him, but in the end it wasn't necessary. As Pink went past Dan, he reached out, and shoved him hard against the stack of metal kegs. They clattered to the ground, rolling in all directions, with Tommy Pink sprawled groaning on top of them. They had Pink and Grace bang to rights. And yet the show wasn't over. Not by a long chalk.

Twenty-two

Fifteen minutes after the skirmish behind The Target had all but finished, a dark Toyota saloon pulled to a halt beside the old wooden gate of the pub with a BMW estate police squad car drawing up behind it. Detective Inspector Hogarth stepped out of the saloon and dragged a hand through his unkempt hair. The man looked as irritated as ever, and yet they had done much of his work for him. Eva suspected the moody look was because they had once again proved him wrong. They had yet to share their recording with him, but the look in his eyes said he knew – the PIs had beaten him to it. The only thing they didn't have was the means. The weapon. Nor did they have the confession or the fingerprints. But Eva hoped those things would come soon enough. But there was one other minor comfort for the DI – and Eva knew he would soon remind her – their client's gold was still missing. In Pink and Grace's recorded argument there had been no discussion of any gold or any theft – only of murders, betrayal and treachery. Eva was almost ready to admit defeat. They weren't going to get their fee. But even if they didn't get paid, at least justice would have been done.
"Here you go, they're all yours," said Dan as he pushed Clive Grace staggering towards Hogarth. Hogarth looked at the tall man like he was biblically unclean, stepping aside as Grace came his way, only to palm the man in the direction of his uniformed colleague – the short young constable they'd seen on the beach alongside one of the older uniforms. The young constable seized his man, but Grace looked unwilling to go quietly, and the older PC was forced to get involved.

"Now, now," said Hogarth. "You'll only be making things worse for yourself, Clive."

"Worse?" hissed Grace, with gore still trailing down to his mouth from his nose. "I don't see how it could get any worse than this."

"That all depends on how cooperative you are," said Hogarth. As Grace was shoved down into the back of a police car, Hogarth turned to Dan.

"I see you've been looking after them for me," he said. "I'm sure all injuries there were only caused in self-defence."

"They beat each other senseless," said Dan. "I'm not a thug, Inspector,"

"I'll take your word for it," said Hogarth.

"And you should," said Eva. "These men attacked Dan after we confronted them about what they've been doing. And here's your evidence."

"Evidence?"

"We've got them admitting everything, including who was to blame. The voice memo app on my phone came in very handy. They were discussing a few things I think you'd like to hear."

Hogarth's eyes narrowed. "Taking the law into your own hands again. You should apply for a job on the force, Miss Roberts." Eva handed him her phone, with the voice memo app ready to play.

"No thanks, Inspector. I'm not really one for taking orders," said Eva.

"So I've noticed. But at least you seem to have *some* respect for the law. Unlike others I could mention," said Hogarth.

Dan bristled and shook his head but let the comment pass as Hogarth pressed play on the device. Tommy Pink stood in the back of the yard, the cut above his eyebrow still leaking, his face stark with shock. The man looked like he wanted to throw up. He listened to the recording along with Hogarth, unable to back away, unable to escape being damned by his own words. The horror on his face only deepened. Pink looked away.

"The way you talked on that recording, Tommy, makes it sound like you think you're innocent." Hogarth clicked off the sound file. Pink could barely meet his eyes. "You're not innocent. You're a dirty, scumbag drug trafficker. You deal in death, Tommy. I'll admit it. You had me fooled. But if it means one less scoundrel on the street, I suppose I'll just have to take that on the chin."

Pink looked up and shook his head. "Look. I'm no victim. But I'm no killer either. And I'm not taking the rap for a crime I haven't done – I know what he told you about me killing those men, but it's lies. All of it."

"What he told me…?" said Hogarth. He paused, his mind already ticking. When he shot Eva and Dan a look, their eyes were loaded with meaning. Hogarth's eyes narrowed in response, and his mouth firmed up into a downturned line. But he swallowed and left his questions unspoken.

"I mean it," said Pink. "I didn't kill Norman Peters."

"Save it for the station," said Hogarth. "I know an old-fashioned barrow boy like you loves the sound of your own voice, but Basildon doesn't need to hear it."

"Jordan," said Hogarth. He gave the young officer a nod, and the man started towards Pink. Pink slunk towards the back wall.

"No, you've got to hear me out. Grace would sell out anyone to stay out of trouble. If I'd known that I'd have never worked with the man."

"You know what they say, Tommy," said Hogarth. "Birds of a feather flock together."

Pink held up a palm to keep the PC at bay.

"Listen!" said Pink.

"We hear what you're saying, Mr Pink," said Eva. "We hear what you're not saying too. You didn't mention Carl Renton. And for you, Renton's death remains a big problem if you haven't got anyone else to blame."

Hogarth's eyes narrowed. PC Jordan held back. He stuffed his hands in his pockets and waited for Pink to speak. Pink was quiet and solemn. Eva watched Hogarth as he studied the crook in detail, right down to the way Pink scratched his temple.

"I'm not guilty," said Pink, quietly.

"Of what?" snapped Hogarth. "Of killing Peters? Or of killing Carl Renton?"

"Those murders, either of them," said Pink. "I'm not guilty on all counts.

"So you say," said Dan.

"No!" roared Pink. He turned to Dan, shaking with anger and indignation. "No matter what Grace told you… I didn't do it."

Hogarth looked at Dan.

"Simple as that," said Pink. "I'm no killer. I didn't kill Renton, but it still didn't make any sense him shouting at me about Ubers when he's indulging addicts in his houses and giving money to other kids to help them get high."

"What?" said Hogarth, shaking his head in disbelief.

"Yeah, see. You didn't know. The gossip I heard was that Carl Renton was indulging some rich kids, letting them take Ubers. He was a hypocrite, like the rest of them."

Eva and Dan shared a look. They were thinking the same thing.

"That rumour, Tommy. Where did you hear it?" said Eva.

"I don't know. It's common knowledge, ain't it?"

"No, it isn't," said Eva. "Where did you hear it?"

Pink shrugged.

"He made it up," said Hogarth. "Like he's been making a lot of things up, eh, Tommy?"

"No… Norm told me about that. I thought everyone knew."

Eva's eyes lingered on Pink. She watched his eyes glaze over in regret and resignation.

PC Jordan started to make his approach towards Pink once more.

"You say Clive Grace killed Norman Peters…" said Eva.

"You heard him. You've got it on that recording."

"But neither of you mentioned Carl Renton. His murder is hanging over your head, Tommy. You'd better think about that."

"No, I told you that I didn't kill the man. Think about it. If Clive was capable of killing poor little Norm then he must have killed Renton too. His head was battered like Norm's was. Only difference was it looked like someone had taken a pickaxe to his guts. If I ever had to kill a man, I certainly wouldn't ever do it like that."

Jordan's eyes flicked to Hogarth for the order. Hogarth gave the slightest shake of his head, barely perceptible. They were hearing something important. Something which might make a conviction stick. "How do you know so much about Carl Renton's body, Tommy?" said Hogarth.

"If I tell you, I'm screwed, aren't I?" Pink looked at Hogarth, and then Eva and Dan.

"If you don't tell us, you're still screwed," said Hogarth. "We'll still have you for drug trafficking and probably murder too. Unless that is, you tell us otherwise."

Pink knitted his eyes together before he started to speak. The words came out with a stammer at first, but they soon picked up momentum.

"It was only a few days back. Friday morning. Normski was still alive and well. After a shipment comes in, we haul it in, bring it into the jetty, and then each go our separate ways. Fast. It has to be like clockwork so we never got seen. It was always pitch black, and I was well aware that Norman was a liability sometimes. He was a clutz and he was forgetful. So most mornings after a drop-off I'd go back and check over at the marine centre for five minutes, just to see if any telltale signs had been left behind."

"You went to check that you'd left no evidence," said Hogarth.

"If you like," said Pink, with a shrug. "That morning Norm was there and Clive was there too, which was very handy. It was so early that the street cleaners hadn't made it down yet. And that's when we saw the body. Right there…" Pink paused and took a breath. "We didn't kill Renton. All we did was find him. I just about kept myself from throwing up. I knew it was Carl Renton from the way he always dressed. Checked shirts tucked over his big belly into a pair of old-school straight blue jeans. And soon as I saw him I knew we were in real trouble. If the old bill got scent of that man being killed right by our landing spot – I knew it would bring the heat, they'd shut down the jetty, and probably our operation too. But I never killed the man. Why should we have gone down for that?!"

"The blood patch on the beach?" said Dan.

"Yeah. There was plenty of blood on the beach. We couldn't cover all of it, but we did our best and hoped the rain would wash the rest away. Then I went to get some ropes from my van. I gave the boys the ropes and told them to tie up the body while I checked the jetty for any other problems. By the time I got back, the body was tied good and proper. Norm tied a couple of broken bits of concrete to his waist, and I dragged him out to the water on my jet ski as far as I dare. I let him sink. I didn't do it. All I did was try to clean up what some other psycho left behind."

"What a noble man you are, Tommy," said Hogarth. "Remind me to nominate you for a CBE in the New Year's Honours list. Jordan."

PC Jordan stepped in and took Pink's arm. This time he didn't fight or seek more time. He let Jordan cuff him without complaint.

PC Jordan led Tommy Pink away to one of the police cars at the edge of The Target pub.

"Who did it then, Tommy?" called Dan. "Who killed Carl Renton? And what happened to the murder weapon?"

"Grace must have done it. As for the weapon, I've no idea. Ask him."

They opened the door and started to stuff Pink in right alongside Clive Grace.

Eva had more questions. They were taking the man away too soon for her liking.

Hogarth watched Eva as she headed past him towards the police estate car. "He killed Renton too," muttered Hogarth. "He's blaming Grace, but without a murder weapon or a witness, they can blame each other until the cows come home…"

Hogarth had a point, but Eva had another question in mind. "And what about the gold, Mr Pink. What about the missing gold?"

The man's eyes stayed neutral. In the shadows of the car Clive Grace remained silent.

"What?"

"Stolen gold was found near the marine centre where you were smuggling. It can't be a coincidence. What do you know about it?"

Jordan pushed Pink down into the backseat. He used up his last moment of freedom with a protest of defence.

"I'm just a humble market trader," said Pink.

"And a drug trafficker," said Hogarth. "Don't forget that too."

"But that gold had nothing to do with me. Never did."

Hogarth moved to the car and shut the car door to end the alfresco interrogation.

"Are we done, Miss Roberts?" said Hogarth. "Or would you like me to pass notes through the car window?"

"No. I think we're done," said Eva. "Though I have got one more question you might want to ask them."

Hogarth sighed.

"Pink and Grace conducted another smuggling operation last night, right under the nose of your PCs at the marine centre," said Eva.

Hogarth's eyes turned fiery. "What?"

"Someone who looked a lot like Clive Grace was sent to cause a distraction on the beach to keep your officers busy while the drop-off was made. You might want to ask them about him."

Dan nodded. "I think he could be a guy from one of Renton's rehab houses."

"Probably the same guy who gave The Record the story about Carl going missing in the first place," said Eva.

"I'll add that to my to-do list, shall I?" said Hogarth.

"It might prove worth it," said Eva.

"Your little recording," said Hogarth.

"I'll email you a copy within the hour," said Eva.

Hogarth nodded. The fire in his eyes dulled a little and as he headed back to his car, something in Hogarth's manner transmitted more than a hint of gratitude, but Dan wasn't subtle enough to pick up on it.

"Stay out of trouble, if you can that is," said Hogarth as he opened his car door. "You'd better get hunting for lost gold."

Hogarth shot one last nod and near-smile Eva's way before he turned and climbed into his car.

"He's right. We still haven't got a clue where that gold has gone," said Dan. The cops started their engines and reversed out onto the street and turned back for Southend.

"Yes. I know we've been a little distracted by the small detail of two murders, but even so we should have found something by now."

"You'd think so. But none of those men were thieves. Drug dealers and killers, but not thieves."

"Not quite, Dan. Norman Peters *was* a thief. He must have been. He took that silver snuff case from a dead man's pocket – that was his opportunity. If we believe Tommy Pink about discovering Carl Renton's body then that's the only way he could have gotten it."

"Unless Peters and Grace killed him and pretended they didn't for Pink's benefit. He could have taken it then."

Eva shook her head. "No. If that was true then why didn't they dispose of the body earlier?"

"If they didn't do it why dispose of the body at all?"

"Pink told us that. That body was going to destroy their business, and he would have been in the frame. He'd been seen arguing with the man and he knew it. They had no good reason to leave their murder victim lying on the beach. Pink was telling the truth."

"Which leaves us where? Our only thief is dead. We haven't found Clancy's gold. And if we believe Pink's story there's still a killer on the loose, and no evidence to find the culprit."

Eva looked up at the sky for relief from the oppressive concrete yard.

"Norman Peters isn't our only thief, Dan."

Dan's brow dipped over his dark eyes.

"Joe Clancy? But he only ever stole to feed his addiction and his dealer is dead and gone. Georgie already accounted for the stolen items he used as payment. It was mostly home equipment."

"But not all of it. And we only know about the stuff Joe was willing to tell her about."

"We've been through this. The burglary. That happened when Georgie and Joe were busy upstairs."

"Again, we only know Joe's version. Georgie's version of events is a grey area, Dan."

"No. Joe can't have stolen all that stuff himself. Giving that much gold to a two-bit drug dealer for some Ubers would have been complete overkill. It doesn't make sense. It'd be like paying a million for a fifteen-year-old Ford Fiesta. Joe Clancy is a teenage junkie, but he isn't that stupid."

"We just have to look again. We're not seeing the whole picture when it comes to Joe Clancy."

"More importantly, we're not seeing who killed Carl Renton."

"Then we're coming full circle," said Eva. "But at least the circle is closing."

"But I'd still like this circle to pay," said Dan.

"I'm still working on that," said Eva.

Twenty-three

Elsewhere. The same day.

Something was going on with her. Jamie Blane couldn't tell what it was, not yet, but whatever it was, he knew it wasn't good. None of her secrets were ever good. He had realised something was wrong when she had started smiling again. Smiling. Lauren hadn't smiled at him in that old way for weeks. Months even. But there it was again, that luscious bright smile. The one that used to make him pinch himself. After the agony of losing his wife, Jamie had doubted he would ever be happy again. The job had never ever been enough. But then Lauren turned up in his life, in his office, bringing in cash, bringing in light, and eventually passion. It felt like he'd stumbled into loving her. And not too long after the tragedy, she'd moved in. He wanted her to move in. Needed her to. The number one asset in his South East recruitment office had become the number one all-rounder in his whole life. And for a while it seemed like life wasn't just about work and grief anymore. There was love again and warm nights. But that sweet phase didn't last long.

Jamie couldn't begin to identify exactly when it started to fall apart… but there were two things he knew well. One, he had gotten together with Lauren far too soon. Lust had hoodwinked him too early for him to deal with his grief. And two, Lauren really wasn't the delight he thought she was. No one could be angelic forever. The hard facts of life and routine eventually stripped all illusions away until a lover saw the other person as they really were. Sometimes a man would still love that person all the more. And sometimes, he would only see the absence of what he had thought they were, left with something else in its place.

She was talking to him. She was talking to him but Jamie wasn't listening because he knew it was all lies. But he forced himself to tune in to her words, so he could go through the motions at least as much as she had. She smiled at him again.

"I think I'll go and get a shower. If you don't mind."

"Why would I mind?" he said.

A shower, in the day time, after spending time out for lunch. There was wine on her breath. She'd been out for three hours. Plenty of time to jump into bed and do whatever it was she liked these days.

Jamie Blane knew she also wanted that shower to avoid spending time in his presence. The feeling was mutual, but he didn't like it anyway. She wanted secrets and she wanted control? It wasn't going to happen like that. Blane looked out of their penthouse apartment bedroom window, down at the park below, at the dots walking their dogs, and the hazy blue summer sky. He sipped on a cold bottle of beer and listened to the sound of his lover humming as she slipped out of her clothes, as she switched on the shower and started the hiss of hot rushing water. Her idle humming brought a surge of anger. That damn smile, he thought. Those eyes. "What is it this time?" he muttered. He sipped again before slamming his beer on the table. His temples were tight and his head ached. The office was doing well enough without her. The business was rolling in. Life wasn't perfect. It never was. But none of his problems were insurmountable. In fact Jamie had no real problems apart from the one he was living with. His eyes flicked from the window. He found her mobile phone on the side table beside where she'd dumped her handbag. He licked his lips and then, listening to the running water, made his move. He snatched up her handbag first. He popped the clasp and peered inside, into a tiny world of screwed-up tissues, lipsticks, eyeliners, a purse, a mess of keys, chewing gum and other junk. He noted there were no condoms. Maybe they had got past safe sex already, damn them. But there were no scribbled notes of phone numbers or men's names. But then she knew better than that, didn't she? Blane hissed and dumped the bag on the table. The water was still running in the bathroom but the humming had stopped. Blane paid no attention either way. He picked up Lauren's mobile, and wondered if the tricky bitch had changed her pin-code yet again. He dialled the last one he remembered and was surprised to find that it still worked. The home screen opened on all the usual icons. Messages, emails, web browser, WhatsApp. The whole damn library of a modern person's life. It was almost too much for him to bear, but he decided to check it anyway. Lauren didn't give him any choice, did she? WhatsApp was empty but for the boring work groups he was already a part of – chasing the office boys and girls to ever higher numbers, motivating them and spying on them for the good of all concerned. He scrolled down and found nothing more. The water kept running next door. Facebook. No joy there. She knew he had her under watch and had taken measures accordingly. She kept it clean and safe and boring and fake. He didn't even bother with it. He tried the emails, but they were all work and no play. Lauren and her fake smile. It seemed she was getting very good at this stuff...

But there were always the messages. The phone calls too. He bit his lip with the thrill of the hunt. If he had been listening carefully, he would have heard the change of movement in the bathroom. He would have heard the feet on tiles. The water running, but the water not landing on anyone in the shower, just splashing the tiles like heavy rain. But Jamie was caught up in his own game of hide and seek. Lauren was hiding and he was seeking, and he couldn't wait to find her. The phone calls.

"What?" he said, out loud. He found no less than seven calls to a number with no name assigned to it. Seven calls in a three-day period. And a few of those calls had been returned. He dug a little deeper into the detail. Some of the calls had lasted less than a minute. A couple much longer. His eyes narrowed and he wondered. Calls like that, quick calls, drop calls, calls to arrange meetings, calls to escape detection. Blane ground his teeth and swiped the phone and tapped the messages app. There. He found the very same number had been used for messaging, but he saw no messages. Instead he found a column of blank messages. Which didn't make sense at first, until he realised what it meant. Lauren had deleted the messages. Every single sordid one.
"Bitch…" he whispered.
But he still had that number, didn't he? He pressed the number to dial it. At the other end the phone started ringing. It rang no more than four times before the call was answered. But the nature of the voice shocked him.
"Lauren…? Lauren. What's up? Lauren, is that you?"
He breathed but didn't say a word. A woman's voice. Young-ish, maybe? Concerned too.
"Lauren?"
He listened to her voice, trying to read the unknown woman on the other end, but then he cut the call as soon as the bathroom door opened. Jamie turned around. It was too late. Lauren stood in the doorway, a towel wrapped around her body, her hair dry. The remnants of a smile dropped away from her face. Lauren saw the phone in his hand, watched as it dropped away from his ear. There was no shame on his face, only accusation.

"Jamie. That's my phone. What are you doing? Are you… are you checking up on me again? Jamie… we've been through this."

"Only because you keep so many damn secrets from me." Lauren blinked at him and tightened the towel around her body.

"There are no secrets," she said. But there was a hint of a lie in her voice. "You won't let me have any." Lauren looked at her phone.

"Who is she?" said Jamie.

"What?"

"The woman you've been calling for the last three days. Who is she? Where did you meet her?"

Lauren shook her head.

"Tell me," he snapped. "Tell me, or God help me I'll—"

"Jamie – she's just an old friend. Someone I used to know when I was a kid."

"Really? A friend you've never mentioned before. Never called before either, until now. And so you call her seven times. And after that you delete all your messages so that I can't read them. Some crazy kind of friend that is. A secret friend. Funny, Lauren. I don't think I ever had you down as a dyke. Not until now."

"What? What are you talking about?"

"Secret calls, secret meetings, deleted texts. Like any normal affair. Except this one's a woman. It even makes sense, in a way. That's why you haven't seemed happy for months."

"Happy! You don't want me to be happy! You want me to just exist…"

"I want you to be happy, Lauren. But I want me to be happy too. Turns out that's not compatible with your newfound love interest. Least that explains the lack of condoms in your handbag. Don't suppose you need any."

"Jamie, you're being disgusting. What the hell are you even talking about? I said she's a friend."

"You're lying again."

"Damn you, Jamie. I don't care if you believe me. You make it all up. It's all in your head. Whatever I do, I'm wrong."

"There you go again. Your same old easy way out. I warned you to stop using that against me. And I warned you not to keep any secrets, or to cheat on me, and guess what. You've done both, haven't you? You're destroying our life together."

"What life?!"

"Don't say that, Lauren. You know there have to be consequences."

Lauren stayed silent. Jamie Blane saw eyes full of emotion and a mind full of unspoken secrets. He ground his teeth and charged at her. Lauren backed away and tried to close the bathroom door to block his way, but Jamie reached it too soon.

"Consequences," he said. Blane pushed her back and shut the door behind him. The steam from the shower had filled the room like a cloud trying to blot out what was to about to take place. Outside Lauren's mobile phone buzzed on the chair.

Twenty-four

"Who was that?" said Dan.
"Lauren," said Eva, looking up from hr phone.
"Our next case. Keen, isn't she?"
Eva nodded. "Hmmmm. Weird though. She answered the call but didn't say anything even though I'm sure she could hear me. I heard her breathing."
"You're sure it was Lauren who called? Or maybe it was one of those mistake calls. A call from her pocket."
"No, no. It was her name on the screen, and she was breathing into the phone. I heard her." Eva looked at Dan, understanding his meaning. New worries began to percolate in Eva's mind. "She's in a bad domestic situation, Dan. Lauren says the guy's a totally controlling psycho. Hopefully it was nothing. Maybe she couldn't hear me after all."
Dan shrugged. "Don't panic. She'll call back. She's been pretty good at that so far."
Eva's frown of concern stayed in place, but she resolved to wait. She really didn't want to start dancing to Lauren's tune when she'd already said that they were on another case. And with things finally seeming to be slotting into place, they couldn't abandon it now. With the sudden progress came that familiar old anxiety. One part thrill of the chase, one part fear – and the fear was always inseparable from the excitement. Something told Eva they were getting closer to a truth neither of them were going to like, and Joe Clancy was the one who held the key.

It was early evening. The sky was still bright, but the sun was getting low, stretching shadows to near ridiculous lengths. When they arrived at the Clancy house they were more than pleased to see the jeweller's black Lexus absent from the driveway. He was their de facto boss. And with little progress on his case, it was a relief not to have to make excuses again. Or to explain why they wanted to interrogate his son a further time.

"It's awfully quiet here. You think anyone is in?" said Eva. She looked through the living room window from the garden path. The TV was black and silent, the room dim with the shadows of evening. Dan glanced into the reception room on the other side of the front door. It was empty too.

"They'll be in the house. Joe's quiet anyway. And he'll be suffering. The only other place he could be is losing his wallet again while he tries to find a replacement dealer."

"Let's hope not. He's really too soft for that kind of action," said Eva. "He'd get mugged in a heartbeat."

Dan shrugged. "Good point. Maybe that's how he lost the wallet in the first place."

Eva pressed the bell and they waited on the step. A short time later, a vague shadow appeared in the hallway. Georgie opened the door looking both sleepy and emotional, like it had been a very long day, and her tears had only recently dried. She wiped her eyes and looked at them.

"Not more bad news I hope?" she said.

"Uh. I don't think so," said Dan. "Just a few more questions, that's all. We're getting closer, I promise."

Closer to what, Eva couldn't say. Her suspicions were taking her in a direction Georgie really wasn't going to like. "Is Joe okay?" she said.

Georgie opened the door wide and let them step inside. She nodded. "Kind of. But he's really in pieces. Not that his dad ever seems to give a damn. No doubt he'll probably have booked another of his little shindigs abroad before he asks if Joe is doing okay. At least Carl was good for that. He cared. Even if Joe didn't like the religious stuff, Carl really cared."

"Yes," said Eva. "It sounds like he was a good man."

"You want a drink? Juice, coffee?"

"Water would be good. It's still hot out there."

The girl led them to the smart kitchen at the rear of the house with its black marble worktop and matching floor. She poured them a glass of water each, and stared out into the back garden, vacant and quiet. As she stared out onto the lawn, the girl spoke again.

"After you told Joe what happened earlier – after you left – he became really upset and withdrawn. And I mean a ton more than usual. I tried my best to make him feel better, to see that he had a second chance and all that, but he wouldn't have it. He literally threw up from the shock and grief. I told him to get a doctor but then he shouted at me that I didn't understand and never would. Like he's so damned special. Sometimes I wish I didn't love him like I do. He's so infuriating."

"Yes, relationships can be hard like that," said Eva. Dan raised a questioning eyebrow.

"And he kept saying this one thing over and over. That he'd ruined things for everyone. That he'd ruined things for me, for himself, for Carl Renton, and his father too. *His father!* Can you believe that?! What a joke. As if his father would even notice whatever his son had done."

Eva and Dan shared a knowing glance. "Who knows, Georgie? We all have our secrets. Our shames. Things we know we shouldn't have done. Maybe Joe is talking about those kinds of things."

"And sometimes people make really big mistakes," said Dan. Georgie shot Dan a look. Dan shrugged his shoulders. "I'm just saying, you may not know the full story. It happens."

"I think I know enough to trust Joe over his father."

"And that's good," said Eva. "It's good that you're here for Joe, because soon I think he's going to need you more than ever."

Georgie forced a smile. The girl probably thought Eva meant she was needed to help the boy grieve. But that wasn't what Eva meant at all. "We've got to ask you a few more questions. Just to run over a few details. The closer we get to finding the truth, the more we need to be sure."

Georgie sniffed and folded her arms. "I'll tell you whatever I can. I'll do my best."

"I'm sure you will," said Eva. "That night – last Thursday night. The night of the burglary. Do you know what time you heard that window break?"

"I didn't look. But when Joe came back he said it was one am."

"When Joe *came back*?" said Dan, "Back from where?"

"He'd gone for a pee, remember? He said he was sleeping badly, probably because of his argument with Carl. I knew it was bothering him. He kept getting out of bed that night, but then the glass smashed downstairs and he came rushing in right away. He was in a panic. He said we needed to be quiet because there was someone in the house downstairs. He put the chair against the bedroom door, and then he took out one of his old cricket bats and laid it by the bed. He got back in beside me, put an arm around me and we just lay there waiting, hiding."

"So the whole not hearing anything was a total fabrication," said Dan.

Eva shot Dan a sideward glance. "And did you hear anything after that?"

"Not really. Joe was so good. He told me to relax and not to worry. He stroked my head. He was a real hero actually."

"But you didn't hear anything else? No noises downstairs. No one coming upstairs…?"

"No," said Georgie. "I guess we didn't. I stayed awake a while, but I must have fallen asleep in Joe's arms. Much much later, I heard the front door slam. It was still really early, but there was light outside. I suppose it must have been around five, maybe later. Joe stirred, but I soon went back to sleep. Funny thing was, I noticed that the chair had been pushed away from under the door handle. It was still leaning against the door, but it almost looked like someone had tried to force it open and had given up. I could be wrong. I was a bit panicky the next morning. The chair might have just slipped."

"To be crystal clear, you didn't hear anybody downstairs… and Joe was out of the room when the window got broken… Damn," said Dan.

"Why? What's the matter?" said Georgie. "Joe wasn't out of the room long. I told you everything that mattered the first time."

"It's okay, Georgie," said Eva. "That's why we're asking again now. We need to get a really clear picture."

"You heard the front door slam at five am," said Dan. "That's when you noticed the chair behind the bedroom door had been moved?"

"That's right."

"Did you hear anything or anyone else later that night. Anyone who could have tried the bedroom door?"

"No. After the panic I slept through."

"What about Joe? Did Joe get up again?" said Eva.

"No. That would have woken me up for sure. He was with me the rest of the night. He made me sleep behind him, closer to the window and the wall. Partly because he wanted to protect me, partly from habit. I always slept there so he could hide me in case his dad came in. His dad never switched on the light, so it always worked. I'm pretty petite compared to Joe."

"Then you think Aaron Clancy opened the door?" said Eva.

"Probably not," said Georgie. "He must have come home and slammed that front door at five am. He'd been out at his girlfriend's place all night. Not long after that he must have found his stuff missing because he started ranting and raving about the broken window. That woke me up. It must have woken the whole neighbourhood. He blamed Joe, of course."

"Of course," said Eva.

The nature of the robbery was becoming clearer, though there were minor creases to be ironed out, such as the chair propping against the bedroom door. Had it slipped? Or had the girl been too afraid to think clearly? As Eva was thinking, a loud thud shook the ceiling, and reverberated through the light fitting. Georgie looked up, her eyes filled with panic. "Joe! That'll be him. He's not been right at all…" She ran out of the kitchen into the corridor and bounded up the stairs. Eva and Dan followed closely behind. "Joe!" called Georgie. But there was no answer. She ran into his room slamming the door wide open. They found Joe sprawled in the middle of the floor, one arm folded awkwardly beneath his body, one arm splayed at his side. Eva saw the piles of neat new packets of clothing stacked around his room, some knocked over in his fall. The young man's eyes were closed, his lids flickering as if in dream sleep. Eva's eyes darted around the room and found a small creased piece of manila paper on the boy's bed, and a bottle of Isotonic sports drink spilt beside him, its dark stain spreading across the carpet. Eva pointed at the torn scrap of brown paper and Dan nodded. Eva moved to the boy's side and checked his pulse, pressing her fingers to his neck. His pulse was racing way too fast and he was hot to the touch and sweating profusely. Dan looked down at the shred of paper on the bed. He saw a couple of crumbs of white tablet matter left in the creases. "He's taken whatever he had left. We need to get an ambulance here right away."

"What?" said the girl, looking up at Dan. "Taken what? What do you mean?"

"Just call an ambulance now," said Eva. "Tell them it's a suspected drug overdose."

The girl mouthed the words as she stood up. She ran out of the room and headed for Clancy Senior's study to use the phone.

"If he's taken all of those at once, then he's taken the same amount that killed Norman Peters," said Dan.

Eva knelt down beside the young man and slid a hand beneath his head.

"What have you done, Joe?" said Eva. "What did you do?"
.

***

In the bright white of the frenetic A&E department, white-coated doctors and blue-gowned nurses rushed around looking as focused as Olympic athletes; only here the stakes were greater, and the results of failure much more immediate. Eva, Dan and Georgie stood beside a trolley-bed in the temporary cubicle where Joe Clancy was stationed. There was a monitor attached to him, giving a reading of a fast but stable pulse with an elevated blood pressure. Life and death was happening all around them, but thankfully they were no more than onlookers, even Joe. His stomach had been pumped. He was on a drip to clean out his body and replace lost fluids, and other medication had been provided to stabilise him. His face was grey, much worse than they had ever seen him. His open eyes were dark circled and his lips were pale. But he was alive, and he was awake. Tears still streamed down Georgie's face. Eva was pleased he'd survived but incensed too. Joe Clancy had put Georgie through hell in more ways than any girl deserved. Still she looked at him with earnest, loving, but hard eyes. Even in weakness, Joe Clancy seemed to sense her accusation. He held the girl's hand as she wept.

"How could you?" she whispered. "How could you do that to me?"

"Sorry," he said. His throat sounded sore and weak from the vomiting and the stomach pump.

"Never again," said Georgie. She looked at him, squeezed his hand, and made him swear it.

"Never again," he promised.

"I was so, so stupid," said Georgie. "I never knew you were taking that horrible stuff. But of course you were. It's the only thing that makes sense of it all."

Joe turned his head towards Eva and Dan.

"He's not here is he?" said Joe, his voice frail and croaky.

"Not yet," said Eva.

The boy nodded his head. "When can I go home? I'm not dying. I shouldn't be in this bed. Not with so many other people who might need it…"

"They'll want to keep you in," said Eva. "To make sure everything is okay."

The kid shook his head. "I don't deserve to be looked after. I'm eighteen years old. If I want to I can discharge myself, right?"

"Joe," said Eva, with a voice of warning.

"Soon as I can, I'm going home. No matter what they say."

Eva grimaced. She looked away to the huddle of doctors working on a patient in a cubicle nearby. One of the nurses saw her looking and they swept the blue curtains shut around them.

"You know when it started, don't you?" he said. Joe looked at Georgie as he spoke.

She nodded. "With the clothes," she said. "You did all that to hide it from me. You were taking those Ubers all that time?"

Clancy nodded again. "I kept buying the clothes for appearances sake. I needed a reason for him to keep coming around. I knew you thought I was hoarding the clothes. But I had to let you think what you liked, just so I could get what I needed. Ubers. I tried normal ecstasy once. They were fun. But they're nothing like Ubers. The rush is so nice, you just want more. And if you break them up like I do, you can get little rushes all the way through the day without anyone even knowing you're on them."

"People noticed, Joe. People noticed you were looking ill," said Dan. "Everyone knew something was up with you."

"Maybe. They do wreck your appetite. And your sleep. That's when you start looking rough."

"You're overlooking the chemical content," said Eva. "You don't know what's in them. No one ever does. Or what it's doing to you. Ubers are killing people, Joe. And let's face it, that's what you were aiming for when you took that last batch. Why?"

Eva held his eyes and Joe let loose a long sigh.

"I didn't want to let Carl down like that. Carl believed in me. He believed I could quit the Ubers. He kept coming round to help me. He knew where all my money was going and he didn't want me ruining my life, so he gave me a little pocket money to motivate me. Pocket money, yes, like I was his kid. He said I could have it so long as I didn't waste any of it on that rubbish. It was a way to reward me for weaning myself off. By then he knew my dad only gave me four hundred a month. But I still couldn't help it. All of my money was going on the pills with Norman. Even what Carl gave me. Carl thought I was cutting down, like we agreed, but in the end he saw I was in an even worse mess, and he got angry. Carl wasn't stupid. That night, last Thursday, he faced me down. He said I was lying, and he said he had become part of the problem… Carl Renton gave me my best chance at saving my life and making something of myself, and I threw it back in his face. I'm a scumbag, Miss Roberts. I'm a total scumbag, Georgie. I deserved to die, but I couldn't even do that right, so here I am again, being a scumbag, using up a hospital bed when someone else needs it even more than I do."

"Hey," said Dan, frowning. "Enough of the self-pity. You're alive because these people here saved you. Now it's high time for you to stop being so ungrateful. You could do that for Carl Renton starting right now. Maybe this is your fresh start. Your second chance, Joe. Get it?"

Joe fell silent under Dan's stern gaze. But Dan wasn't going to let him off with a mere silence. He wanted an answer.

"Get it?" said Dan.

Joe gave a single nod and Dan sighed.

"That's the spirit, Joe," said Eva. "And a new start begins with you helping us to fix this."

"Fix it? But it can't be fixed. Carl's gone…" said Joe.
"You can start by telling us everything you know. And this time, please don't leave out a single thing."
The young man coughed and Georgie squeezed his hand.
"Come on, Joe. Tell them," said Georgie.
Joe nodded and began to speak. "After a little while of buying Ubers and the clothes to cover it, I got to the point I couldn't afford to buy them just from my allowance anymore. My allowance was four hundred a month. I know that sounds a lot for someone my age but when you're buying clothes as well as Ubers the cost mounts up quickly. And I didn't even know how much I was in debt to Norman Peters until he told me. He said I owned him hundreds! I'd been paying him all I had, but I still owed him more. And even then, Norm was okay for a little while, but then he suddenly wanted to get paid off. So I had no choice but to start giving him things from the house. Little things at first. Anything I thought might not be noticed…"
"That phase couldn't have lasted long," said Eva.
Among the constant footfall of medical staff and visitors passing along the central aisle between the cubicles, a tall newcomer interrupted a busy nurse. He asked a question. The nurse pointed to a roll call of patient names scrawled on a big white board, then pointed him in the direction of cubicle 10. The cubicle which housed Joe Clancy's bed.
"No. It didn't last long," said Joe.

Aaron Clancy reached the end of the wall which bordered one side of cubicle 10. He saw the girl Georgie with his son's hand in hers. He saw Dan Bradley's back and his son's feet, wearing socks but no trainers. Aaron Clancy took a deep breath and looked up at the ceiling, relieved to hear his son's voice. He was alive. But as the boy's words kept coming, Clancy Senior listened on in grim fascination. He stayed hidden from sight around the corner, rooted to the spot.

"I started to run out of what I thought of as small and inconsequential items from the house. Anything I gave Norm after that was bound to be noticed and missed. But by then Norm was happy with the arrangement. I was buying his clothes and his pills. I guess I was a cash cow, and he was probably making extra money by trading on whatever I gave him for extra cash. At that point Norm said I could have as much as I liked, just so long as I kept paying him with whatever else I could grab from the house. So I did. I knew it had to end one day, but by then, I honestly didn't care. I was hooked bad. I just had to pay him however I could and damn the consequences."

"Which was when you started stealing from your father's private jewellery collection…" said Dan.

Joe winced at the word, stealing.

"Look. I hate myself for it, but what else could I do? I tried to find myself a cheaper supplier, one without the clothes, so I could manage it from my allowance without taking my dad's stuff. But it went wrong. I ended up getting stung for every penny I had, and I just about got away without a beating."

"Which was when you lost your wallet?" said Eva.

Joe nodded. "It was never lost. I had to give it over or they were going to break my leg, so I handed it over just like that. I would have been happy if I'd never seen that bloody wallet ever again. But I was back at square one, worse even, so I had to keep giving Norm my dad's stuff just to stay on an even keel. And that didn't last either."

"Because Norman wanted more cash?" said Dan. "Is that why you faked the burglary?"

Joe frowned. "*What?* You... you *know* about that? How?!"

"We worked it out, Joe." said Eva. "It took us a while, but as soon as we knew everything it became clear.

"But that's not it. I didn't set up that burglary to pay Norman Peters. I would never have done that. The thing with Norm came to an end before I even knew it. There was this one time, about a week back, Norm came to give me another batch in exchange for an item. I had to give him one of the small Celtic pieces. Not the one my dad keeps hassling the police for. Just a small old gold brooch. I had to give him that because I was running out of stuff. Norm was very happy. He gave me an extra couple of Ubers and two pairs of jeans. But while I was dealing with Norm I saw this guy out in the street waiting for him. He was waiting in a car. I thought the guy must have given him a lift, but when I saw Norman get in his own car to drive away I realised I was wrong. The other guy who was waiting for him drove off and followed him. I was going to tell Norm all about it when I saw him next, but I didn't get the chance. That was the very last time he came."

"The guy in the car?" said Dan. "Was he tall, thin, mean and ugly looking, right?"

Joe nodded, his eyed widening. "Yes. That's him."

Aaron Clancy put his hands on his hips and shook his head at the floor. He gritted his teeth and prepared to step around the corner to face his son. Clancy Senior was about to speak when a cocktail of confused feelings held him in check. He hesitated, unsure whether to reassure or to roar. And before he had made up his mind, the questions began once more.
"The burglary, Joe. It happened late that Thursday night. Tell me all about it," said Eva.
Joe looked at Georgie and took her hand in his. "I'm sorry, Georgie. I misled you. It was the drugs. They had a hold of me."
"Misled me?"
"There was no burglary. None at all. You were there that night. You remember I was in a state, a real mess," said Joe.
"Yeah. You really weren't good that night."

"That was my fault. I got cocky about how much of the Ubers I could take. I wanted to edge up a little, enjoy a little more, so I took a half instead of a quarter, and it showed. That's why Carl saw I was out of it. Later, when I started to come down I told you I was ill again. When Carl saw me and we went off to talk, he knew exactly what was going on. He'd seen it all before. He'd wanted me to get straight and come off the stuff for good. But that night he saw through me once and for all. I wasn't coming off the Ubers. I was getting in deeper and deeper I was getting worse. When I saw he was so upset with me, it was like upsetting your grandpa. I was so, so, sorry. I was beside myself, and the chemicals weren't helping. He told me he couldn't stand by and watch me kill myself and he wasn't going to help me do it any longer. He just said he would pray for me. I knew then he was never going to come and see me again. I'd lost a good friend. I'd lost a man who was becoming like another father to me... I just wanted him to know that I appreciated all he'd done. As he was leaving, I grabbed anything I could lay my hands on. Looking back, I was still high. I grabbed a few things, whatever I could find, and I gave them to him in a jiffy bag. I said they were a thank you present. He said he didn't want it. He barely even looked at it but I told him to take it. I watched him saying goodbye to Georgie, and off he went. A little later, when I was coming down I realised what I'd done. I'd given Carl about a half dozen of my Dad's favourite pieces. What he called his centrepieces. I panicked. I knew there was no way that could happen. I guessed faking a burglary was my only way out of it. I couldn't ask Carl for them back and I didn't want to, either. So I set up the burglary. About one am I went downstairs while Georgie was still sleeping... I went outside and I smashed the back window with a rolling pin. Then I rushed upstairs pretending I'd been in the toilet there the whole time. For the burglary to work, everyone had to believe it. Even me, I guess. The lie had to be complete. So I started acting like it was true. I put a chair up against the door… and acted like there was someone in the house. And I got my cricket bat ready to defend myself…"

The light of the hospital A&E ward was dimmed by the appearance of a tall figure at the end of the bed. Joe was the first to look up. He saw his father clasping his own hands. The man's gaze was sincere and upset, yet there was no mistaking the hint of anger and reproach in his eyes.

"Joe…"

The boy yammered and shifted in his bed. Eva reached to steady him.

"It's okay, Joe. Stay calm. It's only your father," she said.

"Have you been there long?" said Georgie, her eyes shining with a hint of panic.

"Long enough," said Clancy Senior quietly.. The girl regarded him and tried to read his face.

"Joe… I'm sorry," said his father. "I only wish… I only wish that you'd told me… I could have helped you. I could have paid for a rehab and some therapy. A proper rehab, not one for the hoodlums like your friend Mr Renton used to run. You really should have told me about the money, Joe. And about the stealing too. I deserved to know."

Aaron Clancy felt the weight of Eva's gaze and met her eyes. "Of course," he said. "I'm very, very glad – extremely glad – that you're alive and well. But I am your father. You should have told me all the same."

Joe Clancy nodded meekly. "I know. I'm sorry, Dad."

"What did the doctors say?" said Clancy Senior.

"They said Joe didn't fully digest all the tablets he'd taken," said Georgie, with a trace of anger. "If it had been much longer, they said he'd probably be dead. But the paramedics got to him in time. Then they pumped his stomach but they want to keep him in tonight."

Joe shook his head at these words, but Georgie carried on. "I think he'll probably be discharged tomorrow. Joe's had a very near miss."

Clancy nodded mildly. In a half-hearted gesture he reached out for his son. He laid his hand on his son's ankle and squeezed for a moment, then looked at Eva.

"So... you didn't find my lost collection, but it seems you did find out what happened to them. I never guessed the cause would be so close to home. You've done all you could, I suppose. If some drug dealer attacked Mr Renton when he was in possession of my centrepieces, I'm sure they will be long gone now. Don't worry. I'll settle my account with you in due course, Miss Roberts."

"All in good time, Mr Clancy. This news comes as a shock for everyone," said Eva.

"Yes, it does. Look." Clancy scratched his nose. The man looked a little lost. "I'm sorry but I'd better go. I've made such an awful fuss about the burglary, that I must go and fix a few things as soon as I can. I shall have to tell the insurance company it was all a mistake. I hope they see the funny side. And I should call the police too. It's all so... so very... awkward."

"Leave all that until tomorrow, Mr Clancy. It can wait," said Dan.

Clancy Senior shook his head. "I'm afraid it can't. Back when I was building my jewellery business, I always used to operate on one principle. It was like a golden rule to me. *Do it now!!* That principle has always seen me in good stead. I think I should do the very same thing in this crisis. Please excuse me. Joe… I'll be back when I can."

Clancy nodded his head and made off with a curt wave to his son. Joe looked ashamed of himself, Georgie angry.

"You hear that?" said Dan, shaking his head. "He's even got a golden rule to follow when his son's in a hospital bed. He's still talking gold, even now."

Eva gave Dan a look of warning for speaking his mind with Joe and Georgie present. But young Georgie nodded her head at Dan's words. "Gold and jewellery. Joe's father lives and breathes nothing else," said Georgie. Eva's mouth twitched at Georgie's words. Her eyes briefly misted in thought.

"What is it?" said Joe. His forlorn gaze caught the look in Eva's eyes, and brought her back to the present.

"Just a thought," said Eva. "Last Thursday night. The night of the burglary. You said you were out of it. Just how out of it were you?"

"Yes," said Joe. "It wasn't my finest hour. I took too much and it cost me a friend. Everything else that happened that night flowed from that."

"I wouldn't say that, Joe," said Eva.

Dan agreed. "You had nothing to do with what happened to Carl, after all."

"No. I had nothing to do with what happened to him *afterwards*. Except that if I had been in a better way, who knows, maybe he would have skipped a night's vigil at the beach. He might have stayed longer at my house. He might be alive today."

Eva shook her head. "Stopping drugs coming into the town was a full-on faith mission for Carl Renton. It was his life's work. I don't think you could have stopped him. But go back a step. You said you were out of it. Your father recalled that night too. He said he came home after your meeting with Carl. He told me his impressions of that evening and he said you were in a bad way, upset and unwell but he said he was due to go back out."

"He wouldn't have cared either way," said Georgie.

"But your father said he went up to see you in your bedroom – to see if you were okay. I think he assumed Georgie had already left to go home, so he came to give you a glass of water and see how you were."

Eva let the words sink in and waited to read a response in their eyes. Joe looked unsure, but there was a strangely confused look in Georgie's eyes. "That's a routine we go through sometimes. I pretend to leave for the day, and then do my level best to avoid him."

Eva saw the girl thinking and carried on. "Aaron told me you were too ill, too upset to take any comfort, so he left you in bed to sleep it off and then went on his way."

"I know I was pretty delirious at times," said Joe. "I'm sorry. I can't remember."

"Well, I can," said Georgie. "And he's wrong. He never came to see Joe. I should know, because I was the one looking after him. Yes, I did pretend to leave the house, but I didn't ever leave. For show, I got ready to go, but when I saw Aaron was excited and keen to get out for his date I knew I wouldn't have to try too hard. He was distracted, so I closed the door and sneaked back up the stairs. With Joe like that there was no way I was going anywhere."

"You don't remember Mr Clancy visiting Joe at all that evening?"

"No. Not at all," said Georgie.

"Do you think he could have and you missed it?" said Eva. The girl's expression grew firm and certain. "No. No chance at all. I'm the one who looked after Joe until he started getting settled. I laid next to him then and I fell asleep. Next thing I remember, was the noise downstairs and Joe telling me we were being robbed!" she said, softly punching Joe's arm. "Now I know you were having me on."

Joe gulped and looked away. Georgie's smile faded.

"Aaron was quite certain that he came to see Joe," said Eva. "He made a point of it." She looked at Dan.

"Then it sounds like he got it wrong," said Dan.

"Probably because he wants to seem a better father than he actually is," said Georgie.

"You're *absolutely* sure he didn't come back?" said Eva.

Georgie met her eyes. "I told you already. Aaron really gets under my skin."

"I noticed," said Dan.

"After Joe's staged break-in, I didn't sleep very well. I had a dream, or maybe just a bad feeling, a feeling that he was going to catch me in bed with Joe. It was such a stupid, horrid feeling. But sometimes dreams can be like that, can't they? Feelings, not pictures. I used to have a nightmare of falling. It was just the same."

Joe reached out for Georgie's hand.

"I blocked the door with the chair, and Dad didn't get back until morning. He didn't see you, Georgie. It must have been the break-in that scared you. My father never knew you were there, I'm sure."

Georgie tried for a smile, but Eva saw the strain of discomfort left by describing the previous Thursday night. Eva tried to reassure her. "Joe's probably right, Georgie. Mr Clancy never knew you were there."

The girl nodded, but Eva could only think of the implications of their words. Aaron Clancy didn't know Georgie was there. He had never known. Which was why he felt able to lie about seeing Joe… Whatever the reason for the lie, his guilt about being a bad father, or something else, it exposed the first obvious crack in Clancy's character. It was one thing being a selfish father. But with all the chaos and crime being inflicted on his family, it was quite another to lie to your own investigator about the night of a crime. Eva saw Dan's brooding face, and realised he was thinking along the same lines. Joe blocking the bedroom door had proved a wise precaution. And now the slipped chair was looking less like a trick of a tired mind, and more like a proverbial tripwire. Maybe Clancy had arrived home at five am… But Eva was sure he had also been back to the house much, much earlier. The price of one lie, was that it tended to expose others.

The nurses asked Eva, Dan and Georgie to vacate cubicle 10 while they ran some checks on Joe's vitals. The three used the excuse to take some air away from the chaos, only to find more chaos outside among the ambulances teeming on the cross-hatched area outside the A&E back doors. They stepped out of the way.

"This is important, Georgie," said Dan. "We need you to be absolutely clear on what happened that night. Crystal clear," said Dan.

But I told you everything already."

"Yes," said Eva. "But put the break-in aside for a moment. Let's think about Aaron for a minute. He said he went to see Joe that evening. Now we know he was wrong about that. He made a mistake. Then he went out on his date…"

"Yes, as soon as he could, about nine pm."

"And then?" said Dan.

"And then there was the supposed break-in, about one. And later on, there… there *was* something…"

"Your bad feeling?" said Eva. "The nightmare you described?"

"Maybe it's connected," said Georgie. "If it wasn't just a feeling, then maybe there might have been another noise downstairs. I remember stirring, I know that much. Like I said, I just put it down to what happened before. The window breaking and all that."

"Do you know the time you were stirred by that noise or bad feeling?" said Eva.

"It was still pitch black. I was scared. I really didn't want to open my eyes."

"It starts getting light around four onwards," said Dan. "Which puts that period between one and say, three forty-five am."

"I don't understand. Why's this so important all of a sudden?" said Georgie.

"We have to be clear about everything, that's all," said Eva.

Georgie gave a single nod, but she didn't look convinced. "And after that?"

"I heard the door slam at five. Or thereabouts. Soon after that, Aaron lost it, like I said. He found the broken kitchen window and all his stuff missing and went stomping and shouting all over the house."

"Thank you, Georgie," said Eva. "I think you've told us all we need to know."

Georgie puffed her cheeks and blew out a long deep breath. "He wants to discharge himself, you know."

"Don't let him," said Eva. "He's in no fit state to go anywhere."

"Honestly, he's stubborn just like his father. If there's any chance he can manage it, there will be no way to stop him."

"Which is exactly why he needs someone like you in his life," said Dan. "Joe's a lucky kid. One day he might even realise it. We need to go."

Eva nodded. "Will you be okay?"

"Someone has to be," said Georgie with a shrug.

"That's the spirit," said Eva. She squeezed the girl's shoulder and then they parted right there on the A&E forecourt. Eva and Dan walked away, gathering pace with every step they took.

"Aaron Clancy is a liar," said Dan.

Eva glanced at him as they walked. "Say it out loud if you want to. If Georgie is right about that bad feeling, Aaron Clancy could be a lot worse than that."

"It's still too subtle," said Dan. "It all comes down to one dumb lie, a chair behind a door and Georgie's bad feeling. If we presented the basis of *that* theory to Hogarth he'd laugh in our faces.

"And he'd be right to," said Eva. "We need more."

"Maybe there's a chance we could find the weapon. Grace's cosh looked the part…"

"At the time, yes," said Eva. "But a weapon like that couldn't have cut open Carl Renton's stomach like that. We're looking at a sharp edged weapon. Trouble is there were metal detectors all over that beach hunting for the Saxon gold. If there were any weapons, they would have been found then.

Dan shook his head. "First off, that blood patch was found on the other side of the marine centre, a good way from where the bulk of those treasure hunters were scanning the sand. Most only checked the section between the marine centre and the bistro."

Eva recalled the beach – the few hunters and youths she'd found there after she had picked her way round the jetty.

"Then the police presence pretty much killed any hunting that side," said Dan.

"Then the police should have found the weapon if it was there," said Eva.

"You're giving the police way too much credit. Norman Peters was beaten up, knocked unconscious and killed with Ubers stuffed down his neck. The blood patch wasn't even found until you picked it up. Who's to say they've even started looking for any weapon."

Eva shrugged. "What would this weapon even look like?" said Eva.

"Carl Renton's head was caved in. It had been bludgeoned as well as cut. Then like you said, his abdomen was a royal mess. It couldn't have been a knife. It was a heavy implement of some kind, like the cosh, but something with a sharp edge. Maybe a short crow bar, or a builder's tool… If the drug traffickers did it, it could have a tool from a boat or a pistol whipping, but that doesn't explain the cut to Renton's gut. And guns aren't always made of metal. There's no reason a polymer based weapon would be found by a detector."

"Okay. Fine. I'm persuaded. We should check the beach again. But that's a heck of a large area."

"We'll concentrate on a few areas. If they wanted to hide a weapon in a hurry, underneath the jetty would have been a good place to start. Or out in the mud. But a killer in a hurry wouldn't have time to think about distance. He'd get rid of it in the immediate vicinity. He'd have to, then he'd run."

"You really want to look for this weapon, don't you?"

"Yes," said Dan. "It could nail the killer, whoever he is."

"Fine," said Eva. "But split the labour. Get some help. Ask Mark and Joanne to help you."

Dan frowned. "And what about you?"

"It's Aaron Clancy. His behaviour bothers me, the way he leaves his son in hospital after he almost dies from a drug overdose. I'm seeing him in a new light."

"He's angry with Joe. Clancy's got his priorities all wrong, I know, but that's just the man we're dealing with."

"But combine that with questions over his lies and possible whereabouts on Thursday night, and it makes me wonder."

"I know what you mean. You know, for a minute there I thought this case might actually pay," said Dan.

"Keep the faith," said Eva.

"I'll bet that's what Carl Renton used to say."
"Probably. I'm going to take a closer look at Aaron Clancy. It's an itch I've got to scratch."
"But you don't even know where he's gone," said Dan.
"No. But I'm hoping he hasn't gone home," said Eva. "I might need to ask Georgie for a little favour."
Dan shook his head. "I used to think you'd make a great cop, and I'd make a great convict. These days, you're just as much of a rule-breaker as I ever was."
"Rules are to be followed if they are helpful. But right now we need to take a more flexible approach. Come on. Let's get this over with before I change my mind."
"Good luck," said Dan, starting on his way.
Eva headed back towards the beeping, howling hubbub of Southend A&E. She hoped Georgie would be able to persuade Joe to help. But if Joe wouldn't, Eva had to hope that Georgie would take the same flexible attitude to the rules as she did.

Twenty-five

It was getting late in the day – the time when the light began to change, moving from bright blue to hues of dark blue through to violet and then red. It wasn't long until sunset, and with a clear sky like this one, the beach should have been a beautiful setting. Except they were too busy to pay much attention. Mark and Joanne had agreed to give up their time to help Dan with the search on the town side of the marine centre – the side where the blood patch had been found on the sand, where Norman Peters' corpse had been hidden under the old wooden dinghy. The small white tent around the blood stain had been removed, as had all trace of the blood itself. The larger tent around the Peters' murder site was still in place and still guarded by a uniformed constable and PCSO. The two uniforms regarded the three of them with more than a passing interest when they arrived, but they also looked distinctly reluctant to get involved in any way. The cops had a job to do and didn't need any extra trouble. That sentiment went both ways and when Dan spoke, he was careful to keep his words low enough so the uniforms couldn't hear.
"The blood patch was about there," said Dan. He nodded towards the site. "Where those grasses start. See the patch there – where the grass is missing? That's where their crime scene tent was."
"If they're gone they must have everything they need," said Mark.

"Looks like they took that whole bloodied section of sand away to their lab," said Dan. "But we still haven't heard about any weapon and I think Hogarth would have clued us in if he'd found one. Which means it's now down to us. If we can find the weapon there's a very good chance that we can ID the killer. If not us, then the police can use it."

"What are we looking for?" said Joanne. Dan saw the glint of excitement in her eye and he liked it. Joanne was like a cross between him and Eva. The girl had his exuberant wild side, and Eva's determination to get the job done. Even after all the trouble Joanne had caused him, Dan couldn't fault her tenacity.

"A blunt implement with a sharp edge. Or maybe two weapons, one sharp, one heavy and blunt. Sounds unlikely. We're not talking a ninja here. We're talking your basic vicious drug dealer-slash-importer. We're looking at brute force and speed. To me that says a single weapon."

"Okay and where do we start?" said Mark as he switched on his metal detector – something Mark said his dad had left behind when he moved out. It was an old gizmo with rust down the length of the tubular shaft and a bottom scanner which looked like an old red camping kettle. The device looked like a refugee from the eighties, which Dan guessed it was.

"Under the jetty. Assuming the killer didn't take it with him, he would have wanted to hide the weapon and discard it quickly."

Joanne nodded. "Yeah. That makes sense. He was probably hoping the tide would bury it before anyone saw."

"I hope so. That thing still work?"

"Last time I tried it I was eight years old and I was on a beach in Clacton. I found a Victorian penny."

"So it likes beaches. Good news."

"I'm surprised it still works."

"Well let's see what else you can find. Try under the length of the jetty. I'll start near the water side, dig around and see what I can see."

Dan left Joanne and Mark to their fun as they started to scan the sand under the edge of the marine centre jetty. Dan padded down the beach until he reached the water's edge. There was a gap between the end of the jetty and the first laps of the sea water. He strained his eyes in the lilac-orange sunlight to pick out any unusual shapes in the glistening muddy sand. The light was fading fast. Pretty soon they were going to need a torch.

***

Eva held her breath as she slotted the key into the front door. She turned it quietly, and felt the lock give with a gentle click. Eva's heart was beating faster than she would have liked. Georgie had secured the key from Joe, in return for promising to help the young man with discharging himself from hospital. He clearly wasn't ready for that, but Eva needed the key more than she wanted to object. Hopefully Georgie would keep Joe in check for a while longer. When Eva arrived at the Clancy house the driveway was empty, just as she'd hoped. And as an extra precaution against being caught, Eva had parked her Alfa Romeo around the nearby corner, on a narrow side road which slinked down one side of Chalkwell Park to join Kings Road, not far from Leigh. It kept her car well out of sight, but at a price. A quick getaway was now out of the question. It was a price Eva was willing to pay. There was evidence somewhere in the house, she was sure of it. Evidence of what was yet to be determined. But Aaron Clancy's unnecessary lies seemed like the start of something – like a loose thread. If Eva tugged and kept pulling, she hoped the whole mystery would unravel itself. If Clancy Senior's gold-laden study told her nothing, then maybe Joe's clothes collection might. But it was Aaron Clancy who fascinated her the most. He had hired them to help him find his collection, not to find Carl Renton. But in Eva's mind, the mysteries of the murder and the gold had always intersected through his son. But it wasn't all down to Joe, Eva was now sure of that. She looked out on the quiet street before she shut the door. Closing off the world outside, Eva hesitantly called out and waited for a response, but there was none. There was nothing but her own fear.

"Keep it together, Eva. It's just a big empty house," she muttered. "Focus."

The house hummed and a chill started on the nape of Eva's neck. She took a breath, glanced out through the distorted glass of the front door window. No car. No sign of Clancy. And on she went. The front room with the decorative items of Clancy's collection was interesting enough, but Eva was relatively certain that the room held no secrets. The secrets were upstairs, along with the phone Clancy used for snooping on calls. She climbed the stairs in the twilight of the house, unable and unwilling to switch on the light because of the risk of being seen from outside. Eva closed her eyes for a few seconds and reopened them to adjust to the lack of light. Better. The white walls of the upper hallway were filled with lilac, gold, red and orange light from the coming sunset. The doors of the upper rooms were all open, except for one. Through Joe's bedroom window Eva caught a view of the sun lowering over the distant Thames, and then the silence prodded her on. She moved towards the closed door, feeling a sudden burst of inexplicable panic. She was already breaking the law and certainly voiding their contract. But going into Aaron Clancy's private study seemed something even beyond that. She felt like a thief. This was a family home after all, or at least it was made to look like one. Eva plunged the handle and opened the door. The room was a mixture of bright colours from the evening light and strong, stark shadows. With a deep breath, she closed the door behind her then moved into the centre of the room and looked around, taking a slow three-sixty to observe her surroundings and what they meant. The trinkets framed on the walls like pinned butterflies, the cabinet of larger, striking items, a mixture of gold and other metals, a mixture of periods and styles. Then there were the books on the shelf beside the bureau. Books about antiquities, gems of the ancient world, as well as books on the history of gold, and official annual catalogues from jewellery and auction houses. Some were decades old others were brand new. Eva traced a finger along a few old spines and rubbed her fingers together. Not a trace of dust. Like the man himself, barely a trace of wrongdoing. And yet he lied. Was the obvious lack of love for his son the only reason she had come to suspect him? Or was her lack of success in finding the gold the real reason she had turned against the man who had hired her? Her doubts mingled with her suspicion. She looked at a small wooden cabinet beside the bureau and opened it. Inside were several folders, and what looked like a stack of blank A4 paper. Eva picked up a few pages. The first was typed in small bold letters. THE DIAMOND CONNECTION a novel by Aaron G. Clancy. Eva flicked through the papers and found hints of a muscular but intelligent adventurer with a liking for gold. After a moment Eva found a luridly written sex scene and the words made her cringe. It seemed Clancy was living several lives at once, some in his imagination, and all of them at the expense of his son. Eva was glad to put the paper back in the stack and shut the cabinet door. She turned to the bureau as the daylight on the walls was dimming. Eva knew she would need light to learn anything more. She walked to the light switch, and was about to flick it on, but then she glanced to the window and changed her mind. Closing the curtains would be another dead giveaway. Instead, she had to be careful. Eva moved the chair away from the bureau and crouched down beside the drawers beneath it. The top drawer had a brass-rimmed keyhole. Eva tugged at the little circular pull handles, but the drawer wouldn't budge. Instead, she tried the drawer below. No keyhole which meant no lock. The drawer opened to reveal a box of small bright items all individually bagged, some stickered and coded in the man's hand. She rummaged among them. Rings. Brooches. Cufflinks. Crucifixes. Things ancient and antique, a few more modern. Beside it were a set of small handwritten catalogues. She picked one and scanned it, but it was too hard to read in the failing light. Eva pulled out her phone and switched on the torch app. A bright star of light shone at the top of her smartphone. She aimed it at the book and started to read the short entries. The book had a handwritten title: 'Smaller Items, Mostly Victorian.' Eva set them aside and closed the drawer. Next she opened the bottom drawer. It was heavy and pulled open slowly. There was a metal clatter inside as she opened it. A jumble of dull but colourful metals stared up at her from inside. The drawer was as much a mess as the cutlery drawer back in the office kitchenette, but here every item was made of gold, or studded with gems and these were not bagged. A much smaller book beside them was titled 'small objects, precious metals and gems. Various Periods.'. There and then she felt a sudden rush of insight. A giddy, exciting and yet terrifying prospect. Carl Renton's hideous injuries on the beach at Thorpe Bay flashed into her mind and Eva shone her torch and began to prod the metal apart with a noisy jangle. Her quick eye couldn't find anything remotely suitable, and certainly nothing bloodied. Perhaps she was chasing up another blind alley but she needed to be sure. After a moment, she gave up and closed the drawer. Outside, a car drew past along Kings Road. It slowed to a near halt as it approached the Clancy driveway. Its orange indicator flashed to take the turning. It flashed a few times and the car started to turn before it abruptly stopped. Looking up from his

Lexus window Aaron Clancy's face was swathed in shadow. For a moment he saw a kaleidoscope of colours reflected from the ceiling of his study. Then the light changed and the colours were gone. His eyes caught the shifting light and saw a sudden brightness within, reflecting from the walls. He stared, open mouthed, then turned the steering wheel straight again, changed gears and dabbed the accelerator. He glided the car past his house only to come to a stop a hundred yards away. This time he didn't indicate. He stared into the rear-view mirror and then quite by chance, he glanced along the side road opposite and saw a familiar small red car parked on a bend. His eyes narrowed and he took a breath. He got out of his car, locked it, and set off towards his house. The last of the sunlight had finally fallen away from Kings Road. The street was already succumbing to the first hints of evening.

"You find anything down there?" said Joanne as Dan approached. Her hair was tousled from the rummaging and graft beneath the structure of the jetty. Mark had gone deeper under the structure, ferreting between the columns with his metal detector whining whenever it came near a rivet.
"Besides mud, you mean?" replied Dan. "Nothing. But if I keep raking through that stuff with my bare hands, sooner or later a razor clam is going to cut me to ribbons. We should have brought a spade and a torch. What about up here? Any joy?"
"We've made about three pounds in loose change so far. If we keep going, who knows? We might have a full tenner by morning," said Joanne.
"Cash but no weapon," said Dan.

"And no treasure either," called Mark.

"That's it. I think we can forget all about finding Clancy's missing gold," said Dan. "Whoever killed Renton probably took it as a bonus. Bet they couldn't believe their luck."

"What now then?" said Joanne. "You're actually saying that you want to give up?"

"Hang on a minute," said Dan. "You know I don't like those words. But I would settle for going back home and getting clean again. Think of it as retreating and regrouping. We need more than a metal detector and our bare hands. Daylight would be good for a start."

Joanne gave a vague nod of agreement.

"If that weapon is here, I suppose a few hours' rest won't hurt, Joanne."

"Then we start again in the morning?" she said.

"What about your day job? Won't the council sack you if you keep ducking out?" said Dan.

"I can hold them off a little while. This investigating business is far more my thing."

Dan laughed. He peered under the jetty. "Mark. Come on out. We'll come out again tomorrow. Go home, get clean and get some rest."

"But we've hardly even started," he said.

"Yes you have," said Dan. "You've done the whole length of the jetty. We'll try again tomorrow."

"Fine, fine," said Mark with a sigh.

They gathered together at the edge of the wide platform area behind the marine centre. The two uniformed policemen watched them the whole way. Their only entertainment for the night was finally leaving them behind. Dan tutted to himself and Joanne looked at him, waiting until he spoke.

"This case. It's beating us. It's like a nut you can't crack open."

"But you don't give up," said Joanne.

"No," said Dan "Though sometimes I think it might be easier if we did."

Joanne gave him a look which said she didn't believe him.

"Meet you here in the morning then?" said Joanne.

"Only if your boss says so. Don't get sacked on account of a wild goose chase."

"My boss doesn't have a choice in the matter."

Dan shook his head and smiled at Mark. "This girl is a bad influence on you," he said. "On all of us," he added.

Mark grinned. "Don't I know it."

Dan waved them off and stared out to the water. There would be no jet ski run tonight. Tommy Pink and Clive Grace were in custody. Shame. Dan felt the need to vent his frustration at something, but no chance. Not even the boxing club was open at this time of night. Dan rubbed a muddy hand across his brow and turned reluctantly to find his car.

***

Eva stood up and aimed her phone carefully, shielding the torch beam from the window with her other hand. She tried the top of the bureau, but the fold-down leaf was also locked fast, and wouldn't budge at all. Just as she'd expected. But the bureau was an antique. She'd seen them before. Eva's father used to have one, a hand-down from her grandfather. It was an antique item, the kind which was opened with a tiny old-fashioned key. It was the kind of key which few would put on a keyring. Simply the wrong sort of key for that. Which had Eva wondering where it would have been stored… She opened the side cabinet again, pushing the awful homespun novel aside to run her hand along the back of the shelf. But she found no key in the cabinet. Was the key buried in the ceremonial tool drawer after all? She opened the drawer with another clatter which seemed to reverberate even louder than before… Or had she heard another noise somewhere in the house? Eva stilled her breath and listened. She heard nothing but that same old pregnant silence. She stood up and moved to the window. Aaron Clancy's car was nowhere to be seen. The driveway was empty. Good. She let her breath go and took a deeper one. Her eyes flicked to the bookshelf and she scanned the tomes there. Nothing, no sign of a dish or anything in which a key might hide. Next she tried the usual alternatives and ran a hand high along the top of the bookshelf, but only got a trace of dust for her trouble. Eva shook her head and in a moment of desperation ran her finger along the framed cabinet of trinkets on the wall beside the presentation cabinet. Her finger nudged against something cool and tiny, and promptly knocked it down to the floor. She tutted and turned her phone torch beam down to the floorboards, and the tiny thing gleamed back at her. An ornate little key, dark and brassy. A grin broke across Eva's face and she swiped it up. She moved to the bureau and unlocked the top lock, then tried the key on the top drawer. Both locks gave with a gentle click. Eva opened the bureau lid and lowered it down onto the wooden supports which were slid out by hand. She gazed around the small internal drawer and compartments and at the mass of catalogues and paper junk dumped in the main section between the pigeon holes. She scanned the compartments, prodding the contents left and right before her eyes settled on the pile in the centre. The pile – the stuff she had assumed as unloved accounting – something about the disorder didn't look right. It looked hurried and inconsistent with what she had come to expect of a man like Aaron Clancy. Eva frowned. The mess of papers and books and pamphlets did seem to have an order to it once she looked more closely… it looked to her like a hastily crafted mound of whatever lay to hand, including a few of the man's prized catalogues. Eva looked at the pile and started to pull out one small catalogue, receipt and clipping after another. She pulled out a bulldog-clipped pile of bank statements and set them aside. The same for a set of programmes for past jewellery auctions. She laid everything aside in a neat pile until all that was left was a battered looking jiffy bag with a torn corner. She pulled the yellow-brown jiffy bag away and was about to look inside when she saw something lay behind it. A dirty silver-grey item which looked like it had been designed to look like braiding or rope, ending in a wider circular footing. Beside the silvery stick was a large dark gold buckle. A square made of two rectangles, thick and weighty, with detailed engravings on all sides. Both looked extremely old. Eva frowned at them. They weren't just old, they were quite obviously ancient. Eva gasped and turned her phone over in her hand. She thumbed the phone screen, opened the web browser app and typed in a few hasty search terms. As she typed, a sound came from somewhere beyond Clancy's study. Eva paused and listened. Nothing but the silent hum. Probably just the pipes or something. She carried on typing... *Items Stolen from Saxon King Tomb Treasures Southend.* Click.

The first hit in the search list was an article written by Eva's most recent nemesis, the young man-stealing harpy, Alice Perry. The article was no more than a week old, written when the pieces first went missing. Without saying it outright, Perry's article had implied that Councillor Audley had been selfish in the extreme and taken a huge risk in borrowing the items from the museum for his so-called fundraising dinner, held at his own Chalkwell home. By the end of the article, she had even hinted the councillor had left the items unguarded when he was drunk and might even have engineered the theft himself. But there was nothing libellous. It was all carefully crafted insinuation, and possibly enough to curtail the man's career, leaving the councillor on the defensive. No wonder the council interfered when the police found Clancy's missing Celtic gold torq on the beach. They were desperate to regain the Saxon gold, feverish to do so. But the explanation behind it now seemed clear. Joe Clancy had given it to Carl Renton with all the rest of his repentance gifts and Renton must have dropped it during the fatal attack. None of which explained what Eva was seeing in Clancy's bureau. She scanned Perry's article until she found the part she was looking for.

"…said to be priceless, the missing items from the King's hoard include the silver corded stem of a goblet and the buckle of the Saxon King's belt. Councillor Audley, who had requisitioned the treasures as the star exhibits for his privately hosted fundraising soirees was unavailable to comment."

Eva read the words again before she gasped. She aimed her phone camera at the two pieces laying in the central compartment, framed by the dark wood on either side and took a snap. Then she hastily folded back the lid to inspect the drawer below. As she slid the drawer open, the handle on the door behind her began to dip, slow and silent.

Inside the drawer at the top of a small pile of ornaments and papers, Eva saw another item wrapped in canvas. The canvas was tied in the middle with a piece of old-fashioned twine. Eva teased at the knot in the twine with her fingernail, and loosened the knot. She bit her lip as she pulled the canvas open. Inside was a substantial piece of ornamental gold, copper and silver. A heavy metal-headed implement with one sharpened edge, albeit much softened by age. The heavy head was connected to the handle shaft with a braiding and twisting of decorative bronze and silver, which stretched down the length to join a complementary gold criss-cross pattern pressed onto a smooth handle of aged wood. The hatchet was marked, damaged and grooved by the centuries. Eva blinked, astonished. Clancy had told her this item had been stolen along with everything else. *But* he had only said so after she had noticed it missing from the nearby cabinet. With a trembling hand Eva pulled down the writing flap of the desk and turned out the contents of the creased-up jiffy bag onto the maroon leather inlay. Behind her the door opened wider, and Aaron Clancy's bright cold eyes stared in as the contents of the jiffy bag tumbled down over the desk. "My God," said Eva. Every single item Clancy had hired them to find lay before her on the desk. Eva opened the catalogue from her handbag to check, but it was a pointless gesture. She already knew. "That's why we couldn't find it," she muttered. "He hired us to chase a lie!"

The voice behind her jolted her like an electric shock.

"Oh, it wasn't a lie, Miss Roberts," said Clancy. Eva spun around to face the man as he leaned into the doorway, his eyes sharp and dangerous. "And if I may say, I'd appreciate you being careful with my precious items. That hatchet for instance, I have no liking for it anymore. I'm going to sell it on as soon as I can find a buyer who'll pay the right sum." Eva's throat tightened, her heart raced and she fought to keep control of herself. She took a breath and stepped back against the desk, guarding the truth it held, blocking a likely murder weapon from Clancy's hand.

"Of course you lied," said Eva, anger and disgust filling her voice. "You had these things the whole time. The whole exercise, hiring us, involving the police – it was a charade – a waste of time."

Eva still held her mobile phone in her hand by her hip. She kept it there, hoping to be unobtrusive. Trying for a sleight of hand she slipped the phone behind her into her palm and cupped it with her fingers.

"Come on, Mr Clancy. I remember you closing your desk back when you said I had a sharp eye. You had these things here the whole time… ever since poor Carl Renton was bludgeoned to death on that beach." Her mind filled with thoughts of the hatchet blade, and the body on the beach. "What did Carl Renton have to die for? For trying to help your son? For trying to save this town from another wave of needless drug deaths?"

The man's eyes sparked at the accusation. An accusation Eva couldn't quite bring herself to say outright. Not yet. Because Eva sensed what would follow. So she put on an act, and glanced back across her shoulder, turning her head to the desk as if she wanted to make sure she had really seen the murder weapon. But instead she stole a glance at her phone and traced her fingers across the sweat-dampened screen. She dabbed the contacts icon and stole the briefest of moments hunting for Dan's name. She looked back at Aaron Clancy and saw a trace of suspicion his eyes.

"Something alerted you to me," said Clancy. "What? Indulge me. I'm a very successful jeweller and a man of good standing. If I wasn't so thick-skinned I might have been offended."

Eva saw a wicked glint in the man's eyes.

"You shouldn't take offence in that regard, Mr Clancy. I never doubted your status. I wouldn't have ever suspected anything if it wasn't for a needless lie," she said.

"A needless lie?" said Clancy, raising his eyebrow. "What lie?"

"When you made a comment about checking in on your son on Thursday night. I really had no reason to doubt you at the time. You might well have checked on your son, he was unwell after all… but that turned out not to be true. I mentioned your visit to Joe – he didn't remember it at all."

"Joe? Joe wouldn't have known what planet he was on, let alone whether I'd visited him in bed or not. Last I saw of him he was delirious and irrational. I had him down as stealing some of my liquor, though I couldn't prove it for sure, like I had my suspicions about some of my missing gadgets. Teenagers do that kind of thing. Didn't you? So long as Joe didn't steal my finest stuff, I really didn't mind too much. It kept him off the streets, or so I thought. Of course, I didn't know then that he'd been stealing from me to fund a drug habit…"

"A deadly habit too, Mr Clancy. Surely you must have heard about the killer ecstasy tablets doing the rounds. They call them Ubers. And just a few can kill. Your son has been taking small amounts of them for a long time. He's been playing with his life."

"As I said, I didn't know."

"But you still thought he was getting wasted under your roof, on your watch and you did nothing about it. You're his father! It's your obligation to know what was going on and to help him. But you've abandoned any duty of care to pursue your wants over his. You're never here. You lead the life of a dilettante and call it work. But your son needed you, and I think you knew you had deserted him. That's why you lied about visiting your son. Because you knew you looked bad. It was vanity!"

"Don't presume to judge me, Miss Roberts. That wouldn't be a good move on your part, would it?

Eva ignored the threat. "But your lie gave it away, Mr Clancy. It was what led me here."

"You couldn't have known whether I lied or not. Joe isn't a reliable witness."

Eva glanced back at her phone once more. Her thumb slid over Dan's name, and prodded at it. But somehow the screen didn't react. The sweat perhaps? Eva's mouth started to dry up. When she looked up Clancy was studying her closely. His brow dipped low over his cold, bright eyes.
"But Joe wasn't the only witness. Georgie told me. You do know what they have is way more than just an ordinary teenage crush, don't you? That girl is devoted to him. And as Carl Renton did, Georgie is trying to make up for the love and care you've denied him."
"Georgie! She was here?!"
Eva blinked at him, reading the man's eyes. She needed to check her phone but sensed his suspicion. One more slip and Clancy would know what she was up to.
"Georgie was always here, Mr Clancy. She slips in when you're not looking. She hides from you because she knows you're not really paying attention. You didn't know, did you. She was even here when you came back very, very early on Friday morning – when you forced your way into Joe's bedroom…"
It was a shot in the dark, but Eva saw the reaction she had wanted in his eyes. Surprise. He saw he had been rumbled. He had come back. *But of course he had.*
"I think I know why you went in his room."
"You're a skilled mind-reader as well as a detective, I see," said Clancy.
"Just a good judge of character with plenty of experience when it comes to liars," said Eva. She snatched one glance down to her hand, saw her thumb over Dan's name, and dabbed it. The screen turned bright white. The call was trying to connect. Eva felt the perspiration prickling at her forehead, her back and under her arms.

"You were angry with Joe, weren't you? Furious, in fact. Because like you said, you didn't lie about everything, Mr Clancy. You *did* think there was a robbery, didn't you? You came home late from your girlfriend's place, and you found the back window had been smashed in. You checked your collection and found your most favoured pieces were missing. The very cream of the crop. You were outraged. Your son only had one job to do, didn't he? The only thing you kept him for, paid him for – and he couldn't even do that right."

The call suddenly connected and Dan's voice came on the line.

"Eva? You done yet?" The voice was faint, but there was no hiding it. Clancy's eyes narrowed and his lips opened. He surged towards her, but Eva backed away. She swiped a hand behind her, knocking Clancy's precious centrepieces off the desk to land on the floor with a clatter. Clancy snarled and yanked at her wrist but Eva managed to pull free. But the violent motion loosed her grip on her phone and sent it flying through the air. It hit the wall, bounced to the floor and the screen turned black and silent.

Dan stood on the threshold of the office, still in the doorway. The old converted shop space was dark, the lights not yet switched on. His face turned grim as he heard the clatter of metal hitting the wooden floor, and the noise of a struggle.

"Eva... what's going on...?" Before he could say another word the line went dead. Dan eyes were wide and bright in the darkness. "Eva!" He turned around, slamming the door behind him, leaving it unlocked as he ran for the car. Before he had reached the car door, his mobile phone was already pressed to his ear.

Clancy stopped by the bureau to collect his precious items from the floor. He picked up Eva's mobile along with them. "Looks like your phone's had it, Miss Roberts. Shame." Eva backed towards the window. The night was advancing quickly. The sky was a varied blur of colours from indigo to blue through to a thin line of subtle orange on the estuary horizon. But there was no comfort in it. Eva could only think of survival
"I thought Joe had failed me, so I went in his room to tell him so, yes. But the door was blocked, which annoyed me even more. Until it gave me pause for thought. A moment to clear my head, shall we say. By the time I managed to push my way into his room, I realised the chair blocking my way meant that Joe had been scared half to death. The robber, so I believed, had scared him during the break-in. It gave me a kind of clarity, and yet it gave me greater cause to be angry too. I never advertised my collection, Miss Roberts. No one knew about it except the few people I told, and a few others who had access to my house."
The man picked up all of his fine items and laid them on the fold-down writing flap. Eva's eyes slipped back to the glinting silver stick and the gold buckle at the back, set between the wooden pigeon holes of the bureau. They gleamed in the ever-diminishing light.

"I wish Joe had been honest with me – even for just once in his life. If he had told me, none of this need ever have happened."

"The murder you mean?" said Eva, saying what had to be said.

Clancy stopped dead. His eyes shone, and he seemed caught in two minds. He gave in and nodded his head.

"If Joe had told me what he did, I wouldn't have gone looking for the man who stole my collection. I would have found another, bloodless way to get it back.

"You thought Carl Renton had stolen from you. And in return you stole his life."

"It had to be him, didn't it? Georgie was young, and far too pathetic and wishy-washy to risk doing anything to upset the applecart here. Neither of them have ever paid much attention to my collection. But Carl Renton was always here, always checking on my son. I'd had my doubts about him before."

"Doubts?"

"The priestly class – sermonising to bolster their own egos, preaching to make up for their own failings in life. Isn't that what these do-gooders are really all about? First, I had him down as an old-fashioned pervert. The man wasn't married, was he? I thought he was interested in my son for the wrong reasons... so I kept an eye on him. Read the reports about his charities. I heard of him offering out Bible quotes like fortune cookies. All very odd, all very suspicious. People never do anything for anyone else without wanting something in return, not ever."

"Not in your world, Mr Clancy," said Eva.

"Renton wanted something and I couldn't work out what it was. Not until the robbery. Then it made sense all at once. From listening to him, I knew Renton liked to conduct his night time vigils. Having already stolen my gold, there was no good reason why the man would be down there, but I had to start the hunt somewhere, and there he was – standing with his back to me, looking out to sea… holding the jiffy bag you saw, full of all my own precious gold… I caught the man red handed."

"You were angry and you felt justified in your anger," said Eva. "He was red handed… but you weren't only after getting back your collection. You wanted much more than that. That's why you went out with a weapon."

"What do you mean?" said the man. Clancy leaned back, palms pressing down on the bureau. His eyes seemed to take on a raptor-like quality. The way he watched her now made her feel cold. Eva supposed he was reliving the moment.

"You believed Carl Renton had lied to you and your son and worse, that he had worked at his lie for a good long time. You had suspected him from the outset, but after a while, you had let things drift because you couldn't prove anything against him." said Eva.

Clancy cleared his throat. "I believed he had milked my son for access and information. He had formed a friendship with my son on false pretences. And as soon as his opportunity came, he struck and stole what wasn't his. I felt entitled to cause him some measure of pain equal to what he had caused us."

"A *measure* of pain? *Equal* to yours? You killed him, Mr Clancy! You told me that hatchet had been stolen when I mentioned it to you, but it had never been stolen, had it? It was missing only because you took it with you that night… Why did Carl Renton die, Mr Clancy?"

Clancy's eyes flashed, and his teeth showed as he spoke. "I told you. That man had abused our trust."

"Trust? But you never once trusted him in the first place."

"He hurt my family and *deserved to be hurt back*."

"Hurt? But he was only ever here to try and save your son's life. He was trying to fulfil the duty you had abandoned!"

"He had my collection in his hands, woman! I saw it – that was all I saw. I was furious. Beyond furious. Those things were mine! He had ripped out the heart of my collection."

"You should have let him speak. Carl Renton would have explained."

"I didn't want to hear his excuses or receive his religious judgement. The man was a thief! *The man had what wasn't his!* I hit him once and I made sure I hit him hard… too hard, in fact. The sharp end did more damage than I had expected. When I saw the collection spill from his hands to the sand, and I saw the blood with it, I knew it was too late to stop. There was too much blood. The situation was beyond saving."

"You never gave him a chance! Your son gave them to him to apologise for letting him down!"

"How was I to know? After the first blow landed, there was only one thing to do. He *had* to be killed. I knew the drug traffickers would be blamed for it. Or some other terrible junkie the man had crossed. This town is full of them. It's full of suspects. All I had to do was keep to the script my son had set in motion with the burglary set-up."

"You hired us…"

"Because Joe asked me to. I knew there was some virtue in it. You two looking for my stolen belongings would have made my position as the victim look far more convincing. And once the insurance claim was initiated, I knew you would make an excellent reference to strengthen my claim."

"You were pursuing an insurance claim? Even after you had killed to get your collection back?"

"If I didn't make that claim, people would have wondered why. And then who knows what else they might have wondered. Just the same as one throwaway comment of mine made you wonder, Miss Roberts. You're clearly a very smart lady. A little too smart for your own good all the same…"

Eva's heartbeat filled her body with a relentless pounding. The sharpness in Clancy's eyes seemed to prod at her, looking for a weakness, an opening which he could exploit.

"Greed, Mr Clancy. This whole case was only ever motivated by your greed. Just like your insurance claim was. You wanted to have your cake and eat it twice over. You let your relationship with your son rot so you could love your golden treasures instead."

"I warned you once, Miss Roberts," said Clancy. Slowly he lifted the flap to close the bureau. Eva watched as the silver stem and buckle were eclipsed from sight.

"I don't care for your warnings, Mr Clancy. You're a hypocrite, a thief, a murderer, and a liar… damned by your own words."

Clancy paused with the writing flap half open.

"What do you mean, damned by my own words?"

"Not just words. Deeds too. *The man had what wasn't his.* That's what you said. But I've seen what you did, Mr Clancy. I saw what was in the bureau. You were the one who stole the treasures of the Saxon King's tomb. You were the one who robbed Councillor Audley…"

The man's face contorted briefly into a smirk.

"Please. Not even Councillor Audley is so stupid as to let them be stolen from his own house."

"I saw them. The Saxon King's missing treasures. They're in your bureau."

"I don't deny it. There seems little point in lying now, does there? Audley was prepared to let his reputation take a trashing if it meant he gets a decent retirement fund in return."

"What?" said Eva.

"I'm a jeweller, Miss Roberts. A good one too. I don't just buy treasures, I sell them too. To the highest bidder I can find. In this instance, China should do nicely."

"Audley engineered the robbery?"

"There was no robbery. It was a transaction. Audley will lose his job, but then he'll end up rich. His stupid little fandango about my Celtic torq was an unnecessary fig leaf, but then politicians are the worst, aren't they? Don't look so shocked, Miss Roberts. If Audley didn't steal them, eventually someone else would."

"You're a sick man, Mr Clancy. The kind of man who just doesn't give a damn about anyone else. You betrayed your son, stole and lied to everyone you know, and you killed the only man who really tried to save your son. And do you know the worst part of it all?"

Clancy lowered his hand to the open drawer beneath the writing flap.

"No. But it sounds like you're going to tell me."

"You've shown no sign of remorse."

"Remorse, Miss Roberts?" said Clancy. "But if I felt remorse then I don't think I'd be able to do it again, would I?" Clancy lifted his hand away from the drawer, holding the criss-cross shaft of the ancient Celtic hatchet in his hand. "There's a kind of a virtue in using this old beast. It's poetic, almost. Living history in a way," said Clancy, admiring the hatchet he held with both hands. "It's ancient, certainly ceremonial. But I fancy that it must once have been wielded as a weapon. Carl Renton couldn't have been the first to be killed by this hatchet… and you, Miss Roberts, probably won't be the last."

Clancy hefted the hatchet in his hand with satisfaction and slowly moved Eva's way. The door was on the right. If she made it past his shoulder, Eva had a chance of escape, but Clancy was tall, and the vicious weapon gave him a longer reach, well beyond what she could easily escape. Instead Eva looked for anything she could use. There was nothing to hand, nothing but heavy books and the framed collection of trinkets. On her left, past the window and just out of reach, was Clancy's trophy cabinet. Some prized positions were empty, their contents still hidden as if stolen. But there were one or two pieces which looked almost promising. Clancy's eyes followed hers, his mouth twitched.

"Don't you dare touch anything in this room. I swear if you lay your hand on so much as one little thing I'll make this even worse."

"I told you, Mr Clancy. I don't like being threatened. I never have. And I never will."

Eva reached a hand for the framed trinkets in the wall behind her. She pulled the whole frame down from the wall and the trinkets spilled, knocking against the glass like hail stones trapped inside. Clancy surged forward then stopped, uncertain, his eyes caught by his treasures in her hand. Eva wielded the frame in front of her. Clancy looked at Eva's eyes and he watched them flare.

"No!" roared Clancy, as Eva hurled the frame at him. There was no chance he could catch it or stop it with one hand, though Clancy did his best to try. He reached with his spare hand and tried to parry with the other, but the frame spun and clattered down to the floor, the frame bursting and the glass shattering over him. The gold brooches, trinkets and rings spilt out with the glass, mingling over his shoes and across the floor. Eva swept one hand down to the mess and snatched up a small shard of glass. The glass sliced the skin of her palm and drew blood, but Eva raised it towards him regardless. She eyed the larger cabinet, and the man's eyes near burst of out his skull.

"Don't you dare!" said Clancy. But it was a trick – a feint. As he stepped towards the cabinet, Eva belted towards the door.

"I'll kill you!" he roared again and swung the hatchet wildly towards Eva's head. As the door opened, Eva felt a heavy whoosh rush past her back. She threw herself headlong into the dim hallway to avoid any injury. Below, bright headlights burst through the front door window, washing the hallway in hard light. A car engine drew to an abrupt halt, and a car door slammed. Eva ran down the staircase towards the bright light. Clancy was right behind her, thudding down the stairs. A welcome shadow appeared at the door and slammed against the wood.

"Eva! Eva, it's me. Open the door!"

She tried the handle, but the door had been locked. "I can't!" she called. Clancy was coming fast. Eva turned away quickly as the hatchet swung for her shoulder. She jinked past the swing and barged into Clancy's torso, pushing past him to run down the hallway towards the back rooms. Dan's shadow disappeared from the glass and Clancy chased after her. Eva turned to face her attacker, backing away into the kitchen, the broken glass in her hand no more than a vain gesture. By now Clancy didn't seem to care about consequences. There was a predatory smile on his face, pleasure at the power he wielded in his hand.

"You should have just got on with the job. You should have said the gold was gone, and that was that. I was going to pay you. You foolish woman. You've really only brought this on yourself, Miss Roberts."

Eva backed further into the kitchen, her heels clacking on the tiles. She looked around for a weapon, but saw only a chrome coloured toaster and kettle. She reached for the toaster, seized it from the worktop and hurled it headlong at Clancy as Dan appeared in the blackness behind the kitchen windows. He hammered at the glass with his fists as Clancy smashed the toaster to the floor with his hatchet.

"You hurt her and I'll kill you!" said Dan.

Clancy grinned.

Eva edged back towards the outer door. Her shaking fingers tried to turn the key behind her hip, but Eva realised she needed to lift the handle first, to yank it up before the key would turn or the door would not open. Her hand fumbled and Clancy stormed towards her, letting out a howl of rage. Eva blinked, took a breath, and pressed her head back to the window in apparent readiness for the pain of death.

Clancy grinned, seeing a final act of submission. She saw the excitement in his eyes. The man tensed his shoulders, his arms followed as they started to sweep upward. She waited for the last instant, the moment the hatchet reached the apex of its arc. Eva slid down the door as fast as she could. Committed, Clancy swung the hatchet down hard. The heavy head smashed the glass to pieces, biting through the double glazing. Glass showered Eva's hair and burst over Clancy's arms and body. He growled and pulled at the hatchet but the tool was caught in the glass. The inner pane was gone entirely, reduced to crumbs. But the hatchet head was caught and held in a hole in the second pane. Clancy yanked hard. The glass cracked but stayed put. He leaned back and pulled again. At any moment Eva knew the hatchet would come free. But she didn't run. She reached up, pushed the door handle high and twisted the key. The lock clicked. Clancy saw what was going to happen. His eyes flared and he pulled at the hatchet with all his might. Outside, Dan heard the mechanism give.

"Eva!" called Dan.

She knew exactly what he meant for her to do. As Clancy yanked the hatchet free and the rest of the glass imploded towards him, Eva darted free past the man's legs. Clancy growled with effort and spun round to follow her. All she needed was time. Just the smallest fraction of time. The kettle was all she had. Eva pulled the kettle free of the cordless dock and threw it at Clancy's face with all her might. Both his hands were on the hatchet handle. He lifted one arm to cover his face, but he was too late. The kettle struck his nose and forehead and brought a grunt of pain. His arms fell limp, and the hatchet lowered. In the same instant the door burst open and smashed Clancy to one side, hammering his torso against the silver-coloured oversized fridge. Clancy collapsed to one side, pressed between the door and the fridge. And Dan kept pushing, gritting his teeth with anger and effort. He used the door as a weapon, driving it hard into Clancy's side and shoulder until the hatchet was dropped and crashed to the tiles. As it landed, the ancient copper braiding snapped and the hatchet head rolled free. Dan pulled the door back, and smashed it hard against Clancy once, and then again for good measure. The second time one of Clancy's bones popped under the pressure and he cried out. Gritting his teeth, Dan flung the door against him a final time and let it go. Clancy tumbled to the floor clutching his chest. Eva looked down at him from the kitchen doorway but the man's eyes were screwed up in pain.
"Eva... you okay?"
"Better now," she said.
Dan offered his hand and they crossed the divide of Clancy's body to hold one another. The sound of sirens hit their senses and the front of the house was blitzed by more bright lights and flashes of blue. More sirens were coming.

"He did it, Dan. He helped the councillor rob the Saxon gold. And he killed Carl Renton because he thought Renton had stolen his treasures from him. Gold is all he cares about. Nothing else. Not even his son."

"And now he's going to lose all of it, aren't you, Clancy?" said Dan, looking down on him with disdain. "Though the truth is I think you lost your son a long time back."

Detective Inspector Hogarth appeared in the doorway and pushed his way inside. His feet crunched on broken glass, and his shoe nudged against the head of the ancient broken hatchet. As the back door was knocked against him again, Aaron Clancy groaned and whimpered. Hogarth looked down in shock, then with one raised eyebrow, he cast a seasoned eye over Roberts and Bradley.

"What the hell have you done this time?" said Hogarth.

"We've caught your other killer," said Eva. "But only just before he caught me."

"What? Hold on. You're saying that *your client* killed Carl Renton?"

Eva nodded. "Not only that, but if you look in his bureau upstairs you'll see that none of his allegedly stolen items were ever truly stolen, Inspector. They're all there. So, I think that means we rose to the challenge. We finally managed to find the gold too. Aaron Clancy wasn't a victim. He was the thief. And he's also in possession of the centrepieces from the Saxon King's tomb."

"*Now* you're kidding me," said Hogarth.

Eva shook her head. "It's all upstairs. I think you'll be needing to pay a visit to Councillor Audley too, mind."

"Oh. And why's that?" said Hogarth.

"The way Aaron Clancy tells it, there was no robbery. Councillor Audley was in on it the whole time. He was prepared to fall on his sword and lose his job, so long as the proceeds of the tomb treasures paid for his pension."

Hogarth looked at them in disbelief. Eventually he nodded as he took it all in. More police appeared on the back garden patio.

"Well, that's a turn up for the books," said Hogarth. "And there's nothing like a mortified politician to cheer me up. Except maybe, a lying, thieving murderer to throw in the cells along with him."

"Clancy's all yours, Inspector," said Dan. "At least, what's left of him."

Hogarth looked down to see the tall man holding his chest.

"He had an accident with the door, I see?" said Hogarth, nodding. "How unfortunate. PC Jordan, pick up this mess will you?" said Hogarth gesturing the PC towards the man at his feet.

Hogarth looked at Eva and Dan, reading the shock and the ordeal from their faces.

"You two just don't know when to stop, do you?"

"Nope," said Dan.

"No. Well, you'd better try and work it out. Because as much as you two can be a royal pain in the backside to a copper like me, I'd rather not be picking your remains up at a crime scene any time soon. Life's too short to waste it on a bunch of scoundrels like this one, trust me. I thought I was getting away from them when I came down here. Maybe not though, eh?" Hogarth sniffed, and let his words sink in. "Okay then. You know I'll be after a formal interview from you two but it looks to me like you need a breather first."

"I'm fine," said Eva, but she was fooling no one.

In the end, Eva gave up. She gave Hogarth a pursed-lip smile and a nod. Hogarth nodded back and returned to his duty, starting with reading the pained Aaron Clancy his rights as PC Jordan held the man against the dented fridge. Eva and Dan retreated to the hallway full of headlights and flashing blues.

"You know, Hogarth might even be right," said Eva. Her voice was like a tired sigh.

"Hogarth? He's never right," said Dan.

"I'm not so sure," said Eva. Dan turned to face her as she spoke. "I don't know how much longer I can keep this up, all this dicing with death…"

Dan hesitated and looked into Eva's eyes. "Well… maybe you could take a break. You could work at the office for a while instead."

Eva shook her head.

"The office? That'd kill me just as well. No. Maybe I need a real change. Something else."

"Whoa, back up. Just take a breath. Now's not the time for making big decisions."

"Isn't it? That bastard out there could have killed me and it's not the first time. It feels like the hundredth."

"Now who's exaggerating?" said Dan.

"Dan, tell me you wouldn't like to take a break from this. *You* were almost killed only a year back. We deserve a life, don't we?"

Dan's face crumpled in confusion. "And what would you do instead then, Eva? Tell me that."

Eva shook her head. She folded her arms and walked to the front door.

"I'm here for you," said Dan. "Always will be. I won't let anything bad happen to you."

"And what about you, Dan?" she muttered. Eva opened the front door onto a world of flashing blue lights, police radios, barked orders, camera lenses and chattering strangers. For a split second, everyone stopped and looked at her. It felt to Eva as if she was at the centre of the world, and yet she wanted to be anywhere else. She looked around in silence, then stepped down off the doorstep and walked away. And the world started up again.

Dan followed on behind. Tonight, he promised himself in silence, he would let the Pinot Grigio flow as freely as Eva needed.

Twenty-six

As expected, the next day was a write-off. The shutters were left down over the ground floor office windows, and what work had to be done was done in the upstairs living room, with the blinds closed. They called Mark and Joanne early to tell them to stay home. Life still felt like a mess, worse still with the tiredness of the booze still filtering through their veins. By afternoon, Eva was brave enough to check the company bank balance. It needed some serious TLC. Another six weeks without a decent paying job, and it would need something more like CPR. Eva winced and closed the banking app on her phone and shut her eyes tight. She recalled her brief shell-shocked chat with Dan on the doorstep of Clancy's house. He was right. As much as she didn't like it, he was right. Eva wasn't made for anything else. No other job suited her, and she could never accept another boss above her. Private investigations had ruined her for a normal life, and yet, Eva still wasn't sure if she could carry on. Dan glanced across at her seeming to read her thoughts. He set down his coffee cup and switched off the TV.
"You want to talk?"
Eva gave him a look. "About what?"
"About what you said last night?"
"Which part?" she said.
"Come on. Any part," said Dan.
"Uh. No thanks. They were dumb knee-jerk things to say. *All* of them."
"You're sure?" said Dan.
Eva's face stayed neutral, but she gave a slow nod. "I'll be okay. *We'll* be okay. I promise."

Dan sipped his coffee, unsure whether to say more or keep quiet.

Eva put him out of his misery by interrupting his thoughts. "I think it's time I tried to build bridges with Lauren Jaeger. That would probably help, wouldn't it? It's time I gave her the benefit of the doubt. The money would be handy too."

"And it might be the catharsis you're looking for."

"I'm not looking for catharsis, Dan. Just a little peace now and then."

Eva picked up her phone and dialled. She was surprised that the call went through so quickly. But when it was picked up no one answered. Just like the last time, Eva heard the sound of breathing. But this time the breathing was rapid and panicky and totally unlike the calm, collected breathing she had heard before.

"Lauren?" she said. Immediately, the line went dead. Eva frowned as she stared at the screen.

"What is it?" said Dan.

"Damn that girl! I was only calling to see if she was okay. I had every intention of giving Lauren a fresh start, making peace. And then she goes and hangs up on me like we're sixteen all over again. I've had it. I'm not in the mood to take any more of this juvenile crap. Case or no case, it's about time I told Lauren Jaeger that she can stick it where the sun doesn't shine."

"Eva wait…"

Eva dabbed the phone, tapping out a quickfire angry text. She pressed send before she even had time to think about it.

Never call me again, Lauren. I grew out of your games a long time ago. Have a nice life. Eva.

Dan watched Eva squirm as she read the text back and Dan rubbed his brow. Whatever text Eva had sent couldn't have been good. And no more than ten seconds later Eva's mobile rang.

Eva stared at the screen, her eyebrows flicking high on her forehead.

"Can you believe this woman? It's her! Calling me! Again!"

"Answer it," said Dan.

Eva looked at him.

"Answer it, Eva. For your own sake," said Dan.

Eva sighed, gave in, and pressed the answer button.

"Lauren? What do you want?" said Eva.

"Eva... wait... the other time... it wasn't me who called you. It was him, Eva. It was Jamie."

"What?" Eva turned rigid. The quiver in Lauren's voice sent a shiver up Eva's spine.

"It's happening, Eva, just like he said. Everything I warned you about is happening. He knows I called you. And because I won't tell him who you are, it's started. Just like he promised. I'm afraid, Eva. I'm scared... you've got to help me! I need you to help me now. I mean it. You've got to help me stop him before someone ends up dead."

Eva fell silent, as her mind teetered on the brink of two possible answers. Either way seemed like a cliff edge. She struggled for a fraction too long, and Lauren's voice became loud and shrill in her ear.

"Eva?!"

Eva took a breath. "Okay. Yes, of course I'll help you, Lauren. Of course."

"Thank God! Please don't make me wait anymore, Eva. I'm scared of what he might do."

"Just hold on. Hold on and I'll be along soon. Be strong, Lauren. I'm coming."

As Eva hung up, the very same words echoed in her head. *Be strong, Eva, Be strong.*

At three o'clock, just as Eva was about to leave, Mark and Joanne arrived at the office door. They turned up like uninvited guests, knocking on the shutters and rattling the door. When Eva and Dan went down to open the door, they found another two very unexpected guests at Mark's side. Eva was feeling grim – as if she was being held together only by the seams of her tweed suit. But she still couldn't help smiling when she saw Joe Clancy and Georgie. Joe looked weak and pale, but the smile on his face was genuine enough. They both looked as if a massive weight had been lifted from their shoulders.

"Eva," said Mark. "I know you had a rough night, but I had to bring Joe around because he has something he wanted to say to you."

"Joe," said Eva. "Georgie. It's great to see you… but look, I'm so sorry. I've got to go and see a client. I'll have to leave in a couple of minutes. It's urgent."

"No problem, Miss Roberts," said Joe. "I knew you'd be in demand."

"I'm very sorry for what happened to your father, Joe," said Eva.

Joe shook his head emphatically and Georgie looked at him proudly as he spoke. "Don't be sorry," he said. "My father deserves everything that's coming to him. He killed my friend… And from what I hear, he almost killed you…"

"As it happens, I think your father came off worse," said Eva carefully.

Joe shrugged and took his time. He lifted a carrier bag from his side and took out a small parcel. "Miss Roberts," said Joe. "I just wanted to give you this…"

Eva took a white paper-wrapped parcel from his hand. It reminded her a little of the awful canvas parcel in Clancy's drawer, but she blinked away the unwelcome feelings. "Open it," he said.

Eva looked around at their faces before she did so, then she slowly unwrapped it to find a small gold Celtic band. Not the large ancient torq the police had confiscated but a smaller decorative clasp to fit a wrist or upper arm. The band had dulled with age.

"This belongs to your father, Joe. I really can't take it."

"Yes, you can," said Joe. "It's only one of his minor pieces. It was in the drawer with all the rest. He'll never miss it. And not only that, I had this one valued especially for the purpose. I'm told its worth two thousand five hundred pounds, so it's not one of his really expensive pieces. Who knows? It might fetch a few hundred more, or a few hundred less. I assume my father owed you at least that amount."

"In the region of, yes" said Eva.

"I would pay you cash, but as you may have guessed, I'm going to be a little cash-strapped from now on. But that's okay. At least I'm not under his watch anymore."

"And that's not all," said Georgie "The rehab called. A guy called Barry from Carl's rehab centre. It turns out Barry had received an email from Carl, saying that he wanted Barry to help him. This Barry only saw the email after Carl had disappeared. He says he'll help Joe get better, with a specially designed outpatient programme, so Joe doesn't have to go into those houses."

"What?" said Dan. "So Carl's rehab project will go on?"
Joe nodded. "Turns out Carl left the rehab projects a lot of cash in his will. Carl lived like he was broke, but he really wasn't.. He didn't see money and gold the way my dad did. And neither do I. I know I'm looked after, Miss Roberts. My father's house is mortgage free. Georgie and I will be living there for the foreseeable future."

"Together. Like a proper couple," said Georgie.

Joe looked suddenly bashful and his face turned pink. "Something like that. Please, Miss Roberts, take that little band and convert it to cash to cover your fee. My father can't pay his dues, so I want to pay them for him."

Eva paused, then nodded. "Only because you insist, Joe. Yes I will," said Eva.

Dan smiled, looking plainly relieved. "One question, Joe," said Dan. "What happens if your old man decides to have you evicted from the house?"

Joe shook his head. "He can't. It's a bit like squatters' rights, you see. I've lived there since I was born, and because the house was mortgage free, I never signed any kind of occupier's waiver. I'm over eighteen years old and because of my time there I might even have a legal claim over the house myself."

"Finally," said Eva. "Some good comes from something bad. Just make sure you take up that offer for rehab, won't you. I don't want to hear you've blasted a whole house on that Uber junk."

Joe nodded. "Definitely."

"Don't worry. That's not going to happen," said Georgie, firmly.

"Thank you, Joe," said Eva. "And thank you too, Georgie."

Eva leaned in for the briefest of hugs before she turned to give Joanne and Mark a parting look.

"I've got to dash. Duty calls," she said. "Lauren Jaeger," she explained.

Eva turned to give Dan the longest look of all. She smiled to show him she loved him and then she walked away. There was no time for regret and no time for hangovers. It was time to get back to work. And who knew? Now Eva had put Lauren in the picture regarding exactly how she felt about the past, Eva dared to hope that the case might not be so bad. And as she walked to the car, Eva was already forming viable strategies to deal with Lauren's boyfriend troubles – and to force a quick win.

But if Eva had had time to reflect, she would have known that every plan she'd ever made had changed when it came up against reality.

Eva had no idea just how bad things were going to get. And someone else was about to call all the shots.

The story continues in Cuts Both Ways…

Thank you for reading Between Two Thieves - the first instalment of the brand new Roberts and Bradley Private Investigator Crime Thriller series. If you enjoyed this book I would be greatly honoured if you could post a short review to let other readers know. Just a couple of short sentences would go a long way. Thank you very much – I appreciate your help.

And if you'd like to get some more highly rated novels, boxed sets, novellas and short stories for free, then simply join the Readers' Group at SolomonCarter.net. It's free to join and once you're in I'll send you links to lots of cool stuff. You can quickly and easily unsubscribe at any time.

All the very best,

Solomon:)

Between Two Thieves

The sixth thrilling series featuring Eva Roberts & Dan Bradley, private detectives

1. Between Two Thieves
2. Cuts Both Ways
3. Play With Fire

More thrilling books by Solomon Carter

The DI Hogarth Secret Fear series – the second DI Hogarth series

1. The Secret Fear
2. The Secret Dawn
3. The Secret Sins

The DI Hogarth Darkest Lies series – The first DI Hogarth series

1. The Darkest Lies
2. The Darkest Grave
3. The Darkest Deed
4. The Darkest Truth

Long Time Dying

The first thrilling adventures featuring Eva Roberts & Dan Bradley, private detectives
1. Out with A Bang
2. One Mile Deep
3. Long Time Dying
4. Never Back Down
5. Crossing The Line
6. Divide and Rule
7. Better The Devil
8. On Borrowed Time
9. The Dirty Game
10. Only Live Once
11. Behind the Mask
12. The Dark Tide
13. Lucky For Some

Luck & Judgment
The second thrilling series featuring Eva Roberts & Dan Bradley, private detectives
1. Luck & Judgment
2. Truth Be Damned
3. The Sharp End
4. Don't Go Gently

London Calling
The third thrilling series featuring Eva Roberts & Dan Bradley, private detectives
1. Rite To Silence
2. London Calling
3. Promise To Pay
4. The Pressure Zone

The Final Trick
The fourth thrilling series featuring Eva Roberts & Dan Bradley, private detectives
1. The Final Trick
2. Taste of Death
3. The Danger Room
4. Killers and Kings

Harder They Fall
The fifth thrilling series featuring Eva Roberts & Dan Bradley, private detectives
1. Harder They Fall
2. The Stone Girl
3. Harvest of Blood
4. Last Man Standing

Also by Solomon Carter
The Last Line thriller series – espionage, international adventure and all out action with Jenny Royal and The Company
Black and Gold – Vigilante Justice short read series featuring Simon 'The Man in the Mask' and Jess. Crosses over with the adventures of Eva Roberts and Dan Bradley, private detectives.
Roberts and Bradley Casebook – segmented short read series available in novel format as 'complete box sets'. Continues the PI storyline onward from Long Time Dying until Luck & Judgment
Flesh and Blood
Rack and Ruin
Two Wrongs

BETWEEN TWO THIEVES
Between Two Thieves Private Investigator Crime Thriller series Book 1
First published in Great Britain in 2019 by Great Leap
Copyright © Solomon Carter 2019
Solomon Carter has asserted his moral right under the Copyright, Designs and Patents Act 1988, to be identified as the author of this work.
This book is a work of fiction and except in the case of historical fact, any resemblance to actual persons living or dead, is purely coincidental.

All rights reserved. No part of this e-book publication may be reproduced, stored in a retrieval system, or transmitted in any form or by any means, electronic, mechanical, photocopying, recording or otherwise, except by a reviewer who may quote brief passages in a review, without the prior written permission of the author.

Printed in Great Britain
by Amazon